Harding McRae

Always / Never

Always/Never

by Harding McRae

Print Edition
ISBN 978-09858494-2-9
e-Book Edition
ISBN 978-09858494-3-6

Please visit:
www.HardingMcRae.com

Other works by Harding McRae:
In The Beginning...

This novel is a work of fiction.
Any resemblance to real persons, living or dead, actual events,
establishments, organizations, and/or locales is solely intended
to give the fiction a sense of reality and authenticity.
Other names, characters, places and incidents are either products
of the author's imagination or are used fictitiously.

Forward

News anchor Howard Beale screamed, **"I'm mad as hell and I'm not going to take it anymore!"** in the movie, *Network,* in 1976. Let me ask three questions:

Are things better today in our polarized America?

Has getting mad accomplished anything?

Did we ultimately ignore the message and were entertained by the messenger?

We are still "taking it." Moreover, we're bored and disinterested, disengaged and selfish, self-centered and covetous. Who cares what the government does? They're just protecting us; it's all for the good, right? What's important is, what's in it for me?

Really?

Writers often daydream or fantasize plots and story lines. I, too, find myself doing that the older I get. This story began as one of those *exercises of flight of ideas*–much like one of those chain letters, or impromptu free association comedy sketches. As I developed the complexities of the story, I also began reading about "fantasy" plotlines and became terrified. Why? Because in my weirdest imagination, I never dreamed anything like it could happen. Let's see if you think this possible.

If we don't get mad as hell about what our governments–not just ours, all of them–are capable of doing or have done, then we deserve what we tolerate. Moreover, we will richly deserve whatever comes next as a result of our tolerance.

This isn't just a book about an illusory medical student and a doctor or two on a quest. It is a lesson about life. That's why, *"Always"* and *"Never"*

I believe we all want to leave this planet a better place than we found it. We simply struggle to find a way to do that. One way is to make our voices heard – individually and collectively. Don't take it anymore. This book is fiction . . .

or is it?

Acknowledgments

I start with the big three–*Faith, Family, and Friends*. Those three define life for me. I have an eternal optimism this country can overcome any obstacle, if it pays attention. That optimism comes from God. I write for complex reasons–and simple ones as well. Certainly, I write for myself as a creative outlet. For my family and friends because I think I have something of relevance to say. Yet, it is more than that. I want to make a difference.

The one person who helps me more than anyone is Max Herr, my editor, friend, and great chef. I'd have him move in if his wife, Martha, would let him. But alas, she has first dibs.

Thanks to my wife, Lynne for her support and friendship, not to mention her proofreading. Many a night she would say to me, "Hurry up! Write the next chapter. I need to know what happens. Hurry up!"

To my many friends, beginning with the real Barbara Zachary–a forty-year friend, critical care nurse, yoga instructor and role model. Thad Mercer, in whose guest bedroom I wrote the first fifty pages or so.

And to Mr. Kim, my Korean compatriot, who read drafts and asked questions. If he didn't comprehend, I rewrote. If he understood, but was confused by the twists and turns, I smiled.

Thanks to Ty Richardson, a long-time theatrical friend and writer, Lynne Richardson (not related), from my music days we have been friends, and Steve Booth, he the longest of friends back to high school. He knows the "real" me–*don't tell!* Steve. Alan Hollingsworth, who encouraged me to write as another friendly competition back to our youth, another brother back to my college and medical school days–who reminded me of the "real" neurosurgeon, Dr. Pritcherman, during our time in medical school.

Other friends and early readers include Susan Kay, Paul Ake, and William F. Williams–thanks for your assistance. And thanks to many others I fear I have forgotten.

Harding McRae
Los Angeles, California
Spring, 2014

I

*S*edate him! God damn it! Can someone SEDATE HIM!" screamed a clearly annoyed medical academic to the gaggle of grunts assigned to care for the unfortunate soul they were currently trying to restrain. "Why now?" angrily muttering under his breath, looking over at the new "team" dealt to him by the Dean.

As the eight students, residents, and paramedical personnel came upon this scene, the patient suddenly broke free of his tormentors and raced down the long hall so typical of academic institutions. Raced, that is, until he encountered a security guard stationed at the door, who drew his weapon, firing into the crazed creature.

There was a sizzling sound of electrons leaping across the fifteen feet that separated the two. The electronic discharge dropped the escapee like a two-hundred pound bag of concrete, as if the hand of God had reached out, placed his thumb upon the head of this wretched man, and smashed him down . . . rubbing him into the floor. He didn't move, temporarily paralyzed by the steadily pulsing current surging through his body. He was awake, but his clenched, spastic mandibular muscles were electro-convulsively frozen, incapable of speech. The guard derived pleasure from the whole experience, intently applying the voltage without interruption.

"Let him up," the professor ordered.

More calmly now, but still irritated he again asked, "Can someone sedate him, please? Two milligrams of *Mezperodol* per protocol." Turning to the team assembled, he noted that they were scattered about the hall generally trying to avoid eye contact with the staff, the patient, and especially the man standing over this woeful creature.

"My name is Stanley J. Pritcherman," he stated while walking around the group, juggling unknown objects in his right front pocket, like Bogart in *The Caine Mutiny*, looking up and down, visually taking measure of his new charges. "You're now on Neurosurgery–Six East. I'm head of this unit, and don't you *ever* forget it."

Locking eyes on me, his eyes cut through mine, his image seared into my brain. "It's my understanding you're assigned to my service for the next few months. What you have just witnessed is a man in the throes of psychosis. An S4, we call it; a schizophrenic resistant to conventional therapy. Hence, the reason why he is here on the neurosurgical service."

"I'm a neurosurgeon. I'm not a psychiatrist," he continued without missing a beat." As a matter of fact, I don't give a damn about shrinks, their approaches to treatment, or their lame rationalizations explaining the actions of patients. I'm a Renaissance man," sneering insidiously as he reached into his coat pocket." A throwback to the twentieth century," he remarked just before tossing something he had taken from his pocket into his mouth, pausing for effect as he walked slowly past the rest.

"I believe modern medicine can fix this man's problem and most of the other problems of society. What I don't believe in are excuses or bullshit lies used to explain why Johnny killed his mother," pacing in front of each of us. "She's just as dead and somebody is responsible. My job is to fix the bad circuit in his brain that caused the malfunction."

"And that's what it is, a malfunction that caused him to kill. Not because his mother didn't love him or let him suck her tits enough," stopping in front of a beautiful blonde I'd never seen before, using his eyes to strip search more than her mind.

"It's a circuit board problem. That's what we know now. Yeah, I'm a Renaissance man," he scowled, then issued a pernicious snicker of a laugh." I believe we *can* influence our children during their upbringing. You know, all that environmental factor crap. But let me tell you something, boys and girls. It's basically a genetic problem. Most computers that have problems come broken from the manufacturer. Once you locate the bad chip, you replace it. Easy as that. Snap in, snap out."

"People are no different. We just don't know how to snap things into their brains. Or, we didn't . . . not until I figured it out. At least, I believe I have. A couple of assholes in research approval don't think I have, but screw them," still standing chin to chin with the blonde. He licked his lips, narrowing his eyes to a squint, "I'll prove them wrong within the year. That's why you're here. To study under the great Pritcherman. Got it?"

He broke off from the blonde, fished what everyone now recognized as a raw onion out of his pocket and took a bite from the center, chewing it loudly, spraying juice everywhere. He had walked over to me again and stared directly at me, his face now two inches away from mine, with breath foul enough to gag a maggot. "Any questions, young Turks?" taking another bite of the pungent *Allium cepa*.

Yeah, I thought, turning my head, nauseous, but determined not to buckle to the smell. *I've got lots of questions. Let's begin with What am I doing here? Who is this cretin? and Who's really snapped?*

Now I wasn't so sure who the psychotic was—the alleged patient, the pompous neurosurgical attending with whom I'd been assigned to study, or me. *Me*, the third-year medical student so out of place and definitely the low man on this son-of-a-bitch's totem pole. Scenes like this made me question why I ever embarked on a medical career in the first place. I never wanted to confront these kinds of patients. Hell, I never wanted to confront *any* patients. What I wanted to do was research. It was some smart-ass in student assignments who thought I would benefit from the diatribes of this maniac.

Stanley J. Pritcherman. I knew what the "J" stood for—*Jerk*. Or, possibly, *jackass*, *japer*, full of *jargon*, *jaundice*, and *jabberwocky*. And so did everybody in the entire school. Pritcherman. A technician, a buzz and zap guy, a . . . a neurosurgeon.

I'm no technician and have no interest in this skullcracker's problems. Just let me finish this rotation and get on to the laboratory, I prayed. People . . . patients . . . everybody makes me nervous, and now this screaming piece of the devil's creation terrifies me. And what am I to make of this deranged being writhing on the floor? I returned to reality with a tearing pain in my left leg. I reflexively withdrew it before looking down to see a three-inch gash in my own flesh mist blood on anyone within a few feet, especially the crazed perpetrator lying on the floor with a meaty red chunk of my leg in his mouth, smiling up at me.

"So numb-nuts," Pritcherman screamed. "Are you gonna stand there and let him eat his way to your ass, or are you gonna move!"

Just then, the messages from my afferent sensory nerve fibers reached my brain. I twisted away and dropped to the floor, grasping my bleeding left appendage with my ungloved hand. As I collapsed, I let out a pseudo-psychotic shriek.

"Get this moron out of here!" Pritcherman screamed. I wasn't at all sure who he was addressing as moron . . . me, the patient, or both of us. My new team members came to my aid, helping me to my feet and limp away from the havoc to an adjoining treatment room. The hall was smeared red with fresh blood, which, it suddenly dawned on me, was the essence of my being. It is an eerie feeling seeing your own blood spraying people and objects. I had a detached perception that it should be more painful than it was, almost as if it were someone else's throbbing leg. Shock, whether emotional or physical, has a numbing effect. I began laughing when I should have cried— laughing, initially in spurts, then uncontrollably, hysterically, and irrationally. As my teammates rapidly became caught up in my delirium, they, too, joined my private joke, only they didn't know why. Pavlov's dogs.

Here were eight strangers laughing over a psychotic patient, who had gnawed a chunk of flesh from the leg of a fellow physician in training. Now what was remotely funny about that?

Several staff members finally bridled my newfound "friend" and placed him on a gurney in four-point leather restraints. As they wheeled him away, he made direct and desperate eye contact with me and silently mouthed, *"Help me, HELP ME! I'm not crazy. I'M NOT CRAZY! HELP ME!"* He strained against his restraints in an effort to maintain that eye contact as his gurney turned the corner. Was this man really psychotic?

"Damn that hurts!" I screamed, as Betadine solution was poured into my wound.

"You students. Gather round. Notice the stellate character to this wound," an unknown female from our cohort intoned, pushing my trunk down onto the table, focusing the overhead light onto my wound. She was clearly the ranking member, with short dirty-brown hair and weary eyes. Eyes that had seen more pain than her years should have allowed. She wasn't the least bit interested in me, only my wound. "Bring me more four-by-fours and a suture set."

"Excuse me, but it's *my* leg you're talking about. Could I—"

"Lie down! I gotta cleanse the wound and explore it for foreign bodies." She was so authoritative. Zachary was the name on her lab coat, Dr. Barbara Zachary.

"How the hell would a foreign body get into the wound . . . my leg, from a bite?"

"Could be he spit something in there or maybe he even vomited," she offered matter-of-factly. "With any luck, the gastric and biliary secretions will protect you from infection." Several of my colleagues backed away from the examining table in disgust.

"Get used to it," she added, with a smirk. "There's nothing pretty about trauma."

"You said infection, Doctor? Dr. Zachary, is it?" Now I was actually becoming concerned. "I've had a tetanus immunization. Shouldn't that protect me from—"

"From rabies? Or, Ebola virus? Or maybe even *Pasteurella*?"

"*Pasteurella?* I've never even—"

She was laughing out loud now, "Good God. Are you a rookie, or what? *Pasteurella multiforme* is a feline bacterial infection transmitted by a cat bite. That pervert didn't look like a cat. More like a rabid dog, or a wolf, but I doubt he's rabid. And Ebola? Didn't you complete basic sciences? Have you ever heard of Ebola being transmitted by a bite? Didn't they teach you anything?"

"*Ow!* What the—" I cringed as she poured a witch's brew of antiseptic into my jagged wound.

"Well, I'll be damned," she exclaimed. "Would you look at this," pulling a yellow-white foreign body from my wound." It looks like a tooth! The son-of-a-bitch broke a tooth off on your leg. Probably hit the bone!"

"What!"

"I'm kidding, uh, Quinton, is it?" glancing at my name tag for the first time. " You're a gullible one, aren't you Quinton? Have you ever even been on a clinical ward before?"

"Well, I—"

"I didn't think so. How many others haven't either? Let's see. From the looks on all your faces, and the fear of blood, I'd say only *you* have any experience." She was staring directly at the blonde. Staring, but without Pritcherman's malice.

"Can I see that tooth?" the blonde asked my savior, Dr. Zachary. Zachary was 5'7" tall, an understated beautiful woman in her early thirties, this one, too, exuded self-confidence. She was the only one who hadn't backed away from my hideous leg laceration. "You'd better not close this wound. It might pus out," rolling her eyes disdainfully in Zachary's general direction. "I'd pack it with *Iodoform* and put him on crutches for a few days. Are you a believer in prophylactic antibiotics Zachary?"

"Why? Are you?" Zachary was scrutinizing the blonde's chest. "Is it really Smith, that can't really be your name? Is it an alias, or is that your stage name, princess?"

"Jessica Smith. *Doctor* Jessica Smith, to you," she was dispassionate. "I'll let the princess comment pass. I'm rotating through this nut house just the same as you. I'm from Washington. Georgetown University, here on a fellowship."

"I'm a third-year trauma surgical resident here, Smith," Zachary retorted, packing my leg with gauze. "I guess these studs are my cross to bear since I'm the senior resident."

"*Studs?*"

"Medical students. MS 2s and 3s. Don't tell me you don't have to baby-sit medical students at Georgetown?"

"Oh, we have them," Smith shrugged. "We usually just throw them away if they get hurt. It's easier to get a new one than to fix 'em when they're broken. Right, Quinton?" She rubbed a dressing onto my wound, patting my leg, as she turned to Zachary. "Can I see that tooth?"

"It goes to pathology for analysis," Zachary snapped, dropping the specimen into a small plastic container and twisting the lid closed.

"Pathology it is," Smith calmly responded, rattling the jar. "After I examine it," opening the container just as quickly and pouring the tooth into her hand. With that, she exited the examining room with Zachary momentarily at a loss for words.

"Hey! That's my specimen," she shouted, as Smith cleared the door of the examining room. Zachary was braced to go after her until I interrupted her.

"What about my leg, Dr. Zachary? Should I—"

"Take six hundred aspirin and call me in a year," she fumed.

"That's too long to—"

"It's a joke, Quinton. It's a joke," she was clearly distracted. "Do you have a first name, Quinton?" She sprayed an adhesive bandage over the wound, not waiting for me to answer. "Get him some crutches. And—all of you—meet me in the conference room in forty-five minutes," she demanded. "This bullshit isn't going to stand." She was out the door as quickly as Smith, but in a different direction.

As I lay on the table, I couldn't focus because of the pounding, throbbing sensation in my leg. I was dizzy, nauseous, and diaphoretic. The shock of it all was wearing off. Hell, she didn't even anesthetize me! My leg was pulsating like a hammer, pounding steadily, only the hammer was striking each of my sensory nerves. The human body handles pain in interesting ways. Pain functions as a warning to withdraw from noxious stimuli. If the level of my pain was any indication, the poisonous excitement of this morning's first few moments was not a good omen.

I was left with three others in the room, clearly also students. Two of them I didn't even recognize. Their name tags confirmed they were second-year medical students. The third person was a fellow third-year classmate.

"Let me help you up," he announced, grabbing me under each arm and lifting me to my feet. Yeah, I knew him. This linebacker-Sumo wrestler-turned-medical-student had been an albatross from my first day.

"Damn it, Grigsby. I don't want to stand on my left leg! You heard Dr. Zachary. I'm supposed to be on crutches. How about finding me some?"

"Get them yourself, you pansy-ass piece of puke," he hissed venomously, walking out the door, too.

"Can you guys find me some crutches?" I begged the remaining two second-years. They raced out the door on their first mission to provide aid and comfort to the ill. I collapsed back onto the examining table.

"I gotta stop getting myself into these situations," I muttered aloud, once again sweating bullets.

Now lying alone, I stared up at the institutional green ceiling. *Who the hell is the freak of nature that ruined my day, my leg, and my chance to make a good first impression? If he was so crazed, why did the fear in his eyes seem real, not psychotic? And what he mouthed to me—what was that all about?*

At least I've made one hell of an impression on my colleagues. None of them even knew my name before today, other than Grigsby. Now they know I have a name and what I'm doing on this rotation.

"I've got a name," I whispered. I slowly inspected the pockmarked ceiling. *Counting holes in the ceiling ain't exactly too appealing to a faceless wonder child whose name's unspoken.* I laughed as I recalled the rhyme from a poem I'd written years before.

"I've got a name," I shouted. "Do you hear me, Pritcherman. And Zachary and Smith and Grigsby and all you other bastards. Do you hear me? I've got a name. It's Chauncey Charles Quinton."

— Never Trust Anyone Who Doesn't Know Your Name —

II

As I lay on the table feeling sorry for myself, my self-pity and depression were interrupted by a detached, anonymous, unemotional, and computer-generated page over the intercom. What had been thirty minutes of solitude was disrupted.

Code Blue. Neurosurgery–Six East, site 671. Code Blue. Neurosurgery–Six East.

I'd always found it curious that someone's death, or impending death has to be announced to the world over and over. Surely, someone could devise a silent notification more appropriate for the silence death imposes. My thoughts were drawn back to reality by the droning, repetitive page, as if no one heard it the first time.

Code Blue. Neurosurgery–Six East, site 671.

Wait a minute! I'm on Six East. Am I supposed to go to this Code Blue? I knew what it meant. What I didn't know is whether I have a role to play. Struggling to my feet, or should I say foot, I managed to hop, skip, and jump to the door. As I opened it, people of all sizes and descriptions were running down the hall and around the corner where my assailant had been carted off only half an hour ago. They too, disappeared around that corner, though as they did this time the slamming of equipment and the frantic opening of a door was inescapable. I had to go. I wasn't sure if I was supposed to, but I had to go.

Hobbling down the hall well behind the others, all the while holding my left knee bent as close to a ninety-degree angle as possible, I approached the corner. My pulse quickened as I rounded it. Just two doors past the corner was another door, this one rapidly opening and closing as various hospital personnel poured through it. They each went in, but none came out. I slowly advanced to the doorframe only to have Grigsby thrust the door open, bolting out.

"Big of you to show up, Quinton," spoken as he ran down the hall, carrying a syringe of blood. "I've got to get this blood gas to the lab. I'm helping. How about you?"

He disappeared, but not before giving me the answer as to whether I was supposed to participate in this exercise in futility. I pushed through the door and stood at the back of the room. I couldn't tell who the victim was and, frankly, didn't recognize most of the players.

That was actually a relief. I did recognize Dr. Zachary standing at the head of the gurney. Just then, the patient spewed forth what seemed to me to be an enormous amount of bloody vomit in Zachary's general direction.

"Suction!" she demanded, holding her right hand in the air as her left one thrust a silver metallic scope-like object into the patient's mouth. Now I recognized him! It was my assailant, currently in the throes of death.

I moved closer in time to see her sweep his tongue to the left and hyperextend his neck with a laryngoscope and rapidly place an endotracheal tube into his airway.

"Hyperventilate him. And give him two milligrams of *naloxone* and one milligram of *flumazenil*. Maybe this bastard OD'd. While you're at it—"

"Doctor, this is a neurosurgical service," came the timid response from one of the nursing staff. "We haven't had those meds here in years."

"Well get it, stat! And also two milligrams of *antidol*. Didn't he get *Mezperodol* about an hour ago? Does he have a rhythm?"

"He's straight line, Doctor. Asystole."

"Well, if there's one thing the late nineties taught us, it's that you don't survive asystole," she dropped everything from both hands to the gurney and tore off her gloves. "Time of death, 0945 hours. What a way to start a morning, huh?"

"What the hell happened here?"

Zachary looked up to find Dr. Pritcherman hulking in the door not one foot behind me. I started to get out of his way, but he pushed through before I could stumble out of his way. I grabbed the door jamb to stabilize my position.

"Who killed my patient? Dr. Zachary, what's going on here?"

"Your patient suffered an unwitnessed cardiac arrest. I responded as part of the code team in an attempt to resuscitate him," pausing momentarily, as if to formulate a better response, she added, "Unfortunately, we were . . . unsuccessful."

"This is a young man with a brain fart, Doctor," Pritcherman screamed. "A computer glitch, a bad chip, not a god-damned bad ticker! Hell, he can't be more than forty."

"Thirty-eight, according to his ID bracelet," Zachary responded. "A waste, yes sir. But he is dead."

"Jesus H. Christ! What am I gonna tell the Dean?"

"What are we gonna tell his family?" Zachary retorted.

"Aw, he doesn't have any family. He's homeless. The Dean asked me to treat him as a favor. Jesus, this looks bad."

"Does anybody know anything about him?" Zachary asked of those in the room. By now most had drifted out of the room, leaving Zachary at the head of the bed, Pritcherman at the foot, me off to the side, and the two second-year students who had been attending me. Two nurses were beginning to place a shroud under and around his body.

"Don't touch anything. Leave all the tubes in place," Zachary commanded. "This is a coroner's case."

"The hell it is," Pritcherman bellowed.

"But Dr. Pritcherman, no one knows how or why he died. He *has to be* a coroner's case."

"Look Zachary," he moved closer. "You don't worry about that. I'll talk to the Dean. We don't need a coroner's inquiry over the death of a poor, homeless man. That's not good use of taxpayers' dollars. An autopsy, yes, for medical reasons," he turned and leaned, conspiratorially, into her left ear. "But not for legal ones."

He pulled away and turned, looking directly at me, pulling another onion out of his lab coat. "You! Get him to pathology. I'll handle the rest." As he passed through the door, he turned once more, "And Dr. Zachary. Thank you for your efforts. I'm sure you did all you could."

"The pH is 6.8 with a bicarb of—"

"Grigsby!" Zachary interrupted the breathless third-year. "He's dead. We don't need lab results for a dead man." The frustrated surgery resident pushed passed both of us. " Fifteen minutes. Everyone in the conference room so we can get the rules straight. And someone find Smith, or whatever her name is."

"Good help, Grigsby. You killed this guy," I glared at him after Zachary had left.

"Oh, bullshit. All I—"

"Don't believe me, Grigsby? That's where Pritcherman's going right now, to tell the Dean."

"No! I really didn't!" He charged out of the room after Pritcherman.

As Grigsby left, the two second-years and I made eye contact. There in the room of a dead man the three of us began laughing. What a sight. Three medical students and a corpse. "And he thinks I'm gullible," I choked, breaking up again. "So guys," trying to regain some composure, "What say the three of us examine this guy to see if we can figure out what happened?" I hopped to the bedside just as a battle-ax of a charge nurse hurried in.

"Wait just a minute here! Back off! No medical students are going to mess with a body on my floor," the nurse commanded, pushing me back. She had no need to move the second-years out of the way. They made no attempt to get any closer to the cadaver than where they stood. "Take him to pathology. Then if you want to cut him up or whatever, you'll be in the right spot."

She wasn't joking. In fact, she was leering at me. After a very few seconds, she had waited long enough. "Now!"

We scrambled to load Mr. Doe onto the transport gurney, with minimal help from the battle-ax.

"I'll get you some crutches," the nurse admonished, staring at me with disdain borne of too many years of medical student antics. "Didn't anybody tell you not to walk on it?"

She left the three of us standing in the hallway with our friend lying motionless on the gurney. In mere seconds, she returned with a pair of crutches no one else seemed able to find.

"You two push and the cripple will do the talking. That seems to be what he does best. Now get going. Take the service elevator to the basement, turn right down a long hall, then a left and quick right and you're there. I'm calling path to notify them you're coming. Don't get lost!" She nudged us along in the direction of the elevator, shaking her head as we departed.

"Students," she could be heard to mutter as the elevator doors sealed us in. "Can't find the crap in their ass."

There was a silence that hung over the elevator like a thick, smoggy cloud. Being the senior member of our very junior triumvirate, I felt it was my obligation to break the silence.

"So have either of you ever been to pathology?" I inquired weakly. My query was met by ardent shaking of both their heads. "Have either of you ever seen an autopsy?" Again, anxious denial. I sighed loudly. "Well, if it's any consolation, neither have I," also admitting my own inexperience.

We rode the remaining minute to the basement in not-so-reverent fear of the unknown that lay ahead. Just where the hell was pathology and what would we find there when, and if, we found it? As the elevator doors opened, my two comrades pushed the corpse-laden gurney into the hall. I hobbled off just as the doors began to close. We were now in the depths of this institution of higher learning in search of the morgue.

"We might as well stick together," I offered.

"Why?"

"Well—"

"So you can screw that up, too?"

"Wait just a minute—"

"No, you listen! You stay here and we'll find the pathology suite and come back for you and the stiff," one of the second-years emphatically insisted. "You may be a third-year, but we're not letting you take us down with you."

"Now, what does that mean?"

"It means you stay here, and we promise to come right back."

And with that, the two went scurrying off down the poorly lighted hall and turned right into another corridor, shaking their heads while in private conversation as they disappeared. I leaned against the wall, propping my gimp leg on the morgue wagon.

"Why me?" I sighed. With nothing else to preoccupy me I quickly became aware of my aching leg. "They'd better hurry," I mumbled. Five minutes passed and my two sophomore associates hadn't returned. I tried to pass time studying the hallway but it held nothing of interest. Nothing, other than the gurney carrying a body I was curiously drawn to.

I couldn't stop thinking about the entire event and the patient to which I was now inextricably linked. So young, yet so very dead. Why did he bite me? And what was with the tooth? I found my hands slowly gravitating to the top of the shroud and shortly succumbed to my curiosity. As I unzipped the temporary garment, his cyanotic face emerged.

He did not appear to be at peace in death any more than he had been at the end of his life. I wanted to inspect his mouth for the socket that once held the tooth he felt so necessary to award me. So there I was, having climbed onto the gurney, now hunched over the body and just beginning to explore this man's oral cavity, when I was interrupted by the bellowing voice of a stranger.

"What in the name of God are you doing? Get down from there before I pull you off myself. Have you no respect for the dead?"

"I was only—"

"I don't care if you're the Pope and were giving him last rites. Not in the hall, and not while I'm head of pathology."

As I came down from the gurney I finally managed the wherewithal to look at my accuser. Standing between my two fellow students was a huge specimen of a man, easily six-feet-seven inches with gold, wire-rim glasses appearing even smaller because of his three-hundred pound frame, dangling precariously on the edge of his nose. In less anxious times, his flushed face might cause someone to mistake him for a Santa Claus knock-off, but not today.

I felt his hand clasp the back of my jacket and "help" me down.

"Get out of the way!" *Santa* said, pushing me aside while zipping the shroud over the head again. "You two! Get this man to the morgue before he suffers some other indignity."

As they struggled to accelerate the gurney down the hall, both were staring down at the floor. They refused to make eye contact with me. I hadn't even noticed the two second-years return.

"If you want to study the corpse I can find plenty of jobs for you," bellowed my newest tormenter. "But in the proper place at the proper time. Do you understand . . . Quinton, is it?" pulling me by my name tag.

"Yes sir. I—"

"Now come back this afternoon at four and we'll schedule your participation in your patient's autopsy."

"Oh, he's not my—"

"Four o'clock, Mr. Quinton. I trust you can find something to do until then," he called over his shoulder as he turned the corridor corner. "Four o'clock, sharp."

Geez! I sure do have something to do. The conference room in fifteen minutes. How much time had passed getting the toe-tagger down here. Should I wait for the other two? I can't make another scene, I grumbled. They're on their own. I pushed the elevator button and the doors opened. In no time, I was limping and wobbling outside the conference room door, hesitating to enter. What more could go wrong? I shrugged and attempted to slip into the room unnoticed.

"Glad you could find the time for us, Mr. Quinton," Dr. Zachary sarcastically chided. "And the second-years I've been told were in your party? Where might they be?"

"I'm sorry. I was—"

She cut me off abruptly, "No need to apologize, Quinton. I've got just the thing to keep your eyes focused on your assignment," she taunted. "Since you aren't very mobile, you are assigned to admission history and physical exams on all the new patients. Normally an intern does them and dictates them. Since you're so interested in looking into every nook and cranny you can set up an examining room and check out each and every one of our new players. Oh, and by the way, each of the H&Ps will need to be handwritten since the rest of us will be using all the dictation stations. Any questions?"

"When do I—"

"I didn't think so," Zachary concluded. "You start when we adjourn. This service admits about five new patients a day. And don't forget, all hospital admissions require a rectal examination noted on the chart. And pelvics on the females. That ought to keep that fertile mind of yours occupied."

Turning now to the assembled group. "All of you. There are practice sets for suturing. I expect you to be competent within the week. Quinton here, might have another accident and I'll let you fix him up next time."

Why did I feel this strange attraction to her? Was she kidding? Was this a one day assignment, or forever? After considering the start of my rotation, I shouldn't have even asked. I knew the answer. Forever.

Probably, forever and a day. At least a month. Or . . . forever. Here it is, not even eleven in the morning on the first day of my first clinical rotation in the third-year of medical school and I have already managed to antagonize virtually my entire team, received a battle wound, ended up on crutches, and drew the worst of all scut work assignments. I knew the third-year was a test, but were the stars conspiring against me?

Am I in a worm hole or time warp, or what? Am I the devil incarnate?

No. Just then, *he* walked through the door.

"This is the sorriest group I've ever been forced to teach," Pritcherman bellowed as he burst toward the podium, pushing Zachary aside. "Zachary, as ranking resident I'm sure you're familiar with the rules. Shit rolls downhill. If I'm unhappy, you can damn well bet you'll be unhappy. And I'm very unhappy. You jokers kill off a patient in the first hour or so and now the Dean's trying to crawl up my ass because of it. I won't take it you hear me! You've got about half a second to whip these morons into a team before I—"

He paused, surveying the room, mentally counting heads. Then he exploded. "Where *is* your team anyway? I count you, the cripple, Grigsby and two nurses. Where is the Georgetown fellow and the two second-years? Can't you even keep them all in one place? I've got a stereotaxic procedure at noon. I want you in my office at three, Zachary. You and I are gonna have a little powwow about how to run my service. The rest of you, stay out of the way and don't kill anybody else!"

He flew out of the room, the trailing tails of his lab coat barely clearing the door as it closed. The five of us sat there silently. I actually relished the quiet. It seemed to be the first relief from an otherwise horrible day.

"Well, that was fun," Zachary sighed. She was sitting at the end of the table with her chin in her hands, staring forward, a blank, disconsolate, vacant gaze. Her eyes glassed over, puffy from too little sleep over many months. Her pouty look intrigued me. She would neither give in to Pritcherman nor tears.

"You heard what he said," with a clear lack of emotion. "Shit rolls downhill. I'm begging you people. Help me . . . no, help us all . . . survive the next ten weeks. He's right about one thing. We'd better act like a team or none of us will survive. A team takes care of each other. If you make the person above you look good, then you look good. Can we commit to that?"

"Sure," Grigsby nodded.

"I'm in," I agreed.

"So Quinton, where the hell are the second-years?" Zachary asked. "Does anybody even know their names?"

"Last I saw of them, they were wheeling the dead patient into a path room with some pathologist. A big guy, red hair with a full beard and moustache. About—"

"That's Dr. Zendejas," Zachary interrupted, rather politely this time. "John Luis Zendejas. He's chief of pathology. A good guy. Very easy to work with. Remember the scare over Creutzfeldt-Jakob disease years ago? He's the one who finally found the etiologic agent proving it was a viral infection. One hell of a geneticist, too. Loves to teach. Just make sure you block out plenty of time if you ask him a question. He'll write three papers just to answer *No*."

"So he's the Mad Cow?" Grigsby asked.

"I wouldn't call him that to his face, Grigsby," Zachary suggested. "He was also the developer of the vaccine preventing the spread of it. Some people think he's a little wacky from maybe acquiring the disease. Anxiety or even psychosis is one of its early symptoms. And his ruddy face. That's one of the early side effects of his first vaccine. He's no martyr, but no one would support his research until he proved it was safe by vaccinating himself. That stunt makes him a bit strange by definition."

Subconsciously, she flipped her bangs out of her eyes. On the other hand, I was entirely conscious of it.

"Well, he wants me back at four o'clock for that guy's autopsy," I added.

"He wants you? Are you sure it isn't the other way around?"

"You're right, Dr. Zachary," I admitted. "There's something weird about that dead guy."

"Quinton, this is a neurosurgical service." Leaning forward, she patted me on the cheek and continued, "There's something weird about every part of it—from our attending physician, to the patients, to the staff—no offense to the nursing staff currently in attendance," acknowledging the two nurses on our team. They nodded their assent. "Our job is to get through this learning experience, hopefully, in one piece. That means you and Grigsby are responsible for the second-years and I'm responsible for the two of you."

"What about Dr. Smith? What happened to her?"

"You leave her to me, Quinton," Zachary replied, glancing upward at the ceiling for a moment, then back to each of us. "You leave her to me."

We all sat there contemplating our various roles. It was obvious what our goal was: to survive these next ten weeks. The devil would be in the details.

"And Quinton," Zachary added. "The second-years. Find out their names."

– Never Take Things At Face Value –

III

*M*edical record number 15-0039678. The subject is a thirty-eight-year-old white male weighing seventy-six kilograms. Height one hundred seventy-five-and-a-quarter centimeters. The subject appears to be his stated age. There are visible external signs of trauma to both wrists and ankles linear, band-like contusion-abrasions consistent with hard restraints. Subject—"

"Dr. Zendejas, you started early," I blurted, as I was ushered into the autopsy suite by an assistant.

"Four o'clock to me means ten minutes early young man," stated matter-of-factly by the pathologist without looking from the table. The room wasn't at all what I had imagined. What I had thought would be drab and dirty was brightly lit, like an operating room, with a sterile-appearing stainless steel table in the center and the subject of the moment laid out head-to-toe. The table was somewhat elevated at the head end, but I didn't understand why. There was a microphone hanging down over the table with an activating foot pedal.

"Show our guest how to gown up and put a mask on him," Zendejas instructed his assistant. The smell would have been overwhelming had there not been a large, overhead ventilation system constantly clearing the atmosphere in the room with its laminar airflow. The pathologist finished his descriptive overview of our patient while I dressed: "There are *in situ* two large-bore intravenous lines, an endotracheal tube extending from the oral cavity and chest contusions consistent with an automated cardiopulmonary resuscitation device. The various catheters are removed post-mortem."

As he spoke, his assistant quickly removed all artificial life support materials placed during this poor soul's final minutes.

"Flip him over, John. Let's not miss a knife or anything." The corpse was rolled onto its side and an inspection of the posterior aspect made. "Signs of post-mortem lividity are present as is rigor mortis, indicating the patient's death is consistent with the reported time of death of 0945 hours today. What the hell day is it, John? Aw, hell, add the right date to the report, will you, Shirley," Zendejas chuckled into the microphone. "You know I never know what the day is or where I am," looking up from the table at me. So why are you here, Mr. Quinton?"

"I don't understand why he died. I don't—"

"You've never seen anyone die before, have you, son?"

"No, but my parents—"

"And it frustrates you, makes you crazy. Right?"

"Correct. They were killed."

"That's why you chose medicine as a career. You have a passion to understand life and a need to try and preserve it at all costs."

"No, not at all. I—"

"Do you know how to open a chest, lad? It's called a Rokitansky incision," Zendejas continued. I noticed him holding a scalpel in his left hand. Without further explanation, he placed the blade at the distal tip of the left clavicle and made a slashing incision deep enough to score each of the ribs as he drew the blade tangentially across the left chest to the xiphoid and quickly repeated the maneuver from the right clavicle, making a "V" shaped gash in the cadaver's chest. He completed the task by deeply incising from the xiphoid to the pubis, being careful not to damage any of the internal organs, and creating a large, Y-shaped incision in the process.

"Draw the usual blood samples for post-mortem toxicology and the like, eh, John?" Without missing a beat, John was filling several multi-colored vials and placing them on an adjoining table.

Along the V portion of the Y-shaped incision, Zendejas used a pair of long-handled stainless steel shears–that looked much like garden loppers—to sever each of the ribs in order to fold the rib cage back over the subject's face with skin intact and expose the chest cavity. Just like that, we were ready for the business of the post-mortem examination of the trunk. Within a few seconds, Zendejas had filleted this man's chest and abdomen in such a way as to reveal the glistening inner organs of both cavities. It was all very efficient.

Now I knew why the head was elevated. As this specimen was carefully dissected, the fluids from his various cavities and organs trickled out onto the metallic table and trickled down toward the feet by gravity. As they reached the feet, they passed through a hole in the table into a collection container. Minuscule drops of blood percolated to the surface, slowly drifting to the foot of the table and into the bucket. I concluded autopsy bleeding was certainly less dramatic than the bloodbath of this man's assault on my leg.

"Nothing much here," he murmured. "I should've been a butcher," he exclaimed. "Notice the lungs are pinkish-blue, indicating he wasn't a smoker. There's a frothy fluid indicative of pulmonary edema, probably the result of whatever killed him. Not unusual, eh, Quinton?"

With that, he excised the lungs and heart at their base, rapidly dissected them apart, tossing our patient's heart with a plunking noise onto scales hanging nearby. As it swung gently back-and-forth, his assistant voice recorded the weights of the heart and then of the two lungs Zendejas had next pitched into the scales.

"So what the hell killed this bastard? Any ideas Quinton?"

"Well, it happened—"

"Suddenly? Like it was unexpected?" he smiled at me. "Son, death is always unexpected. Especially to the victim. Next, I suppose, you're going to tell me he shouldn't have died? John, finish up the chest and abdomen. Quinton here wants to crack this man's skull."

"No, I—"

"Take the scalpel and make an incision from one ear to the other at the base of his scalp."

"I couldn't, I—"

"Do it, *damn it!* And don't be one of those pansy-ass internist-types who barely scratch the surface. Cut him, boy! One swift motion and be done. Now divide and conquer!"

With firm resolve, but little skill, I closed my eyes and plunged the scalpel into the back of his head in my first, albeit post-mortem, surgical incision. What, in my mind, I had deemed a vicious gash barely broke the skin of our subject's scalp. And it hadn't even penetrated the subcutaneous tissue to the galea.

"Give me the blade, son," nearly ripping the Bard-Parker from my hand. Zendejas thrust the blade tip first behind the right ear and pulled this surgical sword posteriorly, then circumferentially around his head and back to the left ear. He briskly dissected the tissue beneath his incision away and pulled the man's scalp from the back of his neck forward, gently lancing any straggler strands of tissue that did not give way to his skin-scalping traction. In no time, the skin from the back of the scalp had been stretched down over the man's face revealing a yellow-red, shiny, cue ball dome of a head. "Now take the scalpel and open the tissues down to the bone, Mr. Quinton. And no more timidity. Cut with authority, son. *With authority!*"

I tried with all the strength of conviction to make a valiant effort, but to no avail. The pathologist again grabbed the scalpel from my hand and using his thumb as a scribe against the head, parsed the underlying tissue to the bone. "Bone saw," he called without looking up. The methodical to-and-fro of the vibrating blade was instantly pushed against the cranium and, within moments, the bony skullcap was being lifted from his head. "Hold the scalpel, Quinton," he ordered. "Now that's a fine looking brain!" Zendejas marveled. "Doesn't look grossly diseased. Well, I'll be . . . won't you take a look at that—"

As he spoke, the previously bright lights flickered and died, bathing the entire autopsy suite in an eerie darkness. I found myself trying to see the gloved hand I had instinctively drawn to a few centimeters from my nose. Here I was in the windowless basement of a big-city hospital, on the first day of the third-year of medical school on my first clinical rotation, terrified by the inky still of the coal miner-like pitch-black. In this kind of blind darkness one's other senses take over. The pounding of my heart echoed in my ears, and its rate was accelerating.

"Now isn't this like a horror movie," Zendejas chuckled. "Don't go psycho on me, people. Let's all acknowledge we're all still here. Count off, folks."

"Boo!" his assistant, John, whispered, and then laughed out loud.

"And I'm assuming you haven't died on me, or anything, Mr. Quinton?"

"No," I feebly answered. "But it's still a possibility."

I again checked my night vision by placing my right hand in front of my face until it touched my nose. I could feel it, but I couldn't see it. This was a darkness I had never experienced. My terror was unexpectedly interrupted by another voice.

"I'm alright, too."

"Who's that?" Zendejas asked, also surprised by our unforeseen guest. "Where are you? And where did you come from?"

"I've been interested in this patient's autopsy, too. I didn't want to disturb you. I . . . "

"Who are you?"

"My name's Smith. I'm a post-graduate fellow from Georgetown University. Jessica Smith. I hope I didn't startle anyone."

"How long have you been watching? Aw, what difference does it make?" Zendejas grumbled. "Do you always go around scaring people in the dark?"

"No sir. I'm just as nervous about this as you."

With my other senses heightened, I couldn't help hearing the metallic sound coming closer, although still perceptibly several feet away. What the hell was it, I wondered. Smith was surely the perpetrator of the noise and I stumbled across the room to confirm it. Limping in the dark, I fell over a Mayo stand—a metal surgical table with C-shaped legs—meant to be positioned over a bed for holding instruments. As I crashed to the ground, John and Dr. Zendejas both let out a frightened shout. I felt a hand on my left shoulder and another under my right arm—not trying to help me up, but holding me down instead.

"Are you alright, Quinton?" Smith asked. "You could get hurt in the dark."

"How did you—"

There was an unexpected burning sensation in my right hip. Instantaneously, the room was spinning in spite of the blackness. Within seconds, my consciousness was draining into the murky darkness.

As I drifted into peaceful unconsciousness, I thought I heard myself sputter, "What the—"

"Quinton! Can you hear me? If you can hear me, squeeze my fingers," Dr. Zachary was yelling into the right side of my head. That did nothing but exacerbate the incredible pounding, water hammer of a headache that dominated my return to consciousness. She cradled my head forward in anticipation of me talking but instead was greeted with projectile vomitus to her left ear.

Real good, Quinton, I fought through the haze. *You're really making a great impression on her by puking.* I wretched several times before regaining full awareness of my surroundings. Even in my stupor, I knew I had been moved from what I remembered as my last grounding. *Where was the pathology suite, the darkness, Zendejas? What time was it, and on what day? Where was Smith? Why did she inject me with . . . with . . . whatever?*

"Where am I?" groaning and grasping at my head, but realizing only one hand was free. The other was bound to the bed I was currently occupying with a large bore intravenous line delivering fluids through my right forearm which was secured to an arm board to prevent involuntary movement. "Why am I—"

"A lot's happened since you left us, Quinton," Zachary smirked. "You're becoming a full time job, you know,." Stroking my hair away from my forehead as she subconsciously flipped hers.

"No, I don't know!" I barked in frustration. "I don't even—"

"Slow down, Quinton, slow down. You've had an interesting few days."

"*Days?* Do you mean I've been out for days? Jesus Christ, I've got to—"

"You got to lie back down and let your wounds heal."

"Wounds? Dr. Zachary, I was drugged. I remember—"

"What exactly do you remember, Quinton? Do you remember sustaining a damned impressive contusion to the frontal aspect of your noggin? Look here," she raised a mirror for me to see.

There was a violaceous hematoma of my right forehead that undeniably ached. Ached, pounded, pulsated, and boiled. Still, the boiling was born of believing no one would listen to what I know is the truth. The truth was not coma-induced.

"I didn't hit my head. I tripped and . . ."

"Right," Zachary laughed. "I suppose someone just manufactured the black-and-blue little forehead ditty?"

"Look," I was frustrated. "The lights went out and Dr. Smith was in the room. I stumbled while trying to find out why, or—"

"Or what, Quinton? Or maybe you fell and don't remember much after that? Smith? Why would she be there when you fell?"

"No, damn it! I remember a burning in my right hip and then getting very sleepy. We were in the middle of the autopsy on . . . you know . . . the guy who died yesterday."

"Quinton," Zachary calmly advised, "you've been unconscious for three days. The burning in your hip was the scalpel embedded in your hip when you fell. The damn thing ought to burn," she patted my wound.

"No! I was injected with—"

"Nobody injected you and nobody died yesterday. At least nobody you know about. Are you talking about the psycho who died on your first day?"

"Yes!" I shouted, sitting up and grasping her shoulders. "That's the man. I was at his autopsy when the power failure happened and Smith—"

"Quinton," Zachary lightly slapped my face–actually more a caress than a slap. "Snap out of it! The guy died, but the autopsy was cancelled by the Dean. You've hallucinated the rest, or dreamed it up, or something."

"*No! I was there.* It was started. I was late. Then Dr. Zendejas—"

"Dr. Zendejas?" she looked perplexed. He left three days ago on a long-scheduled vacation to the Cayman Islands. The Dean appointed Dr. Orlando acting head."

"I had the son-of-a-bitch's head in my hand and his assistant was weighing his organs, for God's sake! I screamed. "What's his first name?"

"Who?"

"Zendejas' assistant?"

"I don't know," she arched her eyes. "I think it's John. Why?"

"Don't you see? He was there. He can confirm what I'm saying about—"

"Quinton!" Zachary was clearly exasperated. "You have to rest. Fabrication is a normal consequence of post-traumatic concussion syndrome. Your MRI showed a small right frontal intra-cranial contusion, but no serious injury. It'll take a few weeks to get back to normal. But you will get back to normal," she stated emphatically. "Whatever *your* normal is," she added for insult.

"Where's Dr. Smith?"

"Now that's the first sensible thing you've said. Where indeed," Zachary looked off into the distance, curling her bottom lip. "She's never around when she should be, is she?" She tensed up, with the question, agitated. "I don't know, Quinton. She seems to float about this service without any responsibilities. Pritcherman doesn't pay any attention to her and she damn sure won't listen to anything I say."

There was a measure of futility in her tone that I hadn't heard before.

"That son-of-a-bitch."

"Who?"

"Pritcherman," Zachary answered. "He's so obsessed with his little pet projects that he doesn't see the forest for the trees."

Now she was fuming. "Damn it, Quinton. Get well so I can abuse you again," she snarled, flipping her bangs as she spoke. She was standing at the foot of my bed, ready to exit the room. As she reached for the door, she turned and looked right at me. "A few days ago you said something was weird about this rotation. You're damned right about that, Quinton. Weirder than any I've ever been on," she paused. "Get some rest. I'll get you discharged. You got a roommate or somebody who can take you home, stud?"

"Not really. I live alone."

"Figures," she sighed. "Alright, Quinton. You just lie there for the next thirty minutes and I'll take you home. You do live somewhere, don't you?"

I fell back onto the bed as she left. It was just me and the holes in the ceiling again. I was beginning to tire of counting them. And fantasizing about Zachary. As a matter-of-fact, I was getting tired of a lot of things.

The final indignity of my introduction to clinical medicine was being paraded through the wards of University Hospital in a wheelchair by the battle-ax of a charge nurse who had insulted me only a few days earlier. I swear she found a route to the ground floor that passed by my every classmate on any and every ward.

At each station, she stopped to make some patronizing comment about how hospital policy required me to stay in the chair while I was convalescing. Besides, I had already proved myself a klutz with my self-inflicted buttocks and head wounds, always emphasizing the posterior injury most loudly. My wheeled processional eventually reached the employee parking structure where Dr. Zachary was waiting.

"Did you pass through Idaho on your way?" she scoffed.

"We had to make a couple of stops along the way," I responded, deciding to cut the battle-ax a break, as she might be helpful in the future. A medical student quickly learns who really runs a hospital and it isn't the residents or the attendings.

No, they come and go over the years as regular as the seasons. But the nursing staff is a fixture. They know the idiosyncrasies, the strengths and the weaknesses of all who pass through their domain. To cross one unnecessarily is to commit *seppuku* slowly, surely and most assuredly.

"Thanks for bringing down my cross to bear, Sandy," Zachary smiled. So she knew the battle-ax. "See you tomorrow." Seems she, too, had learned the lesson.

In no time I was strapped into the passenger seat of her vintage 1998 bright red Ford F-150 pickup truck, complete with all the accoutrements of the day—an out-of-date CD player with no old CDs, and push-button radio, permanently stuck in the AM mode, air conditioning that blew warm dust, and mud flaps appended to the wheel wells.

"Where the hell are you from anyway, Dr. Zachary? Mars?"

As I surveyed her vehicle, she could see I was impressed.

"Almost. Oklahoma. In the hill country."

"Hills? I thought Oklahoma was flat?"

"It is," starting the motor and accelerating away from the parking facility. "Unless you go into the northeast corner, the foothills of the Ozarks. There are lakes, and trees and hills. Lush, rolling hills you Yankees know nothing about. Where to, Quinton?"

"Take the interstate south to State Street. Then west for three blocks. I'm in student housing at the undergraduate school."

"Why there? Why didn't you move closer to the medical school?" she was puzzled.

"Well," I hesitated. "I was the last person accepted in my class. I figured I'd flunk out and I didn't want to have to move back in less than a year."

"But you're a third-year now," she countered. "Maybe no one's told you, but you get to stay, Quinton. You're not gonna be thrown out. You can move down here with the rest of your medical colleagues."

"I know, I know. It's just that . . . it's such a pain to move," I protested. "I'm kind of a pack rat. I keep a lot of stuff other people would throw away. Old articles, newspapers, even Internet postings. I can't get past thinking I'll need them later."

"Quinton," she frowned. "That's why God invented libraries and the Internet. I guess you don't believe in the paperless office." She had turned the last corner and parked in the handicapped zone in front of my building.

"I really appreciate the ride. Would you like to come up for a drink?"

"Quinton," she sighed. "I don't have any choice. You can't walk without falling on a knife or something. I'm gonna make sure you get inside your place. I'm not gonna be responsible for another one of your incidents."

"That's unfair. I didn't—"

She held her left index finger across my lips. "Enough. I'm joking . . . but not really," laughing as she spoke. "Besides, you are kinda cute." She helped me back onto my crutches and led me towards the elevator. "What floor?"

"Penthouse."

"Seriously, Quinton. What floor?"

"I'm not kidding. The penthouse," I sheepishly grinned.

"I took over the whole top floor during my junior year in college. I kinda got settled in."

"That must cost a fortune," whistling softly. "So you've got money, huh?"

"Well . . . a little. Or my family did. It's in trust for me. Probably a good idea so I don't have to pay attention to it."

"Yeah, it's nice to only have to cash the checks," she smirked. The elevator opened into a spacious room thirty by twenty feet that served as my kitchen, study and entertainment center.

"Come in and make yourself at home," I hobbled to an overstuffed brown suede couch in the middle of the room. Zachary was walking about the property scrutinizing my not-so-humble abode.

"Not bad, Quinton," she whistled again. "So where's that drink you promised?"

I pressed a remote and a full bar complete with ice machine and various liquors and mixers rose from the floor. With another remote I turned the music down that had started the moment we walked through the door.

"How did it do that?" she asked.

"It recognizes my DNA signature," I answered. "There's a sensor at the front door. It wouldn't have opened if it hadn't recognized me."

"And you installed this yourself?"

"Genetic biology was my major. I'm not as big a bungler as you might think."

"Prove it," she suggested, pouring herself a large, stiff scotch. "What'll you have?"

"Red wine," I replied. "I think tonight a '91 *Silver Oak* is in order. You'll find that in the cellar."

"You've got to be kidding?"

"No. That's the door next to the refrigerator. It holds about fifteen hundred bottles. Do you know *Silver Oak?*"

"I know *of* it. It's a bit rich for my budget. What are you having, Napa, or Alexander Valley?" She found the cellar and was perusing the selections.

"Actually, I was thinking of the *Bonny's Vineyard.*"

"They made that in '91?"

"It's the last year."

"There may actually be some redeeming social value to you after all, Quinton," slamming down her scotch while carrying the Cabernet to the bar. She was quite deft with the cork, opening it while nearly simultaneously pouring herself another scotch. She brought me the wine and plopped down on the couch.

"So Quinton," she continued, coming closer. "What else don't I know about you?"

— Always Look For The Hidden Agenda —

IV

*D*EAD!?* What the hell do you mean, Zendejas is dead?" I bolted from a pain-medication-drunken-induced sleep. "And where the hell are you? When did you leave? I mean . . . how did you, did anything happen? When did you . . . aw, *shit!*" I screamed into the telephone at Zachary.

I was quickly becoming aware of the multitude of pounding body parts–my head, leg, buttocks, and . . . my head–front and back, occipital and frontal, parietal and temporal, down to the very thalamus of my essence. I was a mixture of emotions and symptoms–my heart pounding from fear and excitement, nausea from death and alcohol, head throbbing from all the unanswered questions straining to be asked.

"What happened to Zendejas?" I shouted into the receiver. My mania was quickly replaced with suspicions of why. What about a grand conspiracy that gnawed at the pit of my epigastrium–my gut screamed, *"Foul! Does not compute! Error!"*

"You're telling me . . . the man I only met . . . during an autopsy . . . an autopsy that supposedly never happened . . . is . . . dead?"

As I questioned Zachary, the vertigo finally overcame me. I wandered toward the bathroom and "tossed my cookies" in the general direction of the toilet, missing for the most part. The porcelain throne now held only a small portion of the previous night's folly. *Clean-up would be a bitch.* I struggled again to unleash my fury upon this unyielding, inanimate object and, in my haste to make my deposit, my leg wound collided with its cold, solid edge adding further insult to injury. What a way to start the day.

"Quinton!" Zachary snapped into my ear in a low-keyed, almost exasperated tone. "Maybe we should talk about your . . . um . . . hallucinations. Meet me in an hour at . . . I don't know—"

"Hallucinations?"

"The incident you said happened during the autopsy."

"You still don't believe—"

"Not now, damn it!"

"How 'bout at Zendejas' office?"

"Too crowded."

"What about—"

"Quinton," Zachary cut me off, "Pritcherman's throwing a hissy fit. He's—"

"Because of Zendejas?"

"Of course not," she whispered into the phone. "The prick only mentioned his death in passing. He's so hung up on himself he wouldn't notice if I dropped dead right under his nose."

In the background I could hear Pritcherman screaming Zach's name. "You mean he wouldn't care. What makes that guy tick? I tell you—"

"Gotta go. I'll see you in an hour at O'Reilly's. In the back."

"*ZACHARY!*" Pritcherman screamed, "What does it take to get your attention? Do *I* need to *call you* on the telephone? If you can spare a few moments from your busy social life, we might just complete rounds soon enough for you to make that hot date you were arranging."

Pritcherman was in rare form. Zach didn't realize she'd left her cell phone on and I was the vicarious beneficiary of his vituperative venom. *"AND TURN THAT DAMNED THING OFF!"* There was a fumbling noise and then the call terminated.

Beneficiary, that is, until she disconnected our two-way link. Now my pulse, blood pressure, and other vital signs were up and ready for the day. Pritcherman even rattled me from afar. I was standing and pacing as I listened to what had just transpired. The *adrenaline* surge, really an *epinephrine* burst, had me ready for "fight or flight."

In a few moments, I was dressed and ready to go. Now all I had to do was find something to do for the intervening hour until my rendezvous with Zachary. I was obsessed with the grand conspiracy. I was also becoming obsessed with her as well. In spite of my forehead contusion, I knew I hadn't struck my head. I knew I had attended an autopsy, an autopsy conducted on the corpse of a man who, in life, had once looked me straight in the eyes. Not at Pritcherman, or Zachary, or anyone else. A corpse so previously vital and violent as to take a piece of my leg in a desperate attempt to convince someone, even a perfect stranger, that he wasn't deranged– that he needed his . . . *my* . . . help.

But why? Who was he? What was he trying to tell me? And why would someone want to suppress the results of an autopsy on a homeless degenerate. Or was he? And why am I the only person who gets it? Or do I? What I needed was someone who believed me and my story. But who? I had no close friends, no confidants. The closest ones I thought I had were cohabitants of my nightmare. Who was I going to enlist? Pritcherman? Grigsby? The second-years? Smith? Zachary?

What I needed was to run this whole thing by Zachary in an hour. Any excuse to be with her. *Maybe I really am crazy.* Or maybe I can pose enough questions she can't answer to convince her I'm not.

O'Reilly's is the stereotypical *place* on every college campus, in any college city. Sawdust on the floor, copious pitchers of beer served to all manner of patrons regardless of age, sex, or state of consciousness, bright red-and-white checkered tablecloths with dim lighting guaranteed to hide both identities and grunge on the floor, along with sufficient background noise to mask conversations. It was into this den of iniquity I ventured to wait for Zachary. Finding a booth near the back, I sat, fidgeting, picking at the semblance of food I ordered, and thought about what I could say to convince her something aberrant was in the works.

"That bastard sprayed onion juice all over my face," Zachary shouted, sliding into her side of the cubicle, feverishly blotting her napkin into my water and dabbing her face. "Come here. *Smell me!*" Zach commanded, pulling on the front of my shirt.

"You're okay." Was she ever. In spite of the onion, she smelled wonderful to me. "How'd he do that?"

"Screaming and eating at the same time. There ought to be a law."

"So what happened to Dr. Zendejas?"

"Unbelievable," she sighed. "The poor guy drowned. He was attending an immunology conference down there. He was one of the keynote speakers. When he didn't show up the second day they went searching for him. The coroner had already found him though."

"Where? I mean, in a pool or . . . where?"

"Don't know anything else. It took an act of Congress just to get that much out of Pritcherman."

"How does *he* know?"

"He didn't say," Zachary heaved a deep expiratory sigh. "He made some derogatory, uncouth remark–almost in passing. Nobody else really knew who he was."

"You said you wanted to talk about my hallucinations," I hesitated. "Well, I'm not convinced that—"

"Look, Quinton," she interrupted. "I shouldn't believe anything you say. I'm not sure I do, I just . . . I need to hear what you thought happened again. Something doesn't make sense."

"You're damned right something doesn't make sense," I shouted. "I—"

"Quinton!" she shouted-in-a-whisper. "Keep your voice down. No reason to tell the whole damn world."

"Yeah, yeah. I know," I calmed down. "Sorry. You say there was no autopsy? Then where did you find me?"

"You were found in a stair well leading down from Six East. You'd obviously fallen and struck your head on the concrete steps."

"Who found me?"

"The second-years. I sent them to look for you after they said they'd seen you going down those stairs in a hurry."

"Yeah, I was late for the autopsy. Around four o'clock. When was I found?"

"Sometime after six."

"A.M. or P.M.?

"P.M. Why?"

"And the scalpel?"

"I assumed—"

"That's the problem. You and everyone else just assumed. So did the perpetrator."

"Slow down, Quinton," Zachary cautioned. "I assumed you had it in your pocket. Remember, you did earlier? Practicing suturing? Remember?"

"I had it in my hand from the autopsy on John Doe."

"Really? And you were carrying it in your right hip pocket when you fell, stabbing yourself in the buttocks?"

"Dr. Zachary," I paused. "I'm *left-handed*. If I'd had it in my pocket it would've been in the *left*, not the right?."

Zachary just sat there, quietly thinking about what I'd just said.

"Zach, um . . . did we, uh . . . What exactly happened last night? When did you leave? Did we—"

"Spare me, Quinton," with a ridiculing look. "I'm your resident superior. We had a few drinks. I probably shouldn't have done that. But—"

"But you did have a good time, didn't you?"

"Yes, Quinton, I had a swell time," Zachary grinned. "So did my head. Next time you offer me scotch, give me the cheap crap. That forty-year-old single malt stuff is way too smooth to put down," she smiled. She was twisting her fork in the linguine. She moved closer to me and I began twisting her hair. Leaning forward and grinning, she asked, "You said Smith was there? During the autopsy?"

"Yeah, but Zendejas didn't know about it until the power failure. After the lights went out, Zendejas asked everyone to count off. First, John answered, then me, then Smith. Before that, no one knew she was there."

"Funny," Zach seemed puzzled. "I don't remember a power failure. She certainly never mentioned an autopsy. She—"

"And she won't unless we can catch her in a lie," I interrupted. "I'll bet she won't even acknowledge her presence there since that would support my charge that she drugged me!" I was becoming hyperactive again.

Zachary raised her hand and, without explanation, I knew she was trying to get me to lower my voice.

"Look Zach, I wasn't in the autopsy more than an hour so she had plenty of time to get me into the hall."

"You're jumping to conclusions regarding our little princess."

"She stabbed and drugged me! She's no friend of mine, let me tell you—"

"Nor mine," Zachary groused. "But what's her angle? How does she fit into your little scheme? What's her story? Find that out and I'll bet we solve several mysteries."

"So do you believe me now?"

"It's still a bit too paranoid, Quinton," she confided as she moved away. "I need some time. Let's go find what's-his-name, John, in the path department. He should be able to clear up this mess."

"I'm still on sick leave for a few more days," I reminded her. "You find John. I've got something else to do. Besides, I shouldn't be hanging around the hospital if I'm on disability."

"Call me if anything comes up," she insisted. "And Quinton . . . try and hold the paranoia to a dull roar." Standing, Zach turned to leave. "You get the tab, rich boy," laughing as she walked away.

I wasn't going anywhere just yet. Out came my smart phone, and in no time I was logged onto the Internet through a secure VPN connection. *Let's just run a search on the Cayman Islands . . . vital statistics . . . say, deaths in the last ten days*, I quietly declared. After about fifteen seconds, a list of thirteen decedents appeared. Midway through the list the name made me shudder.

J.L. Zendejas. Age 57. Presumed drowned at sea. No known next of kin.

My cynical side was raising its head again. What's with this "presumed drowned?" Didn't they find a body? What the hell was a three hundred-pounds-plus, fifty-seven-year-old man doing in the ocean? At least, I hypothesized, he was in the ocean, since they could have found his body in a pool. *But how did they know his name or age? Were they guessing, or did they have his identification? And if they did have his ID, was it with him?* As I logged off, it was clear I still had more questions than answers. Until I had more answers I wasn't going to call Zachary.

She had her own crosses to bear. I hoped I was one of them. I limped-stumbled out the door and headed back to my place to sort some things out. It was time to make a few phone calls.

"Quinton! Answer your damn phone!"

"I just did. Where are—"

"Don't say a word," Zachary demanded. "It seems your buddy, John, quit three days ago. He hasn't been around since he and Zendejas had a major falling out." She was clearly angered by the series of events. "I don't believe it. *I just don't believe it!* I'm tired of being jerked around by you and your conspiracy. I'm gonna talk to—"

"*Talk to no one*," I interrupted. "You're not going to talk to anyone. Not yet. That doesn't make sense. Zendejas didn't impress me as the kind of guy who'd have a blowout with anyone. And three days ago? That's when this whole thing started!"

"I'm a surgeon," my new-found companion asserted. "I want answers and I don't want any more plots or intrigue. Just the truth." She was really worked up now. "The pathology secretary can't tell me. You can't tell me. Pritcherman won't, or doesn't know. I think I'm gonna talk to the Dean."

"What if he's involved?"

"Another conspirator, Quinton?"

"Look," I was trying to talk more calmly. "Who sent this guy to Pritcherman in the first place? Who was Pritcherman afraid of when you brought up the coroner?"

"Maybe Pritcherman's involved with the Dean, too, huh Quinton?"

"Maybe."

"*GET REAL!*" she screamed into the telephone. "Another conspirator? I suppose everyone else on this service is involved in your scheme, too?"

"All I'm saying is that going to the Dean exposes what we know and makes us targets."

"And what do we know, Quinton? Targets of whom?"

"I'll tell you what we know," I breathed into the phone. "We know there was something weird about this guy and he ended up dead. Then he ended up in pathology where I saw him start to undergo an autopsy that you say didn't happen, performed by a pathologist who's dead now, too. And he was assisted in that autopsy by a guy who quit after having a job-ending fight with this patsy? Oh, and by the way, Dr. Smith, another weirdo that no one knows anything about, witnessed the autopsy. I'll tell you what we need to find."

"What?"

"That guy's body and examine it."

"Now you're the weirdo, Quinton."

"No, listen," I continued. "Everyone agrees he made it to pathology. Not everyone agrees he had an autopsy. Well whether he did or not should be pretty damned obvious."

There was a long pause. I could almost hear her thinking. She was dotting the Is and crossing the Ts and, in the final analysis, she knew I was right. "Quinton," she finally said. "You're gonna get us both killed, too. I just know it."

"Well? That's what we have to do, right? There's some planning we need to do in advance. Meet me back at my place."

"Yeah, alright," she answered. "But, geez, do you have to be so melodramatic about it?"

"You tell me. Breaking into a necropsy suite at night isn't melodramatic?"

"Okay, it's not melodramatic . . . ," there was an interminable silence. "It's crazy."

Several hours later, Zachary knocked on the front door. I knew it was her, having programmed the DNA security system to recognize her from a sample taken from her scotch glass the night before. I just *love* fingerprints. The great thing about having this kind of doorbell is it leaves a perfect index finger impression on the specially designed scanner, allowing me to trace and log anyone's fingerprints and DNA who comes a-calling. I took hers from the glass, but I had catalogued virtually all the doorbell-ringers over the last few years. By writing a screening program, I was able to automatically answer the DNA signatures of unwanted guests with a cryptic message dissuading them from future solicitations. It worked great on fund raisers, vagabonds and even Grigsby. It also allowed me a heads-up on who was at the door. None of those peep-holes in the door for me. I was high tech.

"Alright, Quinton. I'm here, but I'm not happy about it," as she charged through my portal, I could tell Zachary was studying my security system. "How does this thing work?" she queried me. She was clearly not in the best of moods.

"My, my aren't we a bit crabby this afternoon. I'm happy to see you in spite of your mood."

"OK, I'll lighten up," she grabbed me around the waist. "This damn thing, this break-in you're talking about," she paused. "I've been thinking about it, too. So I called a friend who knows something about locks. He gave me a master key."

"What?"

"I don't know," she paused. "Somehow, it'll open most doors when you don't have the right key."

"What if it's a keyless entry like my place?"

"Then we're up the creek, pal."

"Not necessarily. I've got some other ideas—"

"Quinton, what the hell are you doing in medicine? Why didn't you join the FBI or something?"

"Well, I did, sort of. I'm in medicine to do research. That's detective work of a similar kind. Want a *Dr. Pepper*?" pouring her one without waiting.

"Okay, rich boy. Out with your life's story." She was giving me trouble but I could tell she really did want to know. I was beginning to observe that put-downs were her trademark. Maybe it was the resident-medical student thing, or the surgeon mentality.

Or, maybe she was just as insecure as I was, just in different shoes. She'd taken her beverage and was sitting down.

"I thought we probably covered most of this last night?"

"Who'd remember, Quinton."

I took a long breath, "I don't do well around people."

"What am I, Quinton, chopped liver?"

"No, what I mean is . . . uh. . . I feel uncomfortable poking and prodding. I can barely carry on a conversation without drenching myself in perspiration and self-doubt."

"I did some checking, Quinton," she laughed. "You're no dummy. Undergraduate biology degree with honors, masters in cellular biology. So why clinical medicine?"

"I never wanted this. All I wanted to do was neurobiological research. I've got some ideas."

"Yeah, I know about your ideas."

"No, really," I confessed. "Some asshole assigned me to Pritcherman to widen my experience. Something about '*knowing what the brain does in living people will make you better understand the dead one's cells*' type of theory."

"Let me guess. Someone in student assignments?"

"Right."

"I think they do that on purpose to everybody," she was grinning. "They got me, too. All I wanted to do was go back to the Oklahoma hills and dispense shots and pills to the natives. All I wanted, until I spent my first night of my third-year of med school in the trauma room of the emergency department."

"Oh God, all the screaming and carrying on," I shuttered. "What in the hell interested you there?"

"A twenty-something year old guy stabbed in the heart who came in as a full arrest. The surgery resident cracked his chest in about ten seconds." As she talked, she stood up and began running her hand around my left chest.

"With one motion he'd divided the skin and subcutaneous tissues and entered the left chest, exposing the heart. I'd never seen a real heart before. There it was, less than a foot from my face, but nearly still, quivering, without a sustaining rhythm. Calmly, this guy divided the pericardium and a gush of blood spewed forth, releasing the pericardial tamponade created by the stab wound. The patient's heart spontaneously began to beat again.

"The resident pulled me up on the gurney, forcing me to kneel over that limp body, and guided my hands around the heart. He told me to feel the heartbeat, to feel the essence of life. As I did, the blood flow to the patient's brain must have been adequate to support consciousness, because the guy woke up with me kneeling over him, my hands in his chest, on his heart. I'd ridden a horse before, but this was the bucking bronco ride of my life. I was hooked. I'd just helped save this guy's life. At least the resident made me think I'd helped. To see immediately the results of your endeavors, I mean, this guy went from dead to bronco in a few moments. Now, that was for me. No pill-popping prescription patsy for me. I want to see results."

"So I've noticed."

"I know I'm not the most patient person," Zach confessed. "That's why surgery suits my personality. I want to see results. I'm willing to work hard to get them, but I want to see them, and see them quickly."

"A little preparation will help guarantee we see results," I reminded her. "What are we trying to accomplish? What are we trying to do?"

"Besides getting ourselves in a lot of trouble if we get caught?"

"Seriously," I cautioned. "We cannot afford to get caught. Not only would it expose us to the bad guys but it'd put us at risk as well."

"Who are the 'bad guys,' Quinton? Wait a minute. Now you've got me conspiring. Are there really bad guys? That's basically what we're going there for. If there is no body, and no records, are there really any bad guys?"

"And if there *is* a body, and it *has* been autopsied, wouldn't it prove there *are* bad guys?"

"It wouldn't prove there are bad guys, but it'd go a long way toward convincing me. And I'd agree that something happened, and that somebody had some explaining to do."

Zachary was sitting so close I inhaled her fragrance with each breath I took. I looked up to meet her eyes. As I leaned in toward her, she made no effort to stop me. I may be a nerd, but I know a passionate kiss–I've seen it in movies–and this was our first.

– Always Be Prepared When Venturing Into The Night –

V

I've never been in love," I said, gently twisting Zach's hair as we tried to untangle our limbs.

"Love? Who said we're in love?" Zachary teased.

"Well," I fumbled badly searching for the words. "I mean . . . uh . . . the last few . . . uh . . . hours, I mean, have been . . . uh . . . I mean . . ."

"Quinton!" she mock-shouted and touched my lips with her finger. "I'm kidding you," as she snuggled to get as close as possible. It seemed she was sitting on my lap. Then I realized she wasn't merely sitting. She gently enveloped my manhood, coaxing it into her vault, without once taking her eyes off mine. Our rhythmic movements increased until we reached climax together, collapsing but not separating. I couldn't be apart from her.

An hour later, we both woke up together. The previous two days had been a blur of sex, talking, more sex and more talking. We had more in common than I would've imagined. Even Pritcherman didn't hassle Zachary about being gone. We barely got out of bed–except to shower together and eat a little something. We even took our meals in bed together.

As fabulous as the last few days had been, there was business to take care of. Later that evening, we would be paying a visit to the morgue.

"Zach," I whispered in her ear. "I know I love you. Do you love me?"

She didn't respond, but I could tell she was thinking. The fact she didn't answer was the answer I needed.

"Damn it, Quinton. Act natural," Zachary whispered, several hours later.

"That's easy for you to say," I whispered back. "You're not dressed in a gown, riding in a wheelchair with a ton of equipment pressed against your crotch."

"You're supposed to be in pain. Remember, you have abdominal pain."

"You want me to throw up to make it look more realistic?"

"I'm turning around if you do, Quinton. And no more talking. You're the one who said we'd be monitored."

I groaned once for effect. My head was wrapped in a towel, but I left my recent forehead wound exposed. I'd even glued on a fake moustache and beard. Maybe it was overkill. I didn't want to be recognized. Zachary could legitimately argue she was supposed to be anywhere in the hospital. She was a surgery resident. I was not. Her security ID badge allowed her into places a student couldn't go. But a patient . . . that's another story.

Nighttime in a hospital has its own set of rules. The people who work nights generally do so by choice. They're prone to abhor bureaucracy, authority or the petty turf battles of day. They aren't ghouls, or misfits—just different. They notice things daytimers don't. They accept as normal many behaviors that daytimers would not. They tolerate things creatures of the light cannot. They truly march to the beat of a different drummer.

The personality of an institution changes with the coming of night, as well. Patients are different. Or, at least, they seem to act differently. Their complaints and presentations are odd, novel, and unconventional. Why would someone with a rash for the past two months suddenly feel it necessary to have it treated at two in the morning? What was the woman planning to clean when she mixed lighter fluid with bleach? That, of course, is chemistry. Many of the nocturnal hospital clients believe in better living through chemistry . . . be it alcohol, uppers or downers.

On this night, into the maze of cockatrice-like victims and complainants, mavericks and oddballs, somnambulists and the truly ill, came one additional wheelchair-bound, moaning, hirsute ogre of the night— me. Unlike the others, we weren't there to be seen, but to traverse the labyrinth of the emergency department, preferably without being noticed. At night, that was the only unlocked or unguarded entrance to the hospital. As agreed, once we made it to the ground floor elevator, no further unnecessary conversation would be conducted, at the risk of exposing both ourselves and our purpose. Zach pushed, I moaned—slumped with head bent over an emesis basin. The more I groaned, the faster she bulldozed our path through the congregation of care-seeking combatants.

Like Moses, Zachary parted the way until the service elevator came into view. Video and audio monitors were obvious and intended to both deter and to observe. I'd always wondered whether they were really attached to anything. If so, did anyone pay attention to them? This was not the time to test the question. The bowels of any older institution are creepy enough during the best of times. At three in the morning, slumped over in feigned pain, riding a wheelchair in a poorly lit elevator to the basement morgue of a big city hospital certainly does not qualify as being the best of times.

Even though we were alone on the elevator, my hair follicles were beginning to rise, along with my senses. Strangely, I became aware of my leg and the fact that it wasn't throbbing. This was the first time I recalled being pain-free since the first day. I only hoped I wouldn't need to run on it.

The elevator creaked to a stop, the lights flickering as it did.

"Open, damn it!" I commanded the doors. I definitely didn't want to be on an elevator with the lights out. I had a phobia about small, dark places. After what seemed to be forever, the breach widened ever-so-slowly. As our escape orifice reached about half open, the elevator shuddered and jerked upward about two inches. The doors froze temporarily, and then began again, groaning with the scraping sound of metal-on-metal. The very second the wheelchair could clear the doors, Zachary bounced me through the narrow opening. We were finally free and directed our gaze into the long hall. By day, it was poorly illuminated at best, with wisps of sunlight struggling to find a path through the filthy overhead skylights twenty feet above the floor. At that height, the grime's effect reduced the ambient light to a bare minimum. It was even worse at night; you could see the must in the air, with dust particles suspended in the murky half-light–thanks to fluorescent lamps which were either broken, burned out, or which had been partially painted over. As we neared the entrance to pathology, the pungent odor of formalin increasingly replaced the stale air permeating the subterranean corridor.

We were in the right place, alright. But was it the right time?

"Where's the key?" I whispered. "Give it to me."

"No," Zachary whispered back. "Let's try the back door first."

"What back do—"

"Quiet!" and with that she accelerated the wheelchair down a side hall to an unmarked wooden door. She stopped my chariot with my knees pressed against the door, the lock at nose level. It looked as if it had never been opened–at least not this century. Without speaking, she pressed the key into my hand and I gingerly slipped the tip into the opening, hoping it would work. Inserting it to the hilt, I instinctively closed my eyes and gently jiggled the brass key back-and-forth until it twisted to the right and, with a telltale click, the lock released and I opened the door.

Zachary pushed me forward through the door. Once we cleared the threshold she eased the door closed, and locked it again. We were in! As I sat and she stood, we were both paralyzed for the moment–breathing much more deeply than our recent physical activity should have required. After about fifteen seconds, I mustered the courage to begin exploring our surroundings and switched on the small penlight flashlight I was carrying.

We were in, alright . . . in the janitor's closet. Now the smell of pine was becoming familiar. We tried to quietly navigate the brooms, mops buckets haphazardly strewn about the space. Without too much pandemonium, we found another door, this one on the opposite wall, clearly not leading back into the hall. I switched off my light and slowly turned the knob. The door creaked open into yet another acrid cavity.

The blackness. Instantly, I recalled the utter blackness of this room in the moments following the loss of light during the autopsy. And the distinctive smell . . . of formaldehyde and death. I shuddered . . . it was *déjà vu* all over again, to quote Yogi Berra. I'd been here before–I recognized this room even without being able to see it.

I flicked on my flashlight to confirm what I sensed. We were in the main examining suite–the autopsy room–where I had been rendered unconscious. Zachary sensed my apprehension. "It was here, wasn't it?"

"Damn right." I smothered the words as I spoke. "I've been here—"

"No time for reminiscing, Quinton. We're here to find a body . . . or not." She was much more analytical–more rational, and far less scared. Subconsciously, I began rubbing my right hip. This was where I was assaulted only five or six days ago.

"Right. Let's get on with it," I resolved.

The 5'x5' closet opened into the larger 15'x15' examining area. On another wall was the door leading to the offices and laboratories of the Department of Pathology. I had entered through that portal once before. I assumed I exited–had been removed–through that opening as well. A third wall supported a glass door that led to a small isolation area. Through a closed door on the fourth and final wall of the suite was the unknown.

It's amazing how and what the mind remembers of the past. I'd never noticed the closet door from the inside or the outside. But I remembered being curious about that door on the fourth wall. With our fingers we masked the illumination of our flashlights and slowly proceeded toward that door. Unlike the three other wood-framed doors, this one was a heavy metal gateway–imposing, but not intimidating. It was what you might find on a restaurant's walk-in refrigerator.

I pulled the cold metal handle and with little effort the door released with a depressurizing *whoosh*. Even in the dim light from our flashlights, it was obvious we had entered a meat locker–cold, quiet, and antiseptic. However, there were no roasts or filet mignons in this locker–no butchered poultry, cattle, or swine. This was a meat locker . . . for humans. We were in the storage facility also known as the morgue.

There were stacked cubicles, five high in each column, each containing a body or, at least, provided room for one. Within each compartment was a tray that slid out of the refrigerated wall unit from behind a stainless steel door. Still silent, we looked at each other anxiously. Here we were in the bowels of the morgue at three in the morning, armed with only a couple of small flashlights.

"I think we've found the place, Quinton." the surgeon's bravado no longer evident in her voice. She, too, sensed the macabre circumstance. Trying to snap us back to reality, she began searching her mental checklist. "Well, we've got to look at each one to find your guy, Quinton. Go for it."

"Where should I start?"

"At the top left and work your way down," she answered. "I'll start on the right. You do remember what the guy looks like, don't you?"

I chose not to dignify her insult with a response. Tentatively, I opened my first drawer. It was empty. Over the next five minutes, the stillness of the night was punctuated by the metallic sounds of the trays opening and closing. Inadvertently, we developed a rhythm. Without directly knowing, we both knew if a locker was empty or occupied by the change in rhythm–open, examine, extract, return, then close for the occupied, open, examine, close for the empty. Of the fifty or so chambers, only about ten actually held bodies. We met at the middle of the bottom row–our eyes trained on the other. We opened the last bin together. It was empty, or so we first thought. No body, but unlike the other lockers, at the very back of the tray was a sealed glass jar covered by surgical towels. The jar was accompanied by two small packets, all nearly concealed from view by the towels. Each was labeled with the ID number "15-0039678".

"I think that's his number."

"Why?" she scowled. "It's the first number you've even noticed."

"No, really. When Zendejas was beginning his post-mortem, he was dictating into a tape recorder controlled by a foot pedal. That's when I walked in. I was late. He was rattling off the ID number for the transcriptionist while he was examining the exterior of the body."

"That means a recording exists," Zachary surmised.

"Or a report," I added.

"One or the other ought to be around here somewhere."

"What about the jar?"

"What do you mean?"

"What's in it?" I continued. "Shouldn't we open it?"

"It's sealed. And there's something covering the inside."

"So what?" I had already pried open the lid. I took a pair of pliers from our work kit. As I lifted off the obscuring towel, a human brain was revealed. "Guess what," I was quite deliberate. "It's pretty hard to get one of these without an autopsy."

"Look at the right side," Zachary whispered. "There's a wedge missing."

"For slides?"

"Too big," she countered. "Check the bags."

"Look here," I pointed. "Here's the wedge under that towel in a plastic bag."

I closed the lid after covering the brain in its towel again. "We've got to find the tape."

"Let's see what's in those two packages lying next to the brain wedge bag. They could—"

"*Quiet!*" she whispered. "Listen . . . did you hear that?"

Instinctively, we turned off our flashlights. The noise sounded like it was from the outer office in the adjoining room to the autopsy suite. We were huddled against the bottom tray when the muffled noise seemed to be getting closer. Zachary motioned me into the open drawer. I vehemently declined her offer. She motioned again, this time more vigorously.

"Over here!" she shouted, pushing me into the drawer and closing it. Her shouts camouflaged the sound of the metallic door closing. I knew the latch had sealed. I could hear some of their conversation, but my solitary prison was again pitch black.

"Who the hell are you?" I heard an unfamiliar voice call out.

"I'm Dr. Zachary. I was looking for a body from—"

"Doc, nobody gets in here without permission," a second voice advised. "Who authorized—"

"Look guys. I'm a third-year surgery resident. I've been up all night on a gunshot victim and I don't have time for your games."

Damn it, Zachary! Now's not the time for your surgical attitude, I thought.

"You're going to have to come with us."

"The hell you say—" There was a loud clanging sound and a scream, then more scuffling noises, and, finally, the grunting and groaning of them hustling Zachary out of the room. After her scream, I didn't hear any other recognizable language.

Just as suddenly as they had come, there was profound silence once again. The only difference was I was now locked inside a morgue drawer, sharing the space with a human brain. My prison resembled a coffin, and this was going to test my faith. Remember that phobia? Oh yeah, I remember. I knew I had to stay in here until they cleared the room. But for how long? And where were they taking her? She'd given me the push to provide cover. But why? That wasn't part of the plan. We'd decided if we got caught to play dumb. This was more than dumb.

So how long should I lie here? My palms were perspiring, my heart palpitating, and I was aware of all my senses being in a heightened state. I was also more panicky than I could ever remember. Maybe it was the circumstances. After all, my previous experiences with closed spaces hadn't included anything like my current state of imprisonment. My hands fumbled around the cramped confines touching the cold metal sidewalls trying to feel my way to a lessened state of anxiety. First, I found the jar and the brain slice bag, making sure not to disturb its contents. Then I located the two small packets. We hadn't had the chance to examine them. I touched them, straining to understand their contents. They were padded, preventing tactile analysis, so I slipped both into my pocket.

What was in reality only five or ten minutes allowed me to contemplate my entire life—past, present and future. I did not embrace the concept of one more second in the drawer. With both feet, I kicked as hard as I could against the end wall of the steel compartment. To my amazement and relief, it smoothly sprang open and I came to a half sit-up like a mummy from an old horror movie.

Unlike the clumsy, plodding moves from those films, I was out of my sarcophagus and running towards the outer door in one coordinated motion—so fast that I collided with the heavy metal door and with no thought about running on my wounded leg. No, I wanted out . . . and I wanted out *now!* I exited through the large door into the "safety" of the autopsy suite, now restored to its ink-like obscurity. Upon entering the room, I paused only long enough to regain my sense of direction, then proceeded to the janitor's closet door.

Once back inside that small space there was security, maybe because it seemed familiar, or because of its coziness, or because I thought it represented no imminent danger. I gathered my wits about me and pressed my head to the exterior door, hoping to hear something. Actually, I was hoping to hear nothing.

After an interminable few minutes of silence, I opened the door and found myself alone in the all-too-familiar poorly lit hall. I wasn't waiting for a reception committee, and wouldn't be taking any elevator this time either. I knew where the stairs were and found myself walk-running to them. An hour later, I was back to the true safety of my penthouse apartment. Safe, but full of questions. Zachary. They took my first real love. What do I do about her? Wait to hear from her? Go looking for her and trouble, too, no doubt? The sun was separating day from night again. I . . . *we* . . . had been up all night. I was tired, but too wired to sleep.

I emptied my pocket onto the small kitchen table—the two packets from the morgue, the master key handed to me by Zachary, and the key to Zachary's apartment in case of emergency. I filled a plastic glass with ice and poured myself a *Dr. Pepper*. The cold, bubbly, sweet-tasting soft drink has been my passion since childhood. On a good day, I can easily go through a six-pack. This morning I needed the sugary pick-me-up high. After taking a long slug of my nectar-of-the-gods, I sat down at the table and inspected the manila 3"x5" parcels. Each was marked with the number, #15-0039678. How could I confirm that was the autopsy record number of our victim?

Zach was right. There probably was a recording or a transcript. But I certainly wasn't going to find it now. The notion of going back to the path lab had zero appeal. What about his chart? Was his medical record number the same? All I had to do was get his records. Yeah, that's all. As a third-year medical student I had no idea how to get a medical record or from whom I could get it. I made a mental note to myself to find out about that.

I couldn't stop thinking about Zachary, alternating between a pit-in-the-stomach fear and laughing out loud at how she was likely interrogating them, not the reverse. The tug-of-war going on in my stomach lost out for now to my confidence that she could handle whoever had her.

I opened the first of the two parcels and nearly dropped my teeth. It contained a small specimen jar I'd seen before. In that jar was a tooth–the tooth extracted from my leg after being deposited there in desperation by the soon-to-be-deceased psychotic. I poured it out of the jar onto the table. Nothing seemed unusual. It looked like an eye tooth . . . an upper canine, maybe the upper left. Dental anatomy hadn't been a high point of my medical education to date. I scrambled to find an anatomy book to confirm my findings.

What I kept coming back to was *why? Why* had the tooth broken off in my leg? Was it intentional? Was it planned? Or was it simply an accident? I examined the tooth against a template from my anatomy book. The root was intact with no evidence of breaking off. The enamel was intact as was the body of the tooth. It seems its deposit had not been an accident after all. Had it been an accident, I wouldn't expect the tooth to be in such good shape.

So, *why me?* I couldn't believe it was anything other than random chance. I was in the wrong place at the right time. So *why* did he die? And how? Certainly no clue in his tooth. Placing it aside, I opened the second envelope. In a thin, cylindrical glass tube, I found what appeared to be a microchip. I quickly found my microscope, a required piece of first-year medical school equipment. Holding the clear cylinder under the magnifier, I confirmed it was a microchip and a very detailed one, at that. I was quite familiar with microchips from my undergraduate work in biogenetics.

If only Zach were here to help. She gave purpose to my sleuthing, a reason to care. She'd better be back soon. I paused to consider whether we'd go out for dinner, or stay in. In had the inside track as I fantasized.

Computer sequencing of DNA, and what to do with it, has fascinated me since high school. It seemed so simple. Locate the target gene, chart its sequence, search for disease caused by genetic mutation at the target gene site and fix it with a neutral viral carrier. Simple, in theory. Incredibly difficult logistically. In my early years I became hooked on trying.

By the early years of the twenty-first century, human deoxyribonucleic acid–DNA–sequencing had become routine. Beginning with the establishment of the Human Genome Project in 1990, accurate sequencing of the three billion-plus pairs in combinations of the four chemical bases, Adenine, Thymine, Cytosine and Guanine, abbreviated as A, T, C and G had proceeded at break-neck speed. The correct order of these four chemicals differentiates humans from fruit flies. The chemicals in both species are the same–only the number and order are distinct.

However, understanding the fruit fly was the first step, or, to be accurate, the sequence of the common bacteria *Escherichia coli*. That came first and allowed mankind to unravel a simple organism's reproductive structure. Then in 1998, came sequencing of the microscopic worm, *Caenorhabditis elegans*, to build on and compare to the more complicated organisms which, ultimately, included humans. The human genetic code is embedded in 21,000 or so genes, each gene composed of thousands of base pair sequences.

These four nitrogen bases are actually of two similar chemical compounds, the double-ringed purines–Adenine and Guanine, and the single-ringed pyrimidines–Thymine and Cytosine. They pair off as A-T, T-A, C-G and G-C, a purine attached to a pyrimidine creating a molecule of uniform diameter. Facing inward, the bases spiral about bound by a hydrogenated phosphate group to a five-carbon sugar called deoxyribose. The three compounds–sugar, phosphate, and base–are called a nucleotide, and are bound in long, winding double-strands, first described in 1953 by Watson and Crick: the much-heralded double helix. This brilliant, yet simple, road map for reproduction is common to all life-forms with only minor changes from bacterium to primate. Reproduction of the genetic code is correctly ordered when the double helix separates at each base pair and a new T pairs to an A and so forth.

DNA is the code, our genetic template, with the actual protein production choreographed by ribonucleic acid–RNA. Although similar chemically to DNA, it substitutes the pyrimidine Uracil for Thymine. All this chemistry made me dizzy until I realized how efficient, compact, orderly and elementary it was. The genetic road map is transcribed into messenger RNA, isolated chemically as complementary DNA, or cDNA, which causes the production of life-building proteins.

It still sounds simple until Mother Nature throws a few curve balls. Not all genes are expressed, that is, they don't all produce the building block proteins necessary for life. The trick was to find the three percent that are expressed.

Next, one has to know what is normal and what is abnormal, *i.e., disease-causing*. Then, a vehicle for correcting the aberrant genetic sequence must be designed and, finally, delivered to the source cell to alter the genetic map and thus, cure the identified disease.

I had been too young to help in discovery of the sequencing. Now, however, I wanted into the thick of the battle to actually try to correct disease. What evolved was a realization that disease was not simply a genetic problem. There were environmental factors causing mutations and wreaking havoc on the question of genetic causation. In fact, many times there is only a genetic *predisposition* towards disease. Many other factors helped to create disease. Scientists are increasingly frustrated with a strict genetic approach. With the advent of the computer age, genetic engineers came to the front. Starting in the late 1990s, computers were becoming increasingly more powerful and, simultaneously, smaller. This miniaturization led to a joining of forces between geneticists and computer-scientists. Small, computerized machines, so-called micro-machines, were now being designed to help correct the genetic defects identified.

In order to become a new-age star, one needed a computer-engineering-biology background. This was my entree. I had been a computer geek throughout my under-graduate biology career. Along the way, inventions such as my fingerprint genetic identification system had helped make my life easier. Royalties were a bonus. My little white lie to Zachary about living from a trust fund wasn't entirely true. I was orphaned and my parents had left a trust fund. *Zachary.* I closed my eyes in an effort to remember her face. Where the hell was she? She should've called by now. They must really be giving her the third degree grilling. Smiling, I wondered who was getting the best of that–I wouldn't cross her in a verbal duel.

As an only child, the trust fund was great, but it didn't provide any real emotional support. I was insecure and a social outcast throughout high school. But I never really knew what happened to my parents. They supposedly were killed in a car accident when I was in junior high school.

At least that was the story I was given. I never believed it. For one thing, I couldn't find a record of their accident or any death certificates. For another, when I searched online for their files, I kept getting messages saying their data was classified. They had worked for the federal government, but had been in rather mundane jobs at the Commerce Department. At least that was what I was told. That is probably what started me down the high-tech invention road. I was trying to find out the truth about my parents. I was left with a suspicious nature, a fertile imagination and a geek's knowledge of technology.

A few high-tech inventions offered me a larger revenue stream, but more importantly, they made me feel like I had something to offer society. Now I had a modicum of self-worth. Or, at least, I was taking the tentative baby-steps in that direction. Medical school was a necessary evil for me. It was my next step, and along with frustrations about how to actually repair genes came an ethics debate that continues to rage today. With new technology came the threat of big brother.

Though the issues weren't new, the specifics of the debate were. Throughout history, any scientific advance raised questions concerning the ethics of its use. To build an atomic bomb took millions of man-hours and several years. The debate over its use continues unabated, even today. Now genetic manipulation, or its potential, brought the ethics of technology to a personal level. Should one's medical history be available to the government? Your employer? A possible spouse? After all, before you can fix a problem you have to know it exists. Mandatory genetic testing? Counseling? Penalties for not submitting?

Personal rights versus the rights of a group–these are the issues governments and individuals are struggling with while development of new technologies marches on. The recent marriage of computer technology with biomedical-biomechanical engineering brought these debates to a more personal level. Everyone has an opinion on its use . . . or potential use.

So how did this microchip fit in? Why did we find it with a brain and a tooth? I focused on the portion of the chip near its outer edge. It vaguely resembled a transmitter . . . or a receiver . . . or both, but far more sophisticated than any I'd ever seen before. It almost looked like . . . .

There was a knock on the door. Strange. Not the doorbell like most people, but the hard, rapid pounding of a fist against my front door. I just knew it was Zach and she was pounding in excitement. I rushed to the door. I glanced at the video screen to identify the intruder interrupting my study. It was a blonde female with her back to the camera. Definitely not Zach. *Who was this?* She turned around and her face came into view. *It was Smith!*

"What the—" I grumbled, quickly scrambling back to the table to hide the tooth and microchip. *Why Smith? Why not Zach?* Jumping back in the general direction of the door, I shouted to Dr. Smith to wait just a minute. I activated the digital videotaping system as I opened the door. "May I help you," I asked, trying to pretend I didn't recognize her.

"Quinton, I was told to come here," she snapped while barging through the door. "What the hell is this all about?"

"You tell me, Doctor. I don't—"

"Cut the crap. I don't understand what a third-year medical student has to do with this, but who am I to argue with the great Pritcherman."

"Pritcherman?"

"Yeah, Zachary said she was gonna be out of town for a few days. Pritcherman probably wants her off his service. I guess I'm her replacement. Does that make any sense?"

"No. So who called you? I thought—"

"Zachary."

"You talked to her. Where was she? I mean—"

"How the hell should I know, Quinton. You're not involved with her are you? You know, that kind of stuff . . . there's a rule against it, I'm sure."

"No. I mean . . . Look," I stammered. "What do you know about last night?"

"All I know about last night is it was the first night of good sleep I've had since getting to this nuthouse."

"You weren't at the hospital?"

"*Hell, no!* I wouldn't be here now if that bitch hadn't called me at six in the morning. She kept saying something about having to have her brain examined. If you ask me, you both need to have lobectomies." She sniffed the air in the apartment. "A cripple and a snivel. So aren't you gonna offer me coffee or something?"

"You said Pritcherman. Did you talk to him?"

"Of course not," Smith snapped. "He has his flunkies do his dirty work, you know, Zachary."

She'd wandered over to the kitchen and began rummaging through my refrigerator.

"Zachary said you could explain. Beats the hell out of me. But here I am. So sport . . . what gives?" She poured herself a large glass of orange juice into one of my best crystal glasses, slamming it down on the counter at the finish and sat next to me at the table. "Do you know anything about this, Quinton?"

Without waiting for me to respond, she was standing again. "I didn't think so. You don't know shit. You can sucker her with that injury, but not me," now walking towards the door. "You're back on my service in three days, buck-o . . . Three days. Not one second more . . . got it?"

Before I could answer, she was gone, slamming the door as she went. I went to the kitchen and looked at her juice glass. She'd left a perfect set of fingerprints. I scanned them into my computer and entered a search command. Propping my head up on my hand waiting for the search to finish, I whispered aloud, "It's time to find out who she *really* is."

– Never Start What You Can't Finish –

VI

She was walking ever-so-slowly, not in a straight line, but in small sidesteps, unbuttoning her blouse as she slinked towards me, her head cocked to one side invitingly. As she neared the couch where I was sitting, her tongue intentionally caressed her pouty lips. There was no denying my arousal and no denying I wanted her in the worst of ways. She was now standing over me, pressing her pubis against my right knee. She leaned down, grasped my wrists, and gently lifted them over my head . . . her grip tightening as she pinned them to the top of the sofa. Her eyes were locked on mine, and her pelvic gyrations became more aggressive as she continued to moisten her lips with her tongue. Subtly, rhythmically, she increased the pressure of her pelvis against mine, convincing my groin to join her motion as I ached with sexual desire.

Every muscle in my body was tensed, ready to explode. Her grip tightened again as she pushed her upper torso against my face. With her unbuttoned blouse draped over her shoulders, the outline of her breasts was plainly visible, her nipples erect and firm against the fabric. I was completely dominated by her. I struggled to free myself from her grip and take her, but my efforts were futile–I was her slave, ready for the taking on her terms. My autonomic nervous system was working overtime, every pore open, sweat beginning to glisten.

She thrust her right breast against my mouth, yet as I tried to kiss it, she pulled away. Teasingly, she brought it back again and just as quickly withdrew. Her pace quickened until she finally thrust the nipple into my oropharynx, allowing me to suckle as any newborn would. Nibbling on the mammary's protuberance further aroused her. As she arched her back, her muscles drew taut–signaling her readiness.

I prayed there would be no flight tonight. Tonight she would be mine in the fullest, most primitive sense. She arched further as I continued my attempt at devouring her breasts . . . left, then right. Finally, falling backwards onto the floor, she pulled me along, forcing my full weight upon her. Although our arms were fully extended above her head, my wrists remained captive to this woman's firm grip. My mouth was firmly planted on her breasts, as we accelerating our pelvic thrusting.

She released one of my wrists and with her free hand tore my shirt open, buttons bursting about like popcorn from a popper. She caressed my chest, swirling the hair faster and faster, occasionally pinching one of my own nipples between her thumb and forefinger. Then her hand began traveling south. Even though I was on top of her, she was still the master and I her willing slave. Her hand submerged beneath the waistband of my jeans and she grasped my invigorated genitals. As she pulled gently on my penis, she rolled us both onto our sides, still clasping my right wrist in her left hand. Her mouth moved slowly down my torso, her teeth eventually reaching my belt buckle. She masterfully opened the buckle as well as the top of my jeans. With my free hand, I was able to release my genitals from their confinement within my jeans as her hand continued to massage my glans penis. She enveloped it with her mouth. The gentle pressure she now exerted quickened as she pulled me deeper into her oral cavity.

My hands were now free thanks to her oral distraction, and I slipped my left hand to her knee and slowly, deliberately inched my way up her inner thigh. Her legs were taut and pressed together tightly, but with minimal coercion, she relented. Still pulsating, her groin was now only a few inches away from my fingertips. As I drew closer, her muscles involuntarily relaxed and her legs parted, leaving her mons pubis unguarded. She wore no panties under her pleated skirt. Arriving at the margin of her heaven, my fingers probed the moist and swollen flesh.

Our mouths found each other's as we embraced deeply, lovingly, passionately. Our hands continued to arouse the other, and our breathing synchronized. Her eyes locked on mine as our lips separated ever so slightly. It was time. She guided my erect shaft into her vaginal vault. Becoming one, I—

"Search complete. There is a match," my computer droned—I was the victim of digital coitus interruptus. My neck was twisted awkwardly, arms wrapped around myself in opposite directions, and my head was throbbing again. As my mind returned to a conscious state, I became aware of another part of my anatomy pounding against my pants. I felt the warm, sticky semen erupt from my loins, while involuntarily pumping forward and remembering why. I had been dreaming of Zachary. Now I knew I had to find her. She was the co-star of my dream fantasy.

"Grigsby is at the door. Gregory M. Grigsby," the security system announced, programmed to identify persons at the door I previously catalogued. This particular *alert* had been catalogued as an unwanted intruder alert.

"Grigsby, you could screw up a wet-dream," I muttered. I smiled as I recognized the state of my trousers. And, in fact, he had.

"What the hell does that son-of-bitch want now?" turning off the monitor. No need to let Grigsby in on my investigations. I left him waiting at the door while I found new pants.

I knew he'd wait. What the hell else would he do? He wasn't here on his own. He was here because someone told him to come. But who . . . and why? I'd find out soon enough.

"Grigsby, you piece of shit," I greeted him while opening the door. "From under what rock did you crawl out?"

"Can the crap, Quinton," pushing into the room. "You know damn well I wouldn't be anywhere near your nerd-atorium if Pritcherman hadn't sent me."

"Pritcherman?"

"Yeah, Pritcherman. He's genuinely pissed off about something and I guess it involves you."

"Uncuff my hands, you son-of-a-—"

"Doctor, listen to me," came the calm, but firm reply. "You have a few things to learn about diplomacy, Doc. Let's just say tact isn't your best feature, eh?"

"No, it isn't. In the operating room, we don't tie people up," Zachary seethed anger at the room.

"Not with handcuffs, but you do with your drugs and anesthesia, don't you?"

"That's different. We—"

"Is it really, Doctor? Is it really? Well, this is no operating theatre."

"No, it isn't, gov'nor," she responded with undisguised sarcasm, noting the British accent and the use of theatre for OR. *Who the hell is this guy?* she wondered.

"You Americans," her captor hissed. He was about six feet tall, black, and thinly built, but well-dressed in a navy blue three-piece suit–not your typical hospital security agent, for sure. "You think you own the world. Well, m' lady, let's see if you can practice the sounds of silence for a while. Soon enough you'll know what that really means."

Just what the hell did that mean? Zachary pondered. After being hustled out of the morgue, then quickly handcuffed by what she believed was hospital security, she had been blindfolded, gagged, and turned over to her unknown captors and was driven about thirty minutes to an unknown location.

One of the skills most physicians must train to develop is the power of observation. Zachary had carefully paid attention to the length of time of her incarceration and catalogued as much as she could about the details of her movement. Now she considered the areas within thirty minutes of the medical center where they might have taken her. She was also looking for a hint of their intent. The medical school and its affiliated hospitals owned much of the property for several miles in any direction, she thought. At the perimeter were warehouses and student housing for the nursing and medical schools.

She quickly ruled out the housing areas as impractical, but not the warehouse areas. For all she knew, she could be somewhere in one of the many hospital-affiliated buildings. *I could also be—*

"Quit picking at your bonds, Doc. They aren't coming off for a while," her subjugator cautioned and then quietly resumed reading the papers he was holding until the silence was broken by a coded knock at the door. Turning to his accomplice, he ordered, "Put the blindfold back on her."

Zachary hadn't noticed anybody else in the room, but there was a third person who was now replacing her blindfold. Before it was in place, however, she was able to notice a few things though: he was a large, black man, all of six-feet-five inches, reeking of tobacco, not so immaculately dressed as the other, but also in a suit. Based on their accents, she assumed they both were from somewhere in the Caribbean.

Soon, the door was unlatched and a new, third voice was heard. Although what was said was inaudible, this one definitely was not British. After entering the room, this new unknown said nothing for at least thirty seconds. In those thirty seconds, Zachary strained to make anything out of the visually imperceptible. But even her olfactory and auditory senses failed her at the moment.

"Doctor Zachary, I don't believe we've met," came a soft, almost soothing voice. "I apologize for your current predicament. Unfortunate, but necessary, you see. Necessary, at least, until we establish a few things. Alright?" The question was rhetorical, as he continued, "You see, your unauthorized morgue expedition you claim was for . . . what was it you said?"

"I didn't say," she shot back. "Since when does being out of bounds in this insane asylum warrant blindfolds and handcuffs? And what's with the ride to who knows where? And—"

"In time, Doctor. All good things in their time. For the moment, however, why don't I ask the questions and you provide the answers, OK? Hmmm?"

"No, it's not OK, hmmm. I—"

"*Enough!*" it was said forcefully, but without anger. Lowering his voice to a whisper, "Enough." This time he paused for effect. After about another thirty seconds of silence, he resumed the dialogue, "I don't think you understand your situation at all. Why were you really in the morgue after hours, Doctor?"

"I told you . . . or whoever grabbed me there . . . I was looking, looking for a patient, or at least the report of a—"

"Come now, Doctor. You can do better than that, can't you?" Chuckling ever-so-slightly, "Stick with medicine, Doctor. Acting and lying aren't your strengths, believe me," the leader advised. "Now, once again. What were you doing in the early hours of the morning, in a darkened morgue, with the lights off, a penlight, surrounded by drawers full of bodies? What indeed? Trying to scare yourself, Doctor?" he mocked. "It's not Halloween. So why would anyone in their right mind be in a morgue at night? You are in your right mind aren't you, Doctor?"

Zachary sensed him slowly walking around her. She could feel him coming closer as well. She didn't say a thing for several minutes. Two can play this waiting game, she thought.

"Cat got your tongue, or are you thinking of another lie."

"No. I just don't see any point trying to reason with you. I—"

"Oh, we're not reasoning, Doctor Zachary. Believe me, we're not doing that at all. Think of this as a conducting a preoperative history and physical."

The *preoperative* comment worried her. And this guy seems to know something about medicine, with the H&P reference. "Who are you?" she asked quietly.

"All in good ti—"

"Yes, you've said that already. Who the hell are you?" she screamed.

There was a long pause and finally, a long sigh as he leaned within inches of her face. "You just won't make this easy will you, Doctor? It could be so easy, if you'd—"

"If I'd what, Mister . . . or is it *Doctor?*"

Another sigh, "Jeremy, I believe we'll need to move on here. Can you prepare the good Doctor, please?"

Prepare me? For what? And one of them is named Jeremy, huh? Now Zachary was squirming in her restraints, struggling, albeit in utter futility. Quickly she felt a firm grip on her right arm as she was lifted from her chair.

"Now, luv, be a good one and come quietly. Don't make me have to use force," as he squeezed her arm tighter.

"Jeremy, may I call you that?" Zachary snapped. "Where are we?"

"All good things in time," he mimicked their leader. "All good things in time," dragging her more quickly.

Throwing Grigsby out was the easy part. Finding Pritcherman's office would be a bit harder. Professors' offices in the new University Hospital were impossibly hidden and getting close to them was daunting, even when you knew where you were going–and I didn't. The university prided itself on its building having more halls than the Pentagon. I'm convinced the professors liked their academic hideaways because if students and house officers couldn't find them, all the better! That feeling of impending doom was sneaking into my psyche.

I was already a little late when I began, so my trek through the maze of halls only served to exacerbate my tardiness. I knew I was in real trouble when I came to a "T" in the hall with a sign identifying both left and right directions as my destination: 12 West.

OK. Now what? His office was 12-517, so what the hell? To the right I charged! It soon dawned on me that this was a circular hall and Pritcherman's office was precisely 180 degrees from the right or left. All the exterior doors looked the same, institutionally nondescript slabs save for a different number on each. As I opened the door to enter 12-517, I assumed the interiors were all the same as well.

Wow! I couldn't possibly have been more wrong. Pritcherman's outer office was huge, with recessed lighting, each of the four walls painted a different shade of soft pastel colors, and each sporting a low lying bookshelf neatly filled with texts, journals, and the like. Unlike Pritcherman, this place looked organized. I was impressed.

"Quinton! Is that you? Get in here now!"

"Yessir, it's me." *Where was here?* I wondered. Suddenly one of the walls opened, a secret entry for this most secretive of neurosurgeons.

"Surprised, Quinton?" It was clear Pritcherman relished in surprises, so I was going to try not to act the part.

"No, sir," I lied.

"Bullshit. I watched you on the monitors," randomly waving in the general direction of a bank of video monitors on one of the walls of the inner office, an inner office that was even larger than the exterior.

How does this guy rate? I thought to myself. He must occupy half the floor. Probably 40 by 50 feet, the office divided into a desk and conference table area on the left and a second space I can only describe as Pritcherman's play area on the right. This second area was distinctly separate from the desk and table, with a large, empty space between the two. On one side of his play-space there was a bench-like table with an electron microscope and four separate computer work stations in one corner.

What immediately caught my attention was a 3-D replica of the human brain, at least 20 feet in diameter with small walkways through its parts and an intricate array of flashing, twinkling lights resembling those old style Christmas tree lights I remembered from many years ago. It dominated the room. It was the centerpiece, towering over everything else, at least 15 feet tall as well.

"Now this is impressive, Dr. Pritch—"

"Can the crap, Quinton. You may be impressed, but I'm not–not with you or whatever the hell it is you're trying to pull. You *and* Zachary. Where the hell is Zachary? I'm told you know what happened to her or where she is, or whatever BS excuse the two of you cooked up. I have to have a resident to run my service and I sure as hell don't want that zombie, Smith."

"What do you know, sir?"

"What do *I* know? Damn it, Quinton, I ask the questions, you give the answers," Pritcherman growled. *"How the hell should I know?"*

"I'm sorry, sir. I meant what have you heard?" I didn't want to open a can of worms unless I had to.

"I heard from Smith she's suddenly going to be gone for weeks. Smith gave me some crap about being involved in an accident with you. I thought you were already off from your previous escapade with that seizure patient? She said you could explain, so you'd better start. I can't wait all day, son."

"Doctor, I don't think you'd believe me if I tried," I sighed under my breath.

"WHAT! Speak up! I can't understand your lame-ass excuse. Look, son," he said, lowering his voice into an almost fatherly tone. "I don't really give a rat's ass if you're trying to get into her pants or whatever, but I sure as hell care if you screw up my service. So come clean. I'll give you five minutes to tell me any crazy-ass story you wanna tell. But that's it. And you can guaran-*damn*-tee I'll check out what you say. That's how much time you have to convince me you're on the level."

"Level? At the moment, I don't know up from down, right from left, top from bottom, sir. But if you'll listen—"

"Quinton, which part of five minutes didn't you understand?"

"I'm pretty damn distracted now, with Zachary missing. I—"

"You two got something going there, Mr. Quinton? Getting to know my resident better than—"

"Enough!" I shouted. "Dr. Pritcherman, do you know about Dr. Zendejas?" I had crossed the Rubicon. I had to tell at least part of this to someone, if only to validate I was or wasn't nuts.

"Know *what* about him?" Pritcherman responded with newfound interest. He knew something. I just needed to find out what.

"That's he's dead?"

"QUINTON!!!!"

Now you've done it, I thought to myself. And Pritcherman, of all people. *Of all people?* He was the *only* one right now, I remembered. I quickly crossed the threshold back into my place. *I've got to sort this out.*

Now what? So, let's see what I know and what I don't. And what Pritcherman knows and what he doesn't. To pour a Dr. Pepper or wine? Such a dilemma. What the hell–wine, I decided. Sure, it was four in the afternoon, but I was off for three more days. Three days Smith gave me to figure out this thing.

"Château Montelena," I commanded to the wind without looking up. Another of my favorite inventions appeared. The wine chiller opened and a small robot selected a bottle, transported it to an opener, which deftly peeled the foil cover and extracted the cork in seconds. Zachary hadn't seen this toy. I really missed her even though I'd only known her a short time. She was consuming my thoughts–when Pritcherman wasn't distracting me. I guess my head was bouncing like a tennis ball between the his insanity, and the insanity of not having Zach around. She was becoming my new obsession.

"A fine nose," droned my mechanical companion, in a bit stilted accent, a mixture of French and mechanics.

"Rupert, you've almost lost your accent," I teased. "If you could only join me without getting rusty." Named after my grandfather, this meter-tall *Rupert* glided across the floor with ease and speed. Many thought I built him because I was lazy. The truth was I needed the companionship, the upside and the downside of being a nerd.

"Tonight we work late, Rupy. We've got a lot to do."

"You know I hate that name. Please call me Rupert," my friend answered.

"Sorry. It's a term of endearment, believe me. Like *Zach* for Zachary."

"Of course." Then, after a pause. "You know I don't believe you."

"Search on," I turned on the voice-enabled search computer. "Name, Dr. Jessica Smith. Last location, Georgetown University. All files and aliases." I took a slow, deep mouthful of wine, swished it to and fro, and swallowed. *I'll bet it's a 2008. Seems younger than that though,* I paused. *But good. It's gonna be a long night.*

— Always Know Who's Playing Before You Deal The Hand —

VII

"Results of the search are negative." I stared at the screen. I'd only finished part of the glass. Way too fast a return.

"Run again against all databases. Use DNA sample to confirm identity."

"All databases previously searched. Repeat search in progress. DNA sample confirmed." Another advantage of gathering a DNA sample on the doorbell was it eliminates the need to confirm a search identity in a traditional way, sort of like checking a Social Security Number. DNA was much more discriminating and virtually every person has a unique DNA signature.

There's no way in this day and age anyone returns no results, I was sure. No way. No way, unless someone or something wants to make you that way, *and that something has to be governmental,* I thought. I learned enough from my parents to know that was the case even back when they were alive. They taught me a lot and sometimes I'm not sure they knew they were doing it. Or maybe they did, since it was pretty easy to figure out how to access the government's databases and sources, and I had begun doing that as far back as when I was in high school.

Next I had to outsmart the *federales* so they didn't turn off that access. I was hidden, deep within the Internet and hadn't been discovered yet. The key was being unobtrusive. I searched but never downloaded. I didn't need to after I came up with a way to dump the data without alerting anyone by copying or printing. Then I covered myself by removing the audit trail showing any trace of access. Piece of cake for a nerd like me. The trouble is, I couldn't really show anyone, not for fear of getting discovered–I'd take that risk in a heartbeat–but because I just don't have any real friends to share it with.

"OK, Smith. Who do you work for?" I asked out loud. She was the new key. Is it for the *good guys* or the *bad guys?* Now the problem gets harder. This was no Zachary search. Yeah, I'd run Zach, too. Call me suspicious, but to my relief, my dream lover was spotlessly clean.

"DoD block search," I commanded, while thumbing through a log of my previous searches. This was a log listing previous validation codes. The Department of Defense has a much more robust security firewall that I needed to bypass. Luckily again, my parents had inadvertently left a few clues for me. It took me a few months to figure them out.

"Echo-Tango-Bravo, One-Niner, Delta-Foxtrot" I paused, "Kilo-Seven-Two, Romeo-Hotel."

"Invalid authorization."

"OK, so they changed it again. Plan B," unconsciously rubbing my sore, but improving leg. I quickly brought up another program, one I'd written specifically to search for valid authorization codes. To remain undetected, however, this program took a lot longer to run through a very complex algorithm I'd written to avoid the DoD "bothering" me about my curiosities while covering my search tracks at the same time.

A block search was designed to tell me who or what was blocking the search. Of course, that implied it *was, in fact,* being blocked. I was sure the search was blocked because no righteous medical colleague had ever escaped a search return. They just weren't sophisticated enough to know or care. Smith is being blocked, all right, and I'd bet three of my patents on it.

"Guess I'll have some time to sample the wine," I thought, as I drank a long mouthful. It was opening quite nicely now. The next few hours were a mix of wine, light sleep and arousal. Finally, the computer droned an answer.

"Smith, Jessica Jane. FBI block on credentials. No other identifying characteristics."

"No other characteristics, my ass," I sneered at the monitor as if it would respond." "Not only are they blocking her but it would appear they covered her pretty deeply."

I pestered the computer. "We'll have to put her in the bad column for now." I'll get back to her later. So, I moved on.

"New search. Stanley J. Pritcherman."

"Search completed yesterday," came the response.

"Yeah, I know. Before I talked to him. It's clean," I answered the computer. "But new search on Stanley J. Pritcherman. This time, not routine background. Search acquaintances and colleagues. Pay particular attention to papers written with others, journal articles, text books, even lay publications."

"Searching."

I sipped on the Cabernet. I wished Zachary were here to enjoy it. My mind wandered and with it, my sexual fantasy started to return. *Where was she?* Wherever it was, I'll bet she's giving somebody are hard time about all this. When she gets back, I want us to go away for a week somewhere . . . anywhere. *I want—*

No, not now. I needed to put her out of my mind. *This is work.* I drifted off for a while as the search engine performed its task. A long night, indeed.

"Search complete," the computer awakened me again. What returned was hundreds of articles, textbook contributions and newspaper interviews written by or about Pritcherman. This was no good.

"Repeat search associations only with Zendejas, John Luis." That should shorten the search, I thought.

"Six articles," the computer responded matter-of-factly. I read the list. All six articles were about Creutzfeldt-Jakob disease. As I skimmed the articles, it was clear Pritcherman had done the biopsy work and Zendejas the pathology that led the two to characterize the disease and the deaths it caused. The last article was about the vaccination creation that prevented the disease.

"Wait a minute," I spoke out loud. "Zendejas got all the credit for CJD. I don't remember ever hearing about Pritcherman. How come? He's in all the articles. He's egotistical enough to claim credit for both of them," I mused. Something didn't add up . . . again. I took another sip of cab and rocked back in my chair. "This I gotta think about."

Sometimes I did my best thinking in my sleep. The problem is, when I did that, I woke up abruptly and I usually hurt myself on something. This time, I awakened with a loud crashing noise and found myself on the floor, a broken Riedel wine glass and red wine scattered everywhere around me.

"Damn it! What a mess," shaking off glass and wine. As I cleaned up, I started adding up what I had. Smith is under deep cover by somebody and I'm guessing they aren't friendlies. Wait a minute. How can the FBI not be friendly? This is complicated, I concluded.

I told Pritcherman about Zendejas and the autopsy to see what he knew. He'll think about it, but I really don't know whether to trust him or not. I needed information from him. And look at all the missing folks. Zendejas is dead. Zachary is missing. This autopsy-helper guy, John, is also missing or resigned or wherever he is. Grigsby's an idiot. Add in two harmless second-year med students and what do you have? A paranoid third-year named Quinton. Or am I?

Let's see what else we have. We have another dead man, this one a patient that shouldn't be dead by all accounts. Or is he? Wait–he's dead. I assume the brain slice is his since I helped cut it out of his head. But is it him? And who was *him?* And what about the tooth, the microchip, and that probe–or whatever it is? And what about finding a recording or something to confirm the autopsy?

Now I need to deal with these samples. First, let's see if any have DNA to test. Then, depending on whom it belongs to, maybe I'll get an answer. Looks like I have my day planned out. I looked out the window and noticed the sun was coming up. Two more days before I have to return to the neurosurgery service. Two more days without Zach?

I retrieved the packets I had hidden from Smith when she paid her unexpected visit. I worked on the contents for about thirty minutes.

"Got it!" There *was* DNA on the microchip and the probe. I placed the small samples into separate PCR chambers. PCR, or polymer chain reaction, is a technique that replicates small quantities of DNA so you have a lot more to play with. In a while, I'd have enough DNA to test each.

Then there was that tooth. To get DNA from a tooth, you have to drill into it and extract DNA directly from the root area. I carefully placed the tooth in a vice grip and guided a high-speed drill into the tooth near the top and side at a 45-degree angle. The soft high-pitched screech of the drill only lasted about ten seconds before it struck pay dirt. I extracted a small amount of semiliquid from the tooth's root. Into the PCR chamber this dental sample went.

It would take an hour or two before I'd have enough DNA, so I could now turn my attention to the tape, if there was one.

"This is Dr. J.J. McCord," I spoke assuredly into the telephone, my voice scrambler disguising my identity. Still, I always talked differently even though I didn't need to. The voice scrambler could also have the caller ID appear to originate from anywhere I chose. In this case, I chose Atlanta. "I'm from the neurosurgical department at CDC. With whom am I speaking?" There was a brief pause, then a timid voice at the other end.

"I'm Helen in the department of pathology. May I help you?"

"Yes, you can, Helen," lowering my voice even more. "I'm looking for an autopsy report on a patient performed a week or so ago. This case is under federal investigation. I'm trying to expedite the findings so as to not inconvenience anyone at your facility. We don't want to make a big deal about it, you understand I'm sure. It would be a shame to have the light of publicity shine on your hospital unnecessarily, I'm sure you can appreciate that. So, what I need is a copy of the report on patient, uh," purposefully fumbling around shuffling papers for effect. "Patient ID #15-0039678. You can do that on the Q-T for me, Helen, right?"

"I don't know."

"Helen, could I have your last name and employee number for my records, then?"

"Gee, doctor, can you give me a minute to see if I can find it?"

"No problem, Helen, but this is an important investigation, so, please look quickly while I'm on hold." I waited, holding the phone and also my breath, hoping my ruse would work. Three minutes later Helen was back.

"This is strange, doctor," she hesitated. "There is a digital recording of the autopsy like normal. But," she paused again, "instead of being in its folder, there's a note saying it's checked out to Dean Jankowski. I've never heard of such a thing."

"The Dean? And his full name is?" I queried.

"Dr. Viktor Igorseg Jankowski," Helen volunteered. "But I thought he was on sabbatical for another month or so."

"Helen, you have been quite helpful. I'll contact the Dean myself. No need to transfer. Thanks again," hanging up the receiver. Well, well, well. The Dean? The Dean who is supposed to be on sabbatical? What's up with that, I thought. But a recording exists, or at least existed, Helen confirmed that. Why would there be a tape of an autopsy that never happened?

I returned to the PCR chamber to see if the "stew" had finished cooking. Sure enough, all three specimens were completed. Now that there was enough of each sample to test, I placed each individually into the DNA analyzer. The analyzer sequenced the DNA and compared it to a government database established a few years back by the NIH for use by DNA researchers. It was tightly secured because the argument about who should have access was a political hot potato, given that every insurance company and others in the world wanted to know what results were in the database. Secure, yes, but I had my own access. In a matter of thirty minutes or so, I had the answers.

All three specimens had DNA from the same human being. and the tooth also had my DNA. That was his "gift" to me when he bit me. I excluded my DNA from the evaluation. Since the tooth was "observed" by me to be deposited from the patient from the neurosurgical service whose autopsy I witnessed, I felt I could conclude the brain slice I'd seen in the morgue drawer was indeed his. And because the microchip and probe also had his DNA, I presumed they were also removed from him, probably from his brain, which explained why a wedge of tissue was missing.

More importantly, I now had an ID number to run against the search database. I hurried over to the computer. "Search by DNA database ID," I commanded.

"ID number?"

"15-0039678," I spoke, then stopped almost as quickly. *That's the same number as the pathology ID. Coincidence? I doubt it.*

"No match," quickly came the search answer.

So why or how would the NIH database have the same ID as the pathology department?

"Run aliases," I commanded again.

"Encrypted by DoD."

"Un-encrypt."

"Unable."

"Bullshit," I yelled at the screen. *What the hell is this? So, now the dead, homeless guy is also deep cover DoD?*

Homeless, I think not! And the Dean, who isn't here because he's on sabbatical, asked Pritcherman, as a favor, to take care of him? The guy dies, but there's no body. And the pathologist who performed an autopsy no one admits happened is missing and presumed dead. Now the resident–*my Zachary*–who helped me look into this is missing, while the other resident, or whatever she is–Smith–has an FBI block on her identity. And they think *I'm* crazy?

– Never Let The Truth Get In The Way Of A Good Story –

VIII

Dr. Smith," Pritcherman seemed pleased with himself as we started rounds on my first day back. "Mr. Quinton, here, says you drugged him during an autopsy on my patient. An autopsy you say didn't happen," pacing while struggling to contain his glee. "A real *he said–she said* don't ya think," eyes bouncing from Smith, to me, to the others like a tennis ball being slammed back and forth. "Any thoughts, Doctor?"

His eyes stopped on me as I turned every shade of red there is. "You prick," I muttered under my breath. I guess trusting the good Dr. Pritcherman was a major mistake. Thank God, I only told him a small part of what I knew. Before I could answer, Smith did.

"Mr. Quinton is prone to exaggeration, now, isn't he Dr. Pritcherman," Dr. Smith coolly answered with no hint of nervousness or emotion. "I haven't seen an autopsy in at least three years. I'm the one who found Mr. Quinton in the stairwell in the basement, sir. His head had a large frontal hematoma. Dr. Zachary admitted him for observation after a negative MRI. Maybe that explains his, uh, his . . . hallucinations?"

"Ah, yes, the fair Dr. Zachary," Pritcherman now trained his laser-eyes back on me, narrowing to a squint. "Would you have any idea how she's doing now, Mr. Quinton?"

"I thought you—"

"Enough, Quinton," Smith softly interrupted. Pritcherman locked onto me and began fishing into his pocket. I knew what he was trying to find. Lucky for me he was out of gastronomic venom, but not his verbal poison.

"My office, this afternoon. You and I need to find you another rotation, don't you think, son?"

"What ti—"

"4 p.m. . . . and don't be late this time!"

"Smooth move, Quinton," one of the second-years whispered. The two second-years trailed after Pritcherman and Smith as they left to do rounds on the ward. If I'm going to be off the rotation, I'll be damned if I'm going to waste my time on rounds. So, the entourage went left and I went right. Before the 4 p.m. meeting with Pritcherman, I had the rest of the day to get some answers.

Who is the Dean and what's his connection? Maybe he knows something about Zachary. He has to be in the administration building, I assumed, so I left the sixth floor and headed out the main entrance and across a long narrow walkway. After about a hundred yards, I entered the ground level of the five-story Administration building and found the directory. The entire top floor was designated as the Dean's office. I casually walked through the elevator door and pressed '5' to go see the Dean. A light came on and almost immediately there was a uniformed guard with a large pistol on his hip asking me if I needed help. Intentionally intimidating, *OK,* I thought.

"Yes, I'm going to see the Dean, sir."

"And is Dean Jankowski expecting you?"

"Not exactly."

"Well, sir. Let me call for you. Who shall I say is coming to see the Dean?"

"Tell them . . . Dr. J.J. McCord from CDC." *Hell, I'd come this far, why not?* I thought. The guard disappeared for a moment and then returned.

"The Dean will see you now, sir. See his secretary when you get to five," the guard said, much friendlier than before. He reached into the elevator and pressed "5" after turning a key. The door closed and I was alone in the elevator with about 20 seconds to come up with a plan. The door opened.

"Dr. McCord?"

"Huh?"

"Are you Dr. McCord from the CDC," a pleasant appearing woman of about 50 years asked.

"Oh. No, ma'am. Is this the fourth floor admissions office?"

"No. This is the fifth floor. The Dean is waiting for a Dr. McCord. There must be some mistake."

"The Dean's here?"

"Yes, but you want the fourth floor. The Dean of admissions is who I think you're looking for."

"I'm so sorry. I'll just walk down a floor."

"Well, it's a secure, locked staircase. You can go down, but the door to this floor is locked at all times, so don't try to come back up," she advised.

"No, ma'am. I'm going down to four."

She led me to the stairway door, opened it and watched me for a few seconds, then closed the door. I skipped down the stairs to the fourth floor, noting many security cameras in the stairwell. Too many, it seemed, for a stairwell to a Dean's office. *Make a note,* I reminded myself, then opened the door and entered the fourth floor hall. It was much different. No plush furnishings, only a maze of cubicles and small offices on the outer perimeter. Instead of staying to look around, I reentered the staircase and went down to the ground floor.

Curiously, once below the approach to the fifth floor, there were no more cameras. *Why not?* I wondered. I carefully opened the door. I really didn't want to encounter the guard again. Lucky for me, I was out of the building in no time.

So the Dean was *not* on sabbatical. Even though I hadn't seen him, I could have, if I'd been from the CDC. *Time to do a background search on the good Dean,* making another mental note. I had this sneaky feeling more than a few answers were to be found in the Dean's office. The autopsy recording, for one. And what else? *How am I going to get in there?* Take another mental note. Breaking and entering into the Dean's office. That should help my research career, huh? This one is going to be tougher.

"Intruder alert! Intruder alert!" the front door calmly repeated over and over as I approached my apartment.

"Identify," I queried.

"No identification available."

"Intruder location?"

"Unknown. Not currently on the premises."

Well, that was a relief. Someone had been here but was not here now, my security system was telling me. I held my hand to the doorbell for DNA authentication and the door opened. As I entered, I looked around closely to see if there was a noticeable change. As I walked around, I caught a dark fleeting movement behind me to the left. Suddenly, I felt a piercing pain in my occipital scalp and before I could react, I felt myself losing consciousness and falling to the floor.

Fog . . . Pain . . . Blurred vision . . . Pain . . . Nausea . . . Dizziness . . . Pain . . . Head swelling . . .

I tried to get up. Tried and fell to my knees. Fog . . . Pain . . . Blurred vision . . . Pain . . . Nausea . . . Dizziness . . . Pain . . . Head swelling . . . Unconscious. Slowly, very slowly, it came back to me. I was on the floor of my apartment. For how long?

Fog . . . Pain . . . Blurred vision . . . Pain . . .

No intruder on location. *No intruder on location?* Nausea . . . Dizziness . . . Pain . . . Head swelling . . .

How was the security system wrong?

Pain . . . in the head . . . back of the head . . .

It had to be wrong.

Pain . . . I reached to touch the back of my head. There was a huge lump there. Pain . . . What time is it? What day is it? How long have I been unconscious? I was an ambiguous mixture of pain, curiosity, growing anger, and fear. After about 10 minutes, my mind cleared enough to start seeking a few answers.

Bed. I had to go to bed. Stumbling more than walking, I wove my way down the hall to get to my bedroom. Aligning myself as best I could, I fell backwards onto the horizontal haven to try and get myself together.

"Quinton," the voice softly called my name from out of the darkness. *"AWWWW!"* I screamed at the top of my lungs, sitting up in bed, terrified as to the inquisitor.

"Quinton, Dr. Pritcherman, here."

"How did you get in?" I struggled against the dizziness, holding myself up, with my arms then lifted in fight mode. "Why are you—"

"You didn't make our 4 p.m. appointment and given the story you told at our last meeting, I decided to come find you," Pritcherman responded.

"How did you get in?"

"The front door was wide open," Pritcherman continued walking around surveying the place. "Nice place. How can a medical student afford . . . aw, never mind. I've been watching over your improving level of consciousness, you know. As a neurosurgeon, I have some expertise in that area," his sarcasm was only minimally contained.

It seems everyone is learning where I live. My head was killing me. I struggled to remain sitting upright, propping myself with outstretched arms.

"Lie down while we talk," Pritcherman commanded.

"OK," I was beginning to remember what he said at the start of rounds. "Why did you tell Smith about our talk?"

"Look, Quinton. I didn't tell her anything she didn't already know. She's been snooping around for several days. But I did make her think I didn't believe you."

"You mean you do believe what I told you?" I was surprised.

"I didn't, at least not at first," Pritcherman gently examined my eyes with a penlight. "But I did some checking around of my own. No one will talk about Zendejas. I tried to talk to the Dean about the patient he sent over that died. Nothing. You're a paranoid shit, but I'm a scientist. None of this makes sense."

"Bullshit!" I protested, pushing him away. Maybe it was the head injury or I'd just gotten fed up. "I'm a scientist, too!" I proceeded to tell Pritcherman about my patents, inventions, and DNA expertise in rapid-fire bursts of shouting, finally ending with, "You think I figured this out without a lot of scientific help? Don't answer. Just listen."

Even Pritcherman seemed taken aback at my aggressiveness. I spewed forth about Zachary and me going to the morgue. So now I'd committed myself even more to Pritcherman. "And if I hear one word of this from anyone, especially Smith, I'll find you and you'll wish you'd never heard of me, you obnoxious piece of shit!"

"Well, well," Pritcherman smiled. "Haven't we gone postal today," pausing. "Look, Quinton. You may not believe it, but I'm on your side."

"Prove it."

"How?"

"Get us into the Dean's office."

"Why?"

"I'll tell you, but can I trust you? I mean really trust you?"

"Quinton," again walking to the side of my bed, placing his hand on my chest over my heart. "You can bet your life on it."

"Huh? Maybe I need to call the cops."

"If you're right, this is a lot bigger than the two of us. And cops won't help you. There might be some real danger here," my newly found fellow sleuth answered. "Get some sleep and we'll talk more in the morning. And here," reaching inside his coat, "onion juice is good for reducing the pain of head trauma," he remarked as he began to walk out of the room. "And, for heaven's sake, lock your doors. Someone might try to break in again."

And with that, Pritcherman was gone.

I stumbled to the kitchen in search of an ice bag for my aching head. I hadn't figured on this being a part of medical school. "Computer, run diagnostics on the audit trail. Look for unauthorized tampering. And secure the perimeter. Maximum security alert for the next 8 hours."

Eight hours of uninterrupted sleep later, I bolted awake. Did I really talk to Pritcherman? Was he here? And just what did I tell him? Does my head still hurt? *YES!* A twenty minute, extra-hot shower helped, as did a bowl of *Honey-Nut Cheerios* and a *Dr. Pepper.* Let's just say nutrition isn't my strength in medical education. I dressed quickly and was at the computer once again. I wanted that diagnostic report and I wanted to run the Dean.

After I entered my security passwords, the audit report was waiting on my screen. It confirmed three unauthorized entries, the last being Pritcherman. If I took him at his word and the door really was open, then his entry doesn't count. The first two did. Two? So the "not on the premises" comment was accurate for the first. It didn't tell me about the second . . . the someone waiting for me. The one who knocked me out.

I looked further. I got home at 1332 hours. Pritcherman got there at 1527 hours, about two hours later. Wait a minute! The appointment I missed was scheduled for 1600 hours, so why did he know I wouldn't make it before it was even to take place? Why did he come looking for me? And why was he here early? Is he back on the bad boy list? I've told him everything, oh, Lord, now what? The first intruder alert was at 0814 hours, while I was at rounds. The second was at 1124 hours. I made a couple of assumptions. Unless they were working together, the two intruders didn't meet each other. That is, the first was gone before the second arrived. I'll try to confirm that with the video recording. Second assumption, the second intruder was there for two hours before I got back. So, the second one was waiting for me or taking a long time to find what he was looking for.

I switched to the video of the exterior door. I hoped it would show me someone I could recognize and maybe a timestamp of them leaving. I fast forwarded the digital images to 0814.

I'll be damned if it wasn't Grigsby. That's right! He wasn't at rounds today. What the hell was he doing here? Then a great image of him leaving at . . . checking the timestamp . . . 0821. Not much time to find anything. Was this innocent? If so, why did he break in? Mental note to check Grigsby out again, but with a bit more scrutiny.

I fast-forwarded again to 1124. Nothing. I ran it over and over. *Nothing.* I checked the logs and digital files for tampering. Nothing. I felt my muscles tighten. Someone had broken in and disabled or somehow tampered with both the door entry and video logs, stayed a while and did who knows what, but long enough to assault me. They got in and out unnoticed.

A shiver went through me. To do that meant someone with more than casual skills. If someone got in, what did they leave in terms of monitoring equipment? My sanctuary wasn't safe. I had to get out of here. I started looking everywhere for boxes. I wasn't leaving all this stuff, accumulated over seven years. I started pulling apart all the electronic gear to take. Luckily, the meat, the databases were virtual and resided in the cloud on a secure site. Mental note, who has accessed my databases lately? About an hour later, I had packed up everything I wanted to take, loaded it in my car and was preparing to leave. I set the security system to silent notification to my smart phone and put it on highest alert.

Maybe I'd catch a stray, who knows? I raced down to the PRT car I'd summoned, jumped in and it started driving away. I asked the vehicle to stop and it pulled to the curb. *Where was I going?* Go stay with Pritcherman? Smith? Grigsby? The two second-year students? No. Zachary's place was my best option. Why not? She wasn't using it. I'd never been there although I did have the address. But she's missing. What if the police were looking for her?

Someone could have reported her missing. Maybe seeing the cops wasn't such a bad idea. Or was it? I reminded myself I couldn't let anyone know where I was and needed to start taking more precautions in all my movements. I had a key to her place from our night at the morgue. So getting in wasn't an issue. What to do when I got there was. I could feel this rapidly getting out of hand.

Maybe Pritcherman was right and this was serious.

A silver-haired wig and mustache and a slumped posture provided my new identity. Zach's place was a small, one bedroom apartment with a small front room and even smaller kitchen. Not exactly my castle, but close to the hospital. After dropping off the boxes, my first priority was to secure this place. She'd had no reason to secure it previously, but I did and now she did, too. I installed an entry video camera, security access system with audit log, and DNA doorbell, all similar to mine, in about an hour. Testing it took another half hour, and now I was ready to set up my investigative tools in the front room.

The equipment would take up the entire space and then some. *What about secure Internet access?* I thought. No way a third-year surgery resident needed the kind of access I was used to. That took a few more hours and a trip or two to the local computer supply shop. By early evening, I was ready to go. Grigsby and the Dean were my first targets. I had to get info on Zach. I ached for her help. I ached for her touch, for her kiss, for her sarcasm. It had been too long since hearing from her. I desperately needed to know she was all right.

Whether my databases had been breached was next. But first, I had to re-examine the tooth, the probe, and the microchip. I froze. I hadn't brought them from my place. I'd get thrown off one of those old *CSI* shows for leaving crucial evidence at the scene! I called the PRT and quickly got back to my place and sure enough, right there in the vice grip was the tooth. I retrieved it and placed it into a small plastic specimen bag. I stiffened and lost my breath. I frantically searched the room. Over and over and over again. So, that's what the intruder alert was about. The specimen bag with the microchip and probe was gone.

— Always Count Your Blessings Before You Say Your Prayers —

IX

"Computer, run intruder alert. Did anything happen while I was gone?" I asked the computer.

"No entries recorded. Nominal activity," the computer droned matter-of-factly.

"So, did they not see the tooth, not care about it, or what?" I was confused. I decided to look at the tooth again more closely. This time, I wasn't trying to extract DNA. I wanted to look at the tooth. My visual evaluation confirmed nothing out of the ordinary other than the drill hole where I previously extracted the DNA.

Under the microscope it went. This time I examined it more closely. The enamel or exterior layer of the tooth wasn't real. It was a porcelain-like material. The pulp, or central part of the tooth where normally there are blood vessels and where soft tissue resides, was hollow. When I drilled into the tooth to get to the pulp and extract the DNA I hadn't paid much attention. I did get DNA, probably from the small amount of blood on the tooth. But that was mine. *So where did the other DNA come from?* As I looked more closely at the tooth, it became clear this was a man-made tooth. The central chamber was hollowed out and contained a small amount of liquid, a sample of which I extracted for the DNA testing. It was DNA. *So why was there DNA in this tooth from the patient that was clearly artificially placed?* I bolted to attention. Also inside the pulp chamber was another microchip. A microchip with which we humans don't normally come equipped.

This was getting more bizarre by the minute. I extracted the microchip from the tooth and placed the tooth back into the plastic container. This time I hid it well. Placing the chip under the microscope, I began looking at this very different microchip.

Using microchips for identification of pets and, for a short period of time even humans, began in the late twentieth century. Because of ethical concerns and worries about *Big Brother*, chipping humans quickly fell out of favor. The real and potential problems simply outweighed the benefits. There are two basic components to most chips. First, is storage of information, which has a capacity dependent on how much memory is built into the chip. Second, is a send and receive capability.

Another very common use is for product identification and tracking. Those chips are based on RFID technology, or radio frequency identification device. If a widget has an RFID tag on it, someone with a reader can track where it is, where it's been, and know what it is. That data can be used by the good guys or the bad guys. Normally, there are three basic types of RFID microchips. Active tags have a built-in battery and are capable of transmitting or receiving radio signals. Passive tags don't have a power source, but can derive power from an external source in order to transmit or receive. Lastly are the BAPs, or battery assisted passive tags that need an external power source to wake up, but can transmit or receive once awakened.

Those are the common chips. It quickly became apparent that this was no ordinary chip. In my DNA work, I'd seen lots of variations developed for the unique needs of particular situations. Just what is the unique need of this situation? Why would a human being need to have a fake tooth containing his DNA and a microchip? For what purpose? Why was it so important to deposit that tooth with all its mysteries in my leg? For what purpose, indeed.

This chip had the traditional two components of data storage along with send and receive capabilities. It had a relatively large storage capacity. It also appeared to have passive RFID. But there was a third component I didn't recognize. I needed the answers to a few questions: What's stored on the chip? How do I turn it on to send or receive the data? And what is that third component about?

Let's say I figured out how to turn it on. Now I could also be activating the tracking portion and someone could track me . . . or, more accurately, the tooth. I wasn't sure I wanted to do that just yet.

"What are you . . . why are you . . . ?"

"All good things in time, my princess," came the mocking laugh from one of Zachary's two assailants as she was jostled along toward a door leading to another room.

"Enough" their leader quietly interrupted. "Just get her secured on the table and get an IV into her."

"The hell you say! No IV for me," struggling to break free without success. The blindfold had slipped a bit, but not enough to really see anything. She'd been man-handled through the door and she noticed the smell. It was antiseptic–one she knew all too well. It was the smell of an operating room accompanied by the dull whisper of a laminar flow ventilation system. "Oh, no you don't."

"Now, now, luv. In a minute you'll be asleep."

"Enough. Just get her secured," the previously quiet leader demanded, a bit more forcefully than before. "I'm on a tight schedule." With that, the two quickly and silently threw Zachary onto the table, one she also recognized as an operating table and, using large, brown-leather belts, secured her lower extremities. With a Posey restraint they next bound her torso. All that remained free were her arms.

"I'll get you, whoever you bastards are," she was shouting, clearly terrified. A surgeon, she was now a patient or a victim, or could it be something worse? She felt her right arm being deftly subdued while also being extended at a ninety degree angle to the plane of her body. Once secured to an arm board, it was then tied to the table. She knew this procedure well–this was to be the point of anesthetic injection. Her left arm was similarly restrained at her side. With all the commotion, her blindfold had slipped even more, now allowing her to see glimpses of her captors. The two juniors were both working to complete her bondage and paid little attention, not noticing she was able to observe them. Onc almost seemed familiar, she thought, as she strained to recall from where.

"Get the IV going and let me know when you're ready. I'll be in the other room getting dressed," the leader ordered.

Dressed for what, Zachary struggled to think. She knew for what, but tried to deny she was about to undergo some kind of procedure. Her terror was now worsened by the distracting pain of an 18-gauge intravenous needle rapidly being placed in her right antecubital fossa. Bastards, she thought, wasting a good "big vein" for medications. The surgery resident in her instinctively wanted to preserve as many large veins as possible. You never know when you might need one. "Ow!" she protested, but to no avail as the catheter and tubing were taped securely into place.

"We're ready," came the firm notice to the one in the other room.

She heard distant footsteps now slowly coming closer. "Give her this." She saw a 20 ml. syringe being readied for injection through the IV port. She also saw the third person for the first time. "No," she muttered, "*not you . . .*" as she drifted into an anesthetic fog.

All right now, what's the reason for this tooth chip? I was tumbling the tooth in my right hand like a poker chip, switching it to my left, then pausing to hold it close to my eyes for inspection, and then back to the hands. This went on for a good ten minutes while I thought aloud, or just stared at the tooth. Then it dawned on me. *What was in the tooth was why it was deposited in my leg* by the bite of the erstwhile neurosurgery patient from Six West. Could this be the poor man's only way of letting someone know who he was?

Or was it more than that? Not just who, but what and why he was. I was pacing now. This is above my pay-grade. Whether I liked it or not, Pritcherman had to be told. I needed help and maybe not just psychiatric help, but HELP.

Suddenly, I felt a cold shiver, and a distinct sense of foreboding washed over me. *Zach, I know it's you*, I whispered to myself. *Where are you? What's happening?*

With that, I stopped pacing. "Do I just turn this whole mess over to Pritcherman, or keep going on my own," I mumbled. "Hell no, I don't turn it over to that onion-laced crazy. Besides, I think this may be genetic and I'll bet I know more about that than he does. It's my girlfriend they have, not Pritcherman's," I stated to the world. I was now resolved to double my efforts. *Who was this guy? This Pritcherman?*

Pacing again, I stopped in my tracks. "Hey? How did that tooth get to the morgue?" I asked the room, and resumed my pacing once again.

Smith took it when Zach was fixing my wound. "So how did it go from her to the morgue? I gotta find out who she is," mentally placing a check by her name. "Whoever she is," I continued my checklist, "Pritcherman doesn't seem to know how she fits in, and she's never around when she's supposed to be and is around when she's not supposed to be. And there's some kind of a DoD block on her."

It was still mid-morning, but I cracked open my fifth *Dr. Pepper* of the day. *I've got a few issues*, I thought to myself. *Smith, the tooth's travel itinerary, the Dean, who was that second visitor to my apartment after Grigsby, do*

I really trust Pritcherman–hell, I've got to. *Who else can I trust? Then there's these two microchips and the probe, and where were they, and who took them?* But first and foremost, what I wanted above all else, I said out loud: "Where the hell is Zachary?"

I decided to start with the chip, since I had it and wanted to know more about it before I talked to Pritcherman again.

I began with an assumption that the two microchips talked to each other. *Maybe the data from the first brain chip was sent to the tooth chip where it was stored or sent on down the line,* I theorized. *But what data? And to whom was it sent? Am I being too cloak-and-dagger-like?*

No, I wasn't. After science outran the ethics and the legal system in the early 2010's, I wasn't the only one concerned about *Big Brother.* First, humankind sequenced DNA, next we realized it wasn't the entire answer, as there were proteins that really controlled everything. Those proteins determined what was defective or not, and caused the diseases. All the DNA did was cause the creation of the good or bad proteins. The proteins did the actual damage. Synthesizing artificial proteins had been much harder to do than first envisioned. But now that DNA sequencing was known, Pandora's box was open.

Insurance companies, employers, the government, you name it–everyone got access to the raw data and, depending on their motives, used . . . or should I say, misused . . . the data for their own purposes. The legal protections were talked about *ad nauseum*, but nothing substantial ever happened. That's one of the downsides of divided government–paralysis.

The U.S. has been in the throes of divided government for many years. That paralysis ultimately worked against all parties, because power abhors a vacuum. Into that vacuum stepped those with less than stellar motives–insurance companies, healthcare organizations, basic researchers, and even branches of the government. Did I say even the government?

The government was the worst offender of them all–what a surprise, huh? Not only were there governmental errors of omission, but worse, there were errors of commission. That is, they failed to pass laws to protect us, and then compounded it by abusing us like the insurance and healthcare gods. Talk about adding insult to injury. And there was significant injury.

Although some rights were guaranteed, such as the right to not be turned down for emergency healthcare services, there were more subtle discriminations. Just because one has health insurance doesn't mean you get *Cadillac* treatments. There are many ways to not treat, and not just by benign neglect, to use Daniel Patrick Moynihan's time worn phrase from the 1970s.

One example involves a genetically identifiable disease which has no known treatment. Do you want to know about it? That's an individual decision–one we'd all like to retain. But with free access to the raw data by all, insurance companies and potential employers now have the ability to identify individuals with these genetic diseases, so who's to say you didn't get that job because of it? Once again, science is a double-edged sword.

What seemed so simple in the beginning is actually quite complicated. Just because it's known that cystic fibrosis is a simple DNA mutation that then causes defective protein synthesis doesn't mean there is a treatment for the disease. There are many more examples of "simple" problems that have complex ramifications.

What was so secretive about this chip and the data it contained? That was my mission, for now.

"Time for a more detailed examination of the tooth and chip," I decided. A further look at the tooth didn't reveal much I hadn't already found. But I did pay better attention to the small amount of liquid I overlooked in my initial exam. I took care to extract just the liquid for more than the DNA analysis I'd already completed and set it aside.

It was to the chip I turned my attention. Send and receive, I understood. But what was the rest of the chip's purpose? Back to the microscope I went.

I was a biogeneticist more than an engineer. So my chip-tech skills were marginal. I knew enough to discern the send and receive portions because they are so standardized and I'd used them in my genetics career. But this third part of the chip was an entirely new matter for me. After about an hour of trying to unravel the secrets of the microchip, using my limited engineering wits, I was no closer to its secrets than when I started.

I was leaning back in a rickety, old chair Zachary must have acquired from her family or an itinerant furniture dealer when my contemplations were interrupted by my smart phone. The Caller ID alerted me to Pritcherman.

"Well, this time his timing's pretty good," shaking my head as I answered. "Yes, Dr. Pritcherman, good morning, sir."

"Quinton . . . my office . . . in an hour." He was all business and no hint of the reason. "And I mean one hour, not a minute later, got it?"

Before I could answer, he was gone. So what's this all about this time? I checked my watch, not really knowing how much time I'd spent just sitting in Zach's chair, taking in her essence. *Damn! I'd just said "good morning" and it's three in the afternoon. Isn't it funny, how time slips away?*

This time, I gave myself plenty of time to find my way through the labyrinth of corridors and endless turns, finally arriving at the entrance to Pritcherman's office. I paused a few seconds to collect my thoughts–realizing I shouldn't have done that with all his monitoring equipment when suddenly the door flew open.

"Inside, inside," Pritcherman hurried me. "You're holding out on me, I just know it, son."

"Me?" I protested. "I could say the same thing about—"

"Mr. Quinton," Pritcherman paused for what seemed to be a full minute and he wasn't pacing on his plush, carpeted office floor. "If we're going to get anywhere solving this mystery, then we're going to have to trust each other."

What was he up to? I was suspicious, but he was right.

Where I thought I'd crossed the Rubicon, in fact, I was only knee deep in the water. Time to jump in with both feet. "Dr. Pritcherman, I'm not holding out on you, but—"

"I know you're sandbagging me."

"No, it's not like that. I—"

"It's not like that? Then just how is it, son?"

"Where's Zachary, Dr. Pritcherman? I have this feeling—"

"Smith said she left for a few days, you say she's kidnapped. How should I know? Who do I believe?"

"You'd better believe me," I barked. "She's my friend—"

"She's my resident."

"Well, this is—"

"Look," Pritcherman interrupted. "Personal, Quinton? It's personal to you? Well, it's more than that to me. Nobody, I mean nobody messes with my service." Pritcherman was standing now.

"Sir, did I tell you about the microchip?"

There was a long pause and the restless neurosurgeon began pacing again and reaching into his pocket. "No," was the near silent response. "There's a microchip? From where?"

"Well, when we were in the morgue, we . . . Dr. Zachary and me . . . I can't stop thinking about her. Zach missing has me worried."

"Quinton! The chip," he screamed, back to his neurotypical mania.

"Sorry, the chip. Yes, we found it in the morgue," I continued. "I thought I told you about . . . whatever. Well, it's gone, but I found another one in the—"

"What in the hell are you talking about, another one, and where's the first one?" His pace quickened to the familiar crunch and spray of his onion-spewing bite. "Sit down . . . slow down and let me direct your thoughts, boy. You told me about a probe from the morgue, but no microchip. And now it's gone? And there's a second one?"

I took his recommendation and sat in a mauve-colored, deep chair in front of his desk. "Well, whoever visited me and decided I needed another concussion must've taken the probe . . . and the chip. I—"

"Which chip?"

"I'm getting there. It's—"

"Well get there faster, damn it!"

"When I got back from the morgue to my apartment, I took a quick look at the probe and the microchip. Then I looked at the tooth–I was trying to extract DNA for identification when—"

"You were identifying him from the tooth?"

"I was trying, but when I looked at the tooth a second time more closely, it turns out it's a prosthesis. And in the interior is a chamber that has liquid that was DNA, or is DNA, I should say—"

"Go on, slow down."

I took a deep breath, exhaled and continued. "Inside the tooth there was also a microchip—"

"To be clear, this is the second microchip," Pritcherman sounded exacerbated. "A second one, different from the first one you never told me about?" Pritcherman's sarcasm was not veiled well.

"Correct. Two microchips and a probe."

"Damn-near sounds like a movie title, huh, son."

"A horror movie, sir. So, the microchip—"

"The second one."

"Right. The second microchip has three components. A storage device, a send and receive component, and a third one I can't figure out—"

"Interesting. And you want to know what that third component is all about?"

"Yes," I mustered my courage. "Sir, if you'd quit interrupting me and let me complete a thought I could tell you about—"

"Yes, yes, I know. I'm a loud-mouthed, bastard who can't keep still. I'm sorry, it's not you, son, it's just my style."

"I understand." *What the hell was I saying?* I was actually beginning to sympathize with Pritcherman's idiosyncrasies. "Just let me occasionally get a word in edge-wise," I continued.

"OK, OK. I'll listen–hard for this old turkey. I'm all talk and no show, Quinton. I hope you know that."

I didn't, but I'll take him at his word for now.

"Yes sir. So back to the chip. From my genetics background I had to deal with bio-chips a bit and this one has me baffled. I spent about an—"

"And nothing. . . sorry, go on, I apologize."

". . . an hour, right. Nothing looks familiar to me. And another thing. How'd the tooth with the second microchip get to the morgue? Smith took the tooth from Zachary right after she took it out of my leg. Anyway, the first chip, the one with the probe, I think it works with the second chip. You know, the tooth chip talks to the brain chip—"

"Smith? The what?" Pritcherman interrupted again, but was now standing over me, close enough for the noxious fumes to permeate my nostrils. I turned my head to the left.

"The brain chip we found with the probe—"

"Why do you call it the brain chip? And where are these two chips, anyway?"

"I brought the tooth chip with me. Here. You take it," I gave it to Pritcherman. "I call the other one the brain chip because we found it next to the wedge of brain in the drawer—"

"BRAIN!! You never mentioned brain, Quinton! Only a probe and a chip. He was screaming again now. "From what part of the brain is this chip? And why the hell . . . ," his voice trailed off.

I sat there looking up at him for about fifteen seconds. Then he continued, "Quinton," he said softly, I want that brain."

"I don't—"

"I want the—"

"I want Zachary!"

"I want that brain!" He was emphatic as he turned and reached for his desk phone. "I'll find your sweetheart and you find that brain. Get out of here, now, Mr. Quinton. I'll be in touch," Pritcherman said as he watched me leave his office.

"Dean Jankowski? Dr. Pritcherman from the neurosurgery service is on line two for you. Shall I take a message?"

"No, I'll take it," the tall, thin graying man of about fifty-five spoke to the unseen speakerphone. Adjusting his tie, straightening his perfectly tailored, three-piece designer suit and standing, the Dean picked up his telephone, "Good day, Dr. Pritcherman. How may I be of service to you today?"

"Viktor, we need to talk."

I made it back without incident to my temporary apartment, also known as Zachary's. On the way, I kept looking around and back at what I thought might be another vehicle following mine. Was this paranoia again, or legitimate? Pritcherman hurrying me out and his obsession with the brain consumed my thoughts, keeping me from thinking more about whether I'm paranoid. He wanted the brain. I wanted Zachary. I also wanted to know about the Dean and Grigsby.

Grigsby had been stewing in the back of my mind for a while. Why is it he's summoning me for Pritcherman and also missing rounds? As I cracked open a *Dr. Pepper* and leaned back in Zach's broken-down chair, I considered Grigsby. I've known him for the two-and-a-half-years of our joint medical school careers, but I didn't know anything about him. We'd each taken an instant dislike to each other from the first day.

He correctly identified me as a geek and I identified him as a jock. The stereotype fit–Grigsby wanted to be an orthopedic surgeon, a hulking bone-crusher, as he made clear to everyone who'd listened from his first day. Besides being linebacker size, bull neck, slumping shoulders and perpetually clearing acne, the only thing I knew about him was he constantly put me down to anyone who'd listen. And it wasn't just me he derided, it was everyone. He had an air of superiority without any reason–and he was a kiss-ass.

A more thorough computer search of the Dean would suffice for now. But for Grigsby I decided I'd need to pay him a visit, or more accurately, his living quarters. I would need to make sure he wasn't there–Pritcherman could help–keep him while he is on rounds, maybe? I secretly hoped for a confrontation but knew better. For now, I needed to remain under his radar.

"Computer, run DoD search on Dean Viktor Igorseg Jankowski," I requested. Nothing. "Computer, run DoD search for Dean Viktor Igorseg Jankowski," I tried again, and again, no response. Then I remembered. I hadn't set that up here yet. So I used the old-fashioned methodology of computer query, the touchpad. A few touches and the search began. "Computer, when first search complete, perform a second search of my database. List all access attempts in the last month," giving the command. "That will take a bit," I said, thinking out loud.

I next sent Pritcherman a text message asking him to keep Grigsby occupied for the next two hours. Gathering a few things and dressing in my disguise, I summoned a vehicle to deliver me to Mr. Grigsby's student housing residence near the campus and near Zachary's as well. In a few minutes, I was outside the plain, institutional building where Grigsby resided. No one seemed to follow.

After taking the elevator to the third floor, I found his unit, number 325, and surveyed the exterior quickly, but carefully. Nothing seemed out of the ordinary–just a normal, drab, long hallway and a door similar to all the others on the third floor. I looked for any traces of an exterior alarm and seeing none made my entrance, using another trick of the trade the parents taught me–breaking and entering.

I closed the door behind me and took note of the outer room. The interior was equally drab, with institutional light green paint–how can anyone stand this kind of a place. I needed more color. Continuing my search, there were two doors on the right, one leading to a bedroom and the other a small bathroom. Off to the left of the main room was a small kitchen area and counter. A table next to the counter held a computer terminal and lots of paperwork scattered over the tabletop.

Before the table search, I peeked into the bathroom–filthy, and he wants to be a doctor? Next, the bedroom–very messy as well. Other than the mess, both appeared rather ordinary. Medical students tended to concentrate on little else besides studying, sustained by junk food and caffeine. Walking over to the table, this seemed a good place to begin a more thorough inspection, when I stopped cold and I felt a shiver run up my spine. Sitting on the table next to the computer was a small plastic bag containing the 'brain' microchip and probe. What in the name of Sam Hill was Grigsby doing with it and just who the hell is Grigsby?

My dilemma was whether to take the bag or not. It was clearly visible, so it surely would be missed. Taking it would also let Grigsby know someone had been here, but not who. Screw him! I expropriated the plastic bag into my shirt pocket. Looking through the papers, I saw no medical school notes, but I did see a number of encrypted printouts. Encrypted? Who the hell is this guy? I took one of the papers, from the bottom of the stack, folded it and placed it in my pocket with the bag. Time to get out of here–I was sweating and it wasn't hot.

The post-anesthetic patient was beginning to awaken, starting to bite down on the #7.5 endotracheal tube extending from her oropharynx. She was experiencing eye fluttering and had weak extremity movements.

"You're alright, Doctor. We're here for you," the team leader whispered in her ear. "A little more improvement and we'll get that E-T tube out," turning away. "Maintain the high flow oxygen," he ordered his assistants. About ten minutes passed with little activity beyond observation.

"Let's deflate the cuff, gentlemen. See how she breathes on her own."

Jeremy deftly deflated the cuff. With that, the patient's respirations became noisier as air was now able to escape around the previously protected airway. Most of her ventilation was through the tube, but before the artificial airway could be removed, the patient has to demonstrate she no longer needed the protection of the endotracheal tube placed prior to her surgical procedure.

"What's the pulse oximetry?"

"98%"

"Good enough. Go ahead and pull the tube," the leader instructed. "Let's put her on CPAP for a while just to make sure. She's precious cargo, gentlemen."

With that, the tube was easily removed and the patient, now much more conscious, began coughing as the plastic airway cleared her vocal cords and a form-fitting CPAP mask was applied over her nose.

"You bastards," she hoarsely mouthed, trying to shake off the mask. "And you, you fat prick . . . ," looking directly at the leader.

"Now, now, Dr. Zachary. Such language from a lady," rapidly turning his attention to the others. "We'll activate shortly. Are you ready?"

"Yes, sir. We'll need some time after initiation to calibrate the parameters through," his subordinates advised.

"We'll let her act up a bit to gather a baseline.

They were ignoring Zachary, but she wasn't ignoring them. "Baseline, my ass." She was gaining strength and trying to loosen her restraints. "Let me up . . . AND WHAT DID YOU DO TO ME? My head's killing me."

"Not surprising, good Doctor," the fat bastard answered, matter-of-factly. "I'm surprised you haven't complained about the bandages. You complain about everything else."

She hadn't noticed her head, other than the pounding. But after his comment, her focus shifted to her heavier than normal cranium. "My God, don't tell me I had a craniotomy! You greasy pig! What about your Hippocratic Oath, you fat slime-ball?"

She was on a roll. One thing surgery taught her was how to curse like a sailor–like the boys. Or maybe it was her Oklahoma farm upbringing. Whichever, she knew her way around the slang vocabulary of the day.

"Well, gentlemen. I think we have our baseline—"

"Screw you!"

"Now?"

"I think I've had enough insults for one day. Yes, now. Initiate, please."

With that, the two acolytes hovering in obeisance over a handheld tablet pressed a few commands and Dr. Zachary was suddenly quiet. "What initial settings, Doctor?"

"Protocol thirteen, for now. Let's just keep her quiet until further notice.

Jumping into my vehicle again, I gave a verbal command to take me back to Zachary's, wishing I could increase the speed. The moment the door was released, I bolted out of the car and I ran directly into Smith. I hadn't noticed her following me in another vehicle.

"Quinton, what's with the costume?" she asks.

"I didn't—"

"Never mind, Mr. Quinton. It's not a very good one," interrupting. "Do you want to do this here or inside?"

"Do what?" I'm standing on the curb, it's 68 degrees and the wind is blowing in my face, but I'm sweating like it's Texas in July. As I took off the disguise I looked around to plan an escape attempt.

"Don't be so paranoid," she chided. "And watch out. That paper in your pocket's about to blow away in this wind."

I stuffed the shirt pocket document down firmly, crumpling it. Does she know what it is? "Where's Zachary?"

"How should I know where she is," Smith replied. "Pritcherman sent me to talk to you about getting you off this neurosurgical service." I knew she was lying, because Pritcherman and I had already talked about that. So what was she really up to?

"Quinton. Do you want to go inside or not?" She was nudging me toward the door.

"No, I mean yes, I mean—" I stammered. "You lied to me about Zachary. What about being off the service? I know Pritcherman said he wanted me gone, but—"

"But what? If he wants you gone, you're gone," she interrupted again. She was also gently pushing me toward the entrance.

"You lied. I'm not going into the building," I stood my ground. "Quit pushing me. Whatever you want to say to me, you can tell me right here."

"Quinton," she leaned in close. "Be careful. Neurosurgery can be a dangerous . . . unless you know what you're doing . . . and you don't . . . *you don't!*" Then she whispered, somewhat menacingly, "Just a word to the wise."

With that she turned to get back into her vehicle. Only then did I notice someone else in her vehicle, in the driver's seat. A large, hulking male–Grigsby, most likely. I couldn't exactly see his face, but I could make out the smirk which I'd seen many times before. As they drove away, I was left standing near the entrance, disguise in hand, screaming as they drove away, "You didn't answer my question!" and wondering how much they knew . . . how much I thought they knew I knew . . . *oh, the hell with it!* I threw the mustache and wig into the trash bin adjacent to the building entrance.

I pulled out my smart phone and made a short video of them both. Grigsby seemed very serious as he drove and Smith flipped her hair off her face, tangled by the wind. "I'll study that later," making a mental note, cataloging another "to do" item. I assumed they knew I had the bag, they saw the paper, and now they know I'm staying at Zachary's, so they know I'm on the run. But do they know Pritcherman and I have already talked about my "reassignment?" Do they know we're collaborating?

Are we?

"Let's run the system through some test parameters. Wake her up, Jeremy. But leave the restraints on until we know how she reacts," the leader ordered.

Silently, Jeremy tapped a series of commands into the tablet computer, pressed Enter, and Dr. Zachary's eyes opened. She said nothing and made no attempt to move. Jeremy remained at the computer awaiting further instructions.

"Doctor Zachary," the leader firmly addressed the docile female patient.

"Yes?" She looked directly at him.

"Tell me who you are."

"I'm Dr. Barbara Lynn Zachary, third-year general surgical resident, currently assigned to the Six West neurosurgical service under Professor Stanley J. Pritcherman. I am—"

"Very good, Doctor. That will be satisfactory," turning to Jeremy. "Now upload her updated biographical information, Jeremy."

A few keystrokes and he responded, "Upload complete."

"Dr. Zachary. I'm going to release your restraints now. Please remain on the gurney for now." Turning to Jeremy, he nodded his head and Jeremy released the Posey and other restraints.

"How do you feel, Doctor?"

"Other than a slight headache, I feel fine. May I sit up?"

"Yes," and with that, the leader of the three stepped back and motioned for his patient to sit. As she sat up, he murmured, "Excellent. Most excellent. Release the rest of the leg restraints and let's have her stand up and move about."

Jeremy freed her remaining appendages and she remained sitting on the gurney. "Doctor, please stand next to the gurney and stretch your legs. Tell me how you feel?"

Still in a surgical gown, she slipped easily off the gurney, first standing on both feet with a widened stance. She narrowed her feet, and then lifted each, bending at the knee, one after the other. She made a slight "bunny hop" motion. Then standing on her right leg, she ran the heel of her left foot up and down her right shin.

"No dizziness or feeling of ataxia. No dysdiadokokinesia. I love that word," she stated calmly. "No one ever knows what it means and it sounds so impressive."

"Well, well, Doctor. I do know what it means."

"Oh. Are you in the medical field, too?"

Looking at his two assistants, the leader beamed, "Excellent, gentlemen. I love her ability to make small talk." Turning back to his patient, "Yes, I'm in the medical field. Tell me about your background. Where are you from? That sort of thing."

"I was born and raised in a small Oklahoma farm area, the first in my family to go past community college," Zachary answered. "I graduated with a degree in microbiology and spent two years after college working on the Creek Indian reservation helping at the local hospital. I saw so much disease and under-treated patients that I—"

"Good, Doctor. I'm sure it was inspiring," cutting her off.

"And then medical school and on to a surgical residency here," the leader quickly concluded her thought. "Fine. All well and good. Do you know me?"

"Yes, you are—"

"Jeremy, bookmark her response for deletion from that memory," he interrupted, turning again to his two underlings. "I don't want any institutional personal memory remaining. Only her bio info and upload the profiles of the team on her current neurosurgical rotation. Got it?"

"Yes," Jeremy answered, the other nodding his head while leaning against the wall across the room. The second had been quiet throughout, observing and making notes on another tablet computer. Jeremy seemed to be the only one handling the programming of Dr. Zachary.

"And Jeremy," the leader continued. "Upload the special Smith data I brought you this morning."

At our last meeting, Pritcherman and I had agreed on our individual assignments. *"Smith"* was mine. I decided it was time to let Rupert help me in my tasks. After the intensity of Pritcherman, Rupert was a welcome relief. He didn't interrupt and he didn't debate with me. This was no ordinary robot, like ones developed a few years ago. I was again the beneficiary of my parents' previous "occupations." Beginning with the *Roomba* to clean floor spaces, robotics had progressed in spurts and fits. The future always seemed to be just over the horizon, another decade or so. Primitive predecessors such as PR2 and HERB, the <u>H</u>ome <u>E</u>xploring <u>R</u>obotic <u>B</u>utler performed rudimentary tasks and followed simple commands. They were way too expensive and didn't really do much. They took hours to climb a short flight of stairs and just as long to do primitive tasks.

No, Rupert descended from a completely different developmental track–the government–more accurately, a top-secret part of the government, a.k.a DARPA, the U.S. Department of Defense's <u>D</u>efense <u>A</u>dvanced <u>R</u>esearch and <u>P</u>rocurement <u>A</u>gency. Decades ahead of his publicly known predecessors, Rupert was able to maintain a top traveling speed of four miles per hour, negotiate around furniture and things without wreaking havoc on his surroundings and could carry on a decent conversation, thanks to the descendants of IBM's *Watson.* Thank you, Mom and Dad, for leaving me Rupert's "parent" to study and improve upon, and thank you to whomever they worked for, and who didn't come looking for it to take it back. Rupert was my avocation through college, built of necessity, since I desperately needed a friend. He could *Roomba* the room, too.

"Rupert, I'm going to send you back to our place for a few more supplies."

"No problem. And what would those supplies be?"

"Most importantly, bring back a mixed case of Cabernets–say, Château Montelena, Silver Oak, along those lines, some of the better Bordeaux bottles and maybe a dry white or two for variety."

"You know you must be specific," Rupert lectured. "And?"

"Yeah, yeah, I know. OK, two bottles of Château Montelena, two Silver Oaks, three bottles of Far Niente, two of Sonoma-Cutrer, that's a chardonnay, Rupert, and pick the next three bottles of whatever you encounter," tiring of instructing him. "Check for intruders, or anything unusual. You can take this list with you."

"Affirmative. No need for the list. And should I return here? How much time is allotted?"

"Take as much time as you need."

"Q, you know these kinds of nonspecific answers drive me crazy," the robot droned.

"Not a far drive, Rupert. Just how does a robot go crazy–don't answer," I interrupted myself.

"If there are no other questions, I will take off now," Rupert commented, exiting the room and the apartment.

I was alone and it was quiet. There was time enough to gather my thoughts and develop a plan for "Smith." One thing I knew–it didn't involve going back to the morgue. "Smith" was alive and well. *What about Zach?* I had to put that thought out of mind. Besides, Pritcherman must be looking for her.

Governmental intrusion has been an issue for this country since its inception. The balance between too much and too little intrusion has waxed and waned from the beginning. What's different now is that the myriad intrusions are far ahead of and outnumber the legislative protections. The ethics of the situation are lost in the politics and gridlock of modern two-party governance. There is no ethical standard to a bureaucracy, be it governmental or private sector. Still, the citizenry yearns for protections and chafes under the apathy of its government, no longer operating *for the people*, but seemingly against its own society.

I am a rebel. I refuse to take the indifferent or incompetent "no" for an answer. My natural inclination is to find a way around the establishment, especially the condescending, pompous types–the "I'm from the government and I'm here to help" ones. No, thanks. Don't try to help me so much. Please don't help me at all.

My skepticism was borne of my parents' demise and the lack of truth surrounding the circumstances. Some things about them I knew; other things I only surmised. What was clear was their covert involvement in the affairs of the government I now loathed and feared, the very government I felt was involved in–perhaps even responsible for–their deaths. I'm lashing out against their killers; whether actual or not, in my mind they were the cause. The ethical lapse is my Don Quixote cause, to strike a blow for libertarianism long lost in the maze of administrations consuming more and more of our national treasure and worse . . . our spirit.

Smith was a part of that, I was now sure, the enemy to be vanquished. Yet I know nothing about her. How do I defeat an adversary I don't know? Leaning back in one of Zach's dilapidated chairs, I closed my eyes and thought, *Just what is it I need to know?*

– Never Announce The Prize Before You Add The Score –

X

Pritcherman sank into the chair of the Dean's fifth floor outer office and began fumbling in his pocket, searching for his nervous habit. Before he could find his prize, an inner office door opened, revealing Dean Viktor Igorseg Jankowski.

"Stanley, come in," the Dean warmly ushered Pritcherman into his inner sanctum, patting him on the back as he walked past. "It's been too long, hasn't it?"

"Cut the crap, Viktor," Pritcherman was in no mood for niceties. "We have problems."

"Nothing we can't handle, I'm sure," Jankowski said, ushering Pritcherman to a chair in front of his large, mahogany desk, overflowing with paperwork neatly stacked in piles.

"Would you care for a drink, Stanley?"

"No," Pritcherman snapped. "And it's not as simple as you think. That seizure patient you asked me to operate on. Well, he's dead and—"

"Yes, I know," the Dean stared straight into Pritcherman's eyes, not betraying any emotion. "Sad, but he was—"

"He was on my service, Viktor," angrily interrupting as was his custom. Pritcherman was now pacing, as he was also prone to doing. "No one dies on my service. Not unless I know about it."

"Playing God again, Stanley?"

"Not God, but damn-near!" Pritcherman's pacing broke off the intense stare-down between the two men. "You sent him to me. What the hell happened to that guy? He was young and—"

"I know, I know," Jankowski remained cool, maintaining his visual lock on the pacing neurosurgeon. "Something must have happened. I will make inquiries."

"You do that, Viktor. And while you're making those inquiries, what happened to my resident, Dr. Zachary? And tell me about a Dr. Smith sent over from Georgetown," Pritcherman stood still in front of the Dean. "And while you're at it, tell me about a third-year medical student named Quinton."

"Dr. Zachary. Are you feeling well enough to resume your duties at the hospital? I suggest you go home first," the leader recommended in a fatherly tone, while removing the pressure dressing from her head.

"Yes, home first. Good idea," Zachary dispassionately answered. She walked directly to the door to leave and then paused, "Thank you for your assistance," smiling as she went through the door. As she made her way to the outside, the two assistants walked behind, observing her closely.

"Shall I summon a vehicle?" Jeremy asked the leader over his smart phone.

"Yes, and follow her per our plan. And Jeremy, check on her frequently," he responded.

Zachary sat in the passenger seat of a PRT summoned by Jeremy, and after the door closed it pulled away from the curb. After a short, five-minute drive, the vehicle pulled to the curb in front of her apartment. the same curb where Smith and Grigsby had confronted Quinton about an hour prior.

"Computer, retrieve Jankowski search. No, cancel. First, retrieve database search," I said as I sat down and opened another *Dr. Pepper*. While the fizz settled down in my glass I remotely sent the video file I'd taken of Smith and Grigsby from my smart phone to the computer for storage.

"Database accessed by Quinton, Chauncey Charles at—"

"Besides me, any others?"

"Seventeen access points by Quinton only. No other access logons," the computer answered.

"Good," slowly exhaling. "Load Jankowski search," I commanded.

Watching the confirmation of the video being stored in the computer, it answered, "Jankowski search complete. Parameters on screen."

On screen was a long list of curriculum vitae information I quickly scanned. Nothing seemed unusual for a well-known academic. His biographical information indicated he was fifty-five years old, born in the former communist Poland, medical school in Gdansk, graduated with honors, residency in the United States at Johns Hopkins, studied internal medicine with a subspecialty in neurology.

"How convenient," I said, smirking a bit. "A neurologist refers a patient to a neurosurgeon for surgical ablation of a seizure focus. Routine, huh? Or is that really the reason?" I suspiciously asked the room. The searches indicated stints at the National Institutes of Health, again not unusual for a professor-type, but left open a curious gap of about ten years, several years after completion of his residency and before going to the NIH.

"People don't disappear for ten years. I wonder what that's about," I murmured. "Computer, DoD detailed search on same subject, Jankowski," verbally commanding another search. "Where were you, Dean?"

"DoD detail search, accessing—"

As the computer worked on the new search parameters, I scanned through the video. One of the beauties of digital photography is the ability to enhance, enlarge and easily edit videos and pictures, all without losing much detail. As I looked at the images, I surveyed the background and seeing nothing in particular, I cropped it down to Grigsby and Smith. Enlarging Grigsby first, I saw his pimply face, but nothing remarkable. Why wasn't Grigsby preoccupied by Pritcherman as I'd asked him?

I wondered?

Turning my attention to Smith, she was tossing her blonde hair back as she entered the vehicle. I noticed a red lesion behind her right ear. I looked at the video in slow motion several times–until I was interrupted by the turning of the front door knob.

"Quinton?"

"Zachary?"

"This is my apartment. What are you doing here?"

"Zach, I am so relieved to see you. I –"

"Why are you here?"

"Remember our plan? If there was trouble? Remember I have a key from the morgue," running to her. As I tried to embrace her, she pushed me away, but not before I noticed she had a red, raised area behind her right ear.

Grigsby opened his apartment door and he instantly knew something was up. Before entering further, he paused and reached inside the left side of his lab coat with his right hand, retrieving a Beretta 9mm pistol, the standard military special forces-issue sidearm. Hardly standard medical school-issue. Adopting a defensive stance, he crouched low to the ground, then passed through the door and quietly moved to inspect both doors leading to the bedroom and bathroom.

Satisfied there were no intruders currently on the premises, he holstered his weapon. As he quickly surveyed the apartment, he noted the papers on his desk had been "rearranged." Sorting through them, a smile spread across his face. He took his smart phone out of his pocket and pressed a speed dial number. "He took the bait."

Zachary's return was a mixed blessing. As happy as I was to see her, she didn't seem to care about me at all. Hell, it was as if we'd never met. Besides that, she wanted to know why I was staying in her apartment and I didn't think I should tell her the truth. I made some feeble excuse and she coldly told me to get my stuff and get out. I took most of it. But I left enough surveillance equipment, including the doorbell DNA scanner, to be able to monitor her apartment without her knowing. What I did collect, I dragged out of her place in boxes and was once again at the curb. Something was very wrong.

"Now where do I go?" I was tired, hot and confused. Pritcherman was my safest option. Really? Safest? How about my *only* option in utter desperation? I called him and without telling him why, told him I was coming back to his office. I summoned my PRT. It was 8 p.m. and I was on the street again.

I loved this technology. Introduced only a few years ago, the PRT, or Personal Rapid Transit, completely removes the driver from the traffic equation. Small, light, efficient, and completely digital, these vehicles can carry up to five passengers. Their roll-out began with common routes from the hospitals in the medical center complex to the dorms and other outlying buildings. The system consists of multiple taxi-like vehicles, each traveling over predetermined routes with embedded sensors in the roadway that communicated with the vehicle's onboard computer guidance system. As useful as it was, not to mention being much safer, it was currently a system with only limited utility, and a more expansive system was being planned, based on updating of existing roadways.

The principal difference between PRTs and traditional buses was that the PRTs were "on-call" and could be summoned anytime by the user–there are no set schedules. One may be reserved in advance, and the route can even be changed on the fly, too. It also beat trying to drive Zachary's old truck.

The PRT pulled away from the curbside stop smoothly and eased into traffic. I soon found myself parked in front of Pritcherman's office building. The vehicle had stopped as smoothly as it had started only minutes before. My phone rang and the now familiar voice of my new-found "friend" was speaking excitedly on the other end.

"Quinton, I've got some interesting information," Pritcherman said. "Get back here as soon as you can."

"That makes two of us," I replied. I unloaded the PRT and just as I cleared the door, it automatically closed and the vehicle drove off. I still found it a bit disconcerting to see a car on the move without a driver. Soon, however, I was back in the halls of the medical center offices and nearing Pritcherman's office. Just as I arrived, the outer door opened and he ushered me in.

"That was quick," he said, turning to close the door. "Listen, there's no record of Smith from Georgetown, or any other resident named Smith in the last six months," Pritcherman loudly announced. "I checked with the resident assignment office. Not assigned to my service, not on any surgical service. No Smith anywhere. Such a common name, but not one resident named Smith assigned anywhere in this hospital."

"Sir . . . Zachary . . . she just walked through the door of her apartment where I was staying. Except I might as well not have even been there. She barely recognized me–cold as ice. I'm worried about her. This is getting out of hand. Maybe we should call the police?"

"Why? And stop the fun? No, this is administration's little game of *screw Pritcherman*. That's my bet," Pritcherman was pacing again. "I'll bet it's some kind of a mole, you know, checking up on me. That prick-of-a-Dean. Sounds like him."

"I don't know," I countered. "This is bigger than that. Last time I checked, the Dean or the resident assignment office was not involved in murders."

"We don't know this homeless guy was murdered," Pritcherman grimaced. "Where the hell did murder come from?"

"Look," I slowed my speech and spoke deliberately. "Your patient quickly dies for no apparent reason after being assigned to your service. So an autopsy is performed, except it wasn't, at least not according to Smith. Zachary and I find a brain and then she goes missing. And then guess what? She just showed up at her apartment–where I'm supposedly staying secretly–and hardly recognized me. No 'Hello, Quinton, how are you?' Nothing."

I continued. "I tried to ask her where she'd been, you know, after her disappearance, and she didn't really answer me or say anything about where she'd been or why, or—"

"Maybe she was just on vacation?"

"Are you kidding? Did you approve a vacation for her? Aren't you her supervisor, since she's assigned to your service?"

"I am, and no, I didn't," Pritcherman was standing still now.

"She's acting differently. Something's up, I know it. Whoever took Zachary from the morgue didn't know I was there that night or I'd probably be missing, too."

Pritcherman, in a rare moment, was silent.

"They didn't know I was there because I was hiding in a morgue drawer with the brain of a dead guy who wasn't autopsied. Wonder how the brain got there, huh, without an autopsy?"

"You were in a morgue drawer? I'd have crapped in my pants being in a morgue drawer like a slab of meat," Pritcherman admitted.

"Yeah, and in total darkness, too. And now there's no record of Smith," I continued. "I'm telling you, she's the key to all of this."

We both sat there, allowing the gravity of that last statement to sink in.

"Maybe we *should* call the police after all," Pritcherman finally said, in a voice so uncharacteristically soft I could barely hear him.

We were both staring up at the ceiling when he broke the silence and said, quite vehemently, "Hell, no! These sons-of-bitches aren't gonna screw up my service or this hospital or my reputation. I do have one, you know, Mr. Quinton."

"Yes, sir, I—"

"We've got some work to do, son."

"Yes, and Dr. Smith—"

"Doctor, my ass!" he railed on. "If she's a doctor, I'll chicken-fry her liver! We have to find out what her role is in all this and how she fits in. With both feet, Quinton. With both feet."

Pritcherman motioned me into a chair and sat down in another one next to it. Pulling it closer, he continued, "We're going to have to work together on this, so I need to know I can trust you."

"That's a two-way street, sir. I—"

"Quinton. Stop the 'sir' stuff. If we're gonna be partners, we have to treat each other that way."

Was he kidding? I wondered.

"You're going to find out everything about this *Smith* and I've got a few things on my plate, too. Now get out of here . . . partner," Pritcherman ordered. "And read up on neurobiology. Did you study anything about that during your genetics career?"

"Well, I know a fair amount. I know interactions are mediated by brain chemicals. It's an area of extreme interest in the neurobiology community and—"

"That's what I am, you know. A neurobiologist," he was up and pacing again. "I'm not *just* a neurosurgeon. I'm a research professor as well, remember?"

"Yes, sir, a neurobiologist. Brain chemicals, uh," I struggled to recall. "The connectome, I believe it goes back to the mid-1900's when—"

"Yes, yes, Donald Hebb in 1949. I know, I know. But how does one *form* memories, and then *recall* them or not? That's what I'm talking about."

"Dr. Pritcherman, what got you thinking about memory? I mean, I've only been gone—"

"Long enough for me to lay the foundation for solving this BS, that's what. It didn't make sense and still doesn't . . . but it will!" Pritcherman was now leaning against the wall. "You said Smith had the tooth, but you recovered it from the morgue, right?"

"Yes."

"How'd it get from her to the morgue? And what's the reason you only found a microchip, a probe, and a slice of brain? Why just a slice? Where's the rest of his remains? And now, all of a sudden, anyone who might know is no longer available." He sat down. "Quinton, we need to jog your memory about your time in the morgue, especially about the autopsy. This stinks, and where it smells there's usually a rat."

"Uh, sir," I interjected. "There was a whole brain there. I only took the microchip and probe because that's all I could fit in my pocket."

"So there's a whole brain?" Pritcherman reiterated.

"Yes."

"Then we have to go back and get it," my new partner insisted. "And the slice, too. I want to run—"

"Oh, no," I couldn't stand the thought. "Not back to the morgue, please, no."

"It's settled then."

"No, it isn't."

"Quinton," Pritcherman held up his hand. "Are you scared of a morgue?"

Sighing, I resigned myself to making the return visit. "One more thing, partner," I hesitated. Another Rubicon for me to cross. "I need a place to stay. Can I stay here in your office for. . ."

"Quinton . . . uh, partner . . . Q," Pritcherman was stuttering for the first time that I'd heard. "What the hell do you mean, you need a place to stay?"

"Well, it's a long story—"

"Oh, great. Another long story," Pritcherman dripped with his routine sarcasm.

"Dinner. Here. You're in charge of it. I'll be back in an hour or two. Make yourself comfortable . . . *partner.*"

"See what you can find out about Zachary," I asked.

It was almost 10 p.m. Another late night looms.

Zachary laid down on the bed in her apartment. She was sweating in spite of the air conditioner running at full strength. She seemed unaffected, resting in silence. But affected she was, just not aware of it.

After unceremoniously ejecting Quinton, she paid no attention to the changes he'd made to her living quarters. Sweating profusely, she drank a full glass of water and took two 500 milligram acetaminophen tablets for her pounding headache. The sledgehammer was pulsating with every heartbeat. Intuitively, after about ten minutes she got off the bed and lay supine on the floor with a pillow under her throbbing head. After another few minutes, she rolled onto her left side. Her instincts were correct.

Shortly, she began having left upper extremity rhythmic shaking, lasting about twenty seconds. She moaned out loud then stiffened, as if struck by lightning, and began having tonic-clonic, generalized seizure activity. Biting down on her tongue, she lost control of her gastrointestinal and genitourinary sphincters, and soiled herself with urine and feces. After about two minutes, now unconscious, the violent trembling stopped, her body lying still with loud, sonorous breathing.

This was the plight of the now-post-ictal seizure patient lying on her side as she involuntarily vomited, repeatedly.

Pouring a 1999 Silver Oak into plastic glasses seemed like sacrilege, but plastic was all I could find in Pritcherman's office. "Dinner" this late would have to be delivery Chinese. The vintage Cabernet seemed over-the-top, but it was one of the few bottles I'd been able to retrieve when I had been forced to leave Zachary's so suddenly.

In the two hours I'd been left alone, I'd done some exploring, while setting up for our dinner around a side table about three feet square to the left of his desk. I couldn't find the access to them, but there were clearly several chambers hidden behind the oak-paneled walls. This office was well-appointed, not ordinary in any way for a well-known professor of neurosurgery. I also found some files, but nothing on Zachary. Maybe my partner really didn't know anything about what happened to her.

I heard the outer office door open and, momentarily, Pritcherman briskly walked into the inner sanctum.

"I'm sure you have some thoughts about who Smith is, don't you Mr. Quinton?" He placed a large briefcase on the desk, turning to make eye contact.

"Why don't you call me Q, like everyone else. *Please*," I answered sheepishly. I paused for a few seconds, gathering my thoughts. Pouring Pritcherman a plastic glass of my favorite Cabernet, I handed it in his direction, "You bet I have some ideas about Dr. Smith. She's—"

"She's no doctor," smelling the nose of the Cabernet, and then taking a sip of wine, swishing it around his mouth. "Not bad. Definitely a Napa, not French. And older, I'd say 2000 at the latest," Pritcherman declared. "What's with pouring good wine into plastic glasses?" He opened a hidden cabinet and brought out two Riedel Cabernet stems.

"Good guess. It's a 1999 Silver Oak," I announced proudly refreshing our pour, but into the new stemware this time. "You have Riedel's in your office?" I was surprised. Then it was back to the business at hand.

"Well uh, Smith, who or whatever she is, I think she's up to no good," I continued. "I ran a search on her—"

"Q, I could've run a search on her," Pritcherman interjected with mild annoyance, taking a larger swallow. "1999, huh?"

"You're doing it again . . . interrupting me. I don't think you can do this kind of a search," I responded with a growing sense of ease. "I have a few tricks you might not be aware of."

"Interesting. Who's the professor now, eh," Pritcherman smiled. "And just what do you mean? Spill it, guru. I knew the first time I met you that you were different."

"Oh, you don't know how different, sir, sorry . . . what do I call you? And while we're at it, you know you took me off your service. I still want to graduate medical school–that is my primary goal, you know. So what can you do about that?"

"As to the glasses. I keep a lot of stuff in the office. I pretty much live here. So, what's for dinner?" Pritcherman set down his glass. "Don't worry about being off the service. You're doing directed readings for me," laughing. "Hell, I don't know what you should call me. My ex-wife had a few choice names, but I'm not letting you use any of those!"

"What do your kids call you, or your colleagues?"

"Colleagues? Most of them call me *Asshole*, with a capital A," he said, looking away. Now his tone became more somber. "No kids. I could barely stay married for even a few months. Let's see. How about P?" Then he slowly started giggling, like a school kid. "Q and P. P and Q. Ps and Qs. Get it? Do you know where that old maxim 'Mind your Ps and Qs' comes from Mr. Q?"

"Just Q, sir, not Mr. Q, please, and no, I don't."

"What's English ale served in, you know, that Guinness Stout stuff? In what quantities is it served?"

"Pints and—"

"And quarts," he couldn't help himself interrupting again. "When the rowdies got out of hand, the bartenders would shake their fists and tell them to mind their Ps and Qs–their pints and quarts. That's where it comes from. We'd better mind ours, too, Q," reaching into his pocket.

I knew what he was going for and that was another Rubicon waiting to be crossed, "No! No onions, please," I protested. "You're not ruining a Silver Oak with onions!"

A puzzled look crossed his face; he stopped and then turned a dark shade of red. "Too much?"

"Way too much. Why the hell do you do that anyway?" Rubicon crossed.

"I don't know, my ex said the same thing. I think I started eating them to piss her off."

"I'm guessing it worked."

"Yeah," a bit dejected. "No kidding. Then it just became a habit, I guess. They're good for your heart, though, you know," Pritcherman was waxing philosophic now, lifting his wine glass. "Look. I know I'm not the easiest guy to be around. But in my business, half the patients who go into surgery with me come out a different person. Believe it or not, I hate that.

"I'm the one responsible for taking away their past–their memories. That's partly why I asked you about your memories, son. All in the name of making them better. But is it really?" He was now staring up at the ceiling. Quiet. Sipping.

I decided not to break the mood just yet and just sat there, too. After about five minutes, I recalled, "Counting holes in the ceiling isn't exactly too appealing—"

"What?" I had distracted Pritcherman. "Sorry, I almost started to sound human, huh, Quinton . . . I mean . . . Q." Mood broken.

"You are human, sir," I answered. "Just a bit rough around the edges. It's a neurosurgical stereotype–maybe for a reason," I opined. "We'll work on that. The way I see it, Smith–or whatever her name is–is hiding something and it relates to this case. And—"

"Who assigned her to me anyway?" Pritcherman was thinking out loud. "If she's not from Georgetown, where is she from, I mean, who sent her and why? I'll throw her off my service. Hell, I'll throw her out the—"

"No, you won't!" now I interrupted. "We want to leave her right where she is. Keep your enemies close, sir. Keep her close."

"Mr. Quinton. Q. You sir, are right. You're a sneaky young bastard, aren't you? So now what?"

He was asking me? "Well—"

"We have to go to the morgue—"

"Please, not me again," I protested.

"I want that brain slice," Pritcherman insisted.

"But how? And when?" I wanted to avoid that place like the plague.

"Leave that up to me. I want the damn brain," Pritcherman paused, then pushing back his chair, "I want dinner!" Pausing, "And I want that brain! Let's eat."

"There's a problem, chief," spoken quietly into his phone from inside Dr. Zachary's apartment. "She's unconscious."

"*Not on this phone!* Is Jeremy with you? Can she be moved?" came the unseen response.

"Negative."

"I'll be there in fifteen minutes. Out."

Stealthily, Smith walked down the dimly lit hallway leading to the morgue. It was deserted, as she had expected at 3 a.m. "I'm at the perimeter," she stated quietly to the hidden microphone-earpiece. "No issues."

After surveying the exterior for security, she pressed a code into her smart phone. With that, the four security cameras synchronously pointed to the ceiling and she keyed open the door leading into the outer office of the morgue. The room was pitch-black-dark as she closed the door behind her. Donning a pair of surgical gloves, Smith reached into a small bag under her lab coat and pulled on pair of night vision goggles. By no means standard hospital-issue equipment.

With the addition of the goggles, she easily located the inner door to the pathology autopsy suite. Passing quickly through the morgue and on to the heavy door leading to the refrigerator morgue area, she opened it, entering the cold, dark room and closed the door behind her. She surveyed the wall of drawers and walked directly to one. Pulling open the drawer, she searched through its contents, making a mental checklist as she looked. At the rear of the metal slab was a glass container holding a brain. She noted that the probe and microchip which she knew had been there previously were now gone, but the brain slice remained. She picked up the brain slice and deftly switched it with a similar appearing slice of brain and replaced the container back into the drawer, closing it in one motion. She removed the brain from the jar, placed it into a large plastic Ziploc bag, and hid it under her lab coat. Quietly slipping back out the same way she had entered, she was once again in the outer hallway.

Before exiting the pathology suite, she removed and stored the goggles and gloves. Speaking into the air, she almost inaudibly said, "Mission complete," and swiftly walked down the hall.

There was a knock at the door. "Probably dinner," I said, standing up and heading toward the door.

"Let me look first," Pritcherman countered, moving to his desk. He pressed a button and a video-monitor appeared on the white-painted wall, the deliveryman clearly visible on the monitor outside the entrance to his office. "OK, you can get the food," waving me toward the inner office door. "But don't let him in. And don't let him see in here."

I thought it puzzling to not want a food delivery guy allowed into his office. Another mental note taken. I exited the inner office, closing the hidden door behind me and opened the outer door, paid for and took the delivery food, and then closed the door again. As I returned to the inner office door and Pritcherman buzzed me through.

"We're having Chinese," I advised. "I hope that's satisfactory?"

"Fine, Chinese is just fine," Pritcherman seemed distracted. "So, back to Smith," fidgeting at his desk. "She seems strange and detached to me."

"Well, so did Zachary when she came back," I answered.

"So what?"

"Well," I hesitated. "Both of them have a commonality, I think. At least they do now."

"Huh?"

"I never noticed it before on Zachary, so I think it's new."

"You knew Zachary well enough to notice a commonality with Smith?"

"Zach and I became close when I was convalescing from my head injury. I—"

"Quinton! What's new? The commonality?"

I raised my index finger to signal to Pritcherman he was interrupting again. "Both of them have a red, raised area behind their right ear."

"So?"

"Well," I continued. "What is it? I noticed it on Zachary when she showed up again. I touched her head there before and it wasn't there. And Smith. I saw it on the video I reviewed after she and Grigsby paid me a visit?"

"Smith? Grigsby? They visited? When?" Pritcherman stood up. "You didn't mention Smith visiting. And that pimply-face of a third-year Grigsby was with her? Spill it, Q."

"Where do you want to eat?" I asked. Pritcherman motioned me over to a small table. As I unloaded the delivery food, I took the time to compose my thoughts. "I have a theory," slowly turning to look Pritcherman directly in the eyes, as he had walked close behind me. We were less than two feet apart. "And I think it has to do with the probe."

Smith exited the hospital unobserved and entered the passenger side of a waiting PRT. As it pulled away from the curb, she retrieved her smart phone, no ordinary street-legal phone. She entered a special code and it became active, but highly encrypted. "Authentication Alpha, Foxtrot, Three, Nine, Delta, Ampersand, Two, Theta, Theta," and with that, the phone connected without her dialing.

After two rings, a voice on the other end answered, "Go for rabbit snare execution. Out."

Smith terminated the call and returned the phone to her lab coat pocket. Turning to look at the passenger silently sitting in the back seat, "Well, Dean. We're ready to go," she said without so much as a smile. "Shall I drop you off at home?"

"No," Jankowski responded. "To my office, please. And good work, tonight."

"So you think this probe is involved? Why?" Pritcherman asked, taking another bite of food with his chopsticks.

"Nice touch, the chopsticks. You do keep everything here," I mumbled through my shrimp in lobster sauce. "The probe. Why else would it be in the morgue with the dead guy's brain slice? Same thing with the microchip. They both have to be caught up in all this."

Pritcherman took a bite of snow peas and beef, "Always liked eating beef. In spite of the CJD, I still like it," chewing and swallowing. "Are you saying they came out of the guy?"

"I don't know, but if they didn't come out of the guy, what were they doing in his morgue drawer?" lifting my glass.

"You think the red marks are somehow connected to the probes?" Pritcherman was contemplating the ramifications of the connection, trying not to look too concerned. "And Grigsby," he said, taking another bite. "You said he was with Smith when she visited you. What was that all about?"

Setting down my wine glass, I studied Pritcherman closely as I told him, "She gave me a warning. Something about neurosurgery can be dangerous and—"

"Dangerous?" Pritcherman put down his chopsticks, defensive of his specialty. "What the hell does that mean?"

"She kept trying to push me into my building, it seemed like," I focused narrowly on his face. "She also noticed the paper from Grigsby's."

"What?" Now Pritcherman was staring back into my eyes. "What paper from Grigsby's? You didn't say anything about paper from Grigsby's."

"Oh, sorry," I detected a hint of apprehension in his face. "I paid Mr. Grigsby a visit. Actually, just his apartment. Look what I found there," tossing the small bag containing the 'brain' microchip and probe onto the table in front of Pritcherman. I also opened the piece of paper I'd taken and laid it on the table. "Here. I have no idea what it says, but it was part of a whole stack of papers, all in some kind of code."

Pritcherman looked at both, but didn't touch either at first. He just stared at them. Then he picked up the paper, scanned it, and dropped it back onto the table. Picking up the bag next, he examined it at arm's length. "This is getting complicated. Way too complicated."

— Never Try To Juggle When There Are Too Many Balls In The Air —

XI

*W*ay too complicated, indeed.

As I sat watching Pritcherman stare at the encrypted piece of paper and the bag which contained the microchip, that nauseous feeling I'd had before when I doubted Pritcherman's motives welled-up from my abdomen to my chest. Hoping more wine would dull that sensation, I downed a large swallow, emptying the glass and ending the bottle as well. That was number two. The vino was loosening tongues and lips . . . and probably a few other inhibitions, including my questions about P's inconsistencies.

I was still bothered by why Grigsby wasn't occupied on rounds and what was with Smith when she confronted me. What was that all about? And why did P show up the other day at my apartment about thirty minutes *before* our scheduled meeting? With the loss of inhibitions, did I feel comfortable enough to ask Pritcherman about it?

The ethics of all this was also weighing heavily on me. *What is a medical student and a neurosurgery professor doing investigating what I'm certain is a murder? Not to mention a kidnapping, a disappearance or two, and who knows what else? Even more basic than all that . . . why is my medical school involved with a government agency or the military?*

More and more, that's what this was feeling like to me. This has to be some type of covert government stuff. Aren't there rules against this sort of thing? Yeah, right, *rules.* I'm not surprised at all that my government is dirty. The line between private and public has been blurred for many years, and is being blurred further still. The degree of blur has seemingly increased exponentially. The more we relinquish our privacy in the name of progress, the more the government dishes out phony excuses and abuses the power even more.

What started as government agencies paying for drugs and medical device trials has evolved into virtually no more privately funded studies. No big deal, eh? That is, unless you understand that government involvement means biased reports and results. This has resulted in protocols and drug treatments for diseases that are based on flawed data as the result of the inherent research bias. When combined with the governmental takeover of healthcare payments, all the promises of improvement are doomed. In what should be the age of individualized treatment and care, the citizens of this great country will increasingly be subjected to standardized, "best practices" modicums of care created and pushed by a government that has a vested interest in reducing–or eliminating–the associated costs.

It's cheaper to ignore problems and to push them off into the future. Government is very good at putting off hard decisions–kicking the proverbial can down the road ten years at a time. It isn't surprising that the result of this bureaucratic *closing of the eyes* will impact a generation that can reasonably expect to be the first to have shorter life expectancies than that of its parents. That's why I initially became interested in medicine–to reverse that trend and discover better ways to provide care through better science. *Am I being naive?*

Of course, this premise depends on the belief that our scientific interventions do make a difference. I believe they can and do, when implemented by caring practitioners who are not bribed with incentives by the government to do the wrong thing. Everyone has their price–and some don't even know it.

"Quinton!" Pritcherman snapped me back to reality. "Solving all the problems of the world in that head of yours? We've got a few here that could use your attention, if you don't mind," He said this while opening a third bottle of wine. "That is, if I'm not bothering you?"

Oh, he *was* bothering me and that's part of the trouble. I stared at him, then turned my attention to the table where the microchip bag and coded paper were lying together. What have I done? My doubts about Pritcherman were rising again. One way or the other, I've got to decide to go all-in with him, or pull back big time. I've given both microchips to Pritcherman. So, if I don't trust him, I'd better get the second one back–and maybe the first, too.

"Uh, no, sorry," I fumbled, the result of my internal conflict and too much wine. Was he over serving me on purpose? "No more wine for me tonight, thanks. I'm good," while I watched him pour more anyway.

"Well, I'm having another glass. This is fine juice," Pritcherman whispered conspiratorially.

He was studying me while I was sneaking looks at the table's contents. Maybe there's a middle ground. Trust . . . but verify. I'll get back the microchip, leave the paper and see what he does next. As we locked eyes, I picked up the glass, "OK, maybe a little more. By the way, can I make up a bed in here?"

"Why?" my inchoate partner asked, standing and walking to the far wall. I hadn't noticed previously, but it was relatively uncluttered. He pressed a hidden button and a double-bed unfolded from the wall. "Remember, I said I spent a lot of time here. Now, about Grigsby."

While P lowered the bed, I slipped the microchip into my pocket. This was going to be a hard, late night.

In the bowels of a nondescript office building in San Antonio, Texas, deep within a sub-basement, surrounded by walls lined with supercomputers, rows of analysts sat at their desks with heads down, working without any audible conversation. In open view at the rear of the large room was a glass-enclosed office of approximately 20'x20'. Inside that office sat a well-dressed gentleman of about fifty, working diligently . . . until he was interrupted by the ring of his smart phone. Waiting intentionally for the third ring, he set down his pen, adjusted his college-crest tie and answered without speaking.

"*Jackpot*, here. There's a problem. Another agent with seizures after modification."

"I know who you are," the executive responded. "No need for introductions." A curt, formal, and no-nonsense person. "That is your first complication?"

"Yes, but I understand there are several others in Europe. What's the commonality?"

"You tell me," querried the executive. "You're the professor. Who authorized another agent modification?"

"We had an emergency come up, a rogue need," the caller replied. "I need to examine the others."

"A rogue need? I'll have to notify—"

"I realize that. Records. I need the records," the caller persisted.

"I may be able to get medical records, but there can be no personal examinations. Too much travel exposure."

"Exactly how many others are there?"

"Seven," the manager answered.

"Out of how many total?"

"Forty-two."

"That's a high enough percentage to stop the procedures," the caller warned.

"I'll determine when and if we stop the procedures. And no more rogue operations. Is that clear?"

"Completely. Send me the records. This is getting complicated."

With that, the executive terminated the call.

At 4 a.m. this morning, in an otherwise average-but-upscale suburban Washington, D.C. home, the Director's sleep was rudely interrupted by the phone next to his bed, just another of the innumerable after-hours calls he'd taken in his long career. The phone, however, was not an ordinary one, but a special, all-black instrument with no keypad and only a small light that illuminated on ringing–the only calls on this phone came from a single location. "Good morning," he answered, professionally, as if it were the middle of his workday.

"Sir, we have a breakthrough on *Operation Chestnut*. And a code name on one of the players. It's *Jackpot*, sir."

"Well done. Thank you." The director smiled as he replaced the handset. He laid back down and within thirty seconds his REM sleep was restored.

"Jeremy, start an IV, and draw a couple of clot-tubes for later," the leader ordered, after assessing Zachary's condition as she lay on the floor of her apartment. "If she has any further seizure activity, give her 10 milligrams of *diazepam* IVP."

Jeremy easily inserted an 18-gauge intravenous catheter into her right basilica vein. Taping it to her arm in routine fashion, he turned to the leader, "We brought in a gurney to transport her. Shall we load her?" Zachary was still post-ictal from the seizure, but becoming more aroused.

"Yes, get her ready while I make a call," the leader advised as he turned away from the two assistants. Pressing a speed-dial number, he quickly connected. Into the handset he spoke, "As I suspected. She had a grand mal seizure. We're readying her for transport back to the lab. Will you be joining us?" After a few seconds, he disconnected and placed the phone in his pocket.

"We're ready," Jeremy advised the leader.

"Go ahead and load her. I'll meet you there," swiftly walking out of Zachary's apartment. Pausing at the door, "And be sure to clean up this mess, gentlemen."

The sun was rising as Grigsby opened his eyes after a few hours of sleep. Looking at his alarm watch, he turned off the silent alarm, taking note of the time–0625. Too early yet to call, he thought. In seconds, however, he was out of bed, throwing the covers over the surface and heading for the bathroom. In another moment, he was in the shower, washing off the long night. He shaved in the shower–very efficient and time-saving. Deodorant and a dab or two of acne medication and he was done in the bathroom. He dressed rapidly and took a *Power Bar* from the refrigerator. He was basically wasting time until 7 a.m.

At precisely 7 a.m. he dialed a coded number and, without thinking, rose to his feet in spite of his fatigue. "Are the bananas ripe today?" he asked when the call was answered.

"We're not expecting any today. Only strawberries."

"Thank you," Grigsby responded politely, hanging up immediately.

In one of the secure areas of CIA headquarters in Langley, Virginia, in an office adjacent to the Director's, another phone call disconnected. As he set the phone down on the desk, this anonymous spook smiled. Standing up and brushing off a few donut sprinkles from his blue blazer, the analyst stepped to the doorway that connected his office with that of the Director. Still smiling, he knocked and cracked open the door just enough to look inside.

"We just intercepted a call from the fruit vendor. *Only strawberries* are expected today. And so it starts."

I awakened to noise in Pritcherman's outer office. Looking around, I realized I was in the pull-down bed, still fully clothed–a hard night, indeed.

Surveying the room, it was cleaned up as if no dinner party occurred last night. I know I didn't do it. So Pritcherman not only drank me under the table, but he cleaned up his office as well. I don't remember much after the third bottle was opened. But I did remember taking the microchip. The noise was getting louder. The inner office door opened and Pritcherman threw on the lights. Squinting at him with a scowl on my face, I cocked my head as he began talking.

"Not an early-bird, I see, eh Q?" Pritcherman was walking around, ensuring that nothing was out of place. He was fastidious about his office. "I suppose you'll want to shower now?" Walking over to the bathroom, he located another hidden button, pressed it, and a larger bathroom complete with a shower, sink, and toilet were revealed. "You've got fifteen minutes. We have lots to do today."

Did this guy ever sleep? I wondered. Dragging myself out of bed, he folded it into the wall moments after my feet hit the ground. I mumbled to acknowledge his presence, while he continued tidying up the minor mess I'd created as I slept.

"Fifteen minutes, Mr. Quinton. Fifteen minutes, sharp!" There would be no long, hot shower followed by a *Dr. Pepper* this morning. Maybe some acetaminophen, though, for my head? In a short fifteen minutes I was ready to go. Entering the main room again, I addressed Pritcherman, "So, what's on our agenda today?"

"You don't remember, eh?" he queried, smiling. Pritcherman was clearly proud of himself for besting me in the wine games of the previous night. "We're going to the morgue."

I couldn't help groaning. "Anything else?"

"Yeah," Pritcherman said, "your DoD search on Smith . . . and we talked about you checking on Zachary to see if you can get any more information from her.

Now it was coming back to me, "Right."

"Tonight, however," the neurosurgeon continued. "*I'm* doing the cooking."

"Get her back on the monitors," the leader instructed his two charges. They carried Zachary through the outer lab and into the operating room which now doubled as the intensive care unit. Jeremy and his accomplice gently positioned her on the table and connected her to the monitors. Zachary remained in a stupor, only vaguely aware of her surroundings, and unable to resist or respond.

"Her vital signs are stable, except for mild tachycardia of 110," Jeremy called out to the leader. "Pulse oximetry is 99%. What do you want me to do with the clot tubes we drew?"

"Run a comprehensive metabolic panel, a cortisol level, and save some for—"

In the midst of giving orders, he was abruptly interrupted by a knock on the outer door. Walking to the door, the leader looked out a small viewing port-hole and opened the door. "Dean Jankowski, good of you to join us."

I felt responsible for Zachary, as well as anxious, passionate . . . and lonely. I had to get Pritcherman to focus on finding out what happened to her and who did it. *After all, I'm the one who got her into this.* I exited the

PRT in front of her building. Making my way to the door of her apartment, I used my smart phone to scan the doorbell, tapping a few commands to download the entry logs and video records collected by the security devices I'd previously installed. They might be useful for review later. Opening the door, it was immediately obvious she wasn't there . . . but *someone* had been. The place was a mess, although it looked as if a minimal attempt at straightening up had been undertaken. Things on the floor were still askew.

"Zach," I called out as I walked around the place, trying not to disturb things more than they already were. "*Dr. Zachary!*"

Looking in the bathroom, I was repulsed by the smell of vomit still lingering there. Whoever had deposited that before flushing had done so recently–likely within the last few hours. In the short time I'd lived here, the place was small enough to be able to discover the few nooks and crannies it held. I hadn't been gone long enough for much to change, but change it had. Things that should have been in place, weren't . . . and things that shouldn't have been, were. Zachary had not done this.

I had that bad feeling again. I took out my phone and took a few still pictures to show Pritcherman. Now he had no choice but to listen to me about Zach. As I surveyed the room one last time, I noticed something which should not have been there at all–the cover to an IV needle. *What the hell happened here?*

"This is Dr. Pritcherman. I need to see the Dean later this morning," pacing about his office, while speaking into his phone. The unseen secretary on the other end of the call answered the professor cordially.

"The Dean can see you immediately, Dr. Pritcherman. He was planning to call you later today."

"I'm on my way," the neurosurgeon answered, pulling on his lab coat as he spoke. "I'll be there in ten minutes."

Before leaving his office, he stood in front of his desk and opened one of the drawers and located a button. Pressing it brought a menu to the desktop where he quickly scanned the items and made his selection– *Record Interior.*

Smith sat calmly in the outer office on the fifth floor of the administration building, flicking through one of the many three-month-old magazines on the table. They were a strange mix of pabulum, considering they resided in a prestigious medical school Dean's office. *Modern Teenager, Film Star's Lives*–give me a break, she thought. Whatever happened to world affairs, or history or medical journals? As she casually flipped her blonde hair back, the door opened.

"Dr. Smith," Pritcherman was surprised, but tried to not show it. "Good to scc you again. When you're done here, maybe we should talk about the service?"

"Of course, Dr. Pritcherman," Smith answered coolly, but was just as surprised to see her neurosurgical superior. "I'm at your disposal."

"Really?"

I opened the outer office to Dr. Pritcherman's office with the key he'd given me. It was no ordinary institutional key, but a magnetic stripe card similar to hotel entry keys that can be programmed and re-set over and over, depending on the administrator's preferences. This one, however, was also a biometric key that scanned my irises, uniquely programmed to recognize me. I'd noticed it before, but had not paid any attention to it. Now I wondered, why a biometric entry? And when did Pritcherman program it? Another mental note taken.

I'd promised P a review of Smith's DoD search–guess I'd told him something about my DoD search capabilities. Finding some empty space on a table, I started to set up my computer, then paused. If he monitors his visitors using biometrics, surely he monitors his office somehow. I turned off the tablet and tucked it away, then moved around as if I were looking for something, but really just appearing to be busy for the monitors– if there were any. I guess this meant I'd made a decision not to tell Pritcherman everything. Picking up my backpack with the tablet, I exited the office and went down to the street.

Now where do I go? I was running out of places. As secretive as I am, I was now off to the most public place I could think of–a coffee shop with Internet access–to complete my homework. Walking a few blocks away, I entered a popular *Starbuck's*, found an open table, and fired up my tablet. Although I'd be using a public access point, I was connecting to my secure area in the cloud.

I picked a spot in a corner to limit any wandering eyes and, looking around the room, saw just a few disinterested students and house staff, all of whom seemed tired and beaten down. The safety of numbers and the safety of indifference. But no verbal computer commands–an old habit I'd have to forgo for privacy's sake. Typing a few keystrokes, the computer retrieved the detailed DoD search of Smith I'd ordered and displayed it on screen.

Bingo! The FBI block had been penetrated and Smith unmasked. Actually, Smith was not a Smith at all. She was Anna Jean Dupuy, born 36 years ago in small-town Nebraska. *Yadda-yadda-yadda* history until she got to college at Brown University in Rhode Island, from which she graduated with honors, completing both bachelor's and master's degrees in . . . criminology. *Criminology?* Huh?

Next, Brown Law School, not medical school–no real surprise there. Then a blank screen, nothing. Another disappearance, just like the Dean's, except this one was a gap to the present day. To me, that only meant one thing. Government undercover. But which branch of government? For that matter, which government?

On to Grigsby. Success again. Grigsby actually *was* Grigsby. More *yadda-yadda-yadda*, unspectacular high school stuff. Then, U.S. Military Academy at West Point. *Really? Grigsby?* Well, I'll be damned. After graduation, commissioned as a second lieutenant and assigned to military intelligence with multiple overseas postings, rapidly rising to the rank of major when he, too, disappears from view. Same conclusion . . . government undercover–good for you, pimple-face. Again, which branch and which government?

My dilemma was what do I tell Pritcherman? Enough to make Zach's situation our first priority now. With Grigsby and Smith unmasked, I knew they had more information than they were giving up. But would Pritcherman agree? At dinner tonight, we would have plenty to talk about, only this time I was determined to remember it all.

"Dr. Smith, Dr. Pritcherman, the Dean will see you now," his secretary smiled and opened the Dean's inner office door.

Smith walked directly into the office and sat down in one of the several plush chairs in front of the Dean's desk. Pritcherman paused, and after about fifteen seconds, followed Smith into the office. The Dean's secretary smiled again and closed the door behind the professor. He stood at the door momentarily, surveying the room, noting the Dean was writing, head down at his desk, as if not paying any attention to Smith. Pritcherman wasn't moving until the Dean acknowledged him. Reaching into his lab coat, he retrieved an onion and took a bite, causing the Dean to look up.

"Must you, Stanley?" then looking back down for about five seconds. Putting down his pen, he stared at Smith without a word and finally gestured the neurosurgeon to another of the chairs in front of his desk. "Well, it seems we have a problem, don't we?"

"We?" Smith queried.

"*We*, yes," the Dean answered, looking past Smith. Leaning back in his chair, he locked his gaze onto Pritcherman. "Stanley, I have something to tell you about your dead patient."

"I knew you were—"

"Quiet, Stanley," the Dean held up his hand. "Your patient's seizure may have been iatrogenic."

"What?" Pritcherman was suddenly quiet.

"Unfortunately," the Dean proceeded. "He underwent a procedure at another institution and—"

"What kind of a procedure?" Pritcherman was immediately suspicious.

"Please don't interrupt me again, Stanley," the Dean said sternly. "That's a bad habit you simply must correct. As I was saying, before I was so rudely interrupted," slowing his speech intentionally to frustrate the neurosurgeon. "Another facility placed an implant that apparently caused seizure activity. I referred the patient to you so it could be removed in hopes that the seizure activity would cease."

"Why the hell was it placed there in the first place? I mean, for what reason? And why the hell didn't you tell me this before he arrived?"

"Stanley, you simply must calm down," the Dean was firm. "He died before I could fully brief you."

Smith was sitting without a sound, but couldn't help smiling a bit.

Turning now to her, the Dean asked pointedly, "Did you want to say something, Dr. Smith?"

Shaking her head, Smith remained silent.

"Dr. Smith here has been sent to look into that death I'm guessing . . . right, Dr. Smith?" Still not taking his eyes off of Pritcherman, the Dean waited for her answer.

"I'm here to learn something about neurosurgery, but so far, all I've learned is this is a soap opera-of-a-hospital," Smith impassively responded.

"Here from where?" Pritcherman smirked.

"Georgetown General Surgery—"

"No way, Doctor," the neurosurgeon caustically interrupted. "There's no record of you at Georgetown and the Dean here doesn't know anything about that either." He was standing now and, taking another bite, moved closer to her.

"Sit down, Stanley," the Dean commanded. "There's enough drama without you adding to it with your little antics."

"Antics? I'll show you antics," moving his focus from Smith to the Dean, spewing saliva as he turned. "You want to tell me why you sent Smith here to my service, Dean?"

"I did not send her to you, Stanley," the Dean calmly replied. "Dr. Smith, who *did* send you? No need to continue with the charade of being from Georgetown."

"Gentlemen," Smith said coolly. "If you don't believe me, I suggest you call my residency supervisor, Dr. Jones. I can provide you with his number if you like?"

"Jones?" Pritcherman was spitting as he talked. "Another BS name. Smith, Jones. Give me a break. I've never heard of any Dr. Jones and I know a lot of people from Georgetown."

"As do I, Doctor," the Dean echoed. "And no Dr. Jones comes to mind."

Smith, without missing a beat answered, "Then one of you had best call this number," writing a number on a small piece of paper and holding it up in the air.

Pritcherman snatched it from her grasp, read it and passed it over to the Dean. The Dean took the paper and dialed the number. Someone obviously answered, but the Dean's next words were, "If you'd kindly show yourself out, Stanley."

"Quinton!" Pritcherman screamed as he came bounding through his outer office door. "Quinton, where the hell are you?" yelling even louder.

I stuck my head out of the inner office as he marched through.

"We have an appointment with the morgue, do we not?" He was agitated more than his normal, histrionic self.

"Yes, but sit down for a minute. Unwind and tell me what's got you all amped up?"

"Amped up? I'll tell you what's got me all amped up," Pritcherman paced furiously. "It's Smith, that's what."

"Really?" Do I tell him what I know, I wondered. "Why?"

"She's no doctor," now slowing his pace. "The Dean called me to a meeting with her where we both confronted her about her Georgetown bullshit. She handed the Dean a number to call and that jerk-off Jankowski threw me out of his office before he called. So I still don't know who she is, but she's no doctor."

"Did you ask the Dean about Zachary?"

"I didn't get to her. He threw me out."

"Zach has to be found. You have to help me find her. Somehow Smith knows what really happened to Zachary. And Smith? Well, she's no *Smith*," I answered, deciding to tell him what I knew. "She's Dupuy, not Smith. Anna Jean Dupuy—"

"How the hell did you find that out?"

"I have my ways, remember? And Grigsby—"

"Him, too?"

"No, he's Grigsby, but military, or ex-military or something," I stumbled.

"Geez, this is complicated," P answered, a little calmer. "I can barely keep up. I'm guessing you know more than their names?"

"Yep. It's not gonna make things any easier either."

"Great."

"Smith is a criminologist," I declared. "At least she has a bachelor's and master's degree in it. And a law degree. And a job gap. All this screams government operative to me."

"I'll be damned—"

"She's some kind of an agent and I'll bet it has to do with—"

"With all of this," P interrupted, but this time, it was OK. "The Dean thought so, too."

"I was going to say Zach, but yes. And I'll bet Grigsby's also involved," I added. "US Military Academy–a West Point-type. What'd 'ya think he's doing here? He can't really be a med student."

"That one I know," P reacted. "He's been enrolled here for two years now. I checked."

"Yeah," I grimaced. "I've put up with that oleaginous prick the whole time.

"Greasy, he may be, but he's not so slippery he can get past me," P was ready to take his frustrations out on someone and Grigsby's convenience suited him well. "I'll get him—"

"No," I paused. "It hurts me to say this. We must leave him alone. He may lead us to something . . . or someone."

"Grigsby?" Smith talked into her phone as she walked quickly. "The Dean knows we're up to something. Meet me someplace public."

"How about that bar across from thc hospital?"

"Can you be there in five minutes?"

"Affirmative," Grigsby whispered, and disconnected.

Smith sat quietly at a back table. It was mid-afternoon, so there wasn't much of a crowd yet. Morning classes were long over and afternoon ones not yet out. House officers were still deep into their hospital duties. So Smith had her choice of tables. She didn't have to wait long. Grigsby slid into the booth opposite her.

"Pritcherman and the Dean know I'm not from Georgetown," she started. "I was forced to refer him to *Big Boy*."

"Pritcherman?" Grigsby exclaimed.

"No," Smith answered. "The Dean. I wouldn't tell that SOB Pritcherman anything. I'd die first."

"Let's hope no one does anymore dying. There's been enough of that already," Grigsby replied. "I'm sure *BB* wasn't happy about that."

"Oh, like hell, he wasn't," Smith acknowledged. "But I had no choice. I couldn't hear what he said to the Dean, but at least he got Pritcherman out of there first," smiling with a sense of busting the neurosurgeon. "The Dean actually asked him to leave before he talked to *BB*."

"At least he left," Grigsby concluded.

"Oh, he left," Smith countered. "But Pritcherman's smart enough to know something's up and that's not good for us."

"Q!" Pritcherman shouted from the bathroom.

I could hear the splashing as he urinated. "What did you drink?"

"Diuresis is good for the kidneys," he answered.

"Yeah, yeah," I'd heard enough. "Listen, I've been thinking—"

"Are you ready for the morgue?"

"Why do I have to go," I protested.

"'Cuz I say so," P laughed. "Seriously, I may need someone to distract them. And as a witness."

"Great," I murmured under my breath. "Like I need more publicity."

Bounding out of the bathroom, Pritcherman reeked of onion with a whiff of urine.

"Couldn't you brush your teeth, maybe," I pleaded.

"Oh no," P answered. "It's part of the plan."

"Even the urine? Wait," I wanted to talk to him before the morgue–anything to try and get out of going.

"OK, the urine's a bit much," P agreed, brushing off his pants, turning to the sink to wash his hands.

"Why didn't you keep Grigsby on rounds like I asked you, so I could snoop around without being detected?"

"Quinton," Pritcherman was becoming arrogant again. "I can't occupy someone's time if they aren't there. He never showed up for rounds. Neither did Smith."

"That explains why I just barely missed them both when I left Grigsby's," I surmised. "But aren't they supposed to be there? I mean—"

"Hell, yes, they're supposed to be there!" P yelled. "Lots of strange things are happening. No one listens to me, or even comes to rounds. The Dean tells me the dead guy's from another facility. The—"

"What about Zach?" I interrupted.

"I simply don't know, Q."

"What about the dead guy?" I continued.

"The Dean says he had some kind of a procedure at Elsewhere General and he sent him to me to take care of it. You know, take it out, whatever they put in, or something like that."

I was animated, "Don't you see? Somehow that procedure is connected to the morgue–the autopsy–they wanted the hardware back."

"Who's *they*?"

"Who knows?" I answered. "But *they* are who we're after."

"*They*," P injected, "But first the brain."

"And maybe the probe is what they wanted," I speculated. "We've got the probe. They've already got Zach. They must've taken her back. Maybe that's why they're coming after me now."

"I don't know. All the more reason we're off to the morgue," P was walking towards the door. "Let's go, Q. We've got some dead folks to visit."

"Before we go," I stopped him. "Why did you come to my place the other day thirty minutes *before* our scheduled appointment in your office? I mean, how did you know I wasn't going to make the appointment?"

"Can we talk about that later?" He was walking faster. As we stepped into the elevator in the faculty office building, Pritcherman punched the button for the basement.

"Basement?"

"Yeah," P casually responded. "To take the walkway over to the hospital."

"What walkway?"

"Quinton," P was incredulous. "You know there's a walkway from the offices to the hospital, right?"

"No."

"Well," P was back in professor mode. "It saves a lot of time getting from one building to the other. Especially if it's raining."

"Yes, I can understand that," I answered. "And it's also another exit route for someone wanting to hide from the street, or take a shortcut, maybe?"

"Sure," P agreed. "I do it all the time." We were now walking swiftly through the corridor I knew nothing about.

"Is it only in the basement?"

"Correct. Why?"

"Because whoever deposited me in the stairwell probably exited through the basement and out the office building to avoid the hospital security cameras."

"Maybe," P countered. "But the corridor and the office building has security."

"Yes, but different security personnel. A different bureaucracy. Maybe they didn't connect the two incidents."

"Or maybe they didn't care to," P shrugged, as we arrived at the morgue office doors, definitely a faster trek than my previous trip through the hospital. Messing up his hair and rumbling his clothes, Pritcherman looked quite disheveled and even scarier. "Follow my lead," he advised, opening the door.

So he acts crazier than he really is, I thought. *Crazy like a fox.*

"Who's in charge here now that Zendejas decided to die," Pritcherman screamed, bounding through the door. All eyes immediately focused on him.

"May I help you, sir," a shy secretary volunteered. "Somebody'd better," P roared, striding from desk to desk. "I need to look at one of my dead patients. Who's taking Zendejas' place? I want to talk to the head honcho and I want him now."

While he was busy intimidating the pathology staff, I was looking around. Everything seemed as I remembered it. The poor secretary was now scurrying around trying to find anyone onto whom she could dump Pritcherman. "Sir, could Dr. Orlando help you?"

"Who's he?"

"It's a she, sir," the secretary corrected. "Our interim chief of pathology. May I tell her who's asking to see her?"

"You sure as hell can," P retorted. "You tell her Stanley J. Pritcherman from neurosurgery is here. *And hurry up! I don't have all day!*" He reached for another onion.

Now that I knew what he was doing–for once, I was not on the receiving end of his act–watching Pritcherman was like watching a puppeteer pulling everyone's strings. He was surgically carving up these pitiable folks who probably chose to work in pathology to avoid living people, especially people like Pritcherman. Momentarily, another office door opened and a short, squatty woman about forty-five hesitantly came over to Pritcherman.

"Are you Dr. Pritcherman," extending her hand, ready to shake.

"I am," P intentionally not returning her gesture, but taking another bite of onion and moving closer to her. "I need to see my patient," turning to me, "what morgue drawer, Mr. Quinton, hurry up."

"You can't—"

"Yes I can, Doctor," P interrupted famously. "Oh yes I can. Quinton!" screaming. "What drawer?"

I hunkered down for effect. I could play his game, too. "I think it's 51, Dr. Pritcherman."

"You *think*, Quinton," Pritcherman was on a roll. "You're a medical student, son. We don't pay you to *think*," turning back to Dr. Orlando, "Do I need to call the Dean?" He reached for his phone.

"No, no," Dr. Orlando quickly advised P. "Come with me," as she walked to the cold storage area, and pulled open the heavy metal door. "You'll need to sign some forms—"

"All in good time. You may leave us, madam," P pontificated. "Out! Out!" shooing her along her way. She stood there speechless as he closed the door, leaving the two of us alone in the cold room with the walls of drawers.

A shiver went up my back as I remembered back to my last time here. "Here's the drawer," I pointed.

"The one you spent the night in," P teased. "Wanna climb back in for old time's sake?"

"Not funny," I was not amused in the least. Opening the drawer. I searched around and at the back found the glass jar and the bag, still containing the brain slice. I proudly announced, "Well, P. Here's your brain slice."

"I thought you said the brain was here," Pritcherman asked. Suddenly I noticed its absence, too. "It was, I swear, P . . ."

"Oh, this time I believe you, Q. And they think I'm dramatic."

"P," I continued. "Can you tell anything from just the slice?"

Pritcherman picked it up in the slice and looked at it closely. "Parietal," he muttered to himself."Gotta be parietal," continuing to examine it. After about two minutes, he turned and looked squarely at me, "Q," he paused. "What side of the head did you say you saw that red mark on Smith and Zachary?"

"Right side," I replied. "Why?"

"Because this slice is *left* parietal."

— Always Know Which Side You're On Before Choosing Your Teammates —

XII

Deep in another basement, this one at the center of operations at the Central Intelligence Agency headquarters in Langley, Virginia, in one of the many nameless small conference rooms, six men sat waiting, each fidgeting in his own way–looking at their watches, pretending to make notes, tying and re-tying their shoelaces, or just doodling. All were curious about why they had been summoned by the Assistant Director.

At precisely the designated meeting time, a man of about forty-five walked briskly through the conference room door, studied the occupants, and proceeded to the head of the table.

"You've still got a few crumbs on your coat, Bill," one of the original six commented.

"Damn donuts," Bill Calhoun glumly responded, brushing his front to the laughter of the room. "They're gonna kill me."

Calhoun had battled a lot more than just his weight during his CIA career. From Gulf Wars I and II, to Afghanistan, to China and Russia, *Wild Bill* had been there. Now *Cautious Bill* was out of the field and the number two guy at the agency. But he never surrendered the experiences and fantasies of the field.

"You should be so lucky," another commented. "If I don't get coffee soon I may join you in hell."

"There's coffee," Bill advised.

"Yeah," the second commentator returned volley. "My wife has me on another one of those diets and no coffee's part of it. Women and their diets."

"Now, now," Bill answered, taking his seat at the head of the table. "What would we do without them? Don't answer, you're spooks!" Again, polite laughter.

"OK, I know you wanna know why you're here," Bill continued.

The room became quiet. The six meeting participants gave him their full attention.

"Gentlemen, I believe the NSA is violating USSID 18," Bill began.[1] There were no more smiles in the room. The six were contemplating the meaning. This was a serious allegation with national security and legal implications. "What I don't know is whether it's from the top or just a rogue element."

"Bill, that's key," one of the anonymous attendees spoke.

"If this is from the top, we need to notify the President. That means—"

---

[1] NSA–USSID 18 (United States Signals Intelligence Directive 18) . . . strictly forbids the interception or collection of information about . . ."US persons, entities, corporations or organizations. . ." without explicit written legal permission from the US Attorney General when the subject is located abroad, or the Foreign Intelligence Surveillance Court when within US borders. NSA has declared that it relies on the FBI to collect information on foreign intelligence activities within the USA. NSA's domestic surveillance activities are limited by the 4th Amendment, but these do not apply to non-US persons located outside of US borders.

"I know," Bill noted. "Believe me, I know. Now. Ideas, thoughts?"

"Who knows about this, Bill?"

"Just this room. . . for now."

"Does the Director know?"

"No," Bill sighed. "Not yet. I haven't gone down that road, yet, and won't until I have something concrete. But the time's coming."

"So," another unidentified voice remarked, "it hasn't gone to the President, then, either?"

"Oh, hell no!" Bill raised his tone ever so slightly, and immediately lowered it. "Remember, I'm *Cautious Bill* now. I'd like to finish my career without precipitating an internecine war with the NSA."

Not a sound came from the deadly serious group.

In yet another shadowy conference room, this one at Fort Meade, Maryland, in the bowels of the National Security Agency[2] headquarters, Brigadier General James (Jim) Bitterman, *aka Big Boy* (or *BB*), was sitting alone, waiting for a call. When a phone on the table rang, he waited until the second ring to answer, an old habit–not wanting to appear too anxious. It was also a form of control.

"This is Dean Jankowski. You asked me to call. I always worry about calling you. Is this connection safe?"

"*Jackpot*," the general's tone was exceedingly condescending, "please use only your code name. I move between many locations and I can't be sure where I'll be when you call. I've moved since we last talked." Sighing in disgust, *BB* continued, "We go through this every time. The NSA has the most secure communications in the world. We are the US government's eyes and ears, as you well know. We encrypt the government's codes. I would think your time in Poland would've given you a better appreciation of our capabilities."

"Yes, you encrypt the codes and break them, too," the Dean retorted. "I'm just being cautious. How do I know someone else hasn't broken your code and is listening to me? One never knows anymore. And I'm involved now because of my time in Poland, thank you."

"We break the codes, not the rest of the government. You're being a bit paranoid, *Jackpot*–Dean Jankowski. I wanted you to call for a progress report and to advise you about the medical records we discussed from overseas." *Big Boy* set the agenda.

"I'm listening."

"As am I, doctor," *BB* shot back. "Is there any progress with your latest seizure patient?"

"Well," the Dean hesitated. "This patient is one of our third-year general surgical residents. So we are being very careful . . ."

---

[2] The National Security Agency, or NSA was established in 1952 by Order of President Harry S. Truman and tasked with two missions. Signals Intelligence (SIGINT) and Information Assurance. That is, it gathers information and protects the information and government systems. Practically speaking, this enables a third function, Network Warfare, a military operation.

"Yeah, yeah," the general cut short the Dean. "That's the problem with going outside of our protocol, sir. From now on, we decide here who gets the probe, not you. Now I have to clean up your mess."

"Hardly, sir," Dean reacted with indignation. "You may remember you sent the *now dead* patient to me . . . to clean up *your* mess. If we can get past the insults, clearly there is a problem with this procedure, since so many have had complications."

"Doctor, I need the intel."

"*I*, General? Don't you mean, *we?* So," Dean Jankowski hastened to add, "the ends justify the means?"

"Don't get preachy with me," *BB* instantly shot back. "We're all in this together."

"Yes, when it suits you," the Dean replied. "It's I for the glory and we for the tough going. Nothing focuses one's attention like a hanging, eh, General?"

"Listen, you prick—"

"So we're casting insults again?" The Dean mocked the spy.

BB lowered his voice, "None of this is solving the problem, *Jackpot*. I suggest we concentrate on that, a kind of mutual truce?"

"Agreed," Jankowski pronounced. "Am I getting the European medical records so maybe I can find a commonality?"

"It's not that easy," said *BB* matter-of-factly, and more calmly now. "It's just too risky. You still haven't told me about whether or not there's progress."

The Dean sighed, "She's unconscious most of the time. She continues to have generalized seizure activity not ameliorated by medication. I need more studies and probably a PET scan or an MRI to investigate it further."

"Don't you have that capability?"

"Not without arousing the entire medical center," the Dean reacted. "One of my neurosurgeons is getting suspicious. Nothing I can't handle, but he's becoming a nuisance."

"I can authorize our agents there to take care of your nuisance, if you'd like," *Big Boy* offered.

"Take him out, you mean? Kill him?"

Without hesitation, the general continued, "Dean, that's your choice."

"General, I'd say there has been enough of that already, wouldn't you think?"

Brigadier General James Bitterman stood, looked over at the American flag in his office before answering, "Sir, I am a patriot. My duty is to my country, to confront all enemies and nothing, repeat, nothing will get in the way of that. Not you, not my superiors, and certainly not some piss-ant neurosurgeon. Do you read me, *Jackpot?*"

"Another seizure," Jeremy announced, reaching for the syringe of *diazepam*, rapidly injecting 10 milligrams. Zachary's seizure activity was lasting longer, occurring more frequently, and taking more medication to ablate them each time. Jeremy was becoming apprehensive about the lack of progress. "Chief, how much longer can this go on?"

The leader was sitting at a desk in the corner writing medical progress notes. He looked at Jeremy and exhaled noisily in frustration. "I'm not a neurologist. Since it started when the probe was placed, I'm guessing it will have to come out. That decision's above my pay grade. Don't worry about it. Leave it to me. Something has to happen soon, or I'll push it."

Ten minutes passed after Zachary stopped having seizure activity, becoming post-ictal and now beginning to awaken again. Groggy, and with slurred speech, her eyes focused on her caregivers, "Is this normal? Why am I having seizures? I can't be a surgeon with seizures." She was docile in her comments, pleading.

"Doctor," Jeremy soothed. "We'll find an answer," looking to the leader. "We're making some progress," hoping she wouldn't detect his anxiety. The leader knew he had to intervene–somehow.

Dialing his phone, the leader spoke into the hand piece, "Dean, we have to find an answer. The seizures are more frequent and—"

From the other end, the Dean interrupted, "I know, I know. I've pleaded with *Big Boy* for the records of the others. He's supposed to give me a final answer later today."

"Viktor," the leader countered. "We're doctors. What are we involved in? This was sold to me, and I'm guessing to you, as a matter of national security. Now I'm not so sure."

"Patience. Just a little more patience," the Dean counseled. "I'm frustrated by this, too. But we have our orders. It is a matter of national security."

"Can I sit up?" Zachary begged from her bed.

"Let me help you up, doctor," Jeremy helping her to sit. "Take a sip of water," offering her a cup with a straw.

Zachary took several small sips, "I'm so dry. My head is pounding all the time. Jeremy," her eyes desperate as she found his gaze, "What's happening to me?"

Jeremy looked at the leader still on the phone and their eyes met before he looked back at Zachary. "We're working on something to fix it right now. I promise."

Smith sat in front of the Dean's desk, waiting for him to speak. The Dean looked at Smith without saying anything, trying to organize his thoughts.

Smith broke the silence. "You asked me to come back, Dean," she opened the conversation. "After you hung up with *BB*, did you have second thoughts?"

"No . . . well," the Dean hesitated. "Not exactly second thoughts," pausing once more. "I need your help."

"Of course, I'm part of the team."

"It seems there have been complications with one of our agents and a probe," the Dean spoke carefully. "You have had the operation. I've seen the small scar behind your ear."

"I'm not at liberty to say, sir," said Smith, cool as ever.

"I understand," although he didn't, the Dean accepted the setback for now. "And I assume not done here, I mean, not done in the United States."

"I'm not at liberty to say that either, sir."

Having difficulty containing his frustration, the Dean remarked, "I suppose I shouldn't waste my time asking why not?" Letting out a deep sigh of disappointment, he continued, "Are you at liberty to discuss complications?"

"Yes. If I can help," Smith remained indifferent.

"Have you ever had a seizure?"

"What?"

"A seizure," the Dean repeated." Tonic-clonic, focal motor. Any kind. You do know enough medicine, Doctor, to recognize a seizure?"

"Yes, Dean," Smith remained unruffled. "I know what a seizure is and, no, I've never had one. Why? Have others?"

"Well, yes," the Dean paused. "One that I know of."

"One? Out of how many?"

"I'm not at liberty to say," the Dean smiled. "Shall we stop that nonsense?"

"Touché," Smith countered.

"I don't know how many, but this is not the only patient having suffered seizures. There are several others in Europe. I'm waiting for medical records to review. There must be a commonality."

"Have they stopped doing the procedures?"

"I had hoped so," Jankowski looked gloomy. "But I fear not. They want the intelligence."

"It would appear at any cost."

"It would appear."

"There's nothing you can do to stop it?" Smith was minimally more dynamic, standing to leave. "Don't you have any say?"

"They only want my medical expertise. Not my ethics."

"Are you going to be here long, Dean?"

"Another hour or so," Jankowski responded. "Why?"

"No reason," Smith countered. "No reason at all." With that, she opened the door and left the Dean to his thoughts.

"So," Calhoun now sat in the large office next to his–the office of the Director.

"Concerning *Operation Chestnut*. I have convened an analysts meeting to discuss options."

"Good, Bill," the Director smiled. "We'll get to the bottom of all this. I know I don't need to tell you, but this is quite sensitive. Only your analyst group can know about it for now."

"Understood, sir," Calhoun nodded. "You haven't kicked this up yet, correct?"

"Correct."

"Not to the DNI?" Bill was specific.[3]

"No, and not to the President," the Director reiterated.

Slamming the door behind him, Pritcherman was quite agitated. He almost closed the door on me, as he walked at a near-running pace. Bounding through his inner office door, he threw the bag containing the brain slice on his desk. "Those bastards switched specimens. Why? What are they trying to hide? What?"

"Well, they—"

"Quiet, Q," P paced. "I'm thinking." He went into the gigantic brain model in his inner office, flipped a few switches and it lit up and I heard a low rumbling, buzzing sound. I didn't know whether to follow him or not.

"P," I hesitated. "Should I come in there?"

Pritcherman ignored me, completely lost in his explorations inside his model brain. He kept moving from the right side to the left side, pausing to look at a touch screen inside the model. I couldn't see what he was reading, but I heard him mumbling to himself. "Quinton! Come in here, now!" he screamed, not hearing any of my previous questions.

I wandered into the morass of lights, sounds, white and grey matter with small touch screens on various walls of the model brain. "Where are you?"

"In the RTPJ," Pritcherman called out loudly.

"Where?"

"The right temporo-parietal junction," stepping in front of me. "Do you know what the RTPJ does?" Not waiting for an answer, P continued. "It's part of our memory system that deals with moral judgment."

"Are you suggesting the probe interfered with the moral judgment of patients?"

"Not suggesting it," P countered. "I'd bet money on it. I think they're trying to interface with the patient's memory."

"Why?"

"I don't know," the neurosurgeon mumbled, already moving on. "So why change brain slices?"

"I don't—"

"I'm talking to myself," P said. "I need the amygdala," he declared emphatically. "It's got to be involved, too. And maybe . . ." his voice trailing off.

---

[3] The DNI, or Director of National Intelligence, oversees and coordinates all U.S. intelligence gathering agencies, both military and non-military.

I decided to stay quiet, even though I wanted to say something. Looking around, I began to figure out the touch screens. When you were in an area of the brain, touching on a nearby screen brought up details of function, anatomy, physiology, biochemistry and genetics pertaining to that area.

I couldn't stay quiet about this. "Who wrote all the text?"

"I did," the professor proclaimed. "For various textbooks and articles mostly." Moving around to the other side, he continued, "Quinton, I told you to study up on memory. Well, now I'm sure these yahoos are trying to manipulate memory somehow."

"So what's the send and receive function for? We've got the dead guy's probe," I reminded P "Should we try and turn it on?"

"Not yet," my partner cautioned. "Not until we know what they're up to. We don't want to turn it on and injure someone. Who knows who and what's on the other end. It'd also be nice to know who the hell we're dealing with."

"So, what's the plan?"

He was coming out of the brain and brushed past me. "Right now," he paused. "We think . . . and . . . we eat."

"Dr. Smith," Bill Calhoun greeted her on his smart phone. "I always enjoy talking to you. How are your studies coming along?"

"Not so well lately," Smith was at ease with her caller. "I'm having trouble understanding all this neurosurgery talk. My attending physician hasn't been very helpful."

"I'm sorry for that," Bill answered, with no emotion.

"Have you talked to his superior about that?"

"Oh yes," Smith affirmed. "He wasn't very sympathetic, so I had him call someone in Maryland to approve a tutor for me."

"Maryland, huh? And they helped?"

"Yes," Smith. "I believe so. I'm hungry now, so I think I'll go eat–maybe some fruit. I'm thinking strawberries."

"Good," her friendly phonemate laughed quietly. "Pick them yourself and with care. They should be fresh this time of year. I may go for some strawberries myself. I'll wait to hear how yours are. Let me know if you need anything else. Goodbye."

Smith disconnected and immediately dialed Grigsby.

"Grigsby, where are you? I'm hungry. Wanna go get some strawberries?"

"Tonight we dine Italian," Pritcherman announced. After leaving his brain, P moved to his desk. Pressing another of his unseen buttons, from the floor, an entire kitchen rose.

I gotta explore this place when he's gone, I thought to myself. What other hidden jewels might I find? "Now that's impressive," I exclaimed.

"Just a lowly professor's getaway kitchen," the neurosurgeon chuckled. "If we eat Italian, we drink Italian," opening a bottle with a corkscrew. "Do you know Barolos?"

"Not well," I confessed. "I know they're primarily from the Nebbiolo grape. . ."

"Very good."

"Complex . . . and they need at least ten years in the bottle," I continued. "Speaking of bottles," I segued, "The glass container. Why keep the brain slice in there?"

"No idea," P shrugged. "Probably just the pathology department's routine. Here's the thing though. Even though it's the left side, it came from a brain–it's real. So is it our guy's, or someone else's? I'm guessing our guy's. Otherwise there'd be another dead guy floating around."

"It is the pathology department," I suggested. "If anybody has an extra brain lying around, it'd be pathology."

"Yeah," P countered. "But I'm guessing it's his."

"We can prove that easily. Remember I have his DNA from the tooth and the probe," I advised. "We can compare the DNA."

"Make it so, Number One," Pritcherman was now in full swing on dinner, working fast to prepare fresh pasta sauce from scratch. "Motive and opportunity, Q, motive and opportunity."

"What?"

"Who has the motive *and* the opportunity for all this?" Pritcherman posed the question. "When we know that, we'll know what this is all about."

"It has to be government," I hypothesized. "There are too many people involved now and too much high tech and stealth."

"I'll agree with that."

"Is this bigger than the two of us?"

Pritcherman thought about that for a long while. "I used to think nothing was too big for me," he finally spoke.

"Funny, a neurosurgeon *not* thinking he's immortal, but the older I get, the more mortal I feel." P stood still, contemplating his own words. "Do I want my legacy to be the guy who missed the chance to save his country from a bunch of wackos?"

"How do you know this is our country?"

"Think about it, Q," my partner imagined. "With all the government intervention of the last ten years or so, these paranoid schmucks in Washington have got to be involved."

"I know a little about that," reflecting on my parents.

"Yeah," P put forward the thought. "You've had experience with our wonderful government killing your parents."

"It's not for sure it was our government."

"Get real, Q," P scoffed. "You know it and I know it. Do we want to let them steamroll us?"

"We could get seriously hurt, P," I worried. "Or even—"

"Killed? What a way to go! Maybe a plaque on some secret government wall, you know."

"Could we find Zach? Let's concentrate on finding some answers and not getting killed in the process, huh?"

"You take all the fun out of it," P faux-mocked. "OK, so what questions do you have?"

"Are you really leveling with me?" Without a sip of wine, I decided to lay the cards on the table. "You've got all this stuff in your office. I can't believe you don't have monitoring equipment, too. I've asked and you've evaded. Why the hell did you show up thirty minutes early at my apartment? And when can we find something out about Zachary? You don't seem interested in her. You want me to tell you everything. I'm not sure it's been reciprocal."

"Fair enough," Pritcherman poured the Barolo into my glass and filled his own. Then, walking over to a chair, he motioned me to a chair, too. Sitting for a moment, he spoke more clearly and slowly than I'd heard before. "Quinton, first of all, I live here. That's why all the *stuff*, as you call it, is here. When my wife and I divorced, she threw me out of our house and I already spent so much time here, I decided to fix it up a little. Basically, I moved in. Over time, I guess I added a few more luxuries than what would be considered normal. As to Zach, we have to let this play out a bit." After pausing for another sip of wine, "Yes, there is monitoring equipment in here. You haven't done anything I wouldn't have while I was gone."

"So you were monitoring me. I knew it. Where'd you go, where'd you sleep the other night?" I was skeptical.

"Yes, I monitored you. You'd have done the same. I stayed in the faculty lounge," P answered. "And don't look so surprised."

I wasn't. Nothing about Pritcherman did I remotely consider normal. Maybe that was what I needed in a partner though for this problem—or problems. "So come clean. Where do you activate and view all the surveillance?"

"On the desk," P waved in the general direction. "I'll show you how to operate it if you'd like."

"I'd like," I countered, then easing up. "But I can't stay here if it's where you live."

"Yes, you can," my partner advised. "But I guess I'll need to stay here, too."

"Don't tell me you have a second bedroom."

"No," he laughed. "We can make up a day bed."

"So, why did you come early?"

"That," P sighed, "is a little more complicated."

No kidding. Another complication, I thought. When were those gonna stop? "I'm listening."

"Yeah, I'll bet you are," Pritcherman grunted. "Quinton, you think I'm crazy, don't you?"

The thought had crossed my mind a time or two, "No sir. Not really. Well—"

"Aw, get real. Everybody thinks I'm nuts," P confessed. "They're probably right. But some of it's an act. People tend to dismiss me and when they do, they don't pay as much attention to me."

"Or they pay more."

"Naw," he poked fun at me. "I've done this a lot longer than you've observed in your few short weeks."

"True enough," I conceded. "What's this have to do with coming to my place early?"

"I'm getting there," he reacted. "A little pushy, Q. You see," pausing, "I knew Smith wasn't on the level, that she was up to something, but I just didn't know what. Then I saw her talking to that arrogant shit, Grigsby. Next thing you know, he's gone. That was just after I yelled at you to be in the office at 4 p.m. remember?"

"Do I ever," I remembered alright.

"Sorry about that, partner," P apologized. "So, I got rid of Smith and followed Grigsby. I sent her off on rounds or something and took out after Grigsby. I gave him a good amount of lead time."

"Yeah, I know he came to my apartment, but he left quickly."

"How do you know that?"

"Well," I sheepishly admitted. "I have some pretty sophisticated monitoring equipment at my place, too. So, if you were watching. Who was the second visitor?"

"Grigsby again," P stunned me. "I wasn't there for his first visit–I'd given him a head start, remember. But I found him and followed him back to his place. He was there about thirty minutes, picked up some stuff and a few hours later he was back at your apartment. But I didn't know it was your apartment then. So I sat outside for a while, waiting for him to leave. I was just going to go in and see what he'd been up to."

"I'll be damned," I was stunned alright. "A few hours later? Where'd he go in between?"

"Nowhere. He went back to your apartment, but didn't get out of his car," Pritcherman answered. "He just sat there, made a few phone calls and seemed to be waiting."

"Waiting for help getting past my security," I suggested. "That makes for a new problem. Grigsby wasn't on my security logs the second time. So he knows about the security and knows how to defeat it."

"That means he had help from somebody and probably not Smith, since I had her busy," P surmised.

"Yeah," I agreed. "Don't you ever operate? I mean, how is it you have all this time to sneak around watching Grigsby?"

"Grigsby's not on the level either. Probably government, like you said," P concluded. "I operate," seeming a bit hurt. "And I'm damned good at it, too. But nobody messes with my service, Quinton. Nobody."

"Well, somebody's messing with it now–big time, P," I was sure. "Back to the same question. Is this bigger than us? I think we have to get the police involved about Zach. You tell me?"

"Nobody messes with my service," P was unwavering. "We go after them. You and I. The cops won't care about Zachary. She's *my* resident," he was adamant. "And I'm not crazy."

I didn't say a word. We both sat there considering the consequences of our admissions and latest agreement. After about five minutes, the silence was broken.

"Start the salad, Q."

"Salad? Where's the refrigerator?"

"Here, of course," pressing another button on the countertop, revealing a small refrigerator.

"When do you shop?"

"Ah, Quinton," P pontificated. "You'll never know," pausing. "You'll never know that, or a few other things about me."

If there was a truer statement, I hadn't heard it yet.

"Grigsby," Smith spoke into her phone. "Meet me in the faculty parking garage, level five. I'm near a black Infiniti coupe.

"Black Infiniti coupe, roger. Out."

Smith was standing at the front of the vehicle, with a clear view of the elevator about ten feet away. She saw Grigsby in his vehicle slowly coming towards her position. She motioned him into a parking space on the opposite side, about four spaces down. After parking, Grigsby took up a position closer to the elevator, hidden and covering the other direction, in case someone turned that way when exiting the elevator. Less than five minutes passed before the elevator doors opened, revealing the Dean deep in thought, not paying any attention to his surroundings.

Smith approached the Dean, as he walked to the Infiniti, "Dean Jankowski, could I have a moment?"

"Dr. Smith, you just left a short while ago," the Dean seemed startled.

Smith intercepted his path a few feet from the elevator and, with her right hand, grasped the Dean's left arm and guided him away from the vehicle to the opposite side of the garage. "Just a minute of your time, Dean," she firmly asked, pushing him further away from his car.

Resisting her change in direction, the Dean defied her, "Where are you taking me?"

"If you could just sit in my car for a moment," Smith instructed as Grigsby appeared, blocking his movement, opening the front door to the vehicle he'd recently parked–a gray four-door sedan with tinted windows–leaving the Dean no choice but to comply.

The Dean's posture relaxed, more out of resignation as Smith ushered him into the front passenger seat. "What's this about, Smith?"

Grigsby entered the back seat directly behind the Dean as Smith got into the driver's side. Smith turned to the Dean and locked onto his eyes, "You know what this is about."

"But I thought *Big Boy*—"

"*Big Boy what?*" Smith queried. "I have a proposal to offer you, Dean."

Grigsby patted Jankowski on the shoulders from behind. "We're going for strawberries. We thought you might like to join us," firmly grasping the Dean's shoulders, pushing down firmly. "I think we just hit—" pausing for a beat, "the *Jackpot*."

– Always Look Behind The Curtain To See Who's Pulling The Strings –

XIII

Please, don't hurt me!" Jankowski pleaded, terror now unmistakably visible as Grigsby secured his torso and upper extremities to the back of the car seat. "Don't put that over my eyes." Grigsby paid no attention to his plea, and without speaking applied a blindfold over the Dean's eyes. He reached into the Dean's pocket and retrieved his smart phone. Turning to Smith, he quietly advised, "Go," while pushing their captive's head down.

"Dr. Jankowski, we will only restrain you like this for a short while," Smith tried to reassure him while guiding the vehicle out of the parking space, accelerating down the exit ramps of the five-story garage, and out onto the street. In the twilight of early evening, their passenger wasn't easily visible. After a drive of about five minutes, the two quickly maneuvered the Dean out of the vehicle and through a heavy metal door. Wherever they were, it was quiet, except for the low-pitched hum of the ventilation system. Grigsby directed Jankowski to a nearby couch and sat him down, removing the blindfold but leaving his arm restraints in place.

Grigsby stood over him, intentionally intimidating the smaller and older Dean, until Smith motioned him to back away. Smith slowly walked next to the couch and sat down about two feet from Viktor Igorseg Jankowski. "Dr. Jankowski," she spoke after his eyes had adjusted to the room's sparse illumination. "I know you are confused by all of this but, let me reassure you, we mean you no harm." The tone of her voice was intended to be soothing.

"Dr. Smith," Jankowski replied. "If that really is your name, please do not injure me. I can assure you this isn't the last you will hear of this insult. There are those who will—"

"Doctor," Smith cut short his opening volley, firmly, but swiftly. "I don't think you have any idea of what's going on here and it would be to your benefit to hold your fire until you do." Moving to within inches of his face, her eyes locked onto his without blinking. As she stared coldly into his eyes, she reminded him, "Remember your time in Poland, sir? Well, so do we. You knew someday you would be called. Well sir, it's payback time."

In resignation, Jankowski's shoulders slumped, his head down, as he sunk further into the couch from the weight of what he'd just heard. He thought he could postpone this day with his medical help on the seizure patient. He thought that would be enough, but apparently not. Today began in earnest his side of the bargain with the devil.

"Quinton," Pritcherman declared, putting down a half-filled glass of Barolo. "I've been thinking through dinner about Zachary. She couldn't have just disappeared–we both know that. They took her . . . but why? She's just a surgical resident. Is she mixed up in this, I mean, how? You know, is she with the bad guys?"

"No, she's not with the bad guys," I was emphatic. "Not voluntarily. I think she got caught up in this because of me. I sucked her into this when I talked her into helping me break into the morgue. You know, to try and find the dead guy. Who is this dead guy anyway?"

"Another good question," P answered, taking another sip. "He was sent to me by the Dean, who won't really tell me much."

"We have to find out who he is," I sputtered. "Did I tell you he's deep cover, too?"

"Hell no," Pritcherman stood up. "Are you telling me that son-of-a-bitch Dean sold me a homeless guy who's really another government type?"

"Well—"

"Because if you are—"

"Look," I slowed both of us down. "I don't know for sure, but it seems likely he's not what you were told he is, or was, or . . . you know what I mean."

"I'm beginning to think I–uh, *we*–don't know anything yet," the neurosurgeon sat back down, thinking to himself. After a pause, he looked directly at me, "Q, nobody screws with my service. Not the Dean, not Smith or Grigsby–a couple of residents or whoever they are–not the government, and not—"

"Grigsby's a medical student, not a resident."

"Whatever. He's an asshole," P retorted. "Stop interrupting me. So, who the hell is this dead guy?"

"That's what I was trying to say when—"

"Who is that guy?"

"Well, this all started with him, I'd say, we're back to him," I concluded. "I'm guessing your life was perking along without a hiccup, until this guy showed up. Mine too, sort of. Did I tell you I have no interest in clinical medicine?"

"Quinton!" Pritcherman held up his hand. "The dead guy."

"Right," I blinked, "the dead guy. Everything was going along on cruise control until then. So, we start by finding out who he is, why he was sent here, and by who."

"*Whom.*"

"Huh?"

"*By whom*, you cretin. Didn't you take English? Not by who, *by whom*."

"Whomever," I scowled at the professor. "We know by whom. It was the Dean, but where did the Dean get him? Where are we gonna find out about this guy?"

"From the Dean," P responded. "I guess I owe Viktor Igorseg Jankowski another visit. And this time I'd better get some answers."

"Another thing. Zachary," I added. "When I went back to her apartment, I found this," throwing the IV needle cap onto the table.

"A needle cap?"

"Yeah," I sighed. "I found it on her apartment floor. She's a surgeon and may have a few supplies in her lab coat. But I've never seen a resident start an IV . . . ever. They leave that for med students or nurses. Did someone start an IV on her?" Pausing to exhale before resuming, I slowly explained my consideration. "I think she's a victim in all this. You know, after they took her. If the IV was started on her . . . I mean, why? Were they trying to drug her? You know Smith did that to me. What reason—"

"I guess that does support your story about Smith being the one to inject you, huh? What if Zachary's a patient now, not a doctor?" Pritcherman said what I feared. "The why might be that they're using her for something, not just sedating her?"

"I can't see why they'd release her, then come back and get her again," I mulled over that thought. "So, how does the IV fit in?"

"You can be sure she didn't go willingly," P added. "Maybe that explains the IV. We have to find her. That's all there is to it."

"I'm listening. What are you proposing now?"

"Didn't you say you took some pictures or a video of her place? Maybe there's a clue there," my partner suggested.

"Yes," fumbling around for my tablet. "I uploaded it into the cloud to be safe," retrieving the still pictures and shuffling through them. "Nothing in the pictures stands out. But look."

"What?"

"Notice this pile of stuff here and that one there," pointing to two separate clumps of clothing. "She's a resident. Nothing's that straightened up in a house officer's place. They're a mess. I'm telling you, someone made a quick attempt to clean the place up."

"Why?"

"To cover their tracks," I exhaled again. "But what tracks, P? What's the big picture here?"

"Keep him quiet for a while," Smith ordered Grigsby, rising to her feet from the couch where she sat with the Dean. Walking to the door, she turned to Grigsby, "I'll be right back."

"So, Dean Jankowski," Grigsby patted the Dean on the shoulders, "about my pharmacology grade last semester—" The door closed, leaving Grigsby alone with the Dean.

Smith walked a few paces away from the door and took out her smart phone and speed dialed. A few seconds later, her call was answered. "I've got the strawberries. I think they're ripe. How hard do I push rabbit snare?"

"You do what's necessary, add whipped cream or whatever. This chestnut has to break our way. Whatever means necessary. Just get it done," came the answer. "You have to turn him."

"Understand, sir, eat the strawberries before they spoil or the rabbit gets away," Smith answered. "I may need to go through Poland, to refresh."

"Uh, yes. No problem."

"Thank you, sir. Have a good evening," Smith disconnected and walked back to the exterior door, opening it and entering to find Grigsby clearly intimidating the Dean.

"Enough, Grigsby!" She shouted across the room. Grigsby pulled back from the Dean, annoyed with Smith, but acquiesced.

Smith told Grigsby to take off the restraints and motioned with her head for Grigsby to get up from his position on the couch as she walked to where the two were sitting. Grigsby slowly got up and Smith stood in front of the Dean without saying anything for thirty seconds or so. She smiled and sat down next to Jankowski. "I loved my time in Poland, Viktor. May I call you Viktor, sir?"

"That's fine," Jankowski replied. "When were you there and where?"

"Long after you'd left. Remember I'm younger. After the fall of the communists. Long after. But not you, right?"

"Of course," the Dean snorted. "I know you have my entire history. Let's dispense with the small talk, Smith. What do you want?"

Smith sighed and shook her head. "We're going to be here awhile and I thought I'd just get to know you better."

"Really? And I'm supposed to believe you?" Jankowski was still contemptuous. "How's your probe doing . . . Doctor?"

"You seem most interested in it . . . Dean ," came Smith's semi-mocking response. "Why do you ask about my probe?"

"You seem different. No real problems," Jankowski reacted. "I don't understand why they sent you to get me. Is it so I can examine someone with the probe that doesn't have problems?"

"Why do you say I haven't had problems?" Smith probed.

"Well, have you? It would appear not," the Dean blurted. "Have you had issues?"

Resuming her more friendly composure and ignoring his question, "I was in Gdansk. In the early 2010s. And also Warsaw. I know you know Warsaw from your medical school days, right?"

"Again, you know all of this."

"Yes, but how has the old city changed from your time to when I was there? The free and independent Poland is better now than the communist one?"

"Of course," the Dean sniffed. "Free? Somewhat. Independent? Hardly. They certainly have better motives now, but all that changed was the puppet master. From Soviets to Americans."

"Ah, and so you're not happy with that?"

"The world is supposed to be better for it," he answered, "but I'm beginning to have my doubts. Why does America have to control everything, Smith? You tell me."

"That sir, is for the policymakers, not me," Smith concluded. "I carry out policy. I don't make it. You believe we pull Poland's strings? Your strings, Viktor? Policy is not for you either, right?"

"It would appear you are correct," exhaling loudly as he spoke. "Yes, I believe you are trying to pull my strings. You, or whomever is directing you through your probe. Either way, can we get on with it? As you said, you carry out orders. So what are your orders, Smith? Why am I here?"

"Cut to the chase, Dean?" Smith stood up. "No more small talk, huh? Maybe you're right, Grigsby." She motioned to Grigsby to sit down next to the Dean. Grigsby sat and smiled menacingly at the Dean, patting him on the shoulders again, but saying nothing.

"So, Viktor," Smith began again. "After medical school, you came to this country . . . to Johns Hopkins in Baltimore, I believe. How did that happen?"

"I was a good student," Jankowski insisted. "I know where you are going. You want me to say because you Americans paid for it, arranged it, too."

"Did we, Viktor?"

"Yes, but I wasn't given my residency, I earned it. I just didn't have the resources available to me in Poland."

"So you made your Faustian bargain with the dirty Americans?"

"Hardly," the Dean snapped. "I love this country. I'm a citizen now, too."

Smith looked at the Dean with admiration, "Your father died making Poland free—"

"And to help his family," the Dean added. "He hated the communists after they broke my mother. All he wanted was for my sister and me to live in freedom," his voice trailing off. "They broke my sister. They threw away her precious life," his eyes glistening with moisture.

"I know," Smith softly took the opening. "I'm asking you to be a patriot again and help your adopted country, Viktor. We have a major problem and we need your help."

"So you kidnap me?"

"Asked you to come for a talk," Smith countered.

"Can I walk out now?"

"You can," Smith waved her right arm towards the door.

"But—"

"I'm listening."

"Your sister in Gdansk. Does she still require around-the-clock care?"

Pausing and slumping again, the Dean answered quietly, "You know she does. And I am grateful for the care America provides for my family. Before my parents died, your government helped my father. He was awarded—"

"Yes, Viktor. Our highest honor," Smith almost imperceptibly said, "Your father was a good man and helped save the free world," pausing a few seconds. "Can we count on you to help your country in the same way?"

"I don't understand how I can help."

"The probes, Viktor," Smith replied. "We need your help with the probes."

"But I'm already helping with them. I can't get the records. *Big Boy* hasn't gotten them to me, but says he will. As soon as I get them, I'm hoping to figure out why the seizures are occurring. But I—"

"Viktor," Smith patiently silenced him, raising her hand. "This isn't about *Big Boy*. It's bigger than that. He may even be part of the problem. Much bigger."

"What?"

"General, we have an intercept," came the anonymous caller to General Bitterman at his Fort Meade office.

"Go on," Bitterman, already sitting ramrod straight, tensed further.

"Yes, sir. This is the duty officer on field agent monitoring. I'm Major Edwards, sir. We've been monitoring and the computers analyzed an unusual call from Smith to a number in Langley."

"From Smith? Do we know who was on the other end, Major?"

"Not who, but it was a number we know to be at CIA, sir."

"Go on."

"Yes, something about strawberries and a rabbit snare and a chestnut. Then something about him being important. Also a reference to Poland, sir. Should I get you a print out?"

"No, that won't be necessary. I know what it references. Thank you, Major," disconnecting. Bitterman leaned back in his chair, rubbing his eyes. *What is Smith up to? Do I confront her now or wait a while?* He was lost in deliberation. *Here it is after 8 p.m. on a beautiful night in Washington and I'm still here defending my country*, he reflected.

"Cover their tracks, indeed, Q," Pritcherman wondered out loud as he sipped on his Barolo. "The big picture, you ask?" Let's see, the bastards have one of my residents, killed one of my patients and stole his brain during his autopsy, oh, and that was after somehow taking out a probe no one ever told me about. And they wonder why I'm pissed off?"

"Don't forget about sending Smith here to spy on you."

"And what about that prick-of-a-Dean, who's been less than helpful? Damn Polack."

"Now, now," I cautioned. "No need for stereotyping. That Dean may be able to help us."

"Not so far," P snarled.

"So, what's our plan?" I sensed P was getting wound up again and I wanted to calm him down. "I can do some more snooping on the dead guy, but what about Zachary?"

"You snoop," P ordered. "And then go back to Zachary's and really look around. In the morning, the good Dean and I are going to have another chat."

I took another long sip of Pritcherman's most excellent Barolo. "Good juice, as you say. Big picture, P. Why? Who? Motive and opportunity, you said. We've identified several opportunists, but what's the motive?"

"That my friend and partner, leads us back to the brain," Pritcherman stated, rising as he did so. Silently, he began walking about more slowly than I thought him capable, stopping in front of the brain model and pausing before entering. "Are you coming or not?"

"What about the video?"

"We'll look at it after your memory tour," Pritcherman was almost gleeful. "Come on. I think better when I teach." Disappearing inside his brain model, I heard him ask, "What do you know about memory, Q?"

I had no choice but to follow him into the maze. "Where are you this time?"

"Quinton, let's start with the basics, a refresher for us both." I found the neurosurgeon standing in front of a touch screen. "There are about ten trillion cells in the human body and one hundred billion or so of those are neurons, connected to each other by at least a quadrillion synapses," he was gazing back-and-forth between the screen and the heavens.

"Yes, each is a *connectome*," I feebly offered.

"Do you know who first gave us an accurate picture of the human brain?" The question apparently was rhetorical, because he continued without waiting for me to answer, "Thomas Willis in the 1660s, the Circle of Willis. The blood supply at the base of the brain is named after him. Anyway, we couldn't even tell one neuron from another until Camillo Golgi developed stains that allowed us to see individual neurons in the 1800s. But all that's anatomy. Memory is physiology. How the neurons communicate." P was walking between several areas of his model as he spoke.

"But—"

"Don't interrupt, Q," P was on a roll again. This, apparently, was going to be a one-way lecture, not a Q&A session or a quiz. "Anatomy's important, but physiology is the key to memory. The attributes of the chemical synapses. Then we figured out what happens at the anatomic level of the neuron when those chemicals interact. Do you know what happens, Q?"

"I can talk?"

"Of course," my partner smiled. "Let me speed it up though," he continued. "You have to look at about 100,000 neurons before you can figure out how they communicate. It took until the early 2010s to do that, but now, finally, we know. That's why there's such a revolution in comparing normal connectomes to the abnormal ones in autism and schizophrenia."

"Yes, I'm interested in pursuing the genetics of all that and—"

"Later, son, later," P interrupted and rambled on. "The engram, Quinton. That and where all this is happening. What specific part of the brain?"

I decided I wouldn't say anything until asked. Also, I stood still. Pritcherman was bounding back-and-forth between the right temporo-parietal junction, the amygdala, and the hippocampus–close in the real brain, but a real trek in this *Brobdingnagian* model. I kept getting in his way and almost knocked down several times.

"The hippocampus is critical for long-term memory," P mumbled. "The amygdala mediates fear memories, and the RTPJ is basically your conscience. Put 'em all together . . ." his voice trailed off as he quickly exited this brain. He briskly arrived back at his chair, lifted his glass and finished his Barolo.

"Quinton!"

I trailed behind and sat down, "Yes, my liege," I feigned.

As I took my seat alongside him, Pritcherman stared blankly into space. After a few seconds, he directed his focus to me, locking onto my eyes like radar, as he had previously demonstrated. "These bastards are trying to influence memory in some way. I'm sure of it."

"But why?"

"I don't know," he slurred a bit–the *Barolo effect* beginning to take hold. "But I will. Believe me, I—"

"We."

"Will."

General Bitterman was pacing as the call he placed went unanswered. He disconnected and dialed again. Again it rang, unanswered. Disconnecting and setting down the smart phone, he sat at his desk, perplexed, thinking. He dialed the duty officer, Major Edwards. "Major, do you show any malfunctions or distress messages on Smith's end?"

"No sir," Edwards replied. "Her last call, the one I informed you about was logged at 2312 hours. No activity since."

"Understand. Thank you." He disconnected, now more perplexed than a few moments ago. Why wasn't Smith answering? No outgoing, standard message either, and no encoded distress signal. So why doesn't she answer?

Picking up his phone again, this time he dialed *Jackpot*. Once again, no answer. "What the hell?" the General muttered. After dialing again and confirming Jankowski's no answer, he called Major Edwards back, "Get me any data on *Jackpot*–calls in or out, and figure out if his GPS is on, Major."

After fifteen seconds, the Major responded, "Negative on the GPS and no calls in either direction within the last four hours. I can ping the phone to check for malfunctions?"

"Do it," the General snapped. "How long before an answer, Major?"

"Already back, sir. His phone is functioning normally, no distress signals, no out-of-touch messages activated. Sir, it's basically turned off."

"Would you have a time on the turn off?"

"No, sir," the Major seemed confused. "And that's unusual. It should be logged."

"Thank you, again, Major," the General hung up and was back to pacing about the office again. Too much coincidence, he thought. There was a gnawing feeling in the pit of his stomach.

"No more wine!" Pritcherman was clearly perplexed. "Are they trying to erase an engram or plant a new one? I just . . . don't . . . get it," his voice trailing off again as he looked into space.

"If an engram is a permanent change in response to a stimulus," I asked, "is what they're trying to do permanent? We have to find a way to reverse the effects."

"That's gonna be pretty hard on a dead guy," P was back with me.

"Yes, but there must be others, or they're planning for more, I'm sure."

"Likely," Pritcherman was gloomy. "It shouldn't work," he was adamant. "Memory doesn't reside everywhere, like was thought before 1984. That was demonstrated at USC, when it was shown that surgically removing a few hundred neurons from the interpositus nucleus erased a memory. But that was a rabbit's eye and not a human. We're much more complicated. The norepinephrine and serotonin systems come into play. Not to mention Area 25 and—"

"Got it." I didn't, but I wanted to slow him down. "Maybe genetics has a role?"

"Don't know, but I do know that adult humans don't make new neurons," P insisted. "That's why memory involves creating new branches from existing neurons, new synapses. That's an area of my research."

"Really?"

"After that fat bastard, Zendejas, screwed me on the CJD vaccine, I became interested in memory. Hoped I could ruin his," he wasn't laughing.

"So you and Dr. Zendejas worked together, but he took all the credit?"

"You got it, Sherlock," Pritcherman was not smiling. "We were working with prions, trying to discover whether they were actually transmitting the disease or the effect of it. Not only did I do brain biopsies on living patients, but I isolated the PrPSc[4]. We were going around in circles–as were the rest of the researchers–until I suggested we look at the genetics—"

"Now you're in my area."

"Yeah, well," P went on, "your area, I discovered, showed us that there are several forms of inherited prion disease because of a genetic mutation at the 210 and 232 positions. That led us–me, really–to suggest the vaccine be in two parts. Part I, an inert viral carrier that corrected the genetic defect, if it existed. Part II–the hard part–was the killer portion that converted the abnormal protein to a form the body could clear."

"So Part I was necessary to prevent the patient from redeveloping the problem again. Beautiful!" I did admire his science.

"And elegant research. Thank you," P said with just a hint of humility. "I'm in it to cure disease. Zendejas wanted the credit."

"So there's no love lost between the two of you."

"I can't stand the prick," P interrupted. "When I'd heard the sharks got him, all I could think of was karma. Couldn't have happened to a nicer guy."

"Actually, he was pretty nice to me," I countered.

---

[4] PrPSc is the abbreviation for Prion Protein, scrapie, the disease-causing form of the abnormal protein. Scrapie is the prion disease in sheep, the original prion disease described. Normal prion proteins are indicated as the PrPc. Prions are abnormally folded proteins. The normal protein has been implicated in maintenance of long-term memory. The abnormal form, or prion, has been implicated in several human diseases, including Creutzfeldt-Jakob disease (CJD), Kuru, Familial CJD, as well as other memory disorders, such as Alzheimer's disease.

"Don't be so sure," P replied. "Behind that *jolly old Saint Nick* façade is a genuine horse's ass. He'd step over his dead mother for glory." With that, he opened another bottle of Barolo.

"I thought you said no more wine?"

"Do you believe everything I say, Quinton? You brought up Zendejas. I can't take him on an empty stomach," my partner volleyed. "Besides, I thought we were going to the movies?"

"Let me retrieve the video," as I went to get my tablet computer. "None of this explains the *why*. We may get to the *who*, but *what's* the reason anyone would want to alter someone's memories?"

"Now you're sounding like a scientist. Asking the right questions. *Why, indeed?* Answer that, and I'll bet you find a government behind it."

"Why did you agree to help with the overthrow of communism, Viktor?" Smith was sitting next to the Dean on the couch while Grigsby, seemingly, was disinterested.

"First, I was angry at how they had broken my parents," Jankowski remembered. "But soon I saw a larger reason, not for family, but for my country. Freedom comes at a high price, Dr. Smith. A very high price."

"Freedom, not just for you and your family, but for your country?"

"Yes. It is under a constant threat," the Dean continued. "We must be vigilant–always."

"I couldn't agree more, Viktor," Smith moved closer. "You see, we are under threat again and we need your help."

"Threat? From who? The communists are gone."

"Ah, but there are always those threats from within, sir. As you say, we must constantly be vigilant."

"I don't understand," Jankowski seemed puzzled.

"Who authorized the probes, Viktor? And for what purposes?"

"I was told that was on a *need to know* basis."

"Who told you, Dean? Who is your contact?"

"Isn't it your contact, too? I'm not sure we should be talking about this."

"Viktor," Smith moved closer. "Remember I said 'the threats from within?' What I'm going to tell you is of the most sensitive nature. One of our own may be the threat. Your contact, we believe."

"General Bitterman? But he—"

"Seems like such a patriot? The enemy within, Viktor," Smith persisted. "You have always been a consultant for the CIA?"

"Yes."

"The General has always been your contact?"

"Just since I was re-activated because of the probes. I haven't been active for the last several years until General Bitterman contacted me."

"Were you ever working for the NSA previously?"

"No," the Dean seemed perplexed. "Always for the CIA."

"What do you know about the NSA's mission, Viktor? Do they have field agents like yourself?" It was a rhetorical question. "No, they don't. Didn't that seem unusual to you?"

"I guess I never considered—"

"Never considered who you were working for? That's understandable. You were just trying to help your country again. Right?"

"Yes, Dr. Smith. I only wanted to help. They made such a persuasive case of needing my help."

"So you were not consulted about the probes before they were actually inserted?"

"Oh no," Jankowski shook his head. "The General contacted me because there had been complications and he wanted my assistance in finding and correcting the cause."

"We appreciate your concern and your help, Doctor," Smith locked on to his eyes again. "Viktor, now we need your help. This is not an authorized NSA mission."

"Of course I will help," Jankowski quickly agreed. "Just one question, Dr. Smith. Who, exactly, is *we?*"

Bill Calhoun gently knocked on the Director's door, before opening it, "Burning the midnight oil again I see."

"Come in, Bill," the Director motioned him to a chair. "You have something?"

"Yes," Calhoun slid into the chair. "The NSA likely knows Smith isn't one of theirs by now, and Jankowski, too."

"Why?"

"Well," Calhoun continued, "Since all this NSA snafu started, we've been trying to use different communications. Since all of ours are NSA-created and monitored, I thought we should try and not just tell them our every move. Have an independent, secure network."

"Smart thinking. Sounds like *Operation Chestnut* is moving our way?"

"Well, I wish it were as good as it sounds," Calhoun sat forward and stared at the Director. This communications change is new to our people. I also ordered our folks to monitor the NSA."

"So, we're monitoring them as they monitor us?"

"Basically."

"Geez, this is complicated," the Director shook his head.

"While we were monitoring them, we overheard them telling someone up their chain of command about us monitoring them," Calhoun was even confusing himself. Sighing deeply, he continued, "Anyway, I'm working on a different way to talk to our agents. But for now, I think we have to assume Smith is compromised."

"Grigsby?"

"Don't know yet," the Associate Director replied. "What I do know is the NSA tried to call Smith, then the Dean, and got no answer from either. If their protocols are like ours, and it's a sure bet they are, then they'll have to assume Smith and Jankowski are working for us."

"Do we have our Polish friend in our snare?"

"I can't confirm that yet. Smith is working on him, but I just don't know," Calhoun frowned. "This communications fiasco is a real pain in the ass. And, naturally, there's more."

"Let me know when you confirm Jankowski," the Director ordered. "What else is there?"

"I think I have an ID on who their up-the-chain guy is."

"That would be our first NSA rogue, Bill?"

"Call him what you want, sir. I'll call him Brigadier General James Bitterman."

"What? No popcorn?" I was kidding, of course, but Pritcherman jumped up and pulled out a bag and threw it into the microwave.

"Give it a couple of minutes. You get the movie ready," he ordered.

My tablet accessed the cloud and I loaded the video clip I had downloaded from Zachary's monitor in her apartment when I returned and found the needle cap. "I haven't viewed it yet, but this should tell us what happened to her," I suggested, as the clip started to play.

After the first few uneventful minutes of the clip, P arrived, a bowl of freshly popped popcorn in hand. "Stop it a minute. Let me plug it into a projector." He handed me a Bluetooth dongle and projector and pointed to a blank white area on the wall. "Show it over there."

"Well, I need to fast forward through it," as I connected the projector and aimed it at the wall. "The first part's been like watching golf, pretty boring."

"So fast forward until something interesting comes on," as he stuffed a handful of popcorn into his mouth.

At least it wasn't onions, I thought, as I quickly ran through over two hours of digital video. "I gotta confess, professor. Some of this anatomy is over my head."

"Not when I'm done with you, my boy. You'll be a first-class neuro-anatomist and a neuro-physiologist to boot."

"That should help my career as a neuro-geneticist." I was actually being serious, as the video sped through at ten times normal speed. "Look!" I exclaimed, as Zachary entered the field of view, "we finally have something."

"It's late. Wake me up when there's some action. So far, this movie sucks," P yawned.

A few minutes later I nudged him to look at the clip. "Is that enough action for you?"

We watched as Zachary intuitively arranged herself on the floor prior to the onset of focal motor, then tonic-clonic seizure activity. It was nauseating to watch someone I knew in obvious distress like this.

"Well, I'll be damned," Pritcherman cursed as he sat up. "She couldn't be a surgeon with a seizure disorder. This has to be something brand new."

"That's my friend, my true love, P," I softly whispered.

"It's my resident," my partner added.

In silence, we watched as the seizure activity stopped and she remained unconscious, becoming incontinent and post-ictal. As the video continued, we both moved forward in our chairs in synchrony. First, two figures came into the room and attended to Zachary. One looked vaguely familiar. An IV was established.

"Well, that explains the needle cap," I muttered, nauseous at watching Zachary on the floor.

Presently, a third person entered the room, causing us both to stand in unison. "I don't believe it!" I shouted.

Pritcherman jumped toward the wall, screaming at the video, "*You fat-rat bastard!* Not only aren't you dead, you're involved in all this!" P instinctively put his arm around me. We could only stare at the image of John Luis Zendejas.

— Never Forget, Your Enemy's Enemy Is Not Necessarily Your Friend —

XIV

W e," Smith took a breath before answering, "are the CIA. I believe you worked with us in Poland a long time ago, Dr. Jankowski. Certainly your father was a huge help."

"But I thought you worked for the NSA, like I do, Dr. Smith," the Dean was puzzled.

"I was assigned to the NSA. They think I still am. That's part of the problem, Viktor," Smith confided.

"I don't understand. It's all very confusing. I—" His voice trailed off.

"I'll try to clear it up as we go along, Dean."

"Aren't the NSA and CIA the same? I mean, on the same team?"

"You would think so," Smith agreed. "We were. At least we thought we were."

"My father warned me about getting caught in a spider's web with the Americans. But you were so helpful to him. The CIA got him out of the communist prison. He was broken by then."

"I know," Smith gently comforted. "From what I know, they couldn't get him out sooner."

"Yes," Jankowski acknowledged. "When he was released, he found my mother. She had been tortured, too. They were never the same."

"When we brought them out of Poland to the U.S., we had hoped they could be rehabilitated. We tried to find your sister then, but the security forces had her well-hidden from us. It takes a brave man to stand for what is right, even though no one in his country knows," Smith continued.

"He was a good man."

"Being a double agent is a thankless job, Viktor. Your father served the truth."

"Ah, the truth. You say it like it's so black-and-white, but truth exists in the shadows of gray," the Dean countered.

"Well said, sir. Governments are not monolithic, even totalitarian governments," Smith added.

"By the time the communists were thrown out and I got my sister back, she was more than broken," the Dean was clearly emotional about the conversation. "Why did they have to involve her, an innocent child? I will never forgive them. I've seen firsthand how a person–my sister–can have her mind damaged forever."

"I know—"

"*No, you don't!*" Jankowski raised his voice. "That is why I thought the probes were being used for good, but—"

"What is the purpose of the probes, Viktor? Do you know?"

"By the time I was involved, they were already being used in people," Viktor offered. "I don't know who placed them or where they were placed, other than it was somewhere in Europe. They called on me to sort out the complications."

"So you didn't ask what they were for."

"Oh, I asked," the Dean countered. "But General Bitterman kept turning the conversation back to figuring out the cause of the complications."

"You mean the seizures?"

"And the other problems."

"What?" Smith seemed surprised. "You mean there have been other troubles?"

"Well—"

"It's late, Viktor," Smith smiled. "Let's get you some rest. I need to think about what you've said. We can continue this tomorrow. I'm sorry we can't let you go home, but I promise we will take good care of you." Turning to Grigsby, "Have you made up the Dean's bed in the other room?"

"It's all set," Grigsby replied. Looking at the Dean, Grigsby apologized, "I'm sorry I had to lean on you, sir. I'll make it up to you tomorrow with a fabulous meal and you'll be surprised at how nice I can be."

"Thank you, Mr. Grigsby," the Dean seemed relieved. "One last thing, Dr. Smith. What about your probe?"

"Dr. Pritcherman," exclaimed the surprised operating room charge nurse. "It's 9 a.m. Your procedure was scheduled for 7. You're never late. What's up?"

"Is my patient ready?" a whirlwind blowing through the door . . . the neurosurgeon ignored her comment. "I was unavoidably detained. I apologize."

The nurse raised an eyebrow, speechless at an act of contrition from Stanley J. Pritcherman, the king of arrogance. "What's up with that?" she murmured under her breath. "OR 6, Doctor. But the anesthesiologist hasn't put him to sleep. Said he won't until he knows you're here. Should I—"

"I'll let him know," P interrupted. "I'm changing first." Since when did Pritcherman let anyone know? Or notify anyone of his dressing schedule? Has hell frozen over?

The charge nurse shook her head and mumbled, "Uh, OK. I'll let the OR team know you're here and to get hopping."

"No need. I'll let them know, too." With that, Pritcherman bounded down the hall, snatching a mask from above the scrub sink and stuck his head into OR 6. "Sorry I'm late, all. I'm changing now. " Looking at the anesthesiologist he added, "You can start, Bill. It's T-time."

The anesthesiologist looked over at the team of three nurses attending the fifty-ish year old patient lying on the operating table. All three nurses were masked and gowned in preparation for the surgery, but the anesthesiologist could read their group astonishment even through the masks. *What is up with Pritcherman?*

After a moment, however, Dr. William Chesney–*Bill*–the senior anesthesiologist at the university, turned his attention back to his patient. Chesney drew the short straw this morning, meaning he had the pleasure of working with the much-feared neurosurgeon–a task most others avoided like the plague. Maybe it wouldn't be such a bad day after all.

Pritcherman quickly changed and began scrubbing in anticipation of his surgery. Shouting to the room, but in a nicer voice than any in the operating area had heard, "Has anyone seen my two medical students? I'd hoped to show them a few things about neurosurgery this morning."

The charge nurse couldn't stand it and broke the spell for all when she said, "Dr. Pritcherman, we sent them back after they waited for an hour or so. What's with your mood this morning? Do you want me to find the students?"

"What do you mean my mood? It's just good, old me," P laughed as he spoke. "Sure, call and have the two sent back. Maybe I can teach them something this morning."

Shaking her head again, the charge nurse left to find the wayward second-years, muttering to herself as she left. No one knew how to react to the "new" Pritcherman, but all prayed it would last. About ten minutes later, the two students timidly entered the scrub area to find Pritcherman singing to himself while he scrubbed his hands and arms.

"Either of you ever scrubbed-in on a surgical case?" Not waiting for the two students to answer, Pritcherman continued. "I'm sure you've read all about scrubbing. Notice how I start at the tips of each finger and work my way up. Water runs downhill, so we never let our hands tilt downward–always up. Germs go where the water goes. Use this to get under your fingernails," utilizing a pointed plastic sword included in the scrub brush kit. "And scrub for about five minutes on each hand. What do I call you two?"

"I'm—"

"I know," P laughed again. "*Frick and Frack.* Come on! Get to scrubbing. You two are going to assist on a neurosurgical case today."

The two students did their best to imitate their mentor and after he was satisfied with their effort, he motioned for them to follow. Pritcherman pushed through the door with his back into the operating room, holding his arms up at midchest level. The two students apprehensively followed. "Ladies and gentlemen of the operating room, this is Frick and Frack," chuckling louder still. "Let's show them how we take care of a surgical problem and maybe teach them a thing or two about the OR at the same time."

The lead OR nurse helped Pritcherman gown and glove, afterward applying his headlamp. Then, turning her attention to the students, she helped them fumble through the same procedure with distinctively more effort than with Pritcherman. Not wanting to break the mood, she quietly talked to them about what was right and wrong about their gowning and gloving technique. After completion, she ushered them to the table, admonishing them gently not to touch anything unless told to.

"Notice the good Dr. Chesney has already anesthetized this gentleman. Note the endotracheal tube to maintain his airway and provide oxygen. I'll let him explain the details of anesthesiology to you later. That said, let's crack this guy's skull and fix his problem. Ready?"

Frick and Frack seemed petrified, standing a foot or two away from the table, taking care not to touch anything. The room was a cool sixty-eight degrees, yet they were lightly perspiring. Pritcherman was conspiring with the unknown circumstances of the operating room to stress the hell out of these two medical students.

"Belly up to the bar," Pritcherman exhorted the pair. "You can't see anything from over there. Sandy," Pritcherman continued, "how long have we worked together?"

The charge nurse responded, "I've been here eight years, Doctor. It's Sandra, please, not Sandy."

"Potatoes, po*tah*toes," the neurosurgeon laughed. "Have I ever treated the OR staff to pizza?" Not waiting for her answer, he continued, "So, let's do it today. Reach into my scrub suit back pocket and find my wallet. Grab a credit card and order as many pizzas as it takes to fill up your bellies. Drinks, too. Oh, and get some of those cinnamon doodads for dessert. I love dessert and then a movie. Saw a good one last night."

Sandra, the charge nurse was fumbling through his back pocket as Pritcherman stood at the operating table. "Got it," she said.

"One other thing," P asked. "Use your cell phone. I don't want the food police knowing you're all eating contraband food."

"You just don't want to pay the junk food tax," Sandra busted him.

"You're correct," P responded. "This government regulation of everything including my bad habits is maddening." He paused a moment before continuing. "One last thing. In my wallet is a phone number to a Mr. Abbouse. It rhymes with caboose. His wife is one of my patients. Could you call him on your cell and tell him I'd like to meet with him to talk about her case this afternoon, anything after 3 p.m. It's such a nice day. Ask him to meet me in Memorial Park. Get a time for me, please."

"Sure," Sandra seemed a bit leery, but decided the better part of valor was not to precipitate an incident with Pritcherman over a few phone calls.

"One other thing, Sandy," Pritcherman asked. "We have a little joke going. He calls me Dr. Jones. Can you tell him Dr. Jones wants to meet with him?"

"OK," she was now more than leery. "Dr. Jones wants to meet with him about his wife's case this afternoon at Memorial Park. He picks the time. That's about it, right?"

"Yep."

She left the room and returned in a few minutes, announcing to the room that a lot of food would arrive around noon. "Mr. Abbouse said 5 p.m.–he'd see you at Memorial Park. Anything else?"

"Answer the damn phone!" Zendejas screamed into his smart phone, pacing the room. The normally jovial pathologist was anything but happy. "Jeremy," he screamed across the room. "Either of you have any ideas about where the Dean's office is?"

Both shook their heads without speaking. John continued charting while Jeremy watched the monitors tracking Zachary's health.

"Well, one of you needs to find him," Zendejas was calming ever-so slightly. "I cannot deal with his seizure activity alone, do you hear me. I can't!"

Both attempted to ignore their leader as he vented. Both were increasingly uneasy with the situation as well. They each stole looks at the leader, hoping he'd suddenly become enlightened with treatment options.

"Stay here and watch her closely," Zendejas commanded as he jumped up and headed for the door. "I'm going to find the damn Dean and bring him back myself."

Jeremy now felt compelled to say something. "I thought you were not supposed to be seen?"

"Yes," Zendejas countered, "and she wasn't supposed to have any complications," as he exited through the door. Neither underling elected to follow him, instead doing as he instructed, returning their attention back to their patient–Barbara Lynne Zachary.

"If she has more seizures while you're gone, what do we do?"

"Give her more *diazepam*–IVP, in 10 milligram increments. But watch her airway. We don't want her to arrest." The door slammed behind him.

The light of day was not the pathologist's time. He preferred the shadows, the night, the darkened pathology suite, even when it was artificially lit. Sometimes the night writes checks that can only be cashed in the daylight. He was feeling abandoned and increasingly desperate. As he walked, he realized he had no idea where he was going. Others–many others–who didn't need to see or be seen by him shared his time in the light.

Just as quickly, he returned to the laboratory space doubling as his operating room and critical care area in the warehouse region. He stepped inside the building, but not back into his lab area. He slowly paced the outer hall, trying to decide. Should he, or not? He decided to cash the check of desperation and retrieve his phone. After a few rings, it was answered.

"I know I'm not supposed to call you, but I can't find Jankowski," Zendejas cupped his hand over the mouthpiece.

"Trying to camouflage your voice is a waste of time, now that you've said his name," snapped General Bitterman on the receiving end of the call. He was clearly frustrated, too. "He doesn't answer me either. So what? He's allowed to eat."

"This patient is having more frequent seizure activity and it's beyond what I can handle. I need backup."

"For now, you'll have to make do," Bitterman instructed without emotion. "Have you heard from anyone else?"

"Like who?"

Sighing into the phone, "Our two friends."

"Who? Oh . . ." the pathologist understood. "Uh, no. Should I—"

"No. I'll get back to you," and with that, the General disconnected. He couldn't find Jankowski or Smith and he surmised neither was just eating. He rhythmically drummed his fingers on the desk, louder and louder until he pounded his fist on the heavy metal government issue, causing several pictures to fall over. He picked up his phone and speed dialed, hoping for an answer.

In a large room in another city, the phone rang. All three heard it, but ignored it initially. Grigsby answered on the fifth ring without saying anything, moving to the corner of the room.

"This is *Big Boy*. I'm looking for *Jackpot*. Any ideas?" Grigsby looked at Smith, then Jankowski. Neither of those two knew the question asked and he hadn't spoken a word in reply. Taking the phone from his ear, he disconnected without speaking.

"Who was that?"

"Wrong number," Grigsby shrugged. "Just a wrong number."

"Quinton! Get up," Pritcherman screamed. "It's 2 p.m. and I've already cracked a skull and maybe cracked more than that."

I couldn't believe it was two in the afternoon, scrambling to look at my watch. I hadn't slept that late since . . . well . . . forever.

"I must've overslept. I thought I set my alarm watch for—"

"Never mind, sleepyhead. Get up. We've got lots to do," P was a whirlwind of activity.

"Orange juice? I believe that's your favorite," as he poured before I could even begin to answer.

"What's got you so wound up this morning?" I mumbled through my haze.

"For one thing, it's afternoon, not morning. I've also decided you need to move back to your place."

"What? Why?"

"Aside from the fact you're driving me crazy, we both need our space," the neurosurgeon commented. "I'll tell you more later."

"Huh?"

"I'll tell you all about that over lunch," pointing to the outside door while motioning with his head. "Understand?"

"Got it," I tumbled out of bed and, taking the OJ, I headed toward the bathroom. "Any other jewels you want to tell me about?"

"Yeah," P called out as I entered the shower. "I'm hungry. Get dressed. We gotta get out of here. Let's go eat."

I was in and out of the bathroom in ten minutes, but not fast enough for my partner, who spent nearly the entire ten minutes chiding me to hurry. As I exited the bathroom in a partial state of dress and awareness, P slapped me on the back around the right shoulder, in the scapular spine area.

"Ow!" I yelped. "What the hell was that for? Why'd you slap me? Have you cut your fingernails lately? That felt like something sharp," as I tried to rub my shoulder, just out of my reach.

"Sorry," P looked sheepish. "Guess I overdid it again. Just trying to get you going." P looked at my back and gently massaged the area for a few seconds. "It looks okay. Just a little red. Hurry up. Get dressed. Let's get out of here."

We were out of the office door and I found myself attempting to keep up with P as he eschewed the elevator and was bounding down the stairs, heading down to the ground level. I nearly slammed into him when he stopped at the stairwell door leading to the ground floor, holding up his hand to stop me.

"Q, we have to be more careful in my office," P was conspiratorial. "This is bigger than we think. They came after you. They could come after me, too. That's why we need to split up. Who's to say my office isn't bugged, or your place, too. You need to move back to your place, and you can't say anything in your place they could use."

"But—"

"I know it's been fun the last few days," Pritcherman continued. "We need to work on our individual tasks separately. Make it harder for them to track both of us. I've come to some interesting conclusions in the OR this morning. I'll tell you about them at lunch. I really am hungry."

"How will we talk to each other if I can't visit you and vice-versa?"

"We'll need to work out a communications plan for emergencies," P concluded. "We can add that to our lunch for dessert." He turned and shot through the door, lab coat and me flying behind him. A brisk five-minute walk transported us to O'Reilly's. It appeared that the university staff liked the dark confines of this college bar and restaurant, too.

We found a table near the back and sat down, with Pritcherman looking in every direction. Before we ordered, P took out his smart phone and dialed, speaking into the handset, "I'd like to see the Dean as soon as possible. Anytime today is good." He spoke with authority. I couldn't hear the other side of the conversation, but his face spoke volumes. "What do you mean he's unavailable? Do you know this is Dr. Pritcherman? You tell that—"

I raised my hand and motioned downward.

Volume lowered, my partner seemed incredulous, "You can't find him? How do you lose a Dean? Never mind. When you hear from him, I insist you tell him I've called and will expect to hear from him in the next few hours."

Having terminated the call, he turned his attention to me. "Unavailable, my ass. I'll bet that bastard's just avoiding me."

"What if he really is?"

"What do you mean?"

"What if he's involved in this thing, too?"

"Yeah," P slowed down a bit. "He did send the dead guy to me," he paused momentarily to weigh the possibilities. "On whose side?"

"Who knows?" I responded. "Add that to our list of unanswered queries. So, what about communications? You said something about an emergency plan?"

"Yes," fumbling in his pocket. "I bought these this morning," tossing two cheap cell phones on the table. "We use these only when absolutely necessary. And," this time he paused for emphasis, "when we use them, we never use our names or locations. Only use it to coordinate a meeting. Now where do we meet?"

"How about here?"

"No. Too obvious," P disagreed. "Do you know Memorial Park downtown?"

"Yeah, but I'm a med student. Do you know how hard it is for me to get—"

"Q. You call a PRT and enjoy the ten minute drive," my partner advised. "You collect your thoughts on the way. To avoid calling too much, let's set up a daily meeting. That way, if one of us doesn't show up, the other knows something's up."

"Good idea," I echoed. "But we need to vary the time each day. Is your OR time the same each day?"

"No, but almost always in the morning. I'll make an effort to keep it that way for now," Pritcherman concurred. "So it's afternoon—"

"Or night."

"Night's probably better. You know, in the dark. Say 7 p.m.?"

"We add fifteen minutes for each day of the week. So Tuesday is 7:15, Wednesday is 7:30—"

"You realize that means Sunday isn't until 8:30?"

"Too late for you, old man?" I teased.

"We'll see who can't cut staying up late, punk," P ragged me back. "Memorial Park is . . . is . . . how about, the fruit stand?"

"Fruit stand?"

"Yeah. You know. I'll meet you at the fruit stand."

"Fine." I didn't really care. "What about Zach? When do I move?"

"As soon as we're done eating. You get moved back in and check on whether you were visited in your absence. Then you work on Zachary."

"What more can I do about her? You have to find the Dean. Surely he knows something. All this sneaking around makes me sick," I confided.

"Just another example of the problem with the slippery slope we've allowed our government to slide down."

"Yeah. But I'd thought of it as a bit more benign—"

"You mean, other than killing your parents? That type of benign?" Pritcherman lowered his voice to barely audible and began his monologue.

"Look, government PRT is rapidly accelerating down that slippery slope . . . and we–the American people–are the ones who allowed it. Not only allowed it, but authorized it. We freely gave away our constitutional rights at the ballot box and in our courts. We've allowed all branches of government to follow suit. We spent the better part of the twentieth century fighting communism and totalitarian governments, only to defeat them and subsequently relinquish the very democracy we expected them to implement.

"What makes this country great, Quinton? Or what made it great? I'll tell you. We specifically enumerate the rights we, as individuals, have and those we don't want the government to have. And we maintain a healthy skepticism of that government in the form of our various and sundry constitutional checks and balances. At least we did until we stopped being vigilant and found cute ways to get around that prolix document.

"All three branches were supposed to be in a constant state of conflict. Sure, one is more powerful for a while, then another. But the balance is always restored. Did I say *is?* I meant to say it *used to be.*" He took a large gulp of soda before continuing. "We let them pass legislation or establish executive regulations, and then let the courts get away with not striking them down. Or we allowed ourselves to get just as burned when they should have passed something and didn't.

"Are you following me?"

"Yes," although I did not admit that I was having difficulty keeping up with the argument. I decided not to interrupt.

"Look at our privacy," P railed on. "We're having to sit in a public bar to avoid being overheard or observed too much, drinking taxed beverages that someone else decided aren't *good* for us, whatever *good* means." Elbows resting on the tabletop, with the index and middle fingers of both hand, he signed quotation marks around the word "good" in the space between us. "Who gets to decide what's *good* anyway?

"Whatever happened to the Declaration's *of the people* or *by the people?* I don't recall voting for taxes on soda or junk food. I rather enjoy a good, greasy burger every now and then. What happened to *all things in moderation?* And another thing! Who gave my government permission to see all my personal data, like DNA, credit cards–*damn! I used a credit card*–and—"

"What?"

"Oh, I bought pizza for everyone in the OR this morning and used a credit card to pay for it," P was becoming enraged. "That rat-bastard will know and add the tax on now."

Pausing for several moments, all the while looking up in the general direction of the ceiling, he finally looked me in the eyes. His eyes penetrated me to my core.

"They know everything about us, Q. *Everything.* Did we vote for that? *No!* We gave it up–allowed it to be confiscated from us–in the name of homeland security, or convenience, or whatever. Make no mistake, we freely and willingly permitted that taking. So how do we get it back?"

"The genie's out of the bottle."

"Yeah, yeah, and Pandora's out of the box, too," my partner calmed down a bit. "It's just not in my nature to roll over on something like this, or anything, for that matter. Maybe this is one chance *we the people* have to get back at them?"

"But who is *them*, P?" Now I was ready to add my two cents. "That's part of the problem. *Them* isn't homogenous. *They* may ubiquitous, but they're not monolithic. We're assuming that *they*," now I was the one signing quotation marks in midair, "are one, big bureaucracy that's all in agreement with each other. Hell, half the time *they* don't have the slightest clue about what the others are doing, let alone agree with it."

"Maybe we can use that to our advantage."

"Like what?"

"What if they aren't in agreement?" P was thinking out loud. "What if, in this case, the left hand disagrees with the right hand? That happens all the time in medicine. Why couldn't it be that way in government? If it is, maybe our job is to enlighten the good guys in government about the bad guys?"

"Yeah, but how do we distinguish the good guys from the bad guys? How do we even know there *are* any good guys?"

Pritcherman, the skeptic, retorted, "Maybe they're all bad guys. Maybe they're all bad, but competing against each other for top honors. One big turf war. I know a thing or two about turf wars. Academia is full of them. After a while, nobody remembers what the issue is, only that the other guys want it, so whatever it is you oppose it. Do you have any idea what this is doing to research? All this government imposed, evidence-based medicine, bullshit?

"Even when the evidence isn't tainted by some special interest funding the research, the *evidence*," more air quotes, "changes from one study to the next. You're too young to remember the cardiopulmonary resuscitation standards from just a few decades ago. First, the *evidence* said to give one drug. If you didn't, you got penalized. Then the next study showed that same drug did harm. So now, you caught grief if you did use it.

"The very nature of science is that it changes as more and better *evidence* is discovered. And government will never, I say again, *never* be able to keep up with the rapid pace of change. How many government types do you know that even attempt to read the literature?"

"None, I'll bet," I nodded my head in agreement. "P, what about our day jobs?"

"Huh?"

"We're both spending all this time trying to figure out what's going on. Meanwhile, I'm supposed to be in medical school and you're supposed to be—"

"You're getting more education about life than you can appreciate, Q. And don't you worry about me. My practice is fine, and I'm in the midst of a research lull right now anyway. Do you recognize the irony of us justifying our freedom while the government takes it away?"

"OK. If we're going to pursue this, we need more help, don't you think?"

"You mean, bring someone else into this? *Hell, no!*" P raised his voice. "Who'd we tell anyway?"

"I don't know," I admitted. "Then, at least, we need more technological help?"

"Quinton, I was born analog and I've been trying to upgrade to digital my entire adult life, but without all that much success."

I smiled at the thought, "I supposed your brain model is analog?"

"Of course not. I didn't say I ignored the digital age. I'm just not on the latest version. You're *Life 4.0* and I'm still on version *2.0*."

"We're both pretty good at not seeing things in ourselves," I observed. "Speaking of digital, you know we never looked at the encrypted page I took from Grigsby's."

"Damn," P cursed. "There's so much to do."

"Don't forget the autopsy report, too," I added. "And the brain and the—"

"We have to get into the Dean's office."

"Do we need to do it soon?"

"Maybe—" P was interrupted by his phone. "Hello?"

As he listened, I could see his neck veins filling, so I raised my hand to try and keep his powder dry. Then the color drained from his face. "You can't find the Dean, but the campus police found his car in the staff parking lot? Jankowski doesn't impress me as a man who walks around campus all night. Did you try his home?"

Another period of silence, then he disconnected. "It appears Dean Jankowski is now *MIA*, too. What the hell is going on here, Q?"

"Good afternoon, sir," Smith addressed the Dean cheerfully. "I see Grigsby's fed you well. Are you ready to talk some more?"

"Your own probe, Doctor," Jankowski remembered back to the previous night. "I must know if you're having complications, too."

"Let's just say my probe hasn't been a problem."

"If I'm to help you, Smith, I want the truth," the Dean was insistent. "In America, I believe it is, *the truth, the whole truth, and nothing but the truth.* That is the price for my help."

Smith looked away, then at Grigsby and turned back to the Dean. "Fair enough. You have that right," she agreed.

"My probe is not active. I have no effect from it, none whatsoever."

"How can that be? Where were you when was it placed?"

"I don't think *where* is relevant."

"I do," the Dean insisted. "You see, if I'm going to trace the complications, I need all the information I can get, in order to look for commonalities. I—"

"I understand," Smith cut him off. "I'm just not at liberty to say where."

"The truth, Smith," Jankowski reiterated. "That is my price."

"Alright," Smith sighed, pausing a moment. "I don't know where, exactly. I was asleep, but it was somewhere in Europe. Possibly Poland."

"Ah, that isn't a surprise," the Dean scowled. "Most of the European probes have been placed in Poland."

Smith looked at Grigsby, "Poland for most, you say, Dean? How many have been placed that you know of?"

"Around forty, forty-two, I believe," Jankowski continued. "Of those, at least thirty were placed in Poland."

Smith continued, "How many complications in those forty or so?"

The Dean, now fidgeting in his chair, seemed uncomfortable, "I don't know, six or seven, I think. They're supposed to be sending me the charts for review."

"Dean," Smith lowered her voice. "There won't be any records coming."

"What?"

"Think about it," she whispered. "This is a clandestine operation. Do you really think they keep records of their mistakes? It's the truth that you want, isn't it? Dr. Jankowski, the NSA has no mission involving field agents–none. Their mission is to gather and analyze intelligence, not to place probes in citizens."

"But if they *are* NSA agents—"

"NSA doesn't have agents," Smith interrupted. "At least, they're not supposed to. They aren't authorized to, and we, the CIA, are trying to get to the bottom of this. Do you understand now, Viktor?"

"Have I done anything wrong, Dr. Smith?"

"This isn't about you," Smith spoke in a more normal voice. "This is about who is doing it, who authorized it, and what we can do to stop it." She looked at Grigsby again. "Will you help us do that, Dean?"

Still looking confused, the Dean took a deep breath and exhaled, "Of course."

"We also need your help in dealing with Dr. Pritcherman," Smith confided.

"Help with Pritcherman? Pritcherman is a loud, arrogant, blowhard," Dean Jankowski concluded. "But he is an incredible neurosurgeon."

"That's part of the problem. He's an obsessive-compulsive neurosurgeon. One who doesn't like things to go wrong on his service. He sees all of this as a personal affront."

"If I were his patient, I would want him to take my demise as a personal affront, Smith."

"Yes, but his snooping around may cause us problems. Can you control him?"

"No one controls Stanley J. Pritcherman, least of all, me," Jankowski was emphatic. "The best way to deal with him is to throw him off the trail. Believe me. He will not be dissuaded, only temporarily distracted."

"What about this medical student, Quinton? What do we do with him?"

"A medical student is interfering with this? Send him off on an assignment, or something," Jankowski suggested.

"It's not that easy," Smith talked softly. "I think he's working with Pritcherman."

"Working *with* him? You mean following Stanley around. No one works *with* him."

"You might be surprised by this medical student. He has a long history of being a thorn in the side of several government agencies. His parents used to work for us."

"Used to?"

"Yes," Smith was quiet for a moment. "They're dead now."

"My father was right. This is a spider's web," the Dean looked resigned.

"He was probably right about many other things, too," Smith added. "It isn't easy betraying your country's government, even when it is a communist one. It's still your country."

"He envisioned larger issues, Smith."

"So do we now, in this time," Smith looked at the Dean directly, making eye-to-eye contact. "Dr. Jankowski, what other complications are you aware of?"

At precisely 5 p.m. Pritcherman arrived at Memorial Park and stood next to an old statute of a local, but now unknown Civil War general. A short time later, a tall, thin man about age forty-five arrived from another direction. He greeted the neurosurgeon, not with a handshake, but with a long bear-hug, as if two old friends were reunited. They made small talk at first, but quickly turned to their mutual interests.

"John, I have a hospital problem," P finally broke the chit-chat. "You're the first person I thought of because of your background."

"I appreciate the call," John Abbouse returned the compliment. "I think of you often, Stanley. So what's this all about?"

Over the next thirty minutes, I listened as best I could while Pritcherman gave Abbouse an overview of everything he could think of relating to the dead homeless guy who didn't exist, the dead pathologist, Zendejas, who wasn't dead, the Georgetown resident, Smith, who isn't a Smith or even a doctor, his resident–and my friend–Zachary, and something about Dean Jankowski, who can't be located–I couldn't hear exactly–and even me.

He left out certain details, mostly due to the volume of story rather than intentional concealment. Abbouse listened intently, asking few questions, in order not to interrupt the neurosurgeon. The conversation drifted back to their wives, and soon each had tears in their eyes.

"I know you miss her," Abbouse comforted his friend, the professor. "I think of my wife every day, every minute. But we both know we have to move on."

"John, I keep being drawn back to her image," Pritcherman was gently sobbing. "Her beautiful smile, her hair. Why?"

"You're the physician. You tell me," Abbouse looked away for a minute, then back at Pritcherman. "Life has dealt us both hands with the tragedies of our wives' deaths. Everyone is given tragedy. It's how you handle it that counts. What's the saying, make lemonade from lemons?"

"You're not giving me that *physician heal thyself* line are you, John?" P sniffed and blew his nose. "Because if you are . . ." he feigned mock threat. "Marianne was my life. How do I go on?"

"Just as Beth was mine," Abbouse comforted, putting his arm around the neurosurgeon. "We honor their legacies by doing the right thing. I do it each and every day of my life, and I suspect you do, too. You're just harder on yourself than I am. Remember, my wife died six months before yours."

"I know," Pritcherman was pensive. "Help me solve this hospital issue, John. Please. Righting that wrong will help me–help us both. This could be bigger than I'm capable of handling on my own."

"I know," Abbouse agreed. "Believe me, I know."

I know, too. Because I followed Dr. Pritcherman to Memorial Park.

– Always Beware Of A Last Minute "Ringer" Joining The Game –

XV

*I*t was dark as I made my way back to Pritcherman's office. I'd packed most of my stuff in anticipation of moving, but had followed him after we returned to his office from O'Reilly's. He'd only stayed long enough to gather up a few things from his desk. His mood had changed as we walked back to the office–he became more distant, but not with me. That tipped me off, I guess. That or some other psychic reason caused me to want to follow him.

I was surprised by his chosen destination, Memorial Park. We had just talked about it in the restaurant. I followed him, but at a distance and that created the problem. While I think I caught the drift of what the two had discussed in the park, the details were lost because of the separation necessary to maintain my stealth. Now, as I left a little earlier than P and had to travel faster to beat him back, I was presented with a fair number of *whys* and one *who*.

I was also left with having to make a decision concerning whether to confront my partner, or not. What was this all about? As I finished organizing my packing, I knew I wouldn't have long to wait as P came through the inner office door, a bit slower than his usual self and more pensive, too. Not the right time, I decided and slipped out of the inner office without him even noticing, or so it seemed. As I cleared the outer door into the hall, fumbling with my suitcase and boxes, I had a strange sense of *déjà vu*, standing there in the hall, thinking about what to do next.

A short time later, I was standing at my apartment's threshold. There was a knot in my abdomen as I considered what had happened in the days of my absence. So much had happened since Zachary and I shared more than our time together. Scanning the doorbell with my phone, it appeared no one had touched the doorbell–*a good omen*, I thought. I entered and quickly looked around. Everything seemed normal. I strained to smell Zach's fragrance, hoping it lingered. I retrieved the logs and they also confirmed no activity had occurred. I breathed a sigh of relief–until I remembered being assaulted just after the logs had told me nothing was up.

I glanced into every room, then set Rupert up and had him do a survey, too. All systems said there had been no intruders. It was nearly 11 p.m. and I was wide awake. I had plenty on my plate. The first thing was to reassess how I felt about my partner, Dr. Pritcherman. I saw a different man in the park. Who was this guy, Abbouse? And Marianne? He said she divorced him, not the ultimate separation. Did this change anything?

"Major, get my *Go Team* up and have them ready to travel in one hour," Bitterman barked his command.

"Yes, sir. Destination?"

"I'll handle that, Major."

"One hour, sir," as the General hung up.

Bitterman was drumming on his desk again, plotting a plan of action. Find Smith, Grigsby and Jankowski, not necessarily in that order, he decided. Depending on what he found, there would be changes to consider and contingencies to plan. Many rollover effects, no doubt. He walked into the other room adjoining his office that doubled as a bedroom, given the amount of time he was there. He changed into a camouflage uniform and headed out.

It was 1 a.m. when he climbed into the cockpit of an attack helicopter, already loaded with his *Go Team* of ten, the rotor spinning at full idle speed. As he took his seat behind the pilot and latched his seatbelt, the helicopter ascended into the dark sky. An hour later, they touched down on the University Hospital helipad, cleared to land as a supposed special organ procurement flight. The team disembarked without a word and descended the back staircase to the basement.

Bitterman wanted to search the morgue himself for any remaining evidence. After satisfying himself there was nothing of substance there, they went back to the rooftop helipad and were airborne again, this time heading for a building only a short distance away in the warehouse district. Smith's brain slice switch, the probe, and microchips were gone. Bitterman assumed they were in Pritcherman's possession. Those, and the encrypted message Grigsby left for them to find, should keep the civilians busy for a while, he surmised.

The team headed straight to the building, aided by GPS coordinates, and, within only a few minutes, they had formed a perimeter around the building. This was accomplished silently and efficiently, with practiced military precision. The team leader and several others burst through the door only to find an empty room with a smart phone sitting on the couch. General Bitterman went directly to that phone, leaving it untouched on the couch, and took out his own and dialed a number in the speed dial directory. The phone on the couch rang. Bitterman turned away as he disconnected the call without speaking.

Pritcherman was right about one thing–being around him all the time *would* drive me crazy. So what did the revelations from the episode in the park alter? It certainly gave me a different perspective on my neurosurgical partner's faux macho image. All the bravado and swagger was not only for show, as he had admitted, but it was a defense mechanism as well. He's afraid of letting anyone get too close again. That explained in part why he chose to throw me out.

In my search for the truth, not much changed in terms of the objective. I had the microchips and probe. P had the wrong-side brain slice along with the encrypted note from Grigsby's apartment. One remaining objective was to find out who was behind the homeless guy's death and why. The objective hadn't changed at all, but the stakes were now much larger.

I have to get Zachary back, but how? Who's got her?

Finding that out would also help solve the mystery of what happened to her. Why the seizures? They have to be new–since she disappeared and reappeared. A new problem coming right after her return means the two are connected. But how? And Pritcherman? How does his memory quest fit in and who is Abbouse? Why was he being so secretive about him? Who is he?

"Rupert, I'm leaving you in charge of a computer search on him."

"Who sir?" Rupert intoned without emotion.

"Who, indeed," I mused. "John Abbouse. Run standard, DoD, and any other special searches you can think of."

"Standard and DoD searches. You know I don't think."

"Well, it's high time you start," I laughed. "Use some of that artificial intelligence, create an algorithm or something, but find out who this guy is."

"Find Abbouse," Rupert echoed. "And you, sir?"

"I am sleeping on it. Rupert, I have complete confidence in you."

"Well-placed confidence," Rupert replied, with a hint of arrogance, I thought.

"Goodnight, Q."

Sleeping always gives me a new perspective on things, so I turned down the covers of my own bed for the first time in a while. In the early morning hours, I stretched and wandered over to a window, staring out at the black stillness of the night. The only sound I heard was the muffled sound of a helicopter on the roof of University Hospital nearby.

"OK, gentlemen," Calhoun convened his CIA analysts early on this summer morning. "I assume you all know about the confirmation that NSA has gone rogue and that General Bitterman appears to be the leader. We don't know if it goes higher up their chain of command, but I'm going to assume that it does. Worst case planning, guys. So, tell me your assessments?"

"Bill," an anonymous analyst spoke first. "I also assume they know we're looking at them."

"Affirmative."

"So, we need to think about what the NSA boys are thinking about doing."

"They have several alternatives, and none would appeal to me if I were in their shoes," another sleuth chimed in.

"They could go after one or all of our people—"

"Not to mention collateral personnel," another added.

"Right. Who knows what they're thinking about this neurosurgeon and medical student."

"Who do they think turned on them, Bill?"

"Well," Calhoun advised, "they must think Smith and Grigsby, for sure, and I'd bet Jankowski, too."

"Did Jankowski come over to us?"

"I'm not sure yet," Calhoun continued. "That was Smith's mission," he paused.

"What does NSA do if they find them? They could certainly eliminate them, but that would attract attention and cause too many aftershocks. They could hide them somewhere."

"Even Bitterman's not crazy enough to kill them," Calhoun suggested.

"Are you sure? Desperate times call for desperate measures," another analyst proposed. "They could also try to turn them to their side. They'd need something to bribe them with or hold over their heads. A reason for them to turn back."

"Are Smith and Grigsby clean?" Someone called out. "We know Jankowski's susceptible. Tell us what you know about them, Bill."

"All things are possible in this game, but I don't think Smith and Grigsby are susceptible to being turned by the NSA."

"Even though they were assigned to NSA?"

"Especially because they were assigned," the Assistant Director insisted. "Grigsby's former special forces, now going to medical school to further that career path. He's got no blemishes anywhere. Great family, great West Point record. And Smith. Any of you recall the incident in Libya a few years back? The lead on that triumph was Smith. She's also a lawyer. That means she's smart enough to know the NSA's in way over their head and in major deep legal hot water. Why would she want any part of that?"

"More than deep water, Bill. I'd say deep shit." No one laughed.

"OK, so let's assume our two aren't touchable," some offered. "Jankowski's the variable here. You think he's already flipped to us? If so, that means he's susceptible to being flipped again. What could they offer him to turn him back to NSA?"

"What do *we* have that could dissuade him?"

"Look," Calhoun was clearly exasperated. "If we can get them all out of the NSA's grasp, I have no doubt we can control the situation."

"So we have to extract them?"

"Yes."

"But who—I mean—how many are we talking about? There are more ramifications to consider."

"Aren't there always?"

"We haven't considered who else is in on Bitterman's scheme," someone offered in from the back. "Someone's been putting in a lot of hardware into people's heads over on the continent. That means the General has medical and logistical help, not to mention field assets. To pull this off would take a shitload of people. And for what reason? We haven't even scratched the surface on that yet—why not? What's the motivation for NSA doing this? What do we know about Bitterman's European agents?"

"Not much," Calhoun conceded. "I'm hoping Jankowski can help us with that, since it's where he became one of our assets years ago. Maybe he still knows people there. I won't know until I talk to him . . . or to Smith . . . or somebody."

"Bill, don't you think the Director should be informed now?"

"Already done," Calhoun informed the room.

"And he's behind what we're discussing?"

"He's the one looking for options," Bill continued. "What I'm hearing is we need to get them under our control as soon as possible. Anything else?"

"Yeah," came another anonymous questioner. "What about the collaterals? The crazy neurosurgeon and the kid?"

"This has the potential to really spin out of control. Way too many problems and effects," Calhoun sighed.

"We have a situation here, sir," Smith spoke quietly into a new smart phone. Grigsby sat behind the steering wheel in the front seat of the nondescript sedan, Smith in the back, sitting to the left of Dean Jankowski. This time, the vehicle was their sanctuary. "We're heading for Sierra, Hotel, Tango, One now. Any chance of a meeting?"

On hearing Sierra, Hotel, Tango, One, Grigsby turned off the freeway and onto a downtown street as the sun began to rise. After a few blocks, he pulled into an underground parking garage and found a vacant space near a staircase.

"Welcome home, Dean," Grigsby murmured. "At least for a while. You'll like this place. It has great toys."

"Mr. Grigsby. I'm more interested in solving all this than playing with toys," Jankowski was rather annoyed.

"By toys, sir, I mean communications and research potential," as the three entered a six-room apartment.

"Oh, those kinds of toys. Good," the Dean seemed pleased. "Smith's already said she didn't know anything about who is doing this in Europe. Do you, Mr. Grigsby?"

"I follow orders, sir. I'm not a policymaker."

"Come now, Mr. Grigsby," Jankowski needled him. "You're in medical school. Doesn't any of this pique your curiosity?"

"It does, but—"

"We're authorized to wait here," Smith cut him off. "And Dean Jankowski," turning to look at him, "We need to keep a low profile. We'll be having visitors soon. Until then, we have work to do. You are with us on that?"

Without hesitation, the Dean answered, "Yes."

Sitting at a large conference table about an hour later, "Honesty, Dr. Smith. You promised honesty. Your probe. Tell me more about what you know."

Smith motioned Grigsby to the table as she took a seat opposite the Dean. She stared at him for at least two minutes, both playing eye tag before she spoke."Dr. Jankowski, what I'm about to tell you is sensitive. Do you understand that?"

"Of course, I—"

"By understand, I mean you realize there is no going back once you know. There are costs."

"What costs, Smith?"

"You're one of us now," Smith moved closer to him across the table. "To tell anyone outside, well, let's just say I would be extremely disappointed."

"I'm a team player," Jankowski snipped. "What do you think I'm going to do? Call General Bitterman?"

"No," Smith smiled to lighten the mood. "But I have to make perfectly clear what the situation is," looking at Grigsby, pausing for a few seconds. "You see, Dean. My probe isn't working."

"You said it wasn't activated," the Dean seemed confused.

"Oh it's not," she smiled again. "And it can't be activated because there is no real probe."

"I don't understand. You said it was placed in Europe.

I—"

"It's a ruse, sir," she continued. "To make them think I was completely under their control as you can see, I'm not," patting his hand on the table. "Were the General or others to find out, well, that's why I would be extremely disappointed. Understand now?"

"Completely," the lamp of knowledge was now lit in Jankowski. "That may be helpful to us figuring out why there are complications."

"Explain."

"You can still act as if the probe is real," the Dean maintained. "You may be able to gather information because they think your probate is real."

"I don't think you fully understand yet, Dean," Smith patted his hands again. "Bitterman thought it was real. He wasn't behind that part of this. Now he knows, or will if he doesn't already."

"Oh, I hadn't thought that through," Jankowski frowned. "Bitterman will know you're compromised—"

"And come after me—"

"And me, too," the Dean concluded.

"And me," Grigsby added.

"We're all in this together," Smith looked back and forth between the two. "Anything else you want to know, Dr. Jankowski?"

"Sandy!" Pritcherman screamed from OR 6. "Who's helping me today on my craniotomy?"

"You usually have a resident, Dr. Pritcherman," the charge nurse responded. "Didn't one come with you?"

"No, not today, sorry."

Sorry? She exhaled, realized his change in mood had persisted into another day. "Should I—"

"Can you do me a favor and call the neurosurgical floor and get Frick and Frack again," as he gowned and gloved up. "It's after 7 a.m. They ought to be here by now. Probably trying to avoid me," laughing into his mask. "I don't really need any help on this procedure, but maybe they'll learn something, huh?"

Sandra ducked out of the room, shaking her head again. *Please let him stay this way*, she prayed.

A few minutes after her call, the two second-year medical students arrived and began to scrub like old pros. She directed them to OR 6, whispering to them that Pritcherman seemed OK again today. Gowned and gloved, with their backs the two much-relieved second-years nimbly pushed through the door to the operating room. Old pros indeed.

"Ladies and gentlemen, I give you again . . . Frick and Frack," Pritcherman joshed, while bowing and sweeping his hand out to the side as a way of introduction. "I trust you two slept well, since neurosurgery generally takes several hours and requires a well-rested, focused mind. Please note, prior to your arrival, this patient had been put to sleep, his head shaved and external landmarks appropriately identified to guide us to our destination today . . . the right parietal and temporal regions of this poor soul's brain. Unfortunately, entering these regions will most likely impact his memory–dramatically and negatively impact it, I fear.

"Also note, EMG monitoring of his cranial nerves has been placed, his head secured in a Mayfield pin-head holder and Betadine prep and sterile drapes placed."

Turning his head and looking askance, "Do either of you have you any idea what I just said?" Without waiting for a response, the neurosurgeon continued, "Tell me what you know about memory, gentlemen."

"No . . . better yet, let me tell *you* what *I* know about it," chuckling out loud. "First, let's open the calvarium and get down to the brain, gentlemen," P advised as he quickly made a ten centimeter, slashing incision with a scalpel through the scalp and carried the incision down through the galeal muscle.

"Today, we'll obtain hemostasis with Raney clips and we'll retract the scalp flap," as he deftly pulled the skin flap just created up and over the medial head. He next drilled four burr holes in the bony skull and connected the holes with a bone saw called a *craniotome*, creating a rectangular bone piece that he removed and threw on the back table. "We'll put that back later, guys. Frick, have you ever used bone wax?"

"Well, I—"

"Don't worry, son. I'm not gonna have you do anything," as he rubbed the remaining bone edges. Without looking up, he extended his gloved hands, "Gelfoam." The scrub nurse slapped a large piece of frothy sponge material into his left hand and he skillfully packed it around the bone. "Ah, the dura mater. What's that Frack?"

"The dura mater is the—"

"So formal," P interrupted. "It's the damn tough fibrous material that keeps the brain in and the bad stuff out. Right?"

"Well, I—"

"Notice how irritated the surface of the brain looks here," pointing to an area of the right temporo-parietal region of the brain, now visible after having opened the *dura* with a pair of surgical scissors. Sighing, he continued, "that's the problem. That irritation hides a tumor below. Bring in the microscope, please."

"*Please?*" muttered the circulating OR nurse, raising her eyebrows. The scrub nurse and anesthesiologist made eye contact. There was obvious consensus of thought about the neurosurgeon's newfound demeanor.

"Good morning, Dr. Pritcherman," I announced as I pushed through the operating room doors. "May I observe, too?"

My neurosurgical partner seemed surprised by my arrival, "Of course, Mr. Quinton. I'm sure your second-year colleagues won't mind. But you'd better know your stuff," motioning them away from the patient's head.

Pritcherman had moved to the operating microscope, a two-headed teaching 'scope and motioned me to the other head. I sat on the stool opposite my mentor. The teaching microscope allows the surgeon to view the operating field through one side and an observer to see the microscopic surgery as it takes place through the other. The beauty of the microscope is the two persons sitting could talk in a way others couldn't hear, with their heads buried close to the microscope head and only inches away from the other.

"That you, sir?" I loudly intoned before lowering my voice. "I need to talk to you about Zachary," I whispered.

"Look at the brain through your side of the microscope," P bellowed, while fiddling with the focusing knobs. After a few moments, the old Pritcherman emerged momentarily as he stood up and screamed, "Damn it Mr. Quinton! You've messed up the focus. Can't you touch anything without screwing it up?"

"I'm sorry, I—"

"Mr. Pemberton," the mercurial neurosurgeon continued. "I need you to go down to radiology and find this patient's latest MRI. His life may depend on it. And Mr. Jenkins. You run to the laboratory and tell them I want the latest C-RP . . . stat! Do you both understand?"

One of the second-years mumbled, "Way to go, Quinton. Screwing up again," as they ran out the door.

"Who the hell are Pemberton and Jenkins?"

"Quinton," P was grinning even through his mask. He motioned me to resume sitting behind the microscope as he assumed his position, whispering, "They're your fellow medical students. You want to tell me something. I figured no one else needs to hear it. Sent them on a wild goose chase."

"That's their names? I never heard anyone call them that. How do you know?"

"Do we blow the door?"

"No need," General Bitterman replied. "They're friendlies. No need to attract any more attention than necessary. When we get there, take up a covert perimeter, repeat, covert. No one obvious. You're with me when I enter. Copy?"

"Covert perimeter. I'm with you, sir."

The helicopter descended into an open area next to another nondescript warehouse. Without words, the team disembarked and took up positions around the building. In a few seconds, none was visible. The General and his subordinate exited the craft and headed to the front door. They found it locked, with a keyless electronic access point.

"Open it," the General commanded.

In seconds, the commando released the door and the two walked through, surveying the entry hall. There were three doors off the hall. They quickly inspected the two closest rooms, finding them vacant. The General's companion crouched next to the third door as the General entered, following him quickly.

"General Bitterman. Am I glad to see you," Zendejas called out as John and Jeremy looked up from their computers. Zachary was lying on the intensive care bed, awake, non-verbal.

"You're the only one, Doctor," Bitterman replied under his breath. "This is the surgical resident you told me about?"

"Yes. She's—"

"Is she still having seizures?"

"More frequently than before, General," Zendejas seemed perturbed at the General's interruption. Jeremy snorted as well.

Bitterman ignored both responses. "We have to get her out of here."

"General, she's not ready to travel. Certainly not long distances. What if she has a seizure en rou—? En route to where? There may be a bad outcome if we—"

"You leave the where to me, Doctor. If she has more seizures, you give her whatever it is you give her to stop them. Bad outcome, Doctor? You think there's going to be a good outcome if you stay here?"

"It's not that simple," Zendejas protested. "She's been having seizures every—"

"Look Doctor," Bitterman cut him off. "You have no idea what danger you're in staying here. I do. So you give her whatever it takes, but you have her ready to travel–and it will be done by helicopter–in thirty minutes. Got it?"

"I will not transport Dr. Zachary as long as I consider her unstable," Zendejas stood his ground.

"Not stable, Doctor?" Bitterman walked to within inches of his face, held that position for a few seconds, then turned away.

"Captain."

"Sir!" moving towards Bitterman.

"Shoot the patient."

"Sir?"

"You heard me. That's an order. Shoot this patient," pointing to Zachary.

Zendejas jumped to her side and Jeremy laid across her trunk. The normally quiet John stood up and grunted. "You will have to shoot me first," Zendejas protested.

"So be it. Captain, shoot Dr. Zendejas *and* Dr. Zachary," the General did not appear to be bluffing.

"You see Dr. Zendejas. Nothing will get in the way of our mission. Nothing. Not you . . . and certainly not a disabled resident physician who is of little use to me."

"Of little use? Use to you? Give me twenty-four hours to get her stabilized."

"Agreed," Bitterman motioned to the Captain to lower his weapon. "Twenty-four hours, and not a minute longer. You are endangering the mission, Doctor. *You, Doctor.* Twenty-four hours!" The General turned and exited with his team member.

As they left, Zendejas, Jeremy and John all instinctively relaxed, though the perspiration continued. "Would he have shot her?" Jeremy asked Zendejas.

"Without a doubt," the pathologist replied. "Can you imagine the consequences?" Zendejas slowly walked around Zachary, thinking, not just about her, but about what had just happened. "Gentlemen, we need help. I'm guessing the Dean is no longer an option, since we haven't seen or heard from him in a while. He wasn't much help to begin with."

"Chief, I'd say we're on our own," John offered.

"Yes," Zendejas agreed. "That changes everything."

"Well, this isn't part of my contract," Jeremy stated flatly, rising as if preparing to leave.

"We're in this together, whether you like it or not," Zendejas advised his subordinate. "If you think you can just walk out on General Bitterman, I'd say he made his solution quite clear earlier. I don't know if that Captain would have acted on his order or not, but I'm damned sure I don't want to test that premise."

"So what do you suggest?"

"We need help. Neurosurgical help," Zendejas sighed. "That means we need to find Dr. Pritcherman."

"Pritcherman?" John raised his eyebrows.

"Pritcherman."

"What's so important you have to interrupt me ruining this man's life, not to mention all his memories?" Pritcherman spoke softly to me. Holding out his right hand to the scrub nurse, but without looking up, "Microdissection forceps . . . and give me the micropolar cautery, too."

"I know what happened to Zachary," I blurted out.

"Softly now, Mr. Quinton," P cautioned, working skillfully. "Dr. Chesney, it's time to give him the *Decadron* and *Mannitol*, please."

Lowering my voice, I couldn't contain my emotions, "P, they kidnapped her, then she was released, acting differently. Next, she had a seizure. Don't you see?"

"What I see is one large tumor right in this poor soul's memory area," grunting and shaking his head, while beginning to dissect around the tumor. "What do you mean about Zachary?"

"She's different and she's having seizures because," pausing and taking a deep breath, "I think they put a probe in her."

Pritcherman looked up from the microscope for the first time and stopped his dissection. "God Almighty," he exclaimed quietly. "She had a flat affect when you talked to her?"

"Yes."

"And you said she didn't seem to know who you were, right?"

"Correct."

"The bastards put a probe in to erase her memory," P sneered. "Or do something. What the hell are they trying to accomplish, messing with someone's memory? We talked about this before, but I couldn't fathom it. Don't they know you can't just put in a probe without *sequelae*."

"*Sequelae?*"

"Consequences. Complications, Q. Don't these morons understand it will affect not only memories, but the serotonin, dopamine and norepinephrine systems, and a whole slew of other problems only the devil knows for sure? Seizures aren't the only problems, I'm guessing.

"Yeah. I'm sure they were thinking about the health effects on their victims," I sarcastically scoffed. "Since Zachary had nothing to do with this—"

"Are you sure of that?"

"I'm sure," I was emphatic. "Zachary wasn't even involved until I dragged her into it. She did it for me. We're more than friends. *Damn government.* They think they can just intrude on anyone at any time. They've injured my girlfriend and—"

"My resident. And—"

"Dr. Pritcherman," I was deadly serious. "This cannot stand. We have to fix her. Could you take the probe out?"

"Probably, but who knows if that would fix her? Besides, who knows what else they did to her," P seemed exasperated. "And there's another small problem."

"What?"

"She's not exactly available to take to the OR, Q. Where the hell is she?"

"*Do you two think you could stop the teaching exercise long enough to finish this man's surgery?*" The scrub nurse was oblivious to the conversation, but not to the long pause in Pritcherman's surgical skills.

"Sorry," P muttered without looking up. "Give me the Cavitron ultrasonic aspirator. Let's get this tumor out and send a section to pathology, even though I know what it is."

Turning his attention back to me, "Q, we have to find that girl–Zachary–your friend."

"Lover."

"My resident. You get the hell out of here and find out where she is. Do your computer stuff. But don't do anything else until I'm finished here. Understand?"

"Perfectly, sir," I answered. "P, one other thing."

"What else?"

"I ran a search," lowering my voice further. "Who's John Abbouse?"

Cautious Bill Calhoun strode into the room–briskly, but without any air of panic or crisis. Studying the occupants and the layout of the room, he motioned the others to the conference table, taking a seat at the head. As Smith, Grigsby, and Jankowski sat down, he addressed them, "Glad to see you've settled in. We have a few things to discuss. Dr. Jankowski, I know Dr. Smith has impressed upon you the sensitivity of this mission, but I'm here in part to convey an even deeper sense of the problems and to assure you, those at the highest level of our government are aware of you, the issues at hand, and have confidence we can arrive at a solution. First though, do you have any questions of me?"

The Dean shook his head to indicate that he did not.

"Let me be clear, Dr. Jankowski," Calhoun continued. "We consider you an integral part of our team and critical to discovering the purpose of these probes, how to fix them, and to prevent any more from being placed. Is that clear, sir?"

"Yes," Jankowski nodded. "Tell me why, Mr. Calhoun. Why are they doing this?"

"That sir, is a damn good question," Calhoun sighed. "We have no idea. But," he paused for emphasis, "no matter what the reason, they are violating their mission statement and the laws of the United States."

"Not to mention their medical ethics—"

"Not to mention their humanity and ethics," the Assistant Director added. "My assignment is to shut down this operation completely. In order to do that, we have to better understand exactly what they are doing. You are our medical expert and I expect expert advice. Are we clear, Dr. Jankowski?"

"Very clear."

"Let's start by having you summarize for us what you know about the medical aspects of this, and feel free to include any speculations you might have, but please tell us what is fact and what is your medical speculation." Calhoun looked at Smith, then the ceiling and back, once more, to Smith. Smith subtly nodded her head.

"First, let me set the scope," Jankowski began. "Factually, we know there are forty-two known probe patients, most placed in Europe, but the timeframe of the placements is not known. I can speculate that it occurred over a relatively short period of time, likely within six months or so. That means more than one physician placing the probes, as I think that number is large enough to exceed one person's capacity."

"You said *physician*, Doctor," Smith asked. "Is that fact?"

"I cannot imagine a non-physician placing these probes. Not only must they have been placed by a physician, but a physician with intimate knowledge of neuroanatomy–such as a neurosurgeon or pathologist. Maybe even a neurologist like myself, but not likely. We are not interventionists.

"That answers the skill set, but not something that has bothered me from the beginning. I can understand someone violating his ethical obligations. But to want to do this implies a new knowledge of neurophysiology and of computers interfacing with the brain—"

"We agree, Doctor. " Calhoun interrupted. "And that is bothersome to us as well, but speculating as to their motives—"

"No, Mr. Calhoun," Jankowski countered. "I'm not speculating as to their motives, but as to their new scientific knowledge. This is way beyond the current level of our science. Which leads me to question. Maybe they *aren't* as knowledgeable as we think about medicine."

"Are you saying whoever did this, isn't medically knowledgeable?"

"I'm saying that *any* physician would have to be naive or insane to place these probes without considering the unintended side effects."

"Or not a physician," Grigsby interjected. "Look, I'm a medical student. So I have some knowledge of this kind of thing. I also can't imagine this happening, whether a physician *or* a non-physician. But since it was done, that implies stupidity or insanity, not naiveté."

"Mr. Grigsby is correct," Jankowski agreed. "It points to someone with an incredible motivation to take such a risk, a huge leap of scientific faith. Who has that motivation, Mr. Calhoun?"

"Another excellent but currently unanswerable question," Calhoun responded. "Facts, people. What other *facts* do we have?"

"Not all of the probe patients have had complications," Jankowski continued. "Only about six or seven. I'm told there are other complications besides seizure activity."

"Where are all the other probe patients?" Smith asked. "Not just the ones with complications, but the others. Have they already been tasked by their handlers?"

"A real Pandora's box," the Assistant Director concluded. "To get to the others, we have to get to the leaders. That's not on your plate, Dr. Jankowski," he said, although he was looking at Smith as he spoke. He returned his attention to Jankowski, "Anything else, Doctor?"

"What if the others are already dispersed? Already sent out?"

"Good point, Doctor, but still not your issue." Again looking at Smith, he ordered, "Find out about the others. Get an analyst team together." Smith silently acknowledged her acceptance of the task.

"Where is Dr. Zachary? The last time I knew of her, she was with Dr. Zendejas and his group," the Dean inquired. "Where is Zendejas? Find him and you will find Dr. Zachary. Am I correct?"

"You are," Calhoun stated clearly. "Again, not on your plate."

"Yes it is, Mr. Calhoun," the Dean disagreed. "Dr. Zachary is a resident at my university, under my charge and I'm also involved in her care. Care she didn't need until all of this started. I feel a moral and ethical obligation to her. That is why I suggest—"

"Suggest?" Calhoun frowned.

"You're right, Mr. Calhoun," Jankowski raised his voice. "*I insist* we find Dr. Pritcherman and have him remove her probe. Get him involved in this. He is the one best qualified to deal with her complications."

"Pritcherman?"

"Pritcherman," the Dean reiterated.

"Pritcherman," sighed Smith.

– Never Forget That When Playing The Game, Every Move Has Its Consequences –

XVI

I'll tell you about Abbouse . . . *later*," Pritcherman seemed stunned at me bringing up his name.

"*Now, P!*" I was adamant.

"Not here," P whispered, finishing removal of the tumor.

"Get this to pathology," Pritcherman said, waving indiscriminately to the circulating OR nurse, as he dropped the tumor into a surgical basin. "Quinton," P continued in hushed tones as he proceeded to close. "What do Zachary and the dead patient have in common?"

"I don't know, but—"

"There must be something," P wrinkled his forehead.

"They both have probes and both have seizures. What's the link?"

"Hell, yes," P exclaimed, then lowering his voice again. "That's why they sent him to me. I thought it was to do a resection of the seizure site. Now, I'm guessing they wanted me to remove his probe."

"Would that stop the seizures?"

"That seems to be their thinking, but I'm not so sure. Seems like an awful lot of experimenting with people going on here," P sighed. "You know, free-lancing."

"Or desperation," I countered.

"Let's close up this guy's head. Meet me tonight at seven for dinner at the office. We need to flesh out more on what they're up to on memory."

Pritcherman quickly irrigated the surgical wound and closed the *dura* with 4-0 *Nurolon* sutures. He packed the site with more Gelfoam–which the body would eventually absorb–and then replaced the bone previously removed and secured it in place with titanium screws and plates. Next, he closed the overlying muscular layer with 4-0 *Vicryl* sutures, and closed the final skin later with staples. On completion, he stood up and bellowed, "Quinton, scrub out and get out of my sight!"

"We have twenty-four hours," the normally passive Zendejas paced as he spoke. "Any ideas on how to get Pritcherman?"

"He won't come voluntarily. Of that you can be sure," Jeremy responded.

"So, you're saying we have to kidnap him?" John queried.

"Or trick him into coming," Zendejas offered. "The best place for that is from the OR."

"With so many people around?"

"All the better," the pathologist concluded. "They're all so used to that "loud-mouthed neurosurgeon they won't pay any attention if he protests and makes a scene. Besides, a little pharmaceutical help may be in order."

"Drugging a doctor in the OR? You've got to be joking," John frowned.

"Not in the OR, but in the dressing room or some adjoining area," the leader continued. "I'm thinking out loud. I can't be seen, so it would be you two."

"Naturally," Jeremy frowned now. "We do the dirty work, you take the credit."

"Now, now," Zendejas raised his hand. "Someone has to monitor Dr. Zachary. Remember, they think I'm dead."

"Not a bad idea," John scowled, looking over at Jeremy.

"Gentlemen, I seem to remember a small matter of monies not being deposited to each of your accounts until I'm satisfied," the rotund chief stood, speaking more forcefully. "Not to mention that my superiors know your families well. Are we clear?"

"Clear as always, your Excellency," Jeremy intentionally poured on the Caribbean accent. "So is that our plan? To take him from the OR area?"

"When?" John asked.

"I'll find out when his next case is," Zendejas dialed his phone. After a few questions, he hung up and turned back to the two subordinates. "He has a case tomorrow morning at seven. It appears things are coming together, eh, gentlemen?"

"Maybe there's a better way," John mused.

"I'm listening."

"The way to attract Pritcherman is to use the medical student for bait. You know how he's protective of his service and his underlings."

"Interesting," Zendejas looked back and forth between the two without speaking for a minute. "Snatching the student, what's his name–Quinton, isn't it–ought to be easier than a screaming neurosurgeon, don't you think?"

"Much."

Jeremy looked up and said, "And more expendable."

Smith was pacing about the living room. "When's Jankowski getting up? Hasn't he been asleep long enough? Does anybody really sleep past noon?"

Grigsby shrugged, while flipping through a medical textbook.

"Check on him."

Grigsby wandered down the hall to an unmarked bedroom and knocked on the door without answer. After knocking several times, he looked back at Smith who was staring at him. She motioned with her head for him to enter. Grigsby quietly opened the door, only to discover an empty room. Running back to the living room. he shouted to Smith, "*Where the hell is he?*"

"You were in this room all morning, right?" Smith demanded. "We took shifts sleeping, but this room was never unoccupied. So he had to get out another way. That weasel of a—"

"Your ass is in deep shit."

"*Our asses*, Grigsby," Smith countered. "Let's find him and both keep them," as she headed for the door. "Why would he leave?"

"I'm guessing to find Zachary or Pritcherman," Grigsby surmised. "He didn't seem too happy with Calhoun's explanation about it not being on his plate."

"I hate freelancers. Damn civilians," Smith fumed. She stood at the door and turned to Grigsby, "We need a plan before we go out looking for him and exposing ourselves as well. Thoughts?"

"I think one of us should stay here. In case he comes back or Calhoun does."

"You stay," Smith agreed. "I'll work my way back to the hospital first. Minimal contact so we don't attract attention. Agreed?"

"Yes," Grigsby walked back to the table as Smith left. He waited a few moments to make sure Smith didn't return. When he was sure she wasn't coming back, he took out his phone and speed-dialed.

"Sir, Smith's out looking for Dean Jankowski. He's somehow no longer under our control." There was a pause while the remote party talked. "No sir, Calhoun is not aware of this." Grigsby listened, then responded, "Yes, sir. This is between the two of us."

"Quinton, make a salad," Pritcherman was shouting as he exited the bathroom. "Tonight we visit the Dean's office," swiftly throwing three rib eyes on the grill. "We're having steak and baked potatoes."

"But I—"

"Don't give me that vegan crap. We need to be manly men, Q. Protein, meat-eater stuff."

"Why don't we just eat it raw and really get back to our roots?"

"Do I detect sarcasm, Quinton?"

"You detect me needing a few answers before I—"

"Yeah, yeah. All in good time."

"Now, P. Who is John Abbouse?" I wasn't going anywhere until P gave me some answers. "And how come you're grilling three steaks? I can't eat that much."

"Why don't you ask *him* who he is?"

"Ask who?"

"Abbouse," P said. "He should be here any minute. Oh, the third steak is for him. Medium OK for you?

"Damn it, Dr. Pritcherman!" I shouted. "You've got to quit all this sneaky stuff. If we're partners—"

The outer office doorbell signaled Abbouse's arrival.

"Seven o'clock. Right on time. Can you get that, Q? The steaks need seasoning."

I sighed loudly, wanting to refuse, then realizing there's no arguing with P. "Sure, why not? What else could happen?"

"I wouldn't say that to John," P cautioned.

As I walked to the outer office I wasn't sure what P's last comment meant. I opened the outer office door and was immediately shoved back into the outer office and thrown up against a wall. Before I knew it, I was handcuffed and being frisked.

"What the—"

"Sorry, son," Abbouse was all business. "I have to be very comfortable with you and make sure you are who you say you are," as he pulled out my wallet and removed my I.D. and lone credit card, then emptied my other pockets.

"Oh, yeah?" I protested. "And just who the hell are you?"

As Abbouse completed his pat down of me, he directed me toward the inner office door, opening it and pushing me through. "Is this the medical student you were telling me about Stanley?"

"Geez, John," P exclaimed. "Such melodrama. I told you to let him know who you were, not scare the shit out of him. Yes, he's the one."

"Sorry, kid." Abbouse apologized as he removed the 'cuffs. "By the way, Stan, he's not wired but he does have a few things of interest."

I shook my wrists out of defiance more than anything and stared at Abbouse. "Well?"

"Well, what?"

"I asked who you are. I meant it. Who are you and what were you two talking about in the park? I saw you there, hugging and then crying. Something about Marianne and—"

"Those are our wives," P softly interjected. "John's wife was a patient of mine and both our wives were in chemotherapy together."

"I thought you said she divorced you?"

"I did. I lied. I don't like talking about it to just anyone," P looked away as a tear trickled down his cheek. "She was my life for over thirty years. Until—"

"Stanley really helped me through my depression after my wife died," Abbouse could tell the emotion was getting to P.

"We helped each other," my neurosurgical partner corrected him. "John, did you bring the onions I asked for?"

"No, please," I pleaded. "No onions. I thought I'd broken you of that?"

"Relax, Q," P laughed. "I'm broken, but I may need them during our break-in. Really, they're for the steaks. Grilled onions."

"He knows about that?" pointing to Abbouse.

"Knows about it? He's going with us."

"What? Who are you anyway?"

"John, let me tell him," P smiled. "Q, I called John and asked him to help us. I did it because this is bigger than the two of us can handle. He's—"

"Well, it's time we finally get some help, but why him?"

"I'm FBI," Abbouse quietly spoke. "Special Agent John Abbouse. That's why I wanted to make sure about you. That you weren't wired."

"P, I thought we were both worried about your office?"

"We were," P agreed. "Until John's people swept it for bugs while you and I were in the OR."

"The office is safe," Abbouse continued, "but we need to get a few things clear tonight."

"Over dinner," P added. "That's why I invited John. You know, to clear up things, get our heads together."

"Maybe to get our heads on straight?" I corrected.

"Sit down, guys. Dinner's served," P waved us in the general direction of the table, placing a large plate of food in front of each of us. "John, would you say grace?"

"Grace?" I mumbled, lowering my head as Abbouse offered a prayer. When he concluded, Pritcherman added a hushed, "Amen." I don't recall any prayers before any of our other meals. Another facet of Pritcherman I hadn't seen before. Both immediately started cutting their meat and eating without another word.

I followed their silent eating for a few moments, but had to ask, "FBI? Are we in trouble?"

"No," Abbouse laughed. "But these other guys are. Look, Quinton—"

"Call me Q. Everyone does."

"OK, Q," Abbouse continued. "You can call me John or whatever. Just keep the FBI thing quiet. Stanley has told me a lot about the medical parts of this. What I haven't told him—and now you—is what I know. We had some knowledge about all this before, but you two filled in a few blanks. Let me do the same."

"More salad, guys?" P asked. "John knows about Zachary getting kidnapped. He confirmed it was Zendejas we saw on the video. The fat bastard isn't dead. He and a couple of helpers have her somewhere close by, hidden, but we won't find her. It seems the good Dr. Zendejas works for the NSA."

"What?" I frowned. "The NSA doesn't have any reason to—"

"To put a probe in anyone?" Abbouse broke in. "I used to think you were right. What we now know is the NSA has violated their mission by using Americans and foreign nationals as field agents to—"

"What a minute," I interrupted Abbouse. "Isn't that against the law?"

"Yes, of course. As is kidnapping, false imprisonment, performing unauthorized medical procedures without informed consent and a whole host of other offenses." Abbouse kept up the recitation of his dissertation, "We caught wind of it when they called on your Dean, Dr. Jankowski, to help."

"What?" Now P was surprised. "So that's how I ended up with the patient? Jankowski sent him to me because of the NSA?"

"Yes," Abbouse answered. "That's also why we need to get into his office."

"It's pretty wired for security. So do you know where Zach is?," I interjected.

"Q, I'm the FBI, remember? We'll get through his security," John was confident. "Besides, I don't really care if they know. Who are they gonna tell? Anyway," he continued, "the Dean may have evidence confirming his work with the NSA and more importantly, who else is involved. It also may help us find your Zachary."

"Finding her is my first priority," I insisted. "And the autopsy records on the dead guy."

"And about the others," Abbouse added.

"What others? P chimed in. "You mean—"

"There are a number others who have been given this probe," Abbouse continued. "We don't know exactly how many or where it was done, but apparently in Europe."

"Not even a guess at how many?" P questioned his friend.

"We think maybe thirty or forty, we're just not sure," the FBI agent speculated. "There's more, however. We do know there are several with complications. Not just Dr. Zachary and the patient the Dean sent you."

"Oh, my God."

"Yes, Stanley. Oh, my God, is right," Abbouse concurred. "So, there's a lot to find in the Dean's office. Mr. Quinton, do you really need to go with us on this?"

"Well, I—"

"John," P cut in. "None of this would be known if it weren't for Q. He's been a lot more than just my partner in all this. He's opened my eyes on a few other things, too. He and Zachary are involved. Let him come."

"OK. Well, another thing you don't know is about Smith," Abbouse seemed uneasy. "Dr. Smith isn't a doctor—"

"I know that."

"She's got a few other credentials though," John continued. "She's a deep cover CIA agent sent to sniff out all of this."

"But don't the CIA and NSA work together?" I asked.

"And the FBI?." Pritcherman added.

"Normally we're all on the same team. You know, the good old U.S. of A." Abbouse exhaled. "But the CIA thinks the NSA has gone rogue on them and they're trying to stop them. That's what Smith and Grigsby are up to."

"Grigsby? We knew he was ex-military, but—" I raised my head.

"That pimply-faced prick," P frowned.

"He's CIA with Smith," John continued. "It gets more complicated. Smith and Grigsby got to the Dean and we believe turned him from the NSA back to the CIA."

"Back?"

"Yeah. You see, he was CIA back in Poland before he came to the U.S. A big help at the end of the cold war, actually. Inactive until recently, when the NSA guys got him involved."

"That explains the ten-year gap," I added.

"I need a blackboard to keep everyone straight," P wasn't kidding. "So Smith and Grigsby have the Dean, Zendejas has Zachary. There are more people running around with probes, you don't know how many, and some of them also have seizures. Is that about it?"

"Yeah, that's about it up to a point."

"Not quite," I chimed in. "Smith has a probe, too."

"That's right," P confirmed. "If she's CIA, did the NSA get to her or—"

"Or the CIA?" Abbouse wondered. "But why would they do that to their own agent? It doesn't make sense."

"Which part of any of this makes sense?" P asked.

"Why?" I couldn't help standing up. "Why are they all doing this? What's the reason, the rationale. What's the end game?"

"Damn good question," Abbouse leaned back in his chair. "I can speculate."

Pritcherman and I were both quiet, letting this all sink in. All I could think to say is, "Now what?"

"Sure, why not," Zendejas unfastened her last arm restraint and unbuckled the leg restraints as well.

"I sure need to pee," Zachary blushed. "Could I have a bedpan?"

"Of course," Zendejas handed her a large metal bedpan. "I'm glad to see you more active. What do you remember of the last two days?"

"Can you help get that thing under me? I feel like I don't have any strength." Zendejas leaned over to lift up her hips to slide the bedpan under them.

Just as he did, Zachary swung with both arms and all her strength, landing the bedpan squarely across Zendejas' right jaw and face, knocking him to the ground. She stood up next to the bed, next to the dazed pathologist lying on the floor, with his head slightly raised and rubbing his face. Her next blow came from above–a well-connected top-of-the-head shot that rendered him completely unconscious.

"No strength, my ass, you unethical moron. Don't ever mess with this Okie," screaming as she stood over him. For emphasis, she struck him a third time with a blow to the side of the head.

She found some tape, removed the IV from her arm and taped a small bandage over the site. Locating her clothes in a hospital bag in the far corner, she dressed quickly, never taking her eyes off the comatose pathologist. She used the remainder of the tape to bind him as best she could. Moving to John's computer, she put the papers she found on Zendejas' desk into her garment bag and exited the room. She looked outside at the sunset, something she hadn't seen in a while and had previously underappreciated. Now what?

Smith had been carefully searching for about three hours. She hadn't found the Dean in the hospital or at his home. She had no idea where to look for Zachary. So she was keying on Jankowski. It was starting to get dark–Smith considered that to her advantage. To her advantage because she thought if he came back to the university, it would be to his office and all the better to do so at night. She knew it was well-secured, but she was undeterred. She entered the building through a back entrance into a stairwell. Even in the early evening the building was empty. University bureaucrats didn't hang around work after hours.

Smith donned the same pair of night vision goggles she used in the morgue a few nights earlier and took out her smart phone. After tapping a few keystrokes, the stairwell security cameras cycled up to the ceiling and she ascended the stairs to the Dean's floor. Before opening the stairwell door, she checked the time–1923. Opening the door, she entered a dark outer office–one she remembered from her previous meetings with the Dean. She surveyed the room and proceeded to the inner office.

On entering, she noted several otherwise invisible laser beams coursing through the office–electronic trip wires that no doubt triggered a silent alarm. Taking out her phone again, she entered a series of keystrokes and the beams turned off. She moved to the large desk and painted a mental picture. What she was looking for would likely not be out and obvious. There were several desk drawers without locks. There were two that were locked. One of these held what she'd come for. While the locks were substantial for a university Dean's office desk, they were no problem for Smith after a few more keystrokes.

Sorting through the Dean's folders and paperwork from the locked drawers took hardly any time, as he was meticulously organized. So organized, he might as well have labeled several folders in large, red letters, *Look Here*, since he had labeled the ones that interested her *NSA* and *Pritcherman*.

How convenient, Smith thought, but not very stealthy. She sifted through all the papers in each folder, photographing each page for later analysis. As she did, she noticed confirmation that Bitterman had instructed the Dean to send the dead patient to Pritcherman for "assessment of possible craniotomy and ablation of intractable seizure activity," along with several other papers that seemed routine. She photographed them all. Under NSA she found several documents describing other agents who had probes placed in Europe, but no names, and only an estimate of their numbers. In one document, she noticed a reference to several patients who suffered from hypothermia as a complication. Jankowski had added several handwritten notes, more speculative than factual, about possible causes–hypothalamic interference, genetic mutation, and a few others that Smith's college-level biology failed to prepare her to recognize. She returned all the documents to their previous location.

What she really wanted was Jankowski, or even better–Pritcherman. But she doubted the neurosurgeon would be anywhere near the Dean's office. If the Dean were looking for Pritcherman, it would be in the operating room or in Pritcherman's own office. She faced a dilemma–stay and wait for the Dean, or move on to find Pritcherman directly. Maybe there was a way to do both.

She set up a small camera behind the Dean's chair, hidden and embedded in an impressionistic painting that hung there. It would capture anyone entering the office and transmit it to her smart phone. After looking around the office for several more minutes, she was satisfied her search was complete, and she slipped out of the inner office and back through the outer office door into the hall, finally retreating into the stairwell she had ascended only minutes ago. She leaned against the wall and took several deep breaths. Breaking and entering never becomes routine.

"Now what?" Abbouse echoed my last question, seemingly incredulous.

"We have dessert." P broke the mood.

"Damn it, P. We can eat any time," I was exasperated. "Mr. Abbouse owes us his best shot at telling us why all this happened. And, I for one, am not leaving here without the satisfaction of that speculation. Agreed?"

"The kid's got spunk, Stanley," John patted me on the shoulder. "Serve up your dessert, Stan and let's talk some more about heading to the Dean's office.

Just then, I was notified of an incoming message from Rupert. Before I left my apartment, I'd tasked Rupert with overseeing a genetic comparison of Zachary and the dead guy that started all this nonsense. This must be the results. "Excuse me just a minute. Can you hold your speculation? I need to see this," I told Abbouse and P. Besides, I needed to calm down after the spunk comment. Looking down at the screen of my smart phone, Rupert had sent me the results of the comparison and it held a surprise.

"I'm guessing John's got more."

"So you want to know why. What's their end game? Their rationale? Is that right, Q?"

"Yes."

"Here's what we think, or more accurately, what we think we know," the Special Agent took a bite of Boston cream pie. "Where'd you learn to cook like this, Stanley?" Wiping his mouth and clearing his throat, "This is a turf war between the NSA and CIA. If one says, black, the other says white. You know. You've both seen it before."

"Are you saying there's no substance to the battle?" P looked up from his dessert.

"Not that I know of," Abbouse continued. "There's probably a reason we are unaware of. My superiors are trying to sort that out. Maybe something to do with Europe."

I looked up from my dessert and glanced briefly at Pritcherman. To me, it didn't make sense. But I wasn't going to say a thing to Abbouse. I knew P well enough to know he saw my look. That was confirmed by silence where normally he would have challenged Abbouse on it. We all finished our pie without saying a word.

"I need ten minutes to clean up the place," P broke the quiet.

"Can I use your microscope, P?" Not waiting for an answer, I moved to the electron microscope in another area of the office. Abbouse just sat there, pretending to look at his smart phone. He was really taking in everything we were both doing.

As I went past the table between the eating area and the microscope, I retrieved two blood samples Abbouse had placed on the table when he searched me. I don't know if he knew what they were and didn't care, since I had others hidden at home.

I first placed the Zachary specimen under the microscope, then our homeless guy. Rupert's comparison search was correct. There was the microscopic evidence confirming the cause of the seizures–an abnormal protein deposited in the cells–harmless in most cells, but not in the brain. This particular abnormal protein was well-known for over a century to precipitate seizures. The modern diet meant that the abnormal protein rarely was an issue.

This left me with several new questions. What was causing the abnormal protein? Since neither patient had seizures prior to their probe placement, I assume it is related to the probes. Examining the dead guy's brain wouldn't be a problem. Zachary's would–at least I hoped it would. I wanted her back–whole. Why did only a few develop seizures? The electron microscope might give me a clue by looking at the internal architecture of the cell. I just know it's a genetic problem.

I have to get inside their cells.

As part of the Rupert study, I'd asked for a DNA comparison of Zachary's normal to her DNA since the probe. I had her normal DNA from her wine glass. Her post-seizure sample came from her secretions I'd obtained from the floor of her apartment. Rupert's comparison detailed several areas of gene mutations in Zachary's specimen from normal. The mutations were duplicated in the dead guy's DNA. That was where the answer would come from. I only had DNA from the homeless guy at autopsy. For the sake of argument, I assumed his mutations were new, like Zachary's. What I needed was a more detailed analysis of the mutated areas.

"P, take a look at this," I called to my partner.

Pritcherman wandered over from his cleaning duties. "Here's the cause of the seizures," directing him to the abnormal protein displayed under the microscope.

"Well, I'll be," he softly exclaimed. "But that doesn't explain why only a few of the probe patients have seizures."

"I know," I answered. "Apparently only a few have the abnormal protein. That's why I had Rupert run a DNA comparison study. A comparison of Zachary's pre-probe and post-probe DNA. Also, DNA from the dead guy. I didn't have any pre-probe DNA to compare to him. But his post-probe DNA has the same abnormal protein as Zachary's. I was confused at first because I was looking for a standard mutation as a cause for the abnormal protein synthesis. An A-T or C-G base-pair deletion or an insertion. That's what took so long—"

"So long for what, Quinton? Get on with it?" P was more interested than perturbed.

"The mutation is a gene fusion abnormality," I proudly stated. About three percent of glioblastomas result from a fusion gene.[5]

"Really?" my partner seemed surprised. "But I thought they were just oncological."

"Yes, most are. But not all," I continued. "That's what threw me off."

"I wonder if they're at risk for a glioblastoma, too?"

"I don't know, P," I was out of my comfort area discussing neurosurgical tumors. "But I'll bet you look into it when—"

---

[5] Glioblastoma is the most common and lethal brain tumor arising in astrocytes, cells that make up the structural supportive tissue of the brain. In the U.S. approximately 10,000 patients are diagnosed annually with a survival time of about fourteen months.

"Are you guys about done?" Abbouse called from the other side of the room."

"Well, what do we have here? A camera, if I'm not mistaken," Abbouse commented. "I wonder who placed it here?"

"And when?" I added.

"Just a minute and we'll know," Abbouse entered a few keystrokes and stepped back. "Wow," he murmured, while instinctively reaching to unholster his weapon. "This was placed in the last hour."

Smith knew the signal loss meant not only that her camera was discovered and she'd get no more intelligence from the three, but it also meant Pritcherman, Quinton and the new guy knew someone else was looking for the Dean. She'd captured enough of a picture to upload it from her phone with a query command, "Identify this person," indicating the third companion. Closing her connection, she also realized there would be nothing positive in staying. She slipped back from the rear of the building and was gone.

Abbouse carefully searched the room again. Finding no one, he holstered his weapon and entered more keystrokes. "Let's see what the forensics tells us."

"Huh?"

"I sent off all the infra-red and stuff to our forensics lab to see if they can identify anything or anyone associated with this camera."

"You can do that from what little info you've got?" I was surprised at the technology.

"Oh, we can do a lot more than that," the agent smiled. "Technology has come a long way, son."

Pritcherman sat down in one of the two chairs in front of the Dean's desk, looking directly at the Special Agent, "John, technology may have come a long way, but the basic intelligence needs are unchanged—*who, what, when, where, why*—am I correct?"

"You are," Abbouse agreed. "Technology just makes it easier."

"Really?" The skeptical neurosurgeon sarcastically reacted.

"Notice, I can also tell you which drawers have been opened recently," pointing to the two locked drawers. "These two," quickly opening them after a few keystrokes on his phone.

"Since they have locks and the others don't, I could've guessed that," P said, not as impressed with technology as our companion.

I sat down in the other chair and listened while surveying the room. After a few moments, I commented, "Is this room wired?"

"Interesting. Let's see," Abbouse countered while waving his phone around the room. "It appears there are several hidden microphones, suggestive of a recording system." Abbouse was sifting through the two recently opened drawers. "Well, look what I found. A couple of files labeled *NSA* and *Pritcherman.* Fancy that," smiling as he looked at Pritcherman.

"Technology found the recording devices, P," I added.

"But I guessed he was recording me several days ago when he called me here," P responded. "Otherwise, why wouldn't he just tell me on the phone what he had to say?"

"Good point," I was beginning to fumble around with the accoutrements on the tabletop between the two chairs while Abbouse superficially inspected the files before putting them in his briefcase, brought along for that purpose.

"Are you taking them? Why not leave them and photograph them instead?" Pritcherman seemed more inquisitive than argumentative.

"Forensics," Abbouse answered. "They get a crack at them first. Besides, I skimmed them. Tells us about what I'd have expected."

"Nothing new?" P frowned.

"Well, I found something new," I said, interrupting the two. I pulled out an unmarked file from the drawer from the table between our chairs. "Unmarked, but look what's inside. A DAT and a transcription."

"DAT?" P turned his head to me.

"Digital audio tape," I replied. "Older technology, P. But you might be interested in it since it's labeled with the autopsy ID from your patient."

I scanned the transcription. "This is a transcription of the autopsy, too." I read on and looked up at Abbouse. "There's a cause of death, John."

"Good," preoccupied with his continuing search of the unlocked drawers.

"Not interested?" I pressed him.

"Oh, I'm interested, but we'll get to it in the lab later."

"Well I'm interested," Pritcherman leaned into me.

Without saying a word, I pointed to the line on the page for cause of death and touched my index finger to my lips to indicate quiet to P.

"What?" P mumbled, staring at the place where I pointed.

I again held up my finger, flipped to a second transcription and pointed to a line of a second autopsy with the same cause of death, but with a name and ID neither of us knew. P frowned and wrinkled his forehead. I slipped the second transcription out of the file and under my leg. After a few seconds, I folded the document under my leg and slipped it into my shoe. I wasn't sure if Abbouse had noticed.

"Well, nothing else much here," Abbouse concluded. "I think it's time to leave, unless you have something else," moving from behind the desk to where we were both sitting.

"Wanna let me have that tape?"

"Sure," P flipped it to the FBI agent. Pritcherman began fiddling around in his pocket. He retrieved two small onions and tossed them into his mouth. "Yeah, let's get out of here. It gives me the creeps."

"Mr. Quinton," Abbouse locked his gaze onto my eyes. "I'll take that transcription as well."

I had a sinking feeling. I knew why P had needed his onions–like a reformed ex-smoker who needs a smoke. I passed the first document to John Abbouse and stood up next to Pritcherman.

"We head back to Dr. Pritcherman's office," our newest companion answered.

"I need to go by my place first to get the Rupert record, if that's OK?" I asked Abbouse as we all headed down the elevator to the lobby.

"Sure," P answered instead. "So, John," I heard him say as I walked away, leaving the two standing outside the Administrative building. "It's just you and me. Now what?"

Zachary knew she didn't have much alone time. She slipped out of the warehouse building into the night. She wanted to find the Dean or Pritcherman, which meant she would first try their offices.

Pritcherman first. Ironically, she felt safer around him. Was that a change, she thought. It took a moment for her to figure out where she was, but since she recognized the area, she realized she was just a brisk ten- minute walk to the neurosurgeon's office. She'd been so close, yet so far, the entire time.

Even though it was night, she hoped he might still be in his office. Finding it proved to be as difficult for her as it had for everyone else, but find it, she did–to no avail. No Pritcherman. So she headed back down the elevator and out, walking the few minutes to the Administration building and the Dean's office–more familiar territory.

She made no effort to conceal herself or her movements. Being discovered by anyone would confirm she was alive, if not necessarily safe. Being discovered by the right person might even offer her safety. Mulling this over as she walked to the entrance, she was confronted by a shadow emerging from the side of the building.

"Dr. Zachary?"

"Dean Jankowski?"

– Never Let Your Adversary Dictate Your Strategy –

XVII

I hurried through the back streets from the Dean's office to my apartment. Even though it was a ten-minute drive, I'd decided to walk rather than ride. A fast walk, but one that gave me time to sort things out again. I hoped P was doing the same—and on the same subject.

What was Abbouse up to? As I walk-ran down the empty streets, I checked the time—12:43 a.m.—another late-nighter.

I knew Abbouse was lying about the documents taken from the Dean's office and I suspected he was not being honest about the NSA motivation we'd discussed over dinner. *Please, P, don't tell this guy anything more. I know he's your friend, but he's not mine.* The return to onions gave me hope—how ironic.

Just then I remembered the second transcription, hidden in my shoe, and retrieved it. I stopped under a streetlight to look it over. No name, but a second ID. That meant a second deadly encounter and I presumed another dead NSA agent.

What also struck me was the same cause of death as our first homeless, dead guy . . . insulin poisoning. *Insulin poisoning?* In two relatively young, healthy patients? Accidental? I doubt it. This poisoning was intentional. They were murdered. Did P realize this, too?

I had to get him away from Abbouse. I folded the document and put it in my hip pocket. I resumed my trek home and, rounding the last corner, dashed upstairs to the comfort of my own apartment. I found Rupert and a bottle of water, and went to my computer, confirming the gene fusion causation in both Zachary and the dead guy's DNA. "Excellent work, Rupert!" I looked at my longtime companion. "Next we need to find a fix, buddy."

"Define fix, sir," Rupert was so formal.

"Loosen up, Rupert. You're gonna be busy tonight," I smiled. "I need you to create and run a program to identify and correct the gene fusion sequences."

"Define correct."

"You define it," I responded. "Parameters for success are length of mutation, susceptibility to viral insertion of a new segment, and whether the abnormal protein synthesis is corrected."

"Understand," Rupert paused. "You want a . . . fix."

Smiling again, I looked him in the artificial eye, "Yes."

Rupert began his computing task while I packed a small bag. Who knows when I'll get back, I decided, taking hygiene items and a change of clothes. "See ya, Rupert. Call me if you need help . . . and when you have results for me."

I secured my apartment, turning to leave when I noticed two figures lurking around my building. One was smoking and the other calmly reading. Since it was now after two in the morning and nothing good happens to me during that time, I had to assume the worst. How do I get past them? Create a distraction.

I slipped back inside and called P. Whispering into the phone, "Listen and don't say anything, P. There are two guys outside my apartment. I'm going to try and get past them using Rupert. If I don't, you need to know there's a second dead patient. That's what the second document's about. Same cause of death–insulin poisoning. That means murder, P. Be careful of Abbouse. I'm not sure about him. He may be involved. Dr. Pritcherman, I don't know who's at your place. If you agree with what I just said, don't say anything for five seconds and I'll know." There was a good ten seconds of silence.

I breathed a sigh of relief and added, "If you don't hear from me, meet me in the park at 8 p.m. tonight. If I'm not there, assume the worst–that they have me."

After ending the call, I programmed Rupert for his starring role in my distraction. I leaned against the door for a moment, hoping this would all go away. I took a deep breath and went through the door again, setting the security parameters and lightly skipping down the stairs to the street. Pretending not to notice the two, I headed in the general direction of the hospital. I didn't have long to wait as the two began moving to intercept me. Just then Rupert opened my window and began *talking* as loud as his program would allow, "Burglary in progress, burglary in progress! Notify police, notify police!" This was followed by an ear-piercing, high-pitched wailing horn for ten seconds and then the entire alert recycling over and over. Lights began coming on everywhere. I tried to speed my pace, but they matched it, finally calling out to me.

"Mr. Quinton," Jeremy called as they closed within fifteen feet. "May we talk to you?"

"No," I screamed back and began running.

"Stop, son!" John screamed back as Jeremy kneeled behind me. I know because I looked over my shoulder just as he squeezed off a shot from his stationary position.

It missed, but the second one hit me in the posterior calf. As I fell, a third shot, this one from the front, whizzed by my right temple, grazing me. Instinctively I grabbed for my right leg as a small amount of blood trickled down my face from the head wound.

Four more shots pierced the stillness of the night, but this time all came from in front of me. *Who's shooting at me from the front?* I'd initially looked back at the two chasing me, looking just in time to see both fall from the frontal gunshots. I whipped my head forward to see a crouching figure behind a nearby building begin to stand and come towards me. I lowered my head as he raced past me to the two. Kicking their weapons away, he checked pulses to confirm his kills and turned to me, making direct eye contact.

"Grigsby?"

"Quinton, this is getting old . . . bailing your ass out," Grigsby spoke as he lifted me like a bale of hay and threw me over his shoulder. Now I appreciated this linebacker. Shifting me to his other shoulder, he reached into his pants pocket and dug out his cell phone, pressing a number on speed dial. After two rings, it connected. "I need a clean-up at Quinton's. Two bananas. Also a lift."

He terminated the call without waiting for confirmation. "Let's get outta here," running back to the safety of a nearby building in which he must have been hiding. "So, Quinton," he barely broke a sweat and wasn't even breathing hard. "What's new?"

"What about my bag?"

"What about it?"

"Can you get it?"

"No. Leave it. Maybe it'll throw them off," Grigsby looked at his watch.

"Who are you, Grigsby?" I asked. "Tell me."

"Now?"

"Now. And where are you taking me next?" I posed the question.

"Where?"

"We have to get you to Dr. Pritcherman," the Dean insisted. "Come on, let's go to my office."

"Is that safe?" Zachary asked.

"Is anywhere? We have to get off the streets," Jankowski advised. "I'll call Pritcherman and make some arrangements for imaging to speed things up."

"Dean Jankowski. I've apparently had continuous seizure activity. Why? I've never had seizures before."

"You underwent surgery for—"

"Surgery! I didn't need any surgery."

"Dr. Zachary," Jankowski spoke quietly. "You've been the victim of a government program. An innocent victim. A probe was placed into your brain—"

"My brain! Who the hell—"

"Doctor," the Dean broke in. "I'm on your side," pausing to let out a deep sigh. "At least I am now."

"Huh? Explain what that means. Explain what it all means, Dr. Jankowski."

Zachary and the Dean entered his outer office proceeded directly into his inner office.

"Someone's been here," Jankowski tensed. "I can tell," turning to leave. "We can't stay here."

"Well I'm not going anywhere—"

Jankowski held up his hand and gently placed it over her mouth. He shook his head sideways and guided her out into the hall. He whispered to her, "Someone's been here and they're looking for both of us. We can't stay here. It's probably wired."

"Who's looking for me? And you, who's looking for you?"

"Dr. Zachary," the Dean sighed again. "A lot's happened in the last few weeks that you know nothing about."

He ushered her down the back stairwell. He glanced up and noted the security cameras were all turned toward the ceiling. "Look," he pointed to the cameras, "someone's pointed them up, disabled them, to insure no one sees who or what went on in my office. Now who would do that, Dr. Zachary?"

"I don't know. I don't—"

"That's right. You don't know about any of this," Jankowski moved closer to her. "You're going to have to trust me."

"Why should I? You just said you were on my side–now. What the hell's that supposed to mean?"

The Dean sat down on one of the concrete stairs, Zachary following his lead.

"I used to work for the government, the NSA. You know who they are, right? They are running a program that places a probe into the brain and you received one. What's the last thing you remember, Dr. Zachary?"

She paused, thinking about what to say next. "I was in pathology with Mr. Quinton, looking for a body."

"That would be the patient I referred to Dr. Pritcherman's service for removal of the probe."

"What?" Shaking her head, she continued, "No, nothing about a probe. We found the dead guy's morgue locker, but only a brain and some metal there. Quinton was just trying to prove he'd witnessed this guy's post-mortem examination. He claims he was drugged during the autopsy and was then told it never happened. I was pretty skeptical myself until we found the locker with the brain and all the other stuff. Then two guys came in and grabbed me . . . even gagged me. I was blindfolded and taken about thirty minutes away. That's the last thing that I remember clearly."

"Well done," Jankowski complimented her memory. "The probe must have been turned off or you wouldn't remember any of this. Do you think the police gag people, Doctor?"

"Of course not. What do you mean–turned off?"

"They weren't police, Dr. Zachary. After they kidnapped you, they placed the probe in order to control you. You began having seizures soon thereafter," the Dean continued. "You're not the first to suffer seizures. It's a complication. There are several others."

"Who is *they*, Dean?" Zachary was more apprehensive. "You keep saying, *they*. They who?"

"Dr. Zendejas for one. He works for—"

"Zendejas!" she shouted. "I knocked the crap out of that fat bastard. The pathologist? What business does a pathologist have doing neurosurgery? And . . . *for the government?*"

Holding his hand up again to quiet Zachary, the Dean continued. "He's an NSA agent. Probably involved in the placing of the European probes as well."

"Europe? Dean, I don't understand."

"There are about forty agents who have had probes implanted. Most are in Europe and a handful have suffered seizures after surgery. You're also in that group. I was called to consult on your seizures, but no standard seizure protocols worked. You were *in status epilepticus.*"

"Why you?" Zachary was focused on the Dean's eyes. "How are you involved in this?"

"I am . . . *once was* . . . an NSA agent as well," Jankowski tried to not look at Zachary. "They kept saying it was the national interest. They—"

"They again," Zachary interrupted. "Who the hell are *they*? How could you, Dean? You're a physician. How could you help them disable me, one of your residents and against my will?"

"A fair question, Doctor. I am so sorry. I should have known," the Dean paused and looked away again. "General Bitterman, he's the NSA project director for all this. He's the *they*. But who knows who's telling him what to do. Please understand. I was told it was in the national interest."

"Just what is the national interest, Dean? And who are you or this General Bitterman to decide that interest involves me? Or gives them–you–the right to invade my privacy and my body?" She was standing over the Dean. "If I wasn't a Doctor, I swear I'd kill you right now."

"You would certainly be within your rights," Jankowski answered quietly. "Before you do, however, please consider that you still are having seizures and still have a probe. Consider also that I am your ally and do have your best interest at heart now, not the national interest. I'm your best hope for fixing both."

Zachary thought about that suggestion for a moment and sat down next to the Dean again. "You bastard," she whispered. She grabbed his collar and pulled him close, "If you so much as look at me wrong, I'll cut your nuts off and stuff 'em in your mouth. Got it?"

"Yes. Absolutely."

"The seizures," Zachary let go of the Dean. "The ketamine vial I found before I—" She raised her voice again. "Wait a minute! Zendejas is who I knocked unconscious. He's the one that was giving me the ketamine. That seemed to work on the seizures. I may have killed him trying to escape."

"Zendejas?" Jankowski smiled. "You struck him? Couldn't have happened to a nicer man," standing up. "Think you can find your way back to where he is?"

"Why would I want go anywhere near there?"

"Because it's a hospital environment and they have the drug you need."

"It's also where they will come looking for me," Zachary concluded. "Not to mention if you're truly on my side, you don't want to be anywhere near there either. By the way, it's not thirty minutes away. I walked from there in about fifteen minutes," she paused. "No, Dean. I will not go back to where that fat, bastard pathologist is."

"So where then?"

"I think I have figured out the mechanism for how they manipulate memory," Pritcherman announced, as he and Abbouse entered his inner office. Before he could say anything else, his phone rang. "Curious," he said as he reached for the phone.

Pritcherman answered the call, then listened without saying a word for about a minute. He stood up and screamed into the phone, "My OR time's been changed? You woke me up to tell me that? You moron," Pritcherman slammed the handset down. Fuming, the neurosurgeon paced a few seconds and then turned his attention back to John Abbouse, who was sitting at the dinner table.

"Problems, Stanley?"

"My OR time is pushed back two hours, so they call after midnight to tell me that. Why couldn't they just wait until morning?"

"Why indeed," Abbouse seemed disinterested. "You were saying you think you know the reason for the memory issue?"

"Yes," P began his dissertation on brain chemistry. "I want you to remember back to your biochemistry days."

"What biochemistry days?"

"Just listen," P was pacing slowly as he talked. "The serotonin network in the brain is one of the chemical mediators of memory, along with norepinephrine and others. The messenger chemical, cAMP–that stands for *cyclic adenosine monophosphate*–causes a temporary modification of *protein kinase A*, which causes MAPK– that's *mitogen-activated protein kinase*–to modify cAMP, which causes a modification of CREB–that's cAMP response element-binding protein—"

"Stanley! What in the name of Sam Hill are you talking about?"

"Listen up," P barely noticed the protest. "When a memory is formed, a protein called ARC–that's *activity-related cytoskeleton-associated protein*–gets activated. It means a memory has been formed or retried."

"Stop!" surrendering, Abbouse held up his hands. "Enough, already. What's this have to do with me?"

"Don't you see, John?" my neurosurgical partner had completely confused his FBI friend. "They're trying to interrupt the chemical mediators by putting those probes into the RTPJ and disrupting memory."

"RTPJ?"

"Yeah, the right temporo-parietal junction. It's where the 'no-fear' memory is located and where they're trying to affect the brain genes."

"Yeah, yeah, Stanley," Abbouse was determined to end this conversation. "OK, you just keep working on that. Are we waiting for the kid to come back, or what? I'm tired."

"Go ahead. Go on home," P responded. "I'm guessing he got distracted by something, he's kind of flighty–probably not coming back. I'll call him in the morning."

"OK," Abbouse stood to leave. "You know best." Walking to the door, Abbouse turned and admonished his friend, "Oh, and Stan, get some rest yourself. You don't need to be going anywhere else tonight. Understand?"

"You mean this morning, John."

"Right. This morning. Good night, Stanley."

Pritcherman looked down as Abbouse opened the door to let himself out.

"Oh, one last thing, Stan," the FBI agent turned to his host again. "May I have the tooth?"

Pritcherman looked up and without hesitating said, "Quinton's got it."

"OK, goodnight."

When he heard the outer door close, he spoke to the security screen, "Activate exterior perimeter security." He stared at the door, thinking about his friend. *I sure as hell can't sleep now.* He was more nervous than usual. He began thinking, am I wrong about John? Where is the tooth? Does Q have it? Do I go after Q? If so, where?

"This time, Captain," Bitterman called out over the headset radio from the helicopter. "Everyone goes in . . . quietly. Everyone. Your orders are to shoot if there is the slightest bit of resistance. Do you copy?"

"Yes, sir," as the helicopter descended onto the empty field next to the warehouse holding Zendejas. The ten-man assault team cleared the attack helicopter in precision form and took up positions outside the exterior door as before. The general exited the helicopter and waved the team in, following behind their entry. They quickly moved to the door where Zendejas and his team were attending to Dr. Zachary.

General Bitterman opened the door, expecting to find activity, but instead found Dr. Zendejas on the floor, awake, leaning on his elbows, holding his head.

"Why are you on the floor?" Bitterman was searching the room, waving to his troops to spread out. "And where are your two assistants . . . and Zachary?"

"I . . . I . . . don't know," Zendejas moaned. "The last thing . . . I remember . . . was . . . Zachary hitting me over the head. She—"

"What time did that happen?"

"Around seven in the evening," as he tried to sit up.

"Tonight?"

"I . . . don't know. What time—"

"Damn it, that means she's been on the loose for seven hours," Bitterman was pacing.

"It's . . . two . . . in the morning?" the pathologist gave in to the nausea, vomiting once on the general's shoes before resuming a supine position. "Where are John and Jeremy?"

"*You tell me, Doctor!* I ought to shoot you where you lie and just be done with you," the general broke off his pacing and stood over Zendejas, wiping the vomitus onto Zendejas' pants. "You had twenty-four hours and I had expected you to fix Zachary so I wouldn't have to shoot her, too. Instead, you managed to lose her. *Damn civilians,*" turning and pacing more.

"Now I remember," the pathologist sat up again. "I sent John and Jeremy after the medical student, Quinton, as a way to get Pritcherman."

"And just why would you want Pritcherman?"

"To help me with the probe," Zendejas said. The fog of his head injury was beginning to lift. As it did, he was remembering more and realized he was telling the general his plan to avoiding this retribution.

"*You village idiot!*" Bitterman was screaming. "Captain, prepare this piece of shit for transport."

"Where are you taking me?"

"Someplace safe," Bitterman sarcastically answered while pointing first to his Captain and then to the door.

"Now?" Zendejas grimaced.

"Now."

"No one will be around this early. Let's start getting you prepared for removal of the probe," Jankowski suggested, standing up.

"What are you saying?" Zachary stood up next to the Dean. "The hospital night shift is usually not very busy," the Dean continued. "So, let's get you a CT and PET scan. They'll be flustered to see the Dean at this time of the night."

"Why not an MRI?"

"Remember the probe," he reminded her. "It's metallic. An MRI might pull it out of your brain."

"Ooh, right, I forgot," Zach shook her head. "This takes some getting used to. Will the pharmacy give you ketamine?"

"If not to me, they will to the anesthesiologist on call."

"Huh?"

"You need surgery," the Dean pressed on as they both walked down the staircase. "You've got to get that probe removed. While you're getting your scans, I'll find Dr. Pritcherman."

At the bottom of the stairs, before exiting the building, Zachary stopped and leaned into the Dean. "I agree, so far, but you'd better remember what I said. One false move—"

"I understand completely," Jankowski said as he opened the door and ushered Zachary through first. They quickly made the walk from the Administration building to the adjoining hospital through the underground corridor. Radiology was only one floor above. They took the stairs.

The Dean arranged for Zachary to undergo the PET scan first, then the CT scan. The PET scan would show function, not as well as an MRI, but the best available given the circumstance. The CT scan would demonstrate anatomy. After satisfying himself that she was in good hands, the Dean went to the OR–a dark, quiet place at this time of night. He found the on-call sleep rooms and gently opened the door. As the door opened, a head popped up and squinted into the light.

"Is it six already?"

Jankowski recognized the voice. "Is that you, Dr. Chesney?"

"Yes," came the groggy response, "Dean Jankowski?"

"I need a favor. Some ketamine, please. Oral if you have it, parenteral if not. Is Dr. Pritcherman scheduled for surgery this morning?"

"I think so," the anesthesiologist sat and rubbed his eyes to wake up.

"He will be cancelling that patient and replacing them with another."

"Are you sure?"

"I'm sure," the Dean was confident. "Make the schedule changes necessary please."

"What's the new patient's name?"

"*Doe* for now," Jankowski answered. "*Jane* Doe. If there are problems, use my name. Just make it happen quietly."

"OK," Chesney was now fully awake and brushing his teeth.

"The ketamine, Doctor," Jankowski persisted.

"Now?"

"Now."

"Them?" I frowned at Grigsby as the ride he'd requested arrived.

"Shut up, Quinton. You talk too much," Grigsby tossed me onto the backseat as the front seat passenger got out of the vehicle. The two stood beside the vehicle, Grigsby, clearly in charge, giving instructions. All I could make out was Grigsby's admonition to be discreet. He sat in the passenger seat and instructed the driver, "You know where to go."

With that, we were in motion, having left the previous passenger at the scene. I couldn't recall their names, but the two second-year med students were our rescuers.

"Quinton, it's a full-time job keeping you out of trouble," the driver/second-year commented. "Shouldn't you blindfold him, Grigsby? He can screw up a wet dream, remember?"

"Aw, leave him alone. He's had a bad few weeks," the sound of Grigsby voice was that of fatigue rather than defender. "He got us what we needed anyway." I closed my eyes out of my own combination of fatigue, frustration, and injury. I was simply giving up, if only for a few minutes. *When will this end?* was all I could think of as I slipped into the peace of unconsciousness.

I was jolted awake when Grigsby lifted me out of the back seat and slung me over his shoulder again.

"Ow! My leg!"

"Shut up, Quinton," Grigsby huffed as he lugged me up several flights of stairs. "You're lucky to be alive. Quit complaining." The second-year followed him with my bag and phone. I'd forgotten the phone had been knocked from my hand by the gunshot.

He opened the door ahead of Grigsby, who deposited me on a couch. I tensed a bit as I noticed Smith talking on her phone. She disconnected and turned her attention to me.

"Well, well. What present did you bring me, Mr. Grigsby?"

"A sack of shit," Grigsby was drinking water from the refrigerator. "Want some water, Quinton?"

"Please. I'm pretty—"

"Lucky to be alive?" Smith interjected. "OK, Quinton. It's *come-to-mama* time. What's your involvement in all this? Who do you work for?"

"What? Who do *I* work for?" I scoffed.

"Come on, Quinton," Grigsby piled on. "You've been a thorn in this mess from Day One."

"You can't be NSA or CIA," Smith added. "So, who are you working for? Make it easy on us all, so we can get you medical attention."

"NSA? CIA? You're full of shit! I'm a third-year medical student. That's all." I was confused and my leg and head were really beginning to hurt.

"Then who's Pritcherman working for? You two have to be on somebody's payroll," Grigsby moved closer and sat down.

"Are you with the Dean and Zendejas?" Smith asked, now standing closer and leaning down in my face.

"Dean Jankowski? Are you kidding, or what? Dr. Zendejas is dead."

"Quinton," Grigsby patted my leg, just above the wound. "Are you just stupid? I can make this really difficult."

"Grigsby. You saved my life, and for that I'm thankful," I confided. "But I'm nothing more than a medical student with a curious mind and a love of freedom and privacy. Is that so wrong?"

"Maybe we all love freedom and our country," Smith agreed.

"You forgot privacy," I reminded her. "I suppose we have different ways of showing what our beliefs are. Who the hell are you two?"

"We'll ask the questions, Quinton," Grigsby advised me. "We're patriots, too."

"And a real funny way of showing it, don't you think?" I braced for their reply.

"You son-of-a—"

"Grigsby!" Smith raised her voice. "Let's remember he's a civilian . . . and he's on our side."

"And what side is that, Smith?" Strangely, the pain seemed to embolden me, but I wasn't backing down.

"Quinton, you certainly know how to get under my skin," Smith smiled as she pulled away from my face. "Any thoughts on what should be done about your leg?"

"And my head," I added. "You're the doctor, right? You tell me."

"Come on, Quinton," Smith chided. "You know I'm not a doctor."

"It was a good dig," Grigsby smiled at her, looking over at me. "I can bandage your head. It's just a graze wound. But your leg looks like it'll need surgery to me. We'll need to get you out of here."

"Not until Calhoun gets here," Smith disagreed. "It's almost dawn."

Grigsby began bandaging Quinton's head wound while Smith was off in the corner talking to the second-year who'd driven us here. I couldn't make out what she was saying, but it appeared as if they were instructions since he was nodding his head intermittently. After a few minutes, he left. Grigsby turned his attention to my leg injury.

"Geez, Quinton. You're lucky. It's a through-and-through with no bone involvement, but it's worse than I thought. It needs to be debrided and washed out."

Calhoun slipped into the room while Grigsby was preoccupied with me. Smith met him at the door and they talked at a low enough volume that, once again, I couldn't hear what was said. I knew about this guy, but had never met him. After a few moments with Smith, he turned and walked to where Grigsby was attending to me.

"Mr. Quinton. You've had quite an ordeal, I hear."

"Yes, sir," I was business-like. "And you are?"

"I'm Bill Calhoun," the CIA Assistant Director replied.

"I'm Smith's and Grigsby's boss you might say."

"I *might?*"

He sat down next to me. "Alright son. Let's cut through the BS. I know who you are, and now you know who I am. What you don't know are a lot of the *whys* and *why nots*. Right?"

He was right about that. "I need surgery on my leg. How am I going to get that here?"

"You're not. We have to get you to a hospital. When it's safe to move you, I've got a helicopter on standby."

"Good," I responded. "Then you've got time to answer a few questions. For starters, how did my medical school get overrun with the CIA and NSA and who knows what other government agencies?"

Paying no attention to my question whatsoever, Calhoun looked at Grigsby and Smith. "Can you handle this until we move him? There are other problems I need to attend to."

Grigsby spoke for them both. "I've got the medical part and Smith has the other."

"Can you sedate him?"

"Now?"

"*No!*" I interjected.

"Yeah . . . right now."

Pritcherman bolted up in the bed as his security system alerted him to a visitor at his outer office door. He strained to see the time on the clock across the room. Five a.m.? This had better be good, he told himself, wiping the mucous from his eyes and moving to the console to view the caller. He was suddenly wide awake when he saw his visitor. It was the Dean. He hurried to the door and quickly ushered the Dean inside and into the inner office.

"Dean, where the hell have you been? Sit down. Do you want something to drink?"

"Stanley, let me first apologize for everything. I—"

"Viktor, what's going on around here? What's happening to our university?"

"Dr. Pritcherman," the Dean leaned closer. "You may be the key to restoring some sanity to all this. I have Dr. Zachary—"

"What? Where?"

"She's in radiology now, getting scans—a CT and a PET scan—before I—"

"Why? How did you get her? Where's she been?"

"Stanley! Please let me finish," holding up his hand to calm himself as well as P. "Dr. Zachary escaped from her captors. Dr. Zendejas placed a probe in her brain in an effort to control her after she was caught breaking into the morgue. She began having intractable seizure activity and I was consulted. No standard medications worked. However, ketamine—remember that old one—seems to work. But, she needs the probe removed—"

"Like the patient you sent me who died," P remembered the start of this all too well. "The patient you weren't honest with me about. Who is doing all this, Viktor? And why?"

"Stanley," Jankowski hesitated for a few seconds. "I was an NSA agent. And before that, I worked with the CIA. It was at their instructions I sent the patient to you for removal of the probe."

"The probe you never mentioned."

"I was getting to it when all this started."

"All this? You mean murder?"

"Murder?"

"Dean Jankowski," Pritcherman puffed up a bit. "If it weren't for Mr. Quinton, you might have gotten away with it."

"No, Stanley. I said I was an NSA agent. Nothing more. And I don't know anything about murder. Smith—"

"Hell, it doesn't matter what I tell you." P decided. "You're not leaving here except in someone's custody. Smith? What's her involvement?"

"She was an NSA agent, but really works for the CIA. She and Grigsby–he's CIA, too–are trying to find out what this is all about as well. I decided I couldn't work for the NSA anymore and they helped me realize the bigger picture. But I don't know whether the CIA is without sin in this either. So I took my leave from them, too."

P knew much of what the Dean was saying from Abbouse's briefing. The Dean was confirming the story from another source, but also being tested for where he stood.

"Escaped? From the custody of the CIA? Huh! That must've been some trick. So where's Quinton?"

"I don't know," Jankowski sat back. "I thought you two were collaborating. I haven't—"

"Where's Zendejas, that piece of—"

"Stanley! I can't stand that kind of talk," Viktor interrupted. "Zendejas and his two accomplices had Dr. Zachary, but they left her alone with Zendejas. She managed to render him unconscious with a bedpan and was able to escape. She came to me . . . was coming back to us . . . when I found her."

Pritcherman laughed out loud at the Dean's characterization of Zachary's assault. The Dean smiled, too.

"Zachary KO'd that fat-rat bastard with a bedpan?" and laughed some more.

"A big metal one, apparently."

"Ah, to have seen that," P mused. "So, let me see if I understand. The NSA sent you a patient for removal of a probe they screwed up and you sent him to me. He died and you don't know why, but the NSA wants you to help them with another probe victim–*victim*, Viktor, *victim . . . one of our residents*–and in that you assisted. But now you say you've flipped back to the CIA–that would be Smith and Grigsby–except that you escaped from them, too, and somehow found Dr. Zachary, whom you now have in radiology getting a bunch of scans?"

"Is that about it, Viktor?" The question was rhetorical. "*No, not quite.* If Mr. Quinton didn't have the normal curiosity of a medical student, none of this would have come to light and the world would be a better place. Right?"

"Well—"

"Well what, Viktor? This is all criminal. Oh, and by the way, you left out the first dead agent, you remember him. He's the one whose autopsy report was in your drawer, but you don't know the cause of death of victim number one or two, right? You despicable prick! I ought to—"

"Dr. Pritcherman," Jankowski was conspiratorial. "There may be a way out of this—"

"Why would I believe you? And even if I did, why would I want to help you?"

"To save Dr. Zachary's life."

"Go on," a suddenly quieter Pritcherman instructed.

"I came to you to remove her probe," the Dean continued. "I've asked Dr. Chesney to move her into your morning slot in the operating room. That's why she's getting the scans."

"How do you know removing the probe will help her? How do you know it won't kill her?"

"Because whatever you are, Stanley, you are a moral, ethical physician—a healer who is interested only in helping others. Yes, I've failed ethically and morally. Don't make my same mistake."

"You still haven't told me what the purpose of these probes is, Viktor."

"I don't know for sure. I—"

"Bullshit! You participated in this and didn't even know what they were for? Tell me another lie."

"I was told it was in the national interest. I was told—"

"And you never thought to question what that interest was? Good God, man," P was livid. "You're playing god and only for the folly of men." Pritcherman sat silently for several minutes staring at Jankowski. Finally, he put his hands on his knees and stood up. "Alright, let's go see her."

"Now?"

"Of course, now. Where exactly is she?"

The next thing I knew, Grigsby was jabbing me in the right deltoid region with an 18-gauge needle attached to a syringe holding a full milliliter of some unknown drug. He didn't have to expend much effort to hold me down, given my leg and head wounds. Besides, I'd pretty much had it with resistance. Within about ten minutes, I was extremely woozy, closer yet to unconsciousness. The rest is . . . .

Calhoun motioned Smith and Grigsby over to the table.

"Why'd you bring him here and not shoot him with the NSA guys?"

"We need him as bait to get Pritcherman," Grigsby answered.

"Refresh me on why we need Pritcherman."

"Sir, to keep this from getting out of hand, we need Pritcherman to take the probe out of Zachary," Smith added.

"This Zachary," the Assistant Director tilted his head and leaned it on his hand, "she's the resident—the collateral damage, right?"

"Yes."

"Why do we need her either?" You cleaned up the mess of the two dead NSA guys, so what's wrong with just taking this Zachary out along with this kid Quinton?"

"Well, for one thing, we don't have Zachary," Grigsby sighed. "Maybe we could use Quinton to lure her, too? I think they're romantically involved. I don't know for sure."

"No, too complicated," Calhoun shook his head. "It wouldn't bring Zachary to us. It would bring a lot of others though. No, way . . . it's too complicated. We have him here now. We'll get her later. Let's deal with him. Understood?"

"Now?"

"Yes, now."

"Dr. Zachary. Good to see you alive," Pritcherman bounded through the radiology door. "I've actually missed you."

"Dr. Pritcherman?" Zachary strained to see from the scanner, her head fixed in place by a helmet-like contraption needed for an accurate scan.

"Lie still and let me tell you what we need to do," the neurosurgeon continued. "I know you've been through a lot, and against your will from what Dr. Jankowski tells me."

"Dean, did you tell him everything?"

"Yes, Dr. Zachary," Dean Jankowski replied. "You are in good hands."

"Here's what I'm proposing . . . and the risks, benefits and alternatives," Pritcherman was all business. "They've put a metallic probe into your right temporo-parietal junction. That's an easy area to get to, but this is uncharted territory, since we don't know much about this probe."

"It can't be too complicated," Zachary's sarcasm cut through the end of the scan." After all, a pathologist put it in."

"Point well taken, Doctor," Pritcherman smiled. "Nevertheless, it is your decision whether to proceed or not. If we do remove it, my concerns would be continued seizures from the injury of its placement. Also, there is the possibility of bleeding and more disruption of whatever synapses in your brain are involved."

"Geez."

"I'm going to be honest with you, this is risky, but not the surgery part. What's risky are the possible complications directly from the probe. From what damage it's already caused going in and the additional damage that will result from its coming out. I'm not concerned about the actual surgery. That I can handle."

"Of that I'm sure, too," Zachary breathed deeply as she was removed from the scanner and able to sit up. "I never wanted to have to undergo neurosurgery, but if it has to be, you are the one who I'd want to do it."

"I'll try to live up to your confidence. In the meantime, I think it's necessary to give you a large dose of the ketamine, an anesthetic-sized dose, to insure no seizure activity during surgery. The procedure won't take long unless there are complications. You do understand the gravity of this. Dr. Zachary, you could die or be severely disabled. I feel I must remind you of that over and over. There's no need for a formal craniotomy. We can use the same small burr hole Zendejas used to place it. But I want you to make this decision with your eyes wide open."

"That bastard," Zachary hissed.

"*Fat, egotistical* bastard," Pritcherman added. "Do you understand? Do you want to proceed?"

"Get this piece of whatever out of me as soon as you can, Dr. Pritcherman. I'm a doctor. I understand the risks. I'd rather be dead or paralyzed than have someone trying to control me—someone I don't even know. Proceed, Dr. Pritcherman. Now, if not sooner, please. And Dr. Pritcherman?"

"Yes."

"Have you seen Quinton?"

"He's the one who solved this mystery," Pritcherman smiled. "You could say we've been partners."

"Please give him a message for me," Zachary weakly returned the smile.

"And that is?"

Zachary lifted her head and made direct eye contact with Pritcherman. "Tell him, . . . Yes."

"What?"

"*Yes.* He'll know what I mean."

Turning to the Dean, the neurosurgeon ordered, "Let's get her to the OR. You have the ketamine there, correct?"

"Yes," the Dean helped Pritcherman push Zachary's gurney down the hall towards the operating room area.

Arriving at the surgical suite, Pritcherman said, "Give her the full dose, as we discussed."

"Now?"

"Now."

FBI Special Agent John Abbouse sat alone in his downtown office on this bright morning, seemingly unconcerned by the world's events. At seven in the morning, he'd been at his desk for some time. Impeccably dressed and groomed, he was reading a memorandum on his desktop computer when his phone rang. After answering, he listened without speaking for several moments. He sat forward and replied, "Good. You know where. But . . . no, wait . . . ."

He listened obediently to his caller.

"Not yet. Not now."

— Always Consider The Future And How Your Actions Now May Influence It —

XVIII

*A*n hour later, just before eight o'clock, John Abbouse answered his phone. An anonymous voice briefly gave him an instruction and hung up. The FBI Special Agent set the phone down and looked up, murmuring to himself, *let the games begin.* Letting out a long breath, he adjusted his tie, more out of habit than need, and picked up the phone again, this time speed dialing.

"Alpha team, *Go*," disconnecting and making another call. "Beta team, assume your positions. *You are No Go*, I repeat, *No Go* until my command." After hanging up that call, he dialed a third number. "Secure the operating area only. Gamma team, you are now active backup." He tossed the handset onto the desktop.

He sat back down and stared out at the room, alone for the moment, knowing he'd just ordered the start of chaos. *Now I know why I learned the Greek alphabet in my college fraternity*, he smiled. Then he broke the silence, *"Forgive me, Stanley."*

"Good morning, Dr. Chesney," Pritcherman greeted the anesthesiologist and the surgical team as he and the Dean wheeled the gurney carrying Zachary into the OR. "Sorry about the change in patients. This one is a top priority for the Dean. You all know Dean Jankowski?" As he looked around the room, no one said a word. "He'll be scrubbing in, but don't let him touch anything," smiling as he spoke. "I don't want a damned neurologist having any chance of bragging about helping on a surgical case. This will be a simple foreign body removal through a previous small burr hole. No need to set up for a formal craniotomy. Simple, quick procedure. Come on, Dean, I'll show you how to scrub while they get the patient ready.

"Dr. Chesney, please administer the ketamine when you're ready." Chesney and the OR team went to work without speaking, preparing Zachary for surgery, none recognizing their patient as a colleague. He would use the IV started for her radiology scans to administer the anesthesia, and in the meantime, he ventilated Zachary with one hundred percent oxygen in anticipation of anesthesia induction. Throughout the entire time, Zachary did not speak.

Pritcherman and the Dean scrubbed and completed their preparations, as did the rest of the OR team. On entering thc room they found Zachary anesthetized, intubated and ready. Positioning her on her left side, the team quickly shaved and prepared the surgery site. Chesney was busy infusing the ketamine. Pritcherman quickly incised the skin down to the previous bony burr hole and opened the *dura*, moving to the microscope, placing the Dean on the teaching second head.

"You do realize we're in unchartered territory here?"

"Yes," Jankowski responded. "Get this over with and let's find someone to tell our story."

"Damn," the neurosurgeon cursed. "Look at the blood coming up from the probe site. He must've come too close to a perforating vein or artery," using suction and Gelfoam in an attempt to control the bleeding." He glanced up at the Dean and noticed several figures at the door, "We have company—don't turn around. I don't recognize any of them . . . and they don't look like medical types."

"What?"

"Yeah," P focused on Zachary's brain as he commented, "They're wearing military fatigues and masks."

The fog began to lift. As I began regaining consciousness, Calhoun's phone rang. He had been discussing my disposition with Smith and Grigsby when he answered the call. He stiffened as he listened, and said, "Yes, sir, I understand. I have everything under control. No, I don't anticipate any problems. It's not like we're overseas." Another pause, and he concluded the call with, "I'll take care of it, sir."

Turning to Grigsby, "Where were we—oh, yes—what to do with Mr. Quinton, our other collateral damage." As he was speaking, the two second-years returned.

"Any problems?" Grigsby asked.

"No."

"We've got another assignment," Calhoun walked closer to the two. "Grigsby will be eliminating the problem with Mr. Quinton with extreme prejudice. Handle it, gentlemen,"

Turning next to Smith. "Find me Pritcherman and the Dean. If we can control all the civilians, we may be able to limit the damage. I told the Director everything was under control. I'm headed back to McLean. Don't let me be wrong." As he stepped toward the door, it suddenly burst open and twenty-five masked and helmeted FBI assault team members swarmed into the room, pointing their assault rifles at Smith, Grigsby, Calhoun, the two second-year medical students . . . and me. I could see at least three or four tightly grouped red dots from the laser sights reflected off each of the other four targets' torsos.

The commander lowered his weapon, "Secure the prisoners. Medics, check out the unconscious one on the couch." Turning his back on Smith and Grigsby, he walked over to the couch where I was lying supine, "Alpha Leader to Top Hat. Alpha party secure. No incident casualties. One subject requiring immediate medical attention. Transporting now."

General James Bitterman was still pacing as his team loaded Dr. John Luis Zendejas onto a gurney for transport to the helicopter. Bitterman was talking to himself, audibly, "This is getting away from me. I've lost one civilian and have another one incapacitated. Maybe I *am* better off taking him out here?" Then shaking his head. This decisive general officer was suddenly indecisive, an unfamiliar circumstance.

As the NSA away team made final preparations to leave, the Captain turned to the General, "We're ready, s—"

There was a loud explosion from a flash-bang grenade tossed into the room, temporarily blinding and disorienting them all. When the smoke cleared, they were all surrounded and subdued under the laser-sighted weapons of another group of masked FBI assault team members. In the confusion, the NSA team dropped the gurney carrying the morbidly obese Zendejas, who rolled off the gurney and onto the floor. Several FBI agents quickly secured the NSA weapons, handcuffed the offenders, and sat them in the corner–all but General Bitterman.

The team leader addressed him directly, "General Bitterman. You and your team are under arrest for violations of federal and military law. Please give me your weapon–slowly, sir–and place your hands on top of your head."

Bitterman hesitated at first, but was persuaded into compliance by the five laser dots trained on his forehead and the other five he could plainly see on his chest. He sighed loudly and handed over his sidearm, butt-end first, and submissively placed his hands on his head. He was quickly handcuffed and seated with the rest of his team.

"Beta leader to Top Hat. Beta party secure. No incident casualties. One very obese head injury victim requires medical attention. Not critical. Transporting all."

"Damn it, I can't stop the oozing from the probe site," Pritcherman was sweating and throwing used sponges everywhere. More suction, Jankowski. How are her vitals, Chesney?"

"Not good," the anesthesiologist replied. "Her blood pressure's down and her pulse is up. And I can't—" Pritcherman felt like an earthquake just struck. "What?"

"Oh, God, she's having a seizure," Chesney shouted, turning to the circulating nurse. "I need ten milligrams of *diazepam*, stat!" He administered the paralytic agent immediately and in about sixty seconds, the violent, generalized shaking stopped.

"That should help your surgical field, but she's still having seizure activity. We just don't see it."

"I know, damn it. I'm a neurosurgeon. I know a paralytic doesn't stop the seizure," Pritcherman snapped, refocusing back on the surgery at hand. "Come on, Zachary. Fight with me!" P heard himself say.

"*SHIT!* She's in cardiac arrest!" Dr. Chesney barked loudly. "Starting CPR. I'm giving her atropine and epinephrine." They rolled Zach onto her back.

Dean Viktor Igorseg Jankowski pulled away from the head surgery and went to Zachary's chest to assist with CPR.

"She's in asystole, Stanley," The droning, high-pitched tone accompanied the flatline trace on the cardiac monitor that was supposed to be beep, beep, beeping to normal sinus rhythm. Waving his hands across the chest of third-year surgical resident, Barbara Lynne Zachary, the Dean terminated the resuscitation. The OR crew stopped CPR and a profound silence descended on the room. More than one tear was shed, quietly, as the cardiac monitor was switched off.

Stanley J. Pritcherman, senior neurosurgeon at his prestigious University Hospital clutched his gloved hands together, and began to pray, "God . . . forgive us for what we have done . . ." The entire operating crew bowed their heads in reverence.

A few moments later, the OR doors swung open and a team of twenty-five masked personnel entered as well, observing the silence, their weapons pointed at the floor. The leader gently spoke, "Doctor Pritcherman, I'm very sorry for your loss. I have orders to take you and Dean Jankowski with me, sir. Will you come this way, please?" pointing to the door.

The OR personnel never looked up as Pritcherman tore off his gloves, throwing them on the floor, and followed Dean Jankowski out of the room. When they entered the hall, the leader quietly spoke, "Gamma leader to Top Hat. Gamma party secure. One casualty. Not incident related. Leaving a debriefing team here and transporting two."

The downtown office of the FBI soon began to fill with the various captives. Zendejas and I were being attended by several unknown medical personnel in the large conference room where we and our fellow detainees had been taken. The sedative I had been given was fully worn off. I was minimally groggy but awake. All of us remained in the custody of their particular FBI teams, but our handcuffs were removed. The others were seated in the conference room at four tables formed into a square, each group of captives separated from the others and guarded by at least five armed personnel standing around their assigned group. The last to be brought in were Drs. Pritcherman and Jankowski. I was relieved to see my partner. But no Zachary. The pit of my stomach tightened.

At the front of the room on a larger table were four large, flat screen monitors, currently displaying the FBI logo, and a podium in front of it. My leg was killing me and my head felt like it was going to explode. They left my head bandage in place. My leg wound was irrigated and a bulky dressing applied while another medic gave me an injection of antibiotics. They mumbled something about needing surgery in the next twenty-four hours. Ironically, I remembered back to when this all started. This is how I felt that first day I met Dr. Pritcherman—headache and an awful leg pain—from the soon-to-be dead guy biting the same leg as today.

John Abbouse stepped up to the podium and the four monitors behind him flickered briefly, then each displayed one of four persons whom I did not recognize.

Abbouse spoke, "For those who don't know me, I'm Special Agent John Abbouse of the Federal Bureau of Investigation, in charge of this operation at the written request of the President of the United States and his National Security Advisor, Sheila L. Rasmussen, on the right end screen. On the other screens are the Directors of the FBI, F. Donald Peterson; the CIA, Webster Trent Scott; and the NSA, General Leslie P. Johnson.

"Let me be clear, since we have civilians with us, there has been a breach of our government and Constitution by many of you here today, and it is in the national interest to resolve this in a way that allows the public to remain confident in its government. Many of you are not here by choice. Although I am an FBI Special Agent, and my Director knows vaguely of my involvement, on this assignment I am working directly for National Security Advisor Rasmussen. All three governmental agencies and some of their personnel have been involved in illegal, criminal, and, arguably, treasonable activities–some more than others, but all are culpable.

"Did you want to add anything, Ms. Rasmussen?"

"Not at this time, Special Agent. Please continue as we discussed."

There was obvious consternation among many in the room and visible in three of the faces on the monitors. "It is my intent to remain as objective as possible, not letting my personal feelings enter into our discussions today." The Special Agent was wearing a wireless lapel microphone that allowed him to walk away from the podium and he was trying to contain his anger.

"To say that I am disappointed, as a sworn federal officer, is an understatement. As a citizen, I am appalled, and as such, demand accountability. There are four civilians involved–Drs. Zendejas, Jankowski, and Pritcherman, as well as a third-year medical student, Mr. Quinton. It is Mr. Quinton who unknowingly uncovered this conspiracy. The rest of you are officers of the government in one way or another.

"That means you all should have known better. Worse, you recruited civilians into this mischief–civilians who likely knew better, but had no sworn allegiance or oath to uphold as you do." Abbouse paused a few seconds, then exhaled slowly. "I insist you all hold your comments unless called on or are asked a direct question. Is that clear?"

All of us silently nodded in agreement.

"You have all been disarmed and searched. All agents are now asked to leave the room and take up a perimeter position outside the door. Thank you for your service."

The assault team members filed out and closed the door. I noticed that Smith, Grigsby, Calhoun, and the two second-years were all together at a table on one side. General Bitterman and Zendejas were at another table, their NSA assault team no longer there to protect them. Zendejas was in a wheelchair. I was lying on a gurney next to Dr. Pritcherman at the back table, my leg still throbbing. I leaned to P to ask him about Zachary when Abbouse interrupted me before we could talk.

"Mr. Quinton," the FBI SAC admonished me, "I told you, no talking unless directly addressed. You are in enough trouble already. I suggest you heed my warning."

"Yes, sir," I answered meekly, pulling back from Pritcherman.

Easing his sternness, Abbouse took a step in my direction, and continued, "You are a brave young man–naive and unsophisticated–and it's hard to argue with your results, Mr. Quinton. Our country owes you a debt of gratitude for your service."

I nodded my acknowledgment without speaking.

"General Bitterman," Abbouse turned to look at him directly. "You are relieved of your command. You will likely stand at court martial at a later time. Your commanding officer, General Johnson, is aware of our actions here." Abbouse looked at the far-left screen directly at the three-star head of the NSA.

"General Johnson, the President awaits your letter of resignation by the end of the day." General Johnson remained stoic and solemn, maintaining his silence, but nodding his assent.

Abbouse returned to Bitterman, "Your assault team is being debriefed and will face internal discipline as needed. You owe this group an explanation for why you initiated this program, General Bitterman. Now, sir."

Brigadier General James Bitterman cleared his throat and continued to sit ramrod straight in his chair, "No sir, I do not, and will not tell—"

"Yes General, *you will*," General Johnson intervened. "You owe an explanation not only to them but to me as well. You violated my confidence and are way out of bounds. As your superior, I will take the fall for your actions, but not without knowing why. *Talk, General, that's an order. Now!*"

Still sitting at attention, he cleared his throat again, "This country is under attack from multiple enemy countries and non-state actors and doesn't even know it. Other agencies, specifically the CIA and FBI, make only a token effort at stopping this attack. Our efforts at NSA have also been half-hearted and incomplete at best. We are being penetrated daily by cyber-attacks on our government, our institutions, and our infrastructure. This program is a counter-terrorism effort fully compliant with the law, if not with your express knowledge and control, General Johnson."

"Under what authority, General?" Johnson was shifting in his chair.

"The Congress of the United States, sir," Bitterman confidently answered. "After the 9/11 attacks, you are aware of the I.A.O. being established by DARPA. This program is an authorized continuation of that program, sir."

"General Bitterman, the Information Awareness Office was defunded by Congress in 2003–as you are well aware–and even if it were not, as Director of NSA, Congressional actions and funding are my responsibility, not yours. You are insubordinate," General Johnson was fuming.

"Sir. I refer you to the joint House and Senate Special Committee for—"

"Did you know about this, Ms. Rasmussen?"

"I'll withhold comment for now, General," came the National Security Advisor's non-committal reply. "Continue, Mr. Abbouse."

"General Bitterman, assuming for the moment you were, in fact, authorized to establish—"

"*Authorized to continue an existing program*, sir."

"Don't interrupt me again, General. You will have ample time," Abbouse snapped. "Under what authority do you have the right to kill U.S. citizens? Not only does that violate our Constitution, but even the I.A.O. program, when it existed, only authorized gathering of information and only on known or suspected terrorists. The Department of Defense Appropriations Act signed into law on October 1, 2003, expressly terminated that office at that same time. Nothing remotely related to it ever authorized domestic surveillance, General. You are way out of bounds."

"I will stand by my program, as authorized by Congress in the—"

"Your program, General?" Abbouse was now standing next to the brigadier. "*Your program*, sir? That is precisely the problem. This is your program, not the NSA's nor any other branch or agency of our government. You violated the chain of command and, I will assume, the Executive branch knew nothing of it. No further comment is required of you at this time, General. You, sir, make me ill."

Abbouse turned away and slowly approached Bill Calhoun, Assistant Director of the CIA, then stood quietly for a few seconds. "So you sent agents in to find out what all this was about, Mr. Calhoun. Correct?"

"I sent agents to investigate. An attempt to interdict what I believed was an illegal program. Yes, sir," Calhoun felt he was on stable grounds.

"Illegal, you say?"

"Yes, sir," Calhoun answered without emotion. "The CIA had an interest in the NSA's I.A.O. projects, such as the Human ID project and others. Our concern was they were violating their mission by using domestic citizens as their guinea pigs. Still, the concept of long-range biometric identification technologies could be most valuable to us. It wasn't high priority to us, but we did send an agent."

"Not high priority, you say? Then why was your agent sent in undercover?" Abbouse tilted his head.

"Not a priority, that is, until he turned up missing."

"And General Bitterman was less than enthusiastic about the CIA becoming involved?"

"I would categorize that as an understatement," Calhoun smirked.

Bitterman strongly reacted, "In order to penetrate our various enemies, we devised this probe program, allowing our agents to gain access to our adversary's secrets and techniques. The probes were designed for storage and control of the agents. I did not want the CIA interfering with that."

"Under what authority is the NSA allowed to implement field agents? You are specifically prohibited from gathering intelligence, especially domestically," Abbouse countered.

"No sir. That is your opinion. NSA and Congressional special counsels have ruled otherwise," Bitterman asserted.

"I'm not aware of that," General Johnson interjected. "Why am I not aware of this?"

"You are," Abbouse turned to his face on the monitor. "You are playing the innocent here, General Johnson and playing it well. But not accurately, sir."

Turning in the general direction of Dr. Zendejas, Abbouse walked over to him and spoke. "Dr. Zendejas, you conducted an autopsy several weeks before. Do you remember the one I am referring to?"

"Well, I do many autopsies—"

"Not on patients with insulin poisoning, Doctor," Abbouse interrupted. "Does that jog your memory? Maybe I can help you. You see, this patient was a government agent and he wasn't a diabetic. That means he was murdered, Doctor. Any thoughts on that?"

"No comment. I wish to assert my Fifth Amendment right to—"

"Come now, Doctor," Abbouse smiled. "This isn't a court of law and this proceeding will never see the light of day. In this room, you have no Third, Fourth, or Fifth Amendment rights, or any others for that matter." As he spoke, Abbouse moved close to Zendejas' wheelchair and now leaned over talking just inches away from his face.

"You are in deep shit, Doctor," he slowly articulated each word. "Right now, you are on the hook for murder . . . unless you suddenly remember who really did it?"

"I don't—"

"You don't know? But General Bitterman does, right?" Abbouse walked back toward the General. "You needed the CIA agent to go away, didn't you General? Which part of the law are you going to hide behind for murder?"

"He was going to blow the cover off the entire operation. The agent was collateral damage," Bitterman snapped.

"So you called Dr. Zendejas?"

"Not me," Zendejas chimed in. "He was dead when he got to pathology. I was told it was a routine autopsy on someone who received too much insulin."

"No," Abbouse sighed. "It wasn't General Bitterman either, I don't suppose. But who was this guy?" The Special Agent walked to the next table. "Mr. Calhoun," Abbouse now trained his focus on him, "did you want to tell us about that routine autopsy? Did you want to weigh in on that?"

"Not really," *Cautious Bill* didn't flinch.

"This is like pulling teeth," Abbouse said to the room, then leaning into the Assistant Director, "We'll get to teeth later. You knew where your missing agent was and what happened to him didn't you, Mr. Calhoun?"

"Yes."

"But," walking to the monitor in front of General Johnson and addressing him, "You called General Johnson—not General Bitterman—to inquire, shall we say, about his demise? Did you have thoughts on that, General Johnson?"

"Look," Johnson was clearly shaken. "This CIA agent was about to blow up this probe project. I couldn't allow that to happen. I worked that out with Mr. Calhoun. It was unfortunate that he died, but necessary to protect the overall project."

Abbouse paused a moment, and was letting General Johnson's response sink in. Finally, he almost whispered to the monitor, "That means you knew about this program all along, General Johnson. You just didn't want your deputy, General Bitterman, to know you knew. That way, if and when there were problems, he could take the fall for you. Plausible deniability, right, sir?"

Abbouse was shaking his head as he walked away from the monitor. Walking back to Calhoun, the SAC stood in front of him for at least fifteen seconds without speaking. He stared at the Assistant Director of the CIA deeply, intently, then said, simply, "Why?"

"Excuse me?"

Raising his voice, "Why would you make a deal to cover up one of your agent's deaths, Mr. Assistant Director? I'll bet agents Smith and Grigsby were unaware of the first agent and his demise? Would you care to tell them about your concern for your agents now, sir?"

Abbouse turned to Smith and Grigsby as they sat passively. He knew the message wasn't entirely lost on them. "The casual moral judgments astound me—of both the NSA and CIA top brass—all of you should be ashamed." Taking a step toward Grigsby, "How can you reconcile your CIA actions with your medical career? Or with your Hippocratic oath, Mr. Grigsby? Have you thought about that?"

"Sir, the safety and protection of my country was my highest priority," Grigsby responded. "All others are subordinate to that. Besides, I haven't sworn any oath to Hippocrates yet. It isn't required."

"Really?" Abbouse feigned a smile. "Not required? Do you even agree with it?"

"Not really." Grigsby was his flippant normal self. "We're in a lot more perilous times than ancient Greece. Wouldn't you agree, Mr. Abbouse?"

"Ah, the fiction of youth," the FBI agent mused. "Each generation thinks theirs is in the most peril and ultimately relearns the lessons time teaches every era." Shaking his head, "Do you not risk losing everything dear—your freedom, your values, your ideals, even your family—in a vain effort to protect those very same things?"

Abbouse shook his head in disagreement and took two steps over to Smith. "And now we come to Anna Jean Dupuy, a.k.a. Jessica Jane Smith, MD, of Georgetown University. Whose idea was it to place a probe in you, Dr. Smith, or do you prefer Anna Jean? Wait. I forgot. The probe isn't real, right?"

"Is there a question, Special Agent?" Smith made a good poker player.

"Oh yes, there are a few questions," Abbouse was clearly sarcastic. "Let's start with you attending an autopsy that involved Mr. Quinton. I'm guessing you remember that event. He certainly does. He remembered your attendance with Dr. Zendejas. But I've been troubled by his story from the first. You see, he says you gave him an injection when the lights went out. An injection in his hip and then helped him stay on the floor. Here's my problem with that account. That's at least four hands, Anna Jean, your two and—"

"Grigsby's."

"Now that makes sense," Abbouse continued. "Except I'm still missing some other hands—you know it's hard to turn off lights all the way across the room, hold someone down, give them an injection. So, Anna Jean, who else was there?"

"Dr. Zendejas, and John, his assistant."

"But they were gloved up and had their hands around the dead guy's brain. Oh, by the way, do you know who the dead guy is, don't you? I'm sorry . . . *was?*"

"No."

"Of course not," Abbouse leaned into her face. "He was a very dear friend *of mine*. We went through the FBI Academy together. You see, he was in Europe recently and picked up some metal over there. A probe in his brain. You probably think we lost track of him, but we didn't. We were able to track his whereabouts using a tracking device. So we knew where he was—not precisely, but in the general vicinity—we just couldn't get to him before the NSA did. You remember them—they're the people you used to work for before you didn't.

"Aw, what the hell. Let's just lay all our cards on the table. You work for the CIA, specifically for Mr. Calhoun, who sent you to find out about what happened to my friend. Not exactly find out. More like, make sure he never got out. Right, Anna Jean?"

"If you say so."

"And Mr. Grigsby came along for the ride," Abbouse glanced over at him. "I'll bet you didn't know he was really there to spy on you? Did you know that Anna Jean?" Abbouse used her real name as if he were twisting a knife blade.

"Mr. Grigsby worked for me, yes."

"No, no, Anna Jean, he didn't work for you at all. He was reporting directly to CIA Director Scott, not to Mr. Calhoun, like you," Abbouse twisted his head as he came closer. "Why do ya think he might do that? Doesn't the CIA have a chain of command? Aren't you his superior, Anna Jean?"

Smith was ever-so-slightly beginning to fidget. "This is all very interesting, but rather boring. What's your point?"

"My point is this," turning to face a monitor in the middle, "your handler, Mr. Calhoun, and you were both being double-crossed by your Director. Why would he do that? You see, that tells me this was important. It also tells me higher up the chain thought it was important, too. Did you want to weigh in on that, Director Scott?"

"Negative, Special Agent." The CIA Director responded. Webster Trent Scott didn't get to where he was by divulging information.

There was immediate silence lasting for at least a minute as the Director and Special Agent played a game of visual chicken. Both stared at each other, minimally blinking, each fixed his gaze on the other. Abbouse broke first. "No, I wouldn't expect you would," sighing as he turned away. "So we'll get there by another route."

Turning back to Smith, Abbouse smiled as he approached her this time. "Tell me about Messrs. Jenkins and Pemberton."

"Two second-year medical students assigned to the neurosurgical service," Smith offered indifferently.

"Really?" Abbouse was not feigning belief. "And all this time I thought they worked for you. Was that when you were with the NSA or CIA? They seemed pretty helpful to you. Right?"

"If you say so," exhaling loudly.

Rapidly turning to the two, Abbouse shouted at them, "Who told you to take Quinton to the stairwell? Who told you dispose of the two bodies on Quinton's street? Who told you to administer the insulin?"

Pemberton was the first to blurt out the information, "Grigsby, but someone called him to—"

"Quiet," Smith fixed her gaze on him, as if a pair of scalpels were ready to excise his tongue.

"I'm sorry, Dr. Smith. Did you have something to say?"

Then stepping in front of Grigsby, Abbouse continued the onslaught, "Or do, you, Mr. Grigsby? Who was it that told you to poison both agents?"

"I did," CIA Director Scott responded, relieving Grigsby of the responsibility. "It was my order, and I take responsibility. *Move on.*"

Ignoring the Director's comment, Abbouse leaned into Pemberton and quietly whispered, "You've been in class here for two years. I think you really enjoy medicine. Tell me how you got mixed up in all this, son?"

"I was a fixer for the agency," Pemberton was trembling. "I made things go away. I did it in exchange for scholarship money to go to medical school. I didn't know I was killing them with insulin. I clean things up, but

I don't kill. Because I was in medical school, they knew I wanted to learn so they let me give the medication. But I didn't know—"

"Who is *they*, Mr. Pemberton?"

"Grigsby told me to give the medications, and he called us to carry Quinton to the stairs. And he also called us to get rid of the two black guys."

"You said 'called *us*.' So, it was Mr. Jenkins who helped you?" Abbouse continued.

"Yes," Jenkins interceded. "We both started several years ago as fixers. Nothing important at first, only to earn our scholarships. They knew we wanted to go to medical school. So we did what they asked of us. Mostly grunt work, but it paid the bills. Once we got into medical school, it seems like our responsibilities changed. They became more difficult for sure."

"Like disposing of bodies?"

"Yeah," Jenkins nodded his head. "Grigsby told us he was putting us both in for a citation. We both knew Grigsby was full of shit, but, all-in-all, he was OK to work for."

"Did you feel like Grigsby was your boss or Dr. Smith?"

"Grigsby had been with us through two years of school. Smith only came a few weeks ago," Pemberton added. "Grigsby had us do a lot of menial things in those two years—mostly his laundry and errand-type stuff. Until the last few weeks. Then it seemed like all hell broke loose. Moving dead bodies . . . and Quinton—"

"Moving dead bodies?"

"Sure," Pemberton continued. "Once Dr. Zendejas finished the autopsies, he had us remove the bodies, although he kept a few parts."

"Zendejas had you do that?"

"Well, come to think of it, Grigsby was the one who told us, but Zendejas was there."

"Didn't you think it was unusual for a hospital to dispose of bodies using two supposed second-year medical students? It reminds me of the middle ages."

"It paid the bills," Jenkins interjected.

"So, we've established that you both had a price," the SAC concluded. "It seems you all do."

Walking over to the monitors, Abbouse continued. "We've got the logistics of all this down. What I still don't understand is the reason behind it. The *why?*

I couldn't help it and leaned over to P when I thought Abbouse was looking at the second years. "P. Everyone's here but Zachary. Where is she?"

Pritcherman looked away, not saying a word, with a small tear in his eye. "I'm sorry, Q. I'm so sorry—"

"Stanley . . . er, Dr. Pritcherman," Abbouse turned his attention to my partner. "I'll get to you soon enough. For now, could I have your undivided attention?" Turning back to the monitors, he walked closer to F. Donald Peterson's image. "Mr. Peterson, you are my superior at the FBI–Director, in fact. I have always admired your leadership skills and appreciate your support." Pausing briefly, he resumed his colloquy, "That makes this task all the more difficult. None of this made sense to me . . . until I started thinking about a grand conspiracy. What if all the Directors of our governmental intelligence and law enforcement agencies got together? Now, I thought, that would be impossible," he took two steps backward and exhaled, lowering his head. "But it wasn't impossible, was it, sir?"

"You're a good agent, Mr. Abbouse," Peterson sat forward. "Did you want to tell me more about this grand conspiracy concept of yours?"

"It's the *why* question, sir," John Abbouse persisted. "I couldn't get that out of my head. Then I did some digging. I didn't know whether the conspiracy came first or once all this was in motion and gaining momentum. You see, governments and their bureaucracies aren't always on the same page. In fact, they are frequently at odds with one another. One says the sky is blue and immediately the other says it isn't. That's what I think happened here.

"The NSA started a program and the CIA opposed it. Not so much because they thought it was wrong or illegal, but because the NSA thought of it first. So they tried to defeat it, sabotage it, even take it over. Wouldn't you agree, Mr. Peterson?"

"If you say so, Special Agent."

"Ah, now we have the proverbial *Which came first, the chicken or the egg?* dilemma," Abbouse didn't miss a beat. "But I still don't know what the purpose of all this is!" Raising his voice for emphasis and then lowering it again.

"However, it doesn't really matter to the three of you," turning once again to the monitors. "You three Directors of the CIA, NSA and FBI. You just didn't want either of the other agencies to get the jump on yours—a turf war of inestimable consequence, right? The fact that the Constitution and a gaggle of laws would be, and were being, trod underfoot was of no concern. No, you just wanted to keep this among yourselves and make damn sure the public didn't find out. At least not the public's representatives, the Congress and the Executive branch."

"You're painting with a broad brush, Mr. Abbouse," Peterson looked stern.

"Am I? Ah, but it is an accurate brush, isn't it, sir?"

"Mr. Abbouse, may we come to some conclusions? The President is waiting for me," National Security Advisor Rasmussen asked.

"Yes. Just a few more issues to clear up Madam Director," Abbouse responded.

"I have some questions for you, Mr. Abbouse." Peterson changed his demeanor. "Are you saying the only reason the three heads of our nation's top intelligence and law enforcement agencies are assembled here today is . . . a *turf war?* You'd better have more than that, Special Agent."

"Heard of FutureMAP, Mr. Peterson?"

"I think that's about enough of that," CIA Director Scott interjected.

"The NSA had been researching predictive market techniques, but that was abandoned several years ago," General Bitterman added.

"Maybe so, gentlemen, but that's not the aspect of FutureMAP I'm talking about. And I believe you all know that." Abbouse pointed to the three monitors displaying the directors.

Turning to the fourth monitor displaying the image of the National Security Advisor, "Ms. Rasmussen, that's not what we're talking about, is it? You were aware of FutureMAP as well, weren't you?"

Sheila Rasmussen sat without saying a word, staring out at the room.

"I'll leave that alone for now," Abbouse knew he had touched a most sensitive nerve.

"And so here we are, left with our four civilians–Mr. Quinton, and Drs. Jankowski, Zendejas, and Pritcherman–the innocents, right? Well, OK, my innocents. Let's see what you know about all this, shall we? Each of you has his price, right?"

"I resent the implication, Mr. Abbouse," Dean Jankowski was first to take a bite of the bait. "I have served this country since my younger days, honorably and without asking for thanks."

"No, you didn't ask for thanks, and yes, you had served this country, your naturalized country, long and well," Abbouse responded. "Do you have any idea what it costs to hospitalize your sister, Dr. Jankowski? Take a guess."

"Well, I wouldn't—"

"No need. Suffice it to say that, to date, it's in the millions, and this country gladly pays those costs for the services you provided so many, many years ago. Service, I might add, motivated by your vengeance against your former country, Poland, and its treatment of your parents. But I digress. That monthly check you receive. Do you include that in your resentment, sir? Those tailored suits you are so fond of and the frequent trips abroad? If I'm not mistaken, we pay for those, too, right?"

"Yes," Jankowski was quieter now. "Part of my resentment, but not my motivation, Mr. Abbouse."

"Agreed, but a nice perk nevertheless," the SAC countered. "As I said, everyone has his price."

Turning to Dr. Pritcherman. "You have been one busy neurosurgeon, Stanley," putting his hand on Pritcherman's shoulder, "by way of disclosure, Dr. Pritcherman took care of my wife during her cancer treatments before her death, and I consider him a friend," patting his shoulders, before taking a step away. "And I am also deeply sorry for your loss this morning, Doctor."

"Thank you, John," P tried to smile. "We both made it through a tough time together."

"Ah, that it were so again, Stan," Abbouse seemed more distant. "You see, my friend, you also had a price didn't you?"

"Yes, I'll admit it," Pritcherman was defiant. "All of you were struggling to control minds, but forgot about the soul. What is so important to you that would cause you to give up your humanity?"

"Good question, Stan. But back to you—"

"Yeah. I sold out for the lure of a few trinkets. All my biometrics and speech technology toys were from the government. So what?"

"From what part of the government, Doctor," Abbouse was gentle.

"I don't know. What difference does it make?"

"Because whoever gave it to you owns you. That's why," the FBI agent replied.

"No one owns me," P snapped back.

"Ah, but they do, Stanley. They provided you all the technology under the ruse that you would field test it, right?"

"Yes, the CIA told me—"

"Do you really think the CIA would let you have their technology to test? It's been well-vetted, trust me," Abbouse advised. "No, what they wanted was access to you and your office. Or, more precisely, whoever came and went in your office."

"Yeah, I figured someone had me bugged," the neurosurgeon was growing impatient. "So I put in some counter-technology of my own to—"

"Stanley," Abbouse interrupted. "You thought you could outsmart the CIA or the NSA? Once they had dirt on you, they were going to approach you and involve you in their probe scheme. Oh, by the way, that means it was the NSA that had you, Dr. Pritcherman, not the CIA. Of course, the CIA had the NSA, and we here at the FBI had them both—I think you get the picture."

"Yes, I get the picture," P was about to explode, I could tell. "You're all a bunch of lunatics! You still haven't said why all this happened. And what the hell are you doing letting a friggin' pathologist do neurosurgery? Has anyone considered the moral imperative for all of this versus the risk? I still don't understand what Smith was trying to accomplish with her fake probe. I guess penetrate somebody's security or something. You're all nuts, not to mention paranoid. But all that pales in comparison to your worst offense. You bastards caused the death of one of this university's top surgical residents, Dr. Zachary. While you're doling out responsibility, John, who's taking responsibility for that?"

"*No!*" I cried out loud. It was the first time I'd actually heard that Zachary was dead. P had intimated it, but it hit me like a building had collapsed on me. I couldn't help it and didn't care who saw. This was my government that had done this and I did recognize it. I felt nauseous.

"Mr. Quinton, I am truly sorry. And Dr. Pritcherman, there are no words to convey how sorry I am about the loss of your surgical resident," John Abbouse said. "She was truly an innocent victim in this. I think we in government do owe you an explanation of the *Why*. And I'd like to hear what my colleagues have to say as well."

"*This is a national security issue at the highest level!*" FBI Director Peterson tried in vain to cut off the discussion.

"Come now, sir. This is your national security team—the FBI, CIA and NSA," Abbouse contradicted his boss. "All Dr. Pritcherman is asking is what is the moral imperative?"

"This country is at risk, as General Bitterman said earlier," CIA Director Scott spoke up. "I don't think it will matter what the civilians know. It's their country, too. I'm sure you've heard of the *Stuxnet virus* discovered back in the early 2010s in Iran, and the Pakistanis selling missile and nuclear technology. Cyber-warfare. This is all about interdicting our adversaries preemptively. The probes were meant to allow agents access to huge volumes of data and upload it immediately to our secure databanks—directly from the probes without human intervention. If the agents were caught, we could control them, erase or scramble their memories so even if they were tortured, they couldn't give up secrets."

"It all sounded workable until the probe complications," NSA Director Johnson added. "That's really when things went to hell. We were field-testing the probes as a way to hack into systems. There are about two million viruses introduced to the Internet each month. We were trying to hack the hackers, but in a way they wouldn't realize. It's preemptive as well, as a way to tell more rapidly when they were attempting to attack our infrastructure."

I screamed at the room. "Aren't we legitimizing cyber-warfare by using it when, as a country, we're the most vulnerable? Aren't there limits to technology?"

No one answered my questions. Abbouse stared at General Johnson's monitor for a few seconds before continuing. "So, I—"

"You say you do this to protect our freedoms," I shouted. "Who protects us from you? You bastards killed my girlfriend!"

"Mr. Quinton," John Abbouse looked over at me. "Excellent questions for our policymakers. We'll let them answer those later."

"Two questions," Pritcherman cocked his head. "Why did the tooth have a microchip and what was it for?"

"That FBI agent was a hero, Stanley," John Abbouse answered. "He knew he would be at extreme risk in Europe trying to uncover what all this was about. The tooth was an implant–he had an old injury and had a previous dental implant. We exchanged it in order to track him. It had a few other classified functions, but mostly we wanted to know where he was."

"Yeah, a lot more than just tracking, John. One more thing."

"You've already had your two questions, Stan."

"Indulge me," P wasn't stopping. "How did you know where all of us were?"

Smiling, the FBI agent walked over to the neurosurgeon and leaned in. "We're the FBI. We have domestic surveillance capability. We've had drones up in the sky for the three weeks or so that all this has been going down." Pulling back from Pritcherman, "And Stanley, we just followed the chip you put in Quinton. Remember?"

"*What?*" I stared at P.

"Remember when I slapped you on the back, Q," Pritcherman reminded me. "I wanted to be able to follow you in case you got into trouble. So John, why did your friend bite Quinton?"

"To get rid of the tooth and chip, hoping somebody would figure out what it was. It was built to come out in an emergency. He was desperate."

"His was one hell of an emergency," P agreed. "Why Quinton?"

"Luck of the draw, I guess. Wrong place, wrong time."

Abbouse had been walking around to the other side of the tables, and stopped at Dr. Zendejas' wheelchair. "Speaking of the wrong place–What's your price, Doctor? Let me speed things up. You sold out for fame and fortune. But that's always been your thing. You screwed Dr. Pritcherman on the vaccine for CJD and now you've moved on to bigger and better things. Right?"

Zendejas was squirming in his wheelchair, but remained speechless.

Abbouse just stared at him for a minute or so without speaking. "Do I make you nervous, Doctor? You were ready to move on to bigger and better things, right?"

"I don't know," Zendejas squirmed more.

"Your death by sharks," the agent continued. "Not very original, but it did fool Quinton for a while. Why would you need to be dead, Doctor? Let me suggest that it took you off the radar and allowed you to start a new life and identity."

"Why?" Pritcherman asked. "It's not just to get away from me. How many others have you screwed, you pathetic, fat-rat bastard?"

Staring at Zendejas, "Now, now, Dr. Pritcherman," Abbouse sounded a little patronizing. "It wasn't only you he wanted to avoid. He needed to get away from the Dean, too, right? Did you want to tell us about that, sir?"

"No."

"I'm not surprised," Abbouse patted his head. "How is your bedpan headache, Doctor? Did you all hear about Dr. Zachary knocking him out cold?"

"*Enough!*" the pathologist's ruddy face turning more crimson.

"Oh, it's nowhere near enough, sir," the Special Agent disagreed. "The good Dean isn't quite as righteous as he might have you believe either. It seems he discovered Dr. Zendejas' scheme and has been blackmailing him. You see, gentlemen, an illegal activity completely unrelated to espionage.

"No, the good Dr. Zendejas has been harvesting and selling bone and skin tissue samples from his autopsies on the eastern European market and making a fortune. The Dean noticed our esteemed pathologist professor was performing an excessive number of autopsies under the guise of teaching medical students. Did you want to tell us more about that Dean?"

Jankowski sat quiet and passive, glaring back and forth from Zendejas to Abbouse.

"No, I didn't think you would," moving away from him. "But it might explain to your colleagues why you needed that sabbatical you're supposed to be taking now."

The Special Agent slowly came around to my side of the table. "And so we come full circle to our last civilian, Mr. Quinton. Another of the innocents," Abbouse pulled up a chair and sat by my gurney. "You've been one busy medical student, Mr. Quinton, what with all the research and late night goings on. To your credit, you did open up this can of worms. Does anyone know about Mr. Quinton?"

Looking around the room. John Abbouse didn't see anyone acknowledge the question. "Dr. Pritcherman?"

"Quinton is the only one with an ounce of sanity in this room," P exuded anger. "I thought he was just another nerdy med student. But he became my friend and taught me something about life. He gave me a reason to be alive again. He's a renegade–and so am I–he's a rebel, like me. Courage requires clarity and Mr. Quinton provided that."

"Yes, he's a real Boy Scout, isn't he?" Abbouse's compliments certainly didn't sound genuine. "No, when I asked if anyone knew about him, I meant his background. Mr. Quinton fancies himself a real sleuth, a regular Sherlock Holmes. He comes by it naturally, or should I say, *genetically*, Mr. Quinton? His parents are both dead, but they left him more than their fortune. You see, Quinton's parents worked for the NSA–now he didn't know *that*, but he did know they were somehow connected to the government–and they left him access to a lot of top secret governmental databases. Right, Mr. Quinton?"

"Yes, but I never knew exactly who they worked for. Thank you for clearing that up. Now, I have a few more issues to clear up—"

"Me first, son," the Special Agent cut short my questions. "Believe me, you'll get your shot. Of course, he thought his database access went unnoticed. Not true. We discovered his snooping as part of the T.I.A. program. That's *Total Information Awareness*, Mr. Quinton. A program several have alluded to previously. We've known about you for years–where you go and what you look into. I'll give you credit, son. You've shortened this investigation quite a bit. I'll put a name on where you've been going–it's called E.E.L.D. That stands for *Evidence Extraction and Link Discovery*.

"Your parents worked on *Genisys*, too, but that's another story. It's your parents' contribution to the cyber-war effort. Some of those searches weren't so innocent though, were they? *NO!* And you've lived quite well off several patents–patents actually owned by the government, but we let you collect rather than blow our cover. Who knows? Maybe we'll come after you for back royalties. We are the FBI after all," smiling at me.

Rapidly becoming serious again, Abbouse continued. "I'm sorry about the deaths of your parents. Ironically, it was because of all this, way back at the beginning. Did you want to tell him about their deaths, General Bitterman?"

Bitterman shook his head, indicating no.

"Again, you take the easy way out," Abbouse scoffed, shaking his head. "Your parents died when they were captured by terrorists after their covers were inadvertently blown in Eastern Europe. They were there working on nascent versions of all this about ten years ago. They weren't agents, they were scientists. But they were killed like agents and, I suspect, that may be what led to General Bitterman and his colleagues deciding they needed actual field agents. Comments, General?"

"Your overview is correct, Mr. Abbouse," Bitterman remained sitting at attention.

"So there you have it." Special Agent John Abbouse was not quiet, walking around the room from each table to the next.

He'd started by sitting next to me and ended back next to Dr. Pritcherman.

I couldn't stay quiet. "Well, I have a few more questions. Where's the DNI or the counter-terrorism head? This inquiry seems to be limited to just a few agencies. Only the National Security Advisor is here. I don't get it."

"*Only* the National Security Advisor, Mr. Quinton?" Abbouse mocked. "The others you mentioned are occupied at the moment. I believe you will find Ms. Rasmussen's presence more than adequate."

"OK, then, how is it my government has its tentacles in every aspect of my university?" Pritcherman joined in my inquisition. "There's been an uncomfortable coziness between universities and pharmaceutical companies and researchers for a while. So now we're infiltrated by government, too? Who admitted all these spooks into medical school?"

"Come now, Stanley," Abbouse was patronizing. "Government is the ultimate guarantor for your university. We pay for it. Shouldn't we have some input into who gets in? And what they study?"

"No, I don't think so," P disagreed. "The loss of independence and privacy markedly outweighs the benefits. Especially if you believe our government isn't benign."

"So we're evil now, too?"

"You said it, John. Not I," P rolled his eyes. *"Rescue me, O Lord, from evil men who devise evil plans in their hearts and stir up war every day."*[6] He fumbled through his pocket and retrieved his last small onion, popping it into his mouth, smiling. "You all have agents in each other's agency, don't you? They didn't know the specifics of this operation, but you all were collaborating even though your directors hadn't told you to. Collaborating except when you were trying to one-up each other," squirting onion juice on the disparaging Abbouse.

"You sold out, too, didn't you? Even you–my friend–make me sick, John," P concluded.

I piled on, "Do you people even have any oversight at all? You killed my friend because she's in the way? What happened to our laws? What happened to Congress or the President? Ms. Rasmussen, you seem to know about this. What do you have to say? No. What do you plan to do?"

"*Do*, Mr. Quinton? " The National Security Advisor stared from her monitor directly at me. "I intend to conclude this meeting and keep my appointment with the President on more pressing matters."

"More pressing than murder and a major breach of the Constitution, Ms. Rasmussen?" I persisted.

"Come now, Mr. Quinton," she ridiculed. "A major Constitutional breach? Hardly," she stood, gathering her notes to leave. "The American people are amnesiacs, Mr. Quinton. They have a short attention span as well." She wrinkled her eyebrows, "No, when the next news cycle catches their attention with thirty seconds of nothing about some half-naked starlet on the beach, they will forget about this episode entirely, that is, if they even paid attention to it in the first place. We'll limit what they hear anyway. Amnesiacs. No institutional memory whatsoever," as she stood up.

"Mr. Abbouse, I believe you have this well under control," beginning to exit, turning to look out from the monitor. "I would like to know if anyone predicted this outcome," as her monitor went back to the FBI logo. The other three monitors went to logo as well.

"And so we come to our conclusion," Abbouse walked to the front podium. "Each of you is guilty in some fashion and a few of you have blood on your hands. So we are left with what to do? What to do with each of you?" The agent sat and folded his hands under his chin, still for about fifteen seconds. "Dealing with the professionals is easy. "It's the four civilians that present the problem. Damn civilians."

He exhaled loudly again. "Protecting the country is not for amateurs," he continued. "Stanley, forgive me" Abbouse sighed and stood up, *"Praise be to the Lord, my Rock, who trains my hands for war, my fingers for battle. He is my loving God and my fortress, my stronghold and my deliverer, my shield, in whom I take refuge, who subdues people under me."* [7]

The Special Agent reached into his pocket and retrieved two handguns and slid them across the table–one to Grigsby and the other to Smith. Then he walked out of the room.

The last sound I heard was the distinctively metallic click-click of a nine-millimeter weapon's slide being racked, loading a bullet into the chamber.

---

[6] *Psalm 140:1–2,* The Bible, New International Version (NIV).

[7] *Psalm 144:1–2.* The Bible, New International Version (NIV).

*— Always Remember: Life Is Just A Game By Another Name.
Never Pretend Righteousness Justifies Treachery —*

– Always Wait For The Final Hand In The Game.
Never Think It Can't Happen. Always Ask, "And Then What?" –

*– Never Skip To The Last Chapter Without Reading The Others
. . . Or You'll Miss The Surprise –*

Epilogue

The Information Awareness Office (I.A.O.) actually existed, established in January 2002, by the Defense Advanced Research Projects Agency (DARPA) after the attacks of September 11, 2001 on the United States. Amazingly, it was the brainchild of Admiral John Poindexter (retired), and others. He was its first head, in spite of his conviction for lying to Congress as Ronald Reagan's National Security Advisor in the Iran-Contra scandal of the 1980s. His conviction was later overturned on a technicality, not substance.

The I.A.O.'s mission was to bring together many disparate sources of information through, "Total Information Awareness" (T.I.A.). The program's name was later changed to "Terrorism Information Awareness" when bad publicity attracted Congressional hearings and ultimately led to the program having its funding cancelled by Congress in 2003. Despite the cancellation, many of its components still exist in various operational forms in various other governmental agencies to this day.

The goal of T.I.A. is to integrate, research and develop technologies to "virtually aggregate data, to follow subject-oriented link analysis, to develop descriptive and predictive models through data mining or human hypothesis, and to apply such models to additional datasets to identify terrorists and terrorist groups." [8]

Some of its various component programs were/are:

HumanID–Biometric automatic technologies in development for use at extreme distances. Uses would include crime prevention, homeland (domestic) and foreign defense purposes as well as force protection.

Evidence Extraction and Link Discovery (EELD)–Systems with the ability to extract data from multiple   sources that use multiple formats and levels of security. Pattern recognition is a key component to look for over the many data sources. By analyzing patterns, it is hoped identification of current and future threats can be predicted.

Genisys–Extremely large data repositories is the purpose of this T.I.A. component–not only collection, but analysis in much larger quantities than commercially available. Allowing more flexibility for both users and storage is a goal.

Scalable Social Network Analysis–Program using social networking techniques and analysis looking for key characteristics of terrorists and others.

---

[8] "Information Awareness Office," *Wikipedia* (http://en.wikipedia.org/wiki/Information_Awareness_Office)

<u>Future Markets Applied to Prediction (FutureMAP)</u>–The most worrisome to me. A predictive market technology utilizing market-trading mechanisms to advance predictions of future world events, such as where political instability or national security threats might arise. Their website would allow users to place bets on various aspects of these predictions, *i.e.,* when they might occur, estimates of damages, etc. Thus, a statistical probability of occurrence is generated.

Oregon Democratic senator Ron Wyden said of this program, "The idea of a federal betting parlor on atrocities and terrorism is ridiculous and grotesque." Michigan Senator Carl Levin, then-Chairman of the Armed Services Committee, added, "(the program was) . . . so ridiculous that I thought initial reports of it were the result of a hoax." Then-Senate Majority Leader Tom Daschle said on the Senate floor, "I couldn't believe that we would actually commit eight million dollars to create a website that would encourage investors to bet on futures involving terrorist attacks and public assassinations . . . I can't believe anybody would seriously propose that we trade in death. How long would it be before you saw traders investing in a way that would bring about the desired result?" *Not long*, this author would answer.

<u>Translingual Information Defection, Extraction and Summarization (TIDES)</u>–Very advanced language processing technologies.

<u>GenoaGenoa II</u>–Decision-support tools.

<u>Wargaming the Assymetric Environment (WAE)</u>–Another predictive tool.

<u>Effective Affordable Reusable Speech-to-Text (EARS)</u>–Automatic, very advanced speech-to-text transcription technology with more accuracy than current commercial technologies, such as Nuance's Dragon and others.

<u>Babylon</u>–Rapid, two-way language translation interfaces. Many potential civilian as well as military uses.

<u>Bio-Surveillance</u>–Automatic detection of biologic covert pathogens.

<u>Communicator</u>–Advanced technologies that allow a human user to talk directly to computers even on a battlefield-wireless, mobile and network compatible.

Author's note: "of the people, by the people and for the people—" *Is this?*

Now . . . do you think it can't happen?

– Always Remember: Life, Freedom, And Liberty Are Precious.
Never Forget What Life Has Taught You –

Never Trust Anyone Who Doesn't Know Your Name

Never Take Things At Face Value

Always Look For The Hidden Agenda

Always Be Prepared When Venturing Into The Night

Never Start What You Can't Finish

Never Let The Truth Get In The Way Of A Good Story

Always Know Who's Playing Before You Deal The Hand

Always Count Your Blessings Before You Say Your Prayers

Never Place A Call Unless You Know Who's On The Other End

Never Announce The Prize Before You Know The Score

Never Try To Juggle When There Are Too Many Balls In The Air

Always Know Which Side You're On Before Choosing Your Teammates

Always Look Behind The Curtain To See Who's Pulling The Strings

Never Forget, Your Enemy's Enemy Is Not Necessarily Your Friend

Always Beware Of A Last Minute "Ringer" Joining The Game

Never Forget When Playing The Game, Every Move Has Its Consequences

Never Let Your Adversary Dictate Your Strategy

Always Consider The Future And How Your Actions Now May Influence It

Always Remember: Life Is Just A Game By Another Name.
Never Pretend Righteousness Justifies Treachery

Always Wait For The Final Hand Of The Game
Never Think It Can't Happen. Always Ask, "And Then What?"

Never Skip To The Last Chapter Without Reading The Others
. . . Or You'll Miss The Surprise

Always Remember: Life, Freedom And Liberty Are Precious.
Never Forget What Life Has Taught You